Bombora
MAL PETERS

Dreamspinner Press

Published by
Dreamspinner Press
5032 Capital Circle SW
Ste 2, PMB# 279
Tallahassee, FL 32305-7886
USA
http://www.dreamspinnerpress.com/

This is a work of fiction. Names, characters, places, and incidents either are the product of the author's imagination or are used fictitiously, and any resemblance to actual persons, living or dead, business establishments, events, or locales is entirely coincidental.

Bombora
Copyright © 2012 by Mal Peters

Cover Art by Reese Dante
http://www.reesedante.com

All rights reserved. No part of this book may be reproduced or transmitted in any form or by any means, electronic or mechanical, including photocopying, recording, or by any information storage and retrieval system without the written permission of the Publisher, except where permitted by law. To request permission and all other inquiries, contact Dreamspinner Press, 5032 Capital Circle SW, Ste 2, PMB# 279, Tallahassee, FL 32305-7886, USA.
http://www.dreamspinnerpress.com/

ISBN: 978-1-61372-701-0

Printed in the United States of America
First Edition
August 2012

eBook edition available
eBook ISBN: 978-1-61372-702-7

For my father

THIS novel would not have been possible without the immeasurable love, support, and encouragement of several special people.

First and foremost, Virginia Modugno, my sister, editor, and indefatigable cheerleader for more than a decade, and whose late-night gigglefests I will look forward to sharing over the phone when we're old and crotchety; Dan Di Poce, for thirteen years of never letting an opportunity to make fun of me pass him by, and for being the most inspiring person I know; Dags, for her enthusiasm, original spirit, and brilliant concept art that kept me going when nothing else could; JJM, for making me feel like a superstar, and who cried when I got on the plane; R.C. Smith, for her friendship, endless hilarity, tough love, and willingness to point out even my most spectacular feats of logic fail; Amy Gibbs and Desiree, for the amazing encouragement and invaluable editing; a very special individual who, though she prefers to remain anonymous, was present at *Bombora*'s conception, and whose friendship, kinship, and all other -ships I am ever so grateful to have in my life—you know who you are; Lynn West, Elizabeth North, and my editors at Dreamspinner for their tireless work, and for putting up with my sporadic bursts of OCD; Reese Dante for her arresting cover art; and finally, all others not mentioned here who bolstered my confidence with such wonderful words of praise and enthusiasm, however undeserved they might be.

Finally, to my parents, who despite their differences never wavered in their support or the belief that I could achieve anything I set my mind to; one could truly not ask to be loved more, nor so furiously. I wish my father could be here to see his little girl finally achieve her dream of becoming a published writer, but I feel his presence in every word I write. Except maybe the dirty ones.

—Mal Peters

Bom•bo•ra—[bom báwrə] *n., Australian*—

1. A wave that forms over a submerged offshore reef or rock, sometimes breaking heavily and producing a dangerous stretch of broken water.

2. The hit 1960s surf-rock song performed by the Original Surfaris.

3. A fucking mess.

Prologue

Hugh

CARDIFF-BY-THE-SEA is one of Southern California's best-kept secrets. It may disappear in the shadow of the better-known Welsh city for which it's named, lose itself in the bend of an unremarkable of stretch of coastal highway, but die-hard surfers aren't fooled by such obscurity.

They're kind of like birds that way—if you pay close enough attention, the dude with the shortboard beneath his arm can give you the inside track on what kind of weather to expect over the next few days and when to get the hell out of Dodge, or even if there's an ear infection going around due to some funky lagoon water. Modern-day medicine people, they are. I like to think those old-school surfer dudes knew exactly the treasure they had on their hands when surfing first became a scene out here in California; they anticipated the millions of people who would make the pilgrimage to the West Coast month after month, year after year, to experience what native Californians grow up knowing in their bones. Cardiff is far from the exception.

Although winter is Cardiff's best season, these beaches bring out surfers in droves pretty much year-round, from total beginners to world-renowned athletes, all of them for a taste of some of the best wave action in Cali. Even Rob Machado, one of the most gifted damn surfers going, lives less than a block away from the ocean. On weekends things can get insane, though: just try to find a parking spot somewhere. I suppose that doesn't make it sound like the secret is that well-kept after all, but during weekdays it's quiet as can be. That's when the magic happens, when people turn into converts.

I would know—it happened to me.

Humankind has been attempting to rationalize and explain the draw of the ocean for thousands of years. Millions, maybe. Have we ever really succeeded? Perhaps the only reason no one attempted to capture the beauty of the sun-sparkling sea in the caves of Lascaux is because its beauty could never quite be adequately rendered, like an arabesque pattern conceding its imperfections to a far more transcendent and unknowable God.

Personally, I think water fascinates us because the waves make us untouchable. On land it's hard to run away so no one can find you, but that's not the case in open water, where there are no boundaries and no rules. Where surfers are concerned, as long as you don't purposely endanger another person, you're not accountable to anyone else; the only life you're responsible for is your own. With that freedom comes the realization that "safety" is very relative, and by no means a guarantee out here. But I suppose that's why, when I needed to get away from Phelan Price and my brother Nate, my first thought was to grab my board and hit the surf, to keep paddling until I could see neither hide nor hair of land or my brother's ridiculously fucked-up life. I knew no one would follow.

The late-autumn waves are fierce, with coastal winds whipping the water into a frenzy of chilly foam and salt spray. I struggle to remain seated on my board even without paddling farther out to sea, and every so often a swell approaches and threatens to engulf me whole. When faced with a wall of water rushing toward you, there are only two choices: Go over or under. Swim for your life or drift back to shore. I'm not quite ready to go back to land yet, so instead I dive beneath each wave as it comes, a stubborn refusal that leaves me shivering and winded. The moment of being suspended beneath all that power is breathless and meditative, the seconds ticking away into infinity as the water deafens your senses and every muscle strains to keep you submerged, weightless, until reality reasserts itself and you're thrown back to the surface with a gasp. I can lose myself in that for now. The concentration required to keep me from being swept away by the waves is almost enough to make me forget the disaster that's been brought to my shores, but not quite.

How did things get so complicated?

Before moving to Cardiff, I wasn't much of a surfer. Not much of an athlete, actually, beyond putting in my time at the gym and going for regular runs. I tried it once in Australia on a book tour, despite Nate's warnings that a man of my size has no place on a surfboard; I got talked into taking a few lessons by my publicist, Caroline. Good photo op, yadda yadda, and apparently it's hard to beat Gnaraloo for waves in July. At first I had my doubts they'd be able to find a board big enough for me—they breed us hearty in Alabama—but Caroline pulled it off somehow. She always does. True to Nate's word, though, I almost died. For a while I thought my foray into marine sports would be short, as much for my own safety as to prevent more awkward tabloid stories about Hugh Dorian embarrassing himself in a wetsuit. I had enough I-told-you-so material to last me at least two decades into my professional relationship with Caroline, if we didn't kill each other before then.

That's why Cardiff kind of took me by surprise. My girlfriend, Nell—I don't even know if that's still the right term, since the relationship never technically ended, but "former girlfriend" doesn't sound right either—was from there, and we visited her family a few times while we were dating. Only a few times, though, since it isn't exactly close to where we lived in Berkeley. The plan was to visit more often after college, once we settled into our house in Los Angeles and I got my first book deal, but then the shooting happened, and all that stuff, along with Nell's life, got cut short. Suddenly my only reason to visit Cardiff was the funeral.

I didn't think much about anything beyond what to say and how to act like a normal person until I found myself wandering the town's beaches and sleepy coastal streets and realizing, hey, life here wouldn't be so bad. Quiet. Relaxed. Just how I like it. I've never been one for the crowds, not like Nate. It's probably really cheesy to pick a town based on its proximity to your dead girlfriend's gravesite, but it wouldn't be the first time someone accused me of being a sap.

Besides, that was only part of it. In the bigger cities, enough people recognized me from my book jacket photos, and after Nell's funeral I started playing with the idea of moving someplace secluded to get away from it all, to avoid the tabloids and the showbiz types and do what I supposedly get paid for: write. I also really, really needed to get away from the celebrity scene, which was turning out to be dangerous in more ways than one. I had to distance myself from the deceptive glitter of Hollywood and the person I found I had the capacity to become when escapism turned ugly. Cardiff proved to be that place.

Because I'm not afraid to admit I'm a geek, I can tell you that Cardiff Reef is the cause of such awesome waves. It extends for about a quarter mile south down the coast, over flat, grass-covered rock that becomes exposed when the tide goes out, allowing the daring and curious a chance to wander out and explore all the marine life normally hidden beneath the water. A biologist's dream. Where surfing is concerned, the wave off the reef is usually described as being a little slow, not ideal except for its low tides and the huge swells that move in during the winter season. There's a peak at the southernmost point that, whether or not you're prepared for it, is one badass tube regardless of skill or experience. North of the reef is what's known locally as the Suckouts, swells that can challenge the most seasoned surfer with quick drops and low water levels as the waves empty into the channel. It's no coincidence any surfer worth his salt cuts his teeth here in Cardiff.

Caroline had her doubts about my moving here, probably because she worried about not being able to keep an eye on me, but for the most part I haven't had any trouble. For an author, the ratio of rabid fans to people who don't give a shit is pretty low, and in Cardiff it's almost zilch. At first there was some excitement to have a best-selling author in the neighborhood, especially one with a troubled history like mine, but after threatening a couple of lawsuits, Caroline was mostly able to keep me out of the local papers. Not to mention I'm usually too boring to warrant much attention. With Rob nearby and a couple of other famous musicians and actors who call Cardiff home, I quickly faded into the fabric of everyday life. Hugh Dorian—though around here I go by my real name, Hugh Fessenden—is just another guy with an inflated salary and too much free time on his hands.

Even after Nell's parents eventually moved away, haunted by memories of her childhood, I was welcomed into the community with open arms, if maybe a few more sympathetic looks than I normally like. Pretty much everyone who grew up here knows about Nell and mourns that someone so kind and well liked should have lost her life to a mugging gone horribly awry. I took up surfing because there wasn't much else to do, and it's a nice way to break up the monotony of my day when I'm not out promoting a new book or struggling to justify the recent publisher's advance. Luckily I embarrass myself a lot less out there on the waves than I used to. Some might even call me proficient.

I wish I could say being a well-known author has made for an active social life and lots of friends, but that isn't really the case. For one reason or another, I keep to myself. Privacy is a hard thing to come by in a small town, and I'd hate to make the mistake of divulging too much of my life to the wrong person. Writers, even the famous ones, don't have it as bad as the Brads and Angelinas of the world, but we still see our fair share of public interest. That I'm under thirty and, I suppose, passably attractive seems to make me a natural target for gossip, especially since some of my stuff got optioned for film adaptations.

While I can't say it's something I ever *really* worry about, there have been a few incidents to make me think twice about who I let into the inner circle. I often used to wish Nate lived closer than Ohio, but his own family was a full-time job, especially since Emilia opened her dance studio and Liam started middle school. My mom died when we were little and my dad a couple of years ago from a heart attack, so for the most part I lie low and have fewer than five people on speed dial. I talk to Nate all the time, but brothers don't count; he just harasses me about being a bore, anyway. "How's the free booze and groupies this week? Or did you spend another Saturday beating off to Internet porn by yourself?" is his usual refrain when he calls.

Like I said, no one I really hang out with on a regular basis.

Except, that is, for Phel.

WHAT is there to tell about Phelan? Way too much and not enough. He's both the most unremarkable and the most interesting guy I've ever met. To this day, I have no idea how the hell he wound up in a place like Cardiff—although how does anyone end up here? His story probably isn't all that different from mine. Then again, he could have escaped from a circus for all I know, or fallen from the sky.

I met him on the beach a couple of months ago while on a morning walk with my dog, Callie. He was having some trouble. Beginners take to the surf all the time around here, and normally I don't think anything of it, but Phel stood out a bit more than the rest, wrestling with his wetsuit like it was a live animal and not a piece of neoprene. It being late July, there were a few kids gathered together for lessons, their small bodies zippering easily into the suits before they grabbed their bodyboards and paddled into the surf after their instructor. Certainly there was no rocket science involved, but this poor schmuck couldn't seem to figure out which end of his suit was up—not what you'd call an experienced surfer.

I probably would have continued on my way if Callie hadn't sprinted away from me in her excitement to catch a slow-moving target. Phel looked up when he found himself under the investigation of seventy pounds of Australian shepherd.

"Uh... hey," he greeted me awkwardly, and his nose wrinkled in the universal sign for people who like dogs a lot more in theory than in practice. "Can I... help you?"

The incongruousness of the question made me snort. I decided to rescue him before Callie could get any more friendly, and she whuffed happily as I approached over the sand. "Get back here," I told her with mock sternness, and she played her little game of running back and forth across the beach between us, inviting one of us to chase her around.

Phel wasn't having any of it. "Is this an off-leash area?" he asked peevishly when I got close enough. "I didn't think dogs were allowed to just...." With a look of frustration for the wetsuit, he threw it down on the sand with a lame slap.

"What, judge people's surfing ability?" I asked. The sun was glaring kind of awkwardly from behind Phel's head, and I had to shield a hand over my eyes just to make out a vague impression of his facial expression. From what I could tell, he looked a combination of embarrassed and exasperated. That's Phel down to a T—always too much going on below the surface to get a proper read on the guy. "Don't think many people care round here," I pointed out, "and Callie won't give you half as much trouble as that wetsuit." This earned me a glare, and a little spark of humor made me add, "By the way, it goes ass-side down."

"And you're the expert?" snapped Phel. I shrugged. The gesture drew another grunt of frustration from him, then Phel motioned at the discarded pile. "I just... I've been cooped up for days, and supposedly surfing is the one good thing to do around here. So far it's a disaster."

"Have you surfed before?" I asked neutrally. We both knew I'd already guessed the answer.

In all fairness, Phel called me on it. "What does it look like?"

"Touché." I stooped, half to put the guy out of his misery and half to save him from further embarrassment, then grabbed his wetsuit off the ground and stretched and untangled the neoprene until I held out a neat person-sized article in front of me. "You should get yourself an instructor if this is your first time," I suggested. "Waves can get pretty intense out there if you don't know what you're doing."

"I know even less about where to go for that kind of thing," he answered. "I borrowed the board from… some friends I'm staying with." There was no denying the emphasis on the word "friends" was weird, but I tried not to comment since it would only make him more uncomfortable. Say what you want about writers, but we're pretty good at psychoanalyzing on the spot. I didn't need a psych degree to know Phel was lying to my face about something he didn't want to talk about. However, the fact that I had one didn't hurt. He was definitely lying about something.

"That's cool, man," I said. Before I could think twice about the impulsiveness of the gesture, given my tendency to avoid people, I extended my hand. "I'm Hugh."

Though Phel responded with a proper handshake, something seemed to dawn on him after he spent a couple of moments looking at my face with a puzzled expression. Two guesses what that was. "Hugh Dorian," he said slowly. "I thought you looked kind of familiar, but I'm not great with faces. Plus it's entirely possible I'm just going crazy." His mouth snapped shut at this. Hesitantly, he added, "You *are* Hugh Dorian, right? The writer?"

Next time I'd ask for a smaller jacket photo or, fuck, a composite sketch that didn't quite get my nose right. "Got it in one," I told him instead, trying not to sound bent out of shape. "Here I thought I was undercover." *Please don't ask me for a fuckin' autograph*, I thought.

Now that he'd stepped closer and correctly guessed my identity, I was able to get a much clearer look at Phel's face. He was pretty handsome, I had to admit: scruffy and wild-haired in a rakish way, full lips that probably made a lot of women jealous, huge blue eyes. Not surprisingly, he was shorter than me by a few inches, compact but for his broad shoulders and strong legs. Despite the gruffness of his voice, he was actually pretty young—early thirties was my guess, around Nate's age.

The difference was that Phel looked tired, more tired than I could remember having seen a person look, the exception being myself in the mirror the night Nell died. It made me wonder what stories lay behind the shadows under Phel's eyes, and to be honest, I still wonder. But that day we were just getting our introductions out of the way, and it wouldn't be another few weeks until I worked up the nerve to ask why he was the most miserable guy in San Diego County.

"Sorry for spoiling your anonymity," he apologized. "For what it's worth, you don't look a whole lot like your jacket photo—it makes you look short, for one thing, and kind of smug." At this, I blinked, and Phelan immediately backpedaled. "But you don't look short or smug here, I mean. You're tall and kind of stun—"

"Can I stop you right there?" I interrupted. This was getting ridiculous. The guy spoke like he'd gone to finishing school at Eton but had less tact than Howard Stern. "I think I get the idea." A regretful look crossed Phel's face. Nevertheless, I was glad when he didn't try to apologize again. Instead I surprised us both by asking, "How would you feel about me teaching you how to surf? I wouldn't charge anything, and I'd sleep a lot better at night knowing you won't die a watery death on my watch."

"I can pay in beer," said Phel, and that, as they say, was that.

That first meeting was a little awkward, plagued as it was by Phelan's enigmatic qualities and tendency to talk about his past life like it'd all happened to someone else, but we've been hanging out every day since then, having graduated from early-morning surf lessons to the kind of stuff regular friends do, or at least insofar as I've ever had a regular friend. You know: coffee, football games, movies, beer. We also run together a lot, and the first time I saw his fast, steady gait on the beach as he plowed ahead of me despite my much longer strides, I knew how he got those leg muscles. Phel's kind of a natural athlete, even though he knows nothing about real-people sports like basketball or football, and tons about weird shit like fencing and cricket and polo—and baseball, for some reason, though he dodged the question when I inquired about the source of his info. His knowledge of the Texas Rangers would have made Nate proud. He's even come around to tolerating Callie's high-energy canine demands, after enough of her persistent affection.

While there's no denying he's still the weirdest person I know, at least I understand a few more of the reasons behind that. The purpose of Phelan's visit to Cardiff is so he can rest up and pull himself together before he figures out what he wants to do next with his life—I guess the less polite way to put it is that the dude had a nervous breakdown and retired to Cardiff to recoup.

I've tried to get more of the story out of him, but the most he'll give me is he made a mistake with the wrong person and had the misfortune of getting caught. There's nothing to suggest he knows what even happened to the other guy, but from the sounds of it, that doesn't matter; Phel's family disowned him either way, being the staunch religious types that don't much care for gay love affairs. Phel has never used that word—love—but I can tell by the look he gets when he talks about the man in question that there're still some feelings there, stuff that won't be cured by a few weeks of R & R. I feel bad for him, but that isn't why we're friends. More than anything, I think we understand our mutual need for privacy and a reliable person to have your back.

After all, those things aren't exactly easy to come by, not even in sunny Cardiff-by-the-Sea. I just wish we'd known enough to appreciate them before they got swept away with the tide.

1

Phel

MY DAYS at the Palermo Springs Centre for Addiction and Mental Health all start the same: I wake up around seven, shower, go to yoga, shower, have an uninspiring breakfast of fresh fruit and oatmeal, dress to meet Hugh at the beach for a few hours before lunch, shower, then go to my afternoon session with Willa, my counselor. Evenings I have to myself. For the record, I don't have OCD—it's just necessary to bathe several times a day to keep from smelling pervasively like seawater or sweat in this climate. Growing up, I split my time between the East Coast and the Midwest, so with the exception of New York in August, I'm not exactly built for these kinds of temperatures. No one wants to be the sweaty guy in group therapy, not with all that hugging.

Hugh is fond of mocking the predictability of my days, but Willa says routine can be grounding in times of chaos. There's not much chaos in my life—more like a void—but if a routine can feel like a tranquil island in stormy seas (Willa's words, not mine), I don't see why it can't serve the same purpose if the water around you is totally becalmed and empty. Besides, I kind of like yoga and having nothing else to do each day besides surf and hang out with Hugh and think about why I'm here. I don't just mean here in the philosophical sense, though that's part of it. Mostly I mean this slip of a town called Cardiff-by-the-Sea.

I came to Palermo on the recommendation of my sister, Aurelia. Turns out she spent some time here while I was away at college, when her drinking got just a little too out of control. Our parents thought she went to Bali for a month, when really they were the reason she needed rehab in the first place. Not hard to see how that could happen, since dealing with our mother and father can be intense on a good day, but

I'm the first to report that *not* dealing with them isn't necessarily better. We all hate our families until they're gone, or they ask us not to come back, and suddenly we realize why Donne went on about how no man is an island. Woe betide the poor asshole who discovers he *is* an island after all. Which is to say, I'm that asshole.

It took being disowned at thirty-two to realize how little I had going for me besides my family and my job. The other incident I don't like to talk about, the one that put me here, was a rash and ill-advised way to break out of my dull existence in the Midwest. Gay love affairs, especially poorly planned ones with married men, never go over well when your family is oppressively Catholic. Turns out there's a reason I've never been known as "the spontaneous one," because all spontaneity had to offer was a broken heart, some frozen bank accounts, and a big fat nothing in place of the life I used to have. Probably not even Nate—that's his name, the asshole—would take my calls anymore, were I to actually pick up the phone and dial.

Willa tells me I don't show enough appreciation for the little things, like the fact that I'm alive and healthy and in full control of my mental faculties, but as much as I like the woman, sometimes I think Willa is full of shit. She *has* a family, and a gorgeous one at that—I've seen her husband at the pool enough times. Rumor has it she had an Oxy addiction before becoming a counselor, but now she's all about the Zen and the *Eat, Pray, Love*. Elizabeth Gilbert she's not.

But I'm not bitter, honest. I'm getting better.

However morbid this might sound, I wish I'd come to Palermo with a substance abuse problem—at least I would have stood the risk of having a little fun beforehand, or damaged enough brain cells to keep me from remembering everything in living color. Instead I'm stuck in the independent living program with all the other depressives and anger-management cases—talk about the amateur ward. It's somewhere between an outpatient program and a retirement home, with my own private residence on the Palermo compound and the freedom to come and go as I please outside of my mandatory counseling schedule. I guess I'm kind of a sorry excuse for a crazy person—I barely even attempted suicide. Sure, a nervous breakdown is nothing to sneeze at, but I know the other patients probably look at me and think I'm just some melodramatic rich kid who can't get over losing his trust fund. Maybe I am. Maybe I also have a bit of paranoia thrown into the mix.

That could be why I like Hugh so much, because he's got his own issues and isn't constantly on my case to talk about my feelings, or even about his. Occasionally I'm struck by the urge to ask him about his family and his dead girlfriend and anything else he'll tell me, but Hugh keeps that stuff locked up tighter than Fort Knox. I know he has a brother somewhere at the opposite end of the country, and their parents are dead, but that's about it. Part of Hugh's reluctance to divulge information has to do with his celebrity, which I understand, and part of it has to do with not being ready, which I also understand. He'll have to have it out with that stuff eventually, though. He's too smart not to realize that.

The same goes for me. But I don't feel judged around him. He knows all about what happened in Columbus—the short version, with names withheld to protect the guilty—and his first response was "The guy sounds like an asshole. I probably would have freaked out too, if a girl treated me like that. You were lucky you got out."

Got out, yes. Came out—not so much, though I more or less agree with Willa that a weight has been lifted from my shoulders. Still, it meant a lot that Hugh took my side without question, without even knowing the other half of the story. I have Willa to make rational arguments about how I should have seen the break-up coming, should have predicted it'd blow up in my face. Hugh is there to teach me surfing and be my friend and tell me that everyone bets on the wrong horse sometimes.

The whole thing with Nate started off in what I thought was a completely innocuous way. And if innocuous isn't the right word, because affairs so rarely are, then at least it wasn't anything sinister. I thought I had my money on Secretariat, and instead found myself with a Phar Lap. After the arsenic poisoning.

I was splitting my time between Chicago and Columbus, managing the Midwest offices of my family's advertising business. For the obvious reasons, I liked Chicago a lot better, especially since that's where Aurelia lives, but my attention was most often needed in Columbus, where the biggest number of things seemed to go wrong without someone to oversee the process. That the responsibility fell to me was just family obligation and bad luck.

It's not a bad town, Columbus, just a little boring for anyone who isn't a student or into tailgate parties, or who doesn't start hyperventilating every time the Buckeyes come up in conversation. (No, I'm not one of those people.) My time in the city was spent either at our offices downtown or my apartment on Parkview Ave., not including places like the gym or the grocery store.

On that one particular Friday, I was actually getting ready to drive to Illinois the next day, happy to leave Ohio behind. I considered Chicago home; it's where my friends were. There weren't many people I hung out with socially in Columbus—nor in Chicago, being honest— and in retrospect, that was part of the problem. Desperation and boredom can make a fool of anyone. One-night stands were a common occurrence for me, because even lapsed Catholic ad men have needs, and I didn't have much time for dating. Too much effort involved trying to keep my personal tastes hidden from my family. Honestly, Columbus was the last place I thought any of this would happen.

So of course, that's where it did.

Sexual orientation isn't something I ever had to think too hard about. I knew from a young age I was queer, and if my ultrareligious upbringing wasn't enough to shake it out of me, probably nothing would. Disguising my lack of interest in women became second nature early on, and I bore the blind dates and family-arranged meetings with as much equanimity as you'd expect. Never was I anything but polite and friendly to those women. A few of them even figured out I wasn't interested in them not because of their clothes or hair or personality, but for another fundamental reason—the lack of dick, for one.

My point is that, when I decided to go out for a couple of drinks and unwind after work that night, it wasn't to some random breeder bar, but rather a gay local called Foxley's. Their meal service was decent, but the real attraction was the down-to-earth crowd that flocked there on weekends. It encompassed neighborhood gays, businessmen, and the odd tourist in search of a quiet, old-timey pub atmosphere not overwhelmingly populated by OSU students, which was hard to come by in Columbus. In other words, Foxley's was a place for gay men to paw at each other in a civilized way, without concern for straight judgment or public decency laws. I might like dick, but straight men have never interested me. Although I know plenty of guys who go in for the excitement of feeling they've "turned" someone, that's not for me—I don't want ambiguity about who's checking me out and whether they might be a sexual tourist. The night before a short road trip seemed a perfect time to take someone home, since I could truthfully say I had to be up early the next morning. No muss, no fuss. Or so I thought.

The dinner crowd had mostly cleared out by the time I got there, replaced by those more interested in cruising than the nightly special. It was barely June, and during the summer months, Foxley's always did good business. Things were starting to get busy at the front of the restaurant, which was crammed with men chatting in groups or more intimate couples, a familiar mating dance in full swing. I looked around and smiled at a few people I knew, particularly shy Adam, who was mixing up martinis and pouring wine behind the bar. By no means did I spot Nate right away—it was he, in fact, who spotted me, though not until much later. I settled myself a respectable distance away from the throng of people and ordered a Scotch on the rocks, something I didn't really like but had grown up watching my father drink.

Three or four men paused to say hello or offered to buy me a beer, but for one reason or another, they didn't compel me—this time *because* of their hair or clothes or personality. I started to think about leaving after I'd been there less than an hour. Either no one really appealed to me, or I wasn't as motivated to cruise as I thought. But then this *guy* sat down a few seats away and ordered the same thing, except he drank his Scotch neat and didn't seem to care whether it was top-shelf.

Now, I consider myself a man of restraint, for the most part. No doubt a lifetime of checking my flamboyance at the door saved me from acting like one of those silly fags who faints at the first sign of a hot body or a gorgeous smile. But the minute I saw Nate's face, I would have done a striptease on the bar just to get his attention. After a few minutes, it became clear that wasn't necessary, because Nate cast a lingering glance my way, holding eye contact when I returned his look. I remember thinking he didn't seem altogether comfortable in this environment, then quickly dismissing the thought because he was hot, for one thing, and he was *here*. No one walked into Foxley's without knowing exactly what he'd signed up for.

"All-American" was the first thing that popped into my head when I saw Nate. Tall, athletic, and so beautiful I actually started to feel insecure about my own appearance, Nate looked too much the meat-and-potatoes jock type for a place like Foxley's. And yet, he still managed to turn every head in the place. On the one hand, I was flattered to have caught his eye, but knew I cut a fine figure of my own in my tailored gray Armani. (Seriously, Mom and Dad—how did you not figure it out sooner?) Nate's own suit seemed plain by comparison, but it was dark and he'd already managed to lose the tie and jacket, anyway. All I cared about was getting him to stop staring and come talk to me, so I tilted my head and gave him my best come-hither smile, which Aurelia says could charm the panties off a nun. Or a priest. Whatever. Ducking his head as though to hide a blush, Nate smiled to himself and pushed away from the bar to wander over.

"Hey," he said easily. With his arms on the bar, he leaned forward and met my gaze. Green, green eyes, like a cat's, and no less sharp. His eyelashes were so thick they gave the appearance of eyeliner. Up close he was even more enchanting, tall and freckled and with the most voluptuous lips I'd ever seen. True, my own lips draw plenty of comments from interested parties, but Nate's were as red and shapely as a Dürer portrait, all sharp Cupid's bow and upturned corners. I noticed his fingers drumming a rapid tattoo against his glass and, sensing his nervousness, I smiled a little wider. He cleared his throat. "Can I buy you another drink?"

As far as pickup lines went, it was classic but effective, and I appreciated his directness. "You can," I told him. "We're more or less drinking the same thing anyway." He signaled to Adam for another round, and I propped myself on my elbows against the bar, matching his stance. Allowing myself the opportunity to rake my eyes down his body and ending on a smile to show I liked what I saw, I added, "I haven't seen you around here before."

This drew a laugh, and in spite of myself, I blushed at the brilliance of his smile. Where did you even see teeth that white and perfect, outside of a fucking Abercrombie catalogue? I found myself wondering where the hell this guy had come from and what had taken him so long to find me. "I didn't take you for the type that recycles tired pickup lines," he chuckled.

"Coming from the man who opened with 'Buy you a drink?'" I shot back.

Nate bit his lip around another smile and sighed in resignation, but didn't argue.

I continued, "In this case it's not a come-on, just a statement of fact. Foxley's doesn't get a lot of new faces."

"So you must come here pretty often, then," he observed. Something mischievous twinkled in his eyes. "Either that or you've slept with everyone already."

I waggled my eyebrows and resisted the urge to contradict him the way my good Christian upbringing dictated—defend that virtue! Unfortunately, Nate was off, but not far off; there wasn't much virtue left to defend, if by those standards queers had any to begin with. "Not everyone," I eventually replied, and with a nod acknowledged Adam's reappearance with two fresh glasses of Scotch. I took a quick sip and offered a handshake. "I'm Phel." Those perfect eyebrows shot up, prompting me to frown and withdraw my hand. "Yes?"

He shrugged casually, broad shoulders momentarily fixating me as they flexed beneath the fabric of his button-down. "Oh, nothin'. That's just not the name I expected you to give—you look more like a Jimmy or a James or something. Is Phel a nickname?"

"Sort of—it's short for Phelan." Surprised this failed to draw a bigger laugh, I added, "My parents had a thing for lavish names; my sister is an equally plain Aurelia. Maybe they just wanted to see how far they could push the envelope before I got the shit kicked out of me at school, who knows?"

"Phel is definitely better," he agreed, "but still—I gotta admit Phelan's pretty sexy. Definitely not a name you'd forget the morning after." I savored his slow smile as much as the mental picture of waking up to a face like that. The way "sexy" rolled off his tongue was even more dangerous than the way he growled my name in a voice like dark brandy. "I'm Nate. Nate Smith."

This time it was he who offered his hand, and I accepted it politely, noting the warmth and firmness of his grip, the slight awkwardness with which he gave his name. Probably a fake, but it's not like I could judge—my last name was so well known I didn't bother to give it out. The "Phelan" was a big enough risk to anyone who bothered to look at the society pages of *The New York Times* once every few months.

"Nice to meet you, Phel."

"Likewise, Nate." I nodded at our surroundings and nudged him with my shoulder once he finished sipping his drink. Our faces were very close together, and a slow tendril of heat curled through me when I caught him watching my mouth as I spoke. "What moved you to grace Foxley's with your presence this evening?" I asked.

"Curiosity, mostly." Nate must have noticed my back stiffen, because he quickly added, "I'm not from here, so this is all kinda new to me. Didn't know Columbus even had a gay scene. I live about an hour northeast of the city—little town called Mount Vernon. You ever been there?"

"Can't say I have," I admitted. Clearly that was a mistake on my part, if the rest of Mount Vernon looked anything like Nate. "You picked the right place, anyway.... Most of the other gay bars around here are either lame, or skeezy, or both. At least Foxley's is halfway respectable, and Adam likes to mix 'em strong." Mouth twitching, I suggested, "Maybe you should *start* a gay scene in Mount Vernon. With a face like yours, people might actually pay attention—and I'm sure you're not the only fag in the suburbs."

Nate gave a careful pause I couldn't interpret, which he attempted to hide behind his glass of Scotch. "That probably wouldn't go over so well," he answered tautly. "Besides, I like Columbus. It's nearby, and a helluva lot more interesting than Mount Vernon." With a smile and a glint in his eye, he added, "Plus, you're here."

Unable to help myself, I rolled my eyes at the cheesy line, earning a laugh. Good to know Nate had a healthy sense of irony, or didn't mind a little teasing. As someone who'd been accused of being too literal and serious on multiple occasions, I appreciated someone who wasn't afraid to laugh at himself—or me, since I probably needed to lighten up.

It was too early to tell whether Nate would understand my biting brand of sarcasm, so I settled on sauciness instead, it being the more obvious—though not necessarily less dangerous—route. Something my father taught me at a young age was to never undervalue your talents, be they few or many, great or small; as such, I have always valued my intellect and strategic reasoning. I am also, however, quite adept at using tone of voice to my advantage. I inherited my father's deep growl, something that surprises a lot of people, given my relatively slight frame. Nevertheless, it's effective at getting people to listen to me, if not flat-out obey.

In a split-second decision, I elected to turn it on Nate, lowering my voice to a much quieter decibel as I slid a hand around to the small of his back and murmured, "What do you plan to do with me, now that you've got my undivided attention?" He all but had to press himself against me to catch the words, his breath hot against my jaw as he brought his ear closer to my mouth. His warmth made me shiver.

The question caught Nate off guard—I saw that much in the quick lift of eyebrows and the blush that suffused his cheeks, making that smattering of freckles stand out even more. He hid it quickly, however, and once recovered didn't shy from the challenge of close physical proximity with a near stranger. If anything he seemed relieved, perhaps happy to be back on even footing, certain of my interest.

At the brush of his lips against my ear, I couldn't disguise my shudder or the quick puff of breath I expelled in his direction. Compared to a lot of straight folk, gay men make agreeing to sex a pretty painless and straightforward transaction. The anticipation gave me a feeling like someone had started a motor in my belly, tiny vibrations growing stronger until they were indistinguishable from a racing heartbeat. "I've got a hotel room nearby," Nate informed me.

I stopped to consider the offer. Nine times out of ten, a hotel room is my preference—so much easier than having to consider the alternatives, like if bringing a trick home is the best way to safeguard my anonymity and my possessions. I've never had anything bad happen, but you hear stories, especially in the God-fearing Midwest or southern states, about unsuspecting gays who invite the wrong sort home. A few drag queens and transvestites have lost their lives this way, even in quiet Columbus. The promise of safety gave me a moment's pause, even though I'm normally a good judge of character. Nate didn't set off any warning bells. Most pressing of all was the sudden desire I had to see him amidst my possessions, drinking from my favorite mug, lounging on my sofa. His head against my pillow.

"N-no," I answered slowly, and for a split second our mouths were so close I couldn't have licked my lips without licking his as well. "My apartment is just down the street—I'd very much like to see how you look in my bed." The sight of Nate laid out on my sheets was an afterimage I'd be sure to keep long after his scent faded away in the wash. Tricks weren't something I tended to hold on to, but I had this feeling, this nagging suspicion Nate would be different. I expected those intelligent green eyes to haunt me for a while; already I had a hard time looking away. "Besides, we can make as much noise as we want without worrying about the other guests."

Apparently this reasoning was sufficient for Nate, his expression gone soft and heavy-lidded at my words, and we each finished our drinks in silence before he threw a few bills down on the bar for Adam. I was barely conscious of the men milling around us, pressing close in their effort to navigate the bar or attract Adam's attention. I didn't care about anything but Nate.

"I'll do my best not to disappoint you," he murmured into my ear. He gave a cheeky tug on my tie, fingers lingering against my breastbone for a half beat. "Lead the way."

The promise implicit in the statement made me flush and harden slightly in my pants, my mind already racing ahead of us down the street to my apartment. I saw us hurrying out of the bar, Nate's arm around my waist beneath my suit jacket. We wouldn't stop to kiss the whole way there, not even when the elevator doors slid closed and we were totally alone. No, I wouldn't get to feel that mouth against mine until my apartment door closed behind us and I turned to see Nate unbuttoning the cuffs of his shirt, a man getting down to business.

He didn't disappoint me at all, not that night. In fact, he so far exceeded my wildest fantasies that I never drove to Chicago the next day, content to bend to the suggestion to put the weekend to better and more creative uses. It's not that Nate was some spectacular hard body with a ten-inch cock or a tongue that could work miracles (well, maybe that last one); I've had those types before, and they never lingered in memory longer than a few hours. No, Nate was an average man with a heartbreaking face and a slight air of mystery to him, prone more to observation than talk, like he'd lived his whole life with a silence so deep he couldn't possibly see how words could fill it. There was so much passion in him, however, that for a minute I reconsidered what I was getting myself into. The way he touched me, the way he fucked me, the way he looked into my face afterward like he didn't quite know what to make of the whole thing... it made my skin tingle and burn like an ant beneath a child's magnifying glass.

Dozens of men have warmed my sheets before, but Nate was the first to make me want to stop the whole ride and think about how I'd feel when he walked off, never to be seen again.

Like I said, he didn't disappoint me. Not in the slightest. Maybe that's why it hurt so much when he finally betrayed me; I don't know. Hugh's probably right in saying I was lucky to get out when I did, but I must have developed a wicked case of Stockholm Syndrome; breaking up with Nate felt like cutting off my own arm, tearing away what had become a part of myself. I still check myself for scars sometimes, as though I should see his name branded on my skin when I look in the mirror. Let's just say the fall back to Earth was a hard one. Small wonder, really, I wound up in Cardiff with a suitcase full of Valium and more baggage than a luggage car.

But. That's all in the past now, isn't it?

After yoga and the second shower of the day, I throw on jeans and a T-shirt and grab my wetsuit from where it hangs drying over the bathtub, and shrug off Nate's memory and the foul mood it never fails to put me in. Time to head over to Hugh's.

I'm looking forward to surfing today—Mondays are always best, the beaches quiet and free of weekend crowds. Sometimes I think I'm really starting to get it—I might not be ready for the Suckouts yet, but weather patterns have taken on a new significance that extends beyond "rainy" or "sunny" or "windy." I used to favor bright summer days with gentle breezes and low humidity, but now find myself excited by overcast skies and the threat of precipitation. Beyond a doubt, that's where the best waves come from, and Hugh's now comfortable letting me tackle a few of the bigger tubes off the reef. With that much water splashing you in the face, a little rain is immaterial.

I set out determined to have a good day and not waste more time dwelling on Nate fucking Fessenden. Lucky for me, Hugh lives within walking distance of my little house on the Palermo Springs compound. While far from being a hotbed of excitement, Cardiff is such a beautiful town that it's hard to be in a snit with the smell of the sea in the air and a touch of eternal summer in the breeze, even during overcast days, the palm trees swaying in the wind like perpetual motion machines.

There's a laid-back atmosphere to the whole place I've never experienced in the Midwest or the East Coast. People very much seem to take life in stride here, which I suppose is the perfect quality for a rehabilitation setting. If you walk around long enough, some of that sense of calm starts to rub off. Surfers are a pretty relaxed group at the best of times, but in Cardiff they actually seem... happy. I can see why Hugh settled down here. Once my program at Palermo is finished—soon, now—I think I'll use what money is left to me from the sale of my Columbus and Chicago apartments, and buy something in the neighborhood. I'd be lying if I said I didn't sometimes think about how much Nate would like it here, because he's certainly got the right constitution, but then again, I kind of like that Cardiff is just *mine* and Hugh's, not anyone else's. Funny how much changes in a year.

As I round the corner onto Cape Sebastian Place, past where it veers off from Manchester, a few young guys are making their way to the beach, wetsuits already half-unzipped to their navels, shortboards tucked beneath their arms with easy pride. They can probably tell the weather's going to churn up some nice waves too. We nod at each other in passing, and I wonder if we'll all end up chasing the same tubes together before day's end, or chatting in a floating circle as we wait for the next swell. A couple of them are exceptionally handsome, even to my jaded eyes, and some old part of me halfheartedly hopes we'll see them again. Hugh's house is the third down from the left, so with any luck we'll join them soon.

Sebastian Place is a lovely street, one of the prettiest in Cardiff, in my opinion. It's set at the top of a hill that leads down to the water, and there's a great view in every direction, the ocean to the east and San Elijo Lagoon to the south. No matter how much Hugh wishes otherwise, his house is like an oceanfront palace. There are too many windows and angled terraces, and the Land Rover in the driveway is a quiet reminder the owner isn't short on cash. He said he tried living in a more unassuming house when he first moved to Cardiff, but was hounded by curious townsfolk until he caved and moved to a private corner lot with a single neighbor. Still, the overall effect is one I like. Somehow it doesn't scream ostentatious wealth like some of the residences I've seen around the area, which is to say, Hugh's house is gorgeous, but not the nicest one on the street.

What disturbs me is that Hugh appears to have a visitor: a huge black motorcycle is parked next to the Land Rover, gleaming in the pale sunlight and reflecting the sky back a darker shade of gray. The make and model I recognize instantly—it's a Ducati Sport Classic 1000, beautifully maintained but with an irrepressible attitude. I knew someone who drove a Ducati once, and I swear to God that machine was more precious to him than a child. He called her Lucy and would talk to her in the mornings as though she might actually answer back and wish him good day. All the hairs on my arms and the back of my neck stand up at the sight of that bike, and it's the first time I start to worry, seriously worry, there's something else afoot besides mere coincidence. Swallowing, I mount the front steps.

I ring the doorbell, resisting the urge to walk right into the house the way I always do. My heart is hammering so hard in my chest that my ears ring and my cheeks tingle. Panic. It's just a fluke, I tell myself adamantly—there are plenty of hot bikes in this part of California, where rich folk like to throw money away on something flashy to drive around on the weekend. It doesn't mean anything at all, except maybe I'm not as recovered as I first thought. There's no way, none, that this Ducati is the same one Nate Fessenden used to drive back in Ohio, because that would just be fucking *crazy*.

Shit.

I hear Hugh's booming laugh echo from inside the house. There's a scuffle to get to the door amidst Callie's barking, like the occupants are wrestling to see who will get there first. The answering voice is so instantly familiar, I have to fight my body's immediate fight-or-flight response, which, since I've never so much as punched another person, would probably translate to me puking, then passing out. The door opens as I'm darting my eyes around, palms clammy, throat tight, trying to find the nearest escape.

On the other side, with his hand poised above the doorknob, Nate freezes. No better word for it. Whatever smile brightened his face a second ago disappears like someone slapped it off him, his whole body going so still the rest of the neighborhood seems to quiet in response. Even the birds fall silent, or at least that's what it feels like. All I can hear is blood rushing past my ears as my heart jackhammers a frantic tympani rhythm. For a second neither of us says anything. We don't even blink. Then from behind Nate, Hugh exclaims, "Oh, shit, Phel—I forgot!" in his dopey, clueless way.

Nate doesn't turn to acknowledge his brother's statement. He's still caught staring at me like he's just seen a ghost—which I suppose he has. I think a part of me died the second that door opened and I saw him standing there, like a vision from my worst nightmare.

"You've got to be fucking kidding me," I whisper under my breath, barely loud enough to be heard. But Nate hears, and for an eternity our gazes collide and hold, the two of us too stunned to waver or look away. "This cannot be happening."

The words make Nate's spine straighten a bit more, and those green, green eyes, every bit as dangerous and beautiful as I remember, glint as he steps back to allow me into the house. His expression slides gracefully from surprise into cold challenge.

"Hey," he says in that old down-home accent of his, and gestures for me to enter. "I'm Hugh's brother, Nate. Now who might you be?"

2

Nate

THERE isn't much that ever makes me want to cry, but if I had to name a few things off the top of my head, the thought of Lucy getting dented is one, or something happening to Hugh or Emilia or Liam, or the Rangers losing the World Series at the bottom of the ninth. Luckily only one of those things has ever happened, and that ball game alone was almost enough to make me break down like a freaking baby on the spot. The other stuff would just destroy me. No two ways about it. Hugh actually insists I cry more than any grown man he knows, but I really fucking beg to differ. I have ragweed issues, but even then I like to think my watery eyes are manly, like Charlton Heston's would be if he had allergies. Nothing emotional, no sissy stuff.

But all that changes the second I yank open Hugh's front door and see *him* standing there with that perfect face and those flying-saucer eyes bluer than the fucking sky, looking a bit like he's not far from crying himself.

Phel. Phelan.

He looks different from the last time I saw him, even though that was only… shit, four months ago now. Not so much physically; he's lost weight off his already slim frame, gained a bit more definition in his shoulders and upper body, but it's like the last few months went and scrambled his brains a little or something. Which, maybe. We've all been there. I notice something birdlike and vulnerable that wasn't there when we first met, because the guy I laid eyes on in that Columbus bar was… whoa. That guy was as slick and confident as a modern-day Don Draper, right down to his hair, so self-assured that it could have bordered on arrogance if not for the kindness in his eyes. Phelan possessed a sense of wariness then too, probably from guarding himself for so long, but nothing like this. Of all the words to come to mind when I see his exhausted mouth and ruffled fringe, the first one is "damaged."

And I know, without a doubt, whose fault that is.

The only one whose world is moderately less rocked by this encounter is Hugh, who, with one hand on Callie's collar to restrain her, skids to a halt a few feet behind me. He says, "Oh shit, Phel—I forgot!" in his typical oblivious way.

There'll be time later to figure out how the hell they even know each other—not that my mind isn't already racing, trying to calculate the likelihood Phel somehow figured out who my brother is and stalked him across the country in an effort to get back at me. Right now I'm a lot more concerned with Phel either trying to shank me or run in the opposite direction. Both responses would give away the game pretty fast. Thankfully, he does neither.

He mutters, "You've got to be fucking kidding me," in an undertone not meant for anyone else. "This cannot be happening." I can't help overhear it, and my gaze sharpens at the words.

I want to say, *You and me both, buddy.* I feel myself go stiff and tense at the pure venom in his tone, a stark contrast to the part of me that wants to grab that beautiful face and check that he's real. Among other things. Instead, I manage to keep it together and put on the expression I wore an awful lot during the year Phelan and I saw each other in secret. It hurts to use it against him now, but there's a reason they say the best offense is a good defense.

"Hey," I greet him neutrally, and open the door like it would make my day if he came on in. "I'm Hugh's brother, Nate. Now who might you be?"

Before Phel can take the invitation to throw the first punch, and I can tell from the look on his face that's just what he'd like to do, Hugh insinuates a fraction of his huge body between us, a reminder there's a very thin line to tread here. Phelan's interest in maintaining Hugh's ignorance is as yet unknown, but for the moment he appears settled, giving Hugh the opportunity to clap him on the shoulder and say, "Nate, this is my friend Phel. He moved to Cardiff a few months ago and we've been doing a lot of surfing together. Phel, this is my brother." Hugh has that look on his face that reminds me why I sometimes think of him as a big, eager puppy. A puppy I currently want to abandon on the side of the freeway without any food or water.

Speaking of which, he releases his dog as Phel steps inside, and Callie jumps excitedly and licks at Phelan's fingers like she's in the throes of ecstasy. This more than anything confirms that Phel spends a lot of time here; Callie's a sweet dog, but she never shuts up around people she doesn't know well, and molests those she does.

"Pleased to meet you," Phel answers stiffly, one hand upon the dog's head, and fails to offer the handshake that would make this whole fake introduction a tad more believable. Just like old times, Phel has these moments of borderline social retardation that used to endear him to me, but right now the quirk is nothing short of terrifying. While it's not like we spent the bulk of our time together trading straight-acting tips, sometimes I have no idea how he pretended to be hetero his entire life. "Hugh didn't mention you would be coming to visit.... Forgive my intrusion." Crap, he's doing his God voice again, which is what Phel always does when he has no idea how else to take control of a situation. "I should... go."

"No," Hugh interjects, squeezing his shoulder again. "Nate surprised me too—you couldn't have known. I should have called to say I couldn't make it out today. Still, now that you're here, there's no reason you can't stick around. Right?"

For fuck's sake, Hugh. Trying not to sound too desperate, I say, "Phel here looks like he was just on his way to the beach," gesturing to his wetsuit and towel and the little smear of sunblock at his temple that hasn't quite managed to be absorbed into the skin. A year ago I would have wiped it off for him or been the one to apply it in the first place. The image of slathering sunblock onto that pale back pops into my head unbidden, and I force it back down with something like desperation. "We should let him get on with his business."

This earns me an annoyed look from them both. "Don't be a dick, Nate," Hugh tells me in a flat voice. "Phel and I surf together every day." Well then. To Phel he says, "You don't mind the extra company, do you? Nate's a lot less annoying once you get to know him."

Phel looks absolutely stricken, to the point I'd feel sorry for the guy if I weren't so busy dying on the inside. "I—"

"Awesome. We were just grabbing some snacks in the kitchen. Come on." Expression mulish, save for the parting glare he sends my way, Hugh grabs Phel by the arm and shuts the front door before striding farther into the house, Phelan trailing behind with a look of dread on his face.

"Fuck, fuck, fuck," I curse to myself, and for a few seconds I stare at the space they've vacated, everything silent except for Hugh talking animatedly on his way to the kitchen and the whirr of the AC in the foyer. I don't even know what just happened.

Since when does Hugh choose some random guy over uninterrupted face time with his big brother, who just drove across the country to see him? And since when does that random guy also turn out to be my former gay lover? If there's a God, please oh please don't let them be fucking. The thought is just too damn depressing. Hugh's resolute heterosexuality aside, with the run of shit luck I've been having lately, such a development wouldn't surprise me. Someone really wise once said *fuck my life*, and given the current state of things, that about sums it up. Not that I wouldn't deserve it. There's a special circle of hell reserved for douchebags like me.

Seeing Hugh and Phelan seated at the kitchen island, and Phel sending furtive glances in my direction, I elect to delay further interaction by slipping upstairs to my bedroom. Attached is a private balcony that faces the ocean. A deep breath of sea air goes a long way to calm my nerves and get me thinking straight—no pun intended— though I'm no closer to having any answers than before.

Phel, here? In California? The only place he used to complain about visiting more bitterly than the South was Los Angeles, adverse as he was to the heat and humidity. A Midwesterner through and through. It makes absolutely no sense for him to be here, even excusing the problematical mindfuck, and the odds of him being best buddies with my freaking *brother* of all people are even worse. I know Hugh better than anyone—he doesn't do friends, not like before Nell died, and Phel isn't what you'd call a warm personality. Not unless there's sex involved.

And, I mean, I would know. I spent the better part of a year getting intimately acquainted with the inside of Phelan's bedroom, as well as every square inch of his house, his body, and the deep recesses of his mind. More than that, I got a front-row seat to what makes him laugh and shout and smile and cry, all of which I directly accomplished at one point or another during our relationship.

And, hell. Relationship. There's a concept. Not in just general, though that too, but mostly in reference to Phel. After a year together, I suppose that's what we had—something we never anticipated or claimed to want, but nevertheless managed to achieve. To me it's a word that, even after the breakup or divorce or slammed doors and screening of calls has happened, implies some special connection remains, some invisible cord that tethers you to the other person regardless of time or space. Phel is the first person who made me feel there was nothing left to cling to after it ended, so effectively did he disappear. For months and months he was all I could see. Then he was just... gone. But I'm getting ahead of myself.

I met Phel on a perfectly average day in June, a Friday, notable only because I was in Columbus on a business trip and, later, for the events it set in motion. For the past few years I'd been working at a contracting firm owned by my wife's brother-in-law, Craig, and most of my time was spent meeting with clients and potential clients, a lot of them large corporations or institutions such as hospitals and schools. My primary duty was to charm my way into a deal and make sure the client stayed happy by any means necessary.

The work was different than what I'd expected going in. At first I started off as a carpenter, but Craig, who did me no favors on account of my being the guy to knock up his wife's sister, must have recognized my talents lay elsewhere. I'm the first to admit that, aside from working with my hands, my gift is people. Anyone who knows me knows I can talk my way out of anything about as well as I can talk my way *into* it. Suddenly I was being promoted to project manager, then business manager for the whole company, which was one of the more successful contracting firms in the Greater Columbus area.

As such, I made a lot of trips into the city during the week and on weekends, close enough to Mount Vernon that I could drive home at the end of the day, but far enough away that it wasn't unheard of to stay a couple of nights when wining and dining prospective accounts. Although I didn't mind Columbus as a city, it was a lot bigger and noisier than I was used to, having grown up in small-town Alabama and relocated to equally small-town Ohio. Mount Vernon was practically a hamlet by comparison, which suited my family just fine. I'd been living there with Emilia and our son, Liam, for the better part of a decade, but to be honest, I looked forward to my trips to Columbus.

I know how that sounds. If nothing else, I want to say I never set out to hurt anyone. Not Emilia, not Liam. Certainly not Phel. While that doesn't excuse my behavior or change the fact that people *did* get hurt, none of it was premeditated or malicious—just self-centered and careless. Instead of facing my issues like a man, trying to shoulder the burden myself and minimize the damage to others, I failed to think about the impact of my actions or anything beyond what I wanted in the here and now. No matter what the excuse, cheating ain't anything but an act of selfishness, because in that moment when you're supposed to choose between yourself and them, the people you love, you choose yourself.

I chose myself, my wants. I chose what made my dick hard and my heart beat faster. Sure, Phel's a million times more than that to me now, but if I'd walked away that first night he never would have risen above the station of "hot guy at a bar." So now my family's paying for my fuckup, and me, well… I'm paying too, except that I don't have a right to complain. As far as I'm concerned, I got off easy. But that doesn't change the fact that I was toiling away in a marriage that no longer made me happy like it once did, or like I thought it did. Going to Columbus was a breather, my uncomplicated means of escape. Until I met Phel, that's all it was—an escape. I never went there to cheat on my wife.

Like a lot of marriages with unhappy endings, mine and Emilia's started with a surprise pregnancy. I was nineteen, she eighteen, and what was meant to be an uncomplicated weekend of athletic, no-strings-attached sex culminated in Liam nine months later. Thinking it was the right thing to do, I married her.

She's a nice girl, is Emilia, and Liam got his grabby little hands right in there around my heart within five seconds of meeting. Hasn't let go since. Your perspective changes when you find yourself looking down at this small human who bears obvious parts of you, whether it's your hair or your eyes or the beginnings of the famous Fessenden smile that will go on to break a few hearts. There wasn't really another option; I would never have forgiven myself for walking away a second time, especially not when that family made a place for me with no questions asked. Emilia even suggested Hugh live with us for a year before he went to college. It's not often you find people willing to do that—having all but raised Hugh myself, I know that better than most. Now my kid is about to turn ten, and where the fuck am I?

    I wish I could say I didn't realize I batted for the other team until recently, but that'd be a lie. In a sense, I've always known my interests don't align with those of the run-of-the-mill straight dude I project myself to be, but it took a lot of years of running before I started to come around to the idea. Admittedly, I still have a hard time not hiding it. By the time I started to accept my sexuality, I was already married, firmly entrenched in the lifestyle everyone expected of me. One I expected of myself. Despite having experimented a little before marrying Emilia—nothing more than a few blowjobs or random bar hookups—I really didn't know who I was in that respect, who I wanted to be. I still had a healthy appreciation for a beautiful woman, but even if I found myself checking out her boyfriend at the same time, I wasn't sure I could picture myself in a relationship with a man in the way that seemed hardwired with chicks. Then again, I hadn't had so much luck in the relationship department with women either. Was I bi, gay, or just confused? Damned if I knew. Liam happened before I could really figure out the answer to that question.

    At the time, I hadn't quite managed to outgrow the anxiety that touching another dude's dick established me as card-carrying member of Team Pink. For life. Marrying Emilia seemed the best solution for everyone: she'd get a husband and a father to our kid, I'd be a part of my son's life and have someone awesome to hang out with, and hopefully my years of confusion would stay in the past where they belonged. Shit, even my father's tough-as-nails cop's heart seemed warmed by the sudden addition of a grandson and daughter-in-law before he died. And I was seriously going to fuck that up on a hunch that I might like cock? Hell no. I took my vows seriously. Maybe it's no surprise I eventually cracked under the pressure of keeping that mask in place.

    That weekend in Columbus, I had no plans to do so. Honest. I'd entered a bit of a rough patch in the truce with my non-heterosexually inclined urges, but promised myself I'd do nothing more than look. Looking was acceptable, I reasoned, and it was something I needed, either to confirm my straightness or... I don't know. I guess I never really stopped to think what I would do if I showed up at a gay bar and wanted more, but maybe I figured I'd cross that bridge if and when I got to it.

I did not expect to meet *him*.

The name of the bar was Foxley's. I found the place on the Internet after hours of searching. Columbus's gay scene isn't exactly hopping, but thank God I learned how to delete browser history back when Hugh and I still lived together. Last thing I needed was Liam or, God forbid, Emilia finding all that shit. I went for the quietest watering hole I could find within walking distance of my hotel, and Foxley's promised a laid-back atmosphere free of the aggressive trolling found at most gay bars and clubs. After a day filled with client meetings and phone conferences with Craig, I was in need of a stiff drink and a few hours to unwind. Used to being approached by the fairer sex at most of the sports bars I frequented, I found the prospect of not having to make polite conversation with interested women pretty appealing, this more a byproduct of marriage than my sexuality crisis. By comparison, I thought it'd be easier to tell a guy to fuck off, if it came to that.

I don't really know what I expected when I first walked in the door: male go-go dancers, maybe, or porn playing on the television screens, or a bunch of dudes having sex in plain sight. I was relieved to see all the customers fully clothed and grouped around the bar like civilized people, chatting, watching sports, drinking beer, and looking not at all like the rowdy club-goers you see on television shows like *Queer As Folk*. I guess you can like dick and still harbor misconceptions, huh? A giant deer head mounted on the wall set the tone of the place and, me being from Alabama, helped put me more at ease. I was still dressed for a meeting in my suit and tie, and quickly noticed others who looked like they'd also come from work. My wedding ring was tucked safely away in my suitcase back at the hotel. Feeling naked without it, I must have rubbed my ring finger a few times while I looked around.

A few eyes shifted my way as I took a deep breath and wandered closer to the bar. Their rapid-fire appraisals made me feel like a bull being measured and weighed at a fair, the looks fast turning predatory when I seemed to pass some invisible standard. Now, I'm not blind or prone to false modesty—I know I'm a good-looking guy. I take care of myself and have never hurt for attention. But this was completely different from getting checked out by a group of giggling women with martinis in hand. At least there's an element of coyness there, shyness even, whereas how these men looked at me was pure sex. Like they wanted to eat me off the bone. To my surprise, it was a total trip, and not just a power trip.

Forget feeling up another guy's cock, I thought, *this* is how you tendered your resignation from the heterosexual lifestyle. It was the first time I'd ever set foot in a gay bar, period, and I couldn't claim to have gone there at the behest of a female friend or a group of buddies in search of a laugh. I was there because I wanted to be, because this was where I thought I belonged. The feeling terrified me more than the moment I said *I do* and made Emilia my wife, more than learning I had a kid.

I quickly made my way toward the back of the bar, where I felt I'd draw less notice. Luckily there was already someone attracting most of the attention, chatting to a few other men with his back to me, and I slid into a free spot a couple of seats down. Ordering a Scotch, midshelf but respectable, I settled in to take stock of the whole place, curious about the customers Foxley's tended to attract; the crowd seemed mixed, men in their twenties to upward of forty or fifty. It was hard to get a handle on whether Foxley's catered to a particular clientele, or if it was a locale favored by many regardless of income or social status.

From the corner of my eye, I noticed the dude beside me behaved like he was pretty high up on the food chain, ruling over the small crowd he'd attracted like a king before his court. After a few moments of polite chat, he dismissed his companions and swiveled back around to face the bar with an expression caught somewhere between boredom and melancholy. Curious and with nothing better to do, I tried to get a closer look. And, well… shit.

Damn if he wasn't the most gorgeous person—not man, *person*—I'd ever seen in my life, wearing an impeccably tailored gray suit as easily as he wore his dark hair and incredible eyes, bright even in the dim lighting of the bar. The whole look-don't-touch idea went bust when I let my eyes linger a moment too long on his mouth. Plenty of men have gorgeous lips, cocksucking lips, and I suppose in some circles I'm considered one of 'em. But this man… you couldn't look at a mouth like that and think about anything but sin.

I tried so hard not to stare, but it was too late. He caught me out and turned the full force of those eyes towards me, gaze flicking up and down over my seated form in quick assessment. I couldn't for the life of me look away, though I frantically reminded myself talking to anyone wasn't part of the plan. When a slow smile curled those criminally full lips and he tilted his head in invitation, I was up and wandering closer before I registered my feet upon the ground. My face and neck flamed with the force of my blush. This was retarded; Hugh's favorite joke was that I could impregnate women with a look. Nate Fessenden didn't get embarrassed. *I* was being retarded.

Attempting to man up and bite the bullet, I smiled and said, "Hey," throat tight. At the sound of my voice, his smirk widened and he met my gaze with a hell of a lot more gumption than I felt. "Can I buy you another drink?" I offered. We were both drinking Scotch, from the looks of it, and I was relieved he wasn't holding an appletini or something equally embarrassing.

After that, the details were blurry. His name was Phel—Phelan. I gave a fake name, Nate Smith, which felt awkward and wrong on my tongue but marginally less terrifying than telling him my real identity. Still, intensity crackled between us like something out of the Harlequin novels Emilia read on weekends, heady and thick. It was a sharp reminder I'd never felt anything so potent toward a woman—hell, not even another man. I'd felt it from seven feet away, and the feeling was even stronger up close as I breathed in Phelan's musky, soapy cologne and the subtle scent of whatever product he'd used in his hair.

I was shocked by his forwardness, which was nothing I hadn't encountered before, but never with such... style. Phel seemed uninterested in mincing words about what we both wanted, choosing instead to demonstrate his interest in *me*. No question what we were going back to his apartment to do. I'm a pretty confident guy, but Phelan's self-assuredness blew me away, left me too dumbstruck to do anything but follow him out of the bar. His arm around my waist all but anchored me to the decision I'd taken a scant thirty seconds to make. Amazing how easy it is to cheat, once you get down to it. I wanted him, pure and simple, with more force and more certainty than I'd ever wanted or known anything in my life. Gay, straight, bi... it didn't matter. There was just this, this, *this*.

Fortunately, Phel didn't live far. We came to an old limestone church that looked like it'd been built in the late nineteenth or early twentieth century, and I didn't realize until we walked in the front door that it was a residence, not a place of worship. The interior was gorgeous and masculine, renovated with lots of glass, marble, and steel to offset carefully preserved arched doorways and stained glass windows that hinted what the building had once been. Its effect was of a pastiche palace. Located in the heart of Columbus, this building screamed wealth and status.

As we passed the concierge on our way to the elevators, we were greeted with a nod and a respectful "Good evening, gentlemen." Phel showed no concern if the man noticed our possessive arms around each other, though to be fair we hadn't even kissed yet. After all those flirtatious touches at the bar, Phel's breath hot in my ear when he invited me back to his home, telling me how much he wanted to see how I looked in his bed… holy shit. I was so desperate to taste him I felt drunk with it, but he kept his hands to himself even after we stepped into the elevator, leaning against the opposite wall with this look on his face that promised way more than I could fathom at the time.

Nate Fessenden, I thought, *you are out of your motherfucking depth.*

I tried to distract myself by studying the expert craftsmanship of our surroundings, noting that nothing was shoddy or cheap or half-assed, not like so many cookie-cutter developments these days. Occupational hazard. The building's foyer looked like something worthy of the Pope. Not that I guessed otherwise, but it was obvious Phelan shelled out to live here, and part of me was as curious to see his apartment as I was eager to get him behind closed doors. I had no idea what I'd do once we got there, beyond taking his clothes off and making him moan. Mostly I just needed to get my hands on him.

We rode the elevator up a couple of floors, and it dinged open to reveal a dimly lit hallway. There were only two doors, one at either end, and I followed Phelan to the one on the left. He slid his key into the lock with steady hands and gestured for me to enter with a serene expression. Greeting me was a wide, artwork-lined hallway paneled in rich cherrywood, the light fixtures reflecting back at themselves from the polished marble floors. I could see where the hallway opened up to a large kitchen and dining room, and beyond, an industrial-looking staircase that led to the rest of the house. Work had brought me to some pretty fancy homes in my day, but aside from Hugh's SoCal palace, this was the first time I'd ever been a guest someplace so lavish. I had no idea what Phel did for a living, but it definitely wasn't construction. I glanced over at him with my eyebrows raised when he acknowledged his home with little more than a sigh, for a moment only resembling any old nine-to-fiver returning to the nest after a long day at the office. He tossed his keys into an elaborate-looking metal bowl on the hall table.

Overwhelmed, I indulged myself a moment to take it all in, leaning back against the door and pushing my shirtsleeves up above my elbows. My discarded blazer hung loose in one hand. Though the night air outside was cool, it felt over a hundred degrees inside; I was unbearably warm and growing warmer. My eyes fixed on Phelan's back as he shrugged out of his own suit jacket, looking slim and calm and collected, the thin material of his cherry blossom-pink shirt pulling attractively tight across his shoulders.

The flash of hunger I felt when he turned to look at me must have transmitted, because he was in front of me within seconds, lips inches from mine, hands ready to fist the fabric of my button-down. Those haunting eyes of his were even more incredible up close, lashes as long and full as a girl's, irises bluer than the plumage of one of those birds of paradise you see on the Discovery Channel.

"You're so fucking gorgeous," I breathed incredulously, heart pounding, and my chest ached at the throaty laugh Phel gave in response.

Unexpectedly, almost shyly, his gaze flicked over to the rest of the apartment that was visible beyond the hallway. "Do you want the tour, or a drink?" he asked.

All nerves, I chuckled. "Not really, man." I wouldn't have minded a glass of water and the opportunity to check out the kitchen finishes, compare notes for the renovation Emilia and I had been discussing for a while, but obviously I wasn't going to say that out loud.

My answer earned me a sly smile. "Good." Phel's hands settled lightly upon my chest and slid up to the collar of my shirt. His thumbs proceeded to play with the button at my throat below where I'd undone the first couple. "I wasn't joking when I said I wanted to see how you looked in my bed," he informed me, "but I'd settle for getting you out of these clothes first."

"I'd settle for kissing you first," I countered, swallowing.

He shrugged and leaned forward enough that I felt his breath tickle my teeth; the slightest movement of my head made our noses bump and our lips brush. So fucking close. "No reason we can't accomplish both at once," he amended, and with that there was no more talking, and our mouths finally fused together with all the weight of our anticipation.

Phelan's kisses were way too forceful and dirty for the composed demeanor he'd presented at the bar, and I quickly found myself pressed back against the door with a thigh between my legs, my mouth opening on a gasp to let Phel's tongue inside. He kissed hot and powerful, self-assured, and I felt like I was being claimed or something. *Stop being a pussy*, I coached myself. This I could do, and there was no way I'd let myself be a freaking bystander while my mouth got all but ravaged by someone this insanely hot. "Passive" wasn't how I wanted this encounter to go down in memory. I'd show him forceful and dirty, all right. I could give as much as I took.

Once he worked open the buttons of my shirt and skimmed his palms over my chest, I grabbed Phelan round the waist and turned so our positions were reversed, bearing him against the door. The impact was a bit harder than intended, rattling the wood in its frame. Although I winced at that, Phel inhaled sharply into my mouth, pushing back with his hips but otherwise unable to shove me off. I had a couple of inches and a good thirty or so pounds on him, despite the breadth of his shoulders and his muscular legs, and keeping him in place was enough of a struggle to make it hot.

With one hand around his slender wrists, I was able to pin his arms high above his head, fumbling with his tie and the buttons of his shirt while he purred nonsense at me and bit kisses to my neck and jaw. His chest was beautiful, lean and spare as the rest of him. I couldn't resist the small groan that escaped me as our skin pressed together. By then my body felt like a construction site: nipples hard enough to cut glass, cock swollen enough to pound nails. The last time I'd been this turned-on was… never. Never with Emilia, never with anyone. I couldn't help but think of the first time I'd let another man go down on me, how sharp the arousal had been then too—this was like that, times a billion.

Once we were half-undressed, it was easy to keep going and reach for Phel's belt buckle, the fastenings of his pants. Our lurching hips made progress a bit complicated, but he favored me with a sound of such ecstasy, once I reached inside his boxers and wrapped my hand around his cock, that I probably would have chewed through leather to get to him. I wanted to swoon like a fucking maiden at the feel of that heavy dick in my hand, and he was so wet for me, so hot, I felt the shiver start in my shoulders and travel down to my feet.

Like most good Midwestern boys, Phel was circumcised. It was similar enough to my own that I started pumping my fist up and down his length without having to think too hard about the mechanics. We seemed to like a lot of the same things, if his moans were anything to go by, except for where I preferred a faster jack, he made the most noise when I slowed the pace and concentrated on long, firm strokes from base to tip, pausing to catch and swirl my thumb in the precome easing the way.

The sight of him flushed and vulnerable in my arms just about undid me. After trailing my lips up his neck, I paused to tongue his ear before I pressed my mouth to his once more, I felt almost as wanton as he looked, trying to reap as much friction as possible by thrusting my crotch against my own forearm. As soon as I let go of his wrists, Phelan's hands were everywhere, clutching at my shoulders, my back, my hair. Holding us together. I wanted so badly to make him come right there, but that seemed a bit crass, considering we hadn't made it past the front foyer. Plus I got the feeling he wouldn't be pleased to ruin his expensive suit.

As I started to slow down, Phel made a noise of frustration and cursed, "Fuck, Nate," his hips hitching a little in my direction. "Why'd you *stop*?"

I couldn't suppress a laugh at the pissed-off look on his face. "Because. It's early and I think we're just getting started, yeah?" I had no idea what time it was, nor the day or year. "I really want to see you naked. Besides, I'm sure your dry cleaner will thank me." When he grimaced rather adorably, I released his cock with some reluctance and curled that hand around his side, enjoying the slide of bodily fluids against his skin. "Bedroom?" I suggested.

He nodded and pushed himself away from the wall. "This way," he directed while toeing off his shoes. I did the same and, accepting his outstretched hand, followed him through the kitchen to the stairs.

The staircase was made entirely of brushed steel and glass, obviously a modern addition in a very modern space. But save for a few paintings on the walls, there was nothing to indicate a personal touch, no clue this was Phel's home and no one else's. I don't mean I suspected he might have a partner who lived there, or even a roommate—unlikely—but I didn't see anything of the man in our surroundings. Staged Ikea rooms looked less clinical. Then again, I guess living in a church was statement enough.

We bypassed the rest of the house to reach his bedroom. On the second and third floors were the living room and study. Maybe there were some extra bedrooms in there somewhere, though I reminded myself that I had no reason or need to acquaint myself with his home.

I must have made looking around an obvious undertaking. His voice startled me a little, shaking me out of my thoughts.

"I don't spend all my time in Columbus," Phel explained. This was a weird conversation to be having while half-undressed. "Between here and Chicago, I never really have enough time to make either place feel like a home." He smiled ironically, and I couldn't resist pulling him to me for a kiss, reveling in how warm and buttery he went in my arms. With his hair spiked up in every direction, he looked like pure sex. Pulling away, he nipped at my bottom lip and added, "A friend always helps solve that, though."

On the way to what I assumed was the master bedroom, on the top level, we passed a glass-railed balcony that looked down onto the rest of the apartment, revealing massive arched windows on all sides and a giant fireplace. The grouping of leather couches in the living room made it look like something out of a design magazine. Some adolescent part of me immediately wanted to go have sex on them and rough the place up a bit, leave a mark.

"Nice digs," I said, unable to hide my curiosity. I suppose it must have made me look a little materialistic, but I was desperate to discover something about the other man that would take him from a complete stranger to someone familiar. After almost eight years of marriage, I'd forgotten how unnerving it could be to come home with a virtual unknown, and the extent to which you need to compartmentalize to make it seem normal. "What part of the church are we in?"

"The steeple," Phel told me with a hint of a smile. "The bedroom's through here. I'll give you the tour after, if you like. I wouldn't mind, ah...." Uncharacteristically, based on what I'd seen so far, Phelan blushed and trailed off.

The way his eyes ticked over to the living room a floor below us made me think my idle fantasizing wasn't far off the mark. "Wanna christen the rest of the house, huh?" I offered, taking childlike relish in the pun. I was met by a flash of his eyes and a sharp bite of his lip. Bingo. Nice to know I wasn't the only one with my mind in the gutter. "Haven't lived here long, have you?"

He chuckled. "No, I have. It's just not like me to bring people home. You're the first in a long time—since before I lived here, at any rate." With another subtle inclination of his head, he tugged me toward him and maneuvered us both in the direction of the bedroom.

"What made me different?" I asked. I bit at his earlobe, palming the small of his back. For some reason the idea made me shiver and go warm with pleasure.

A hiss emerged from between Phel's lips as I moved to suck at the juncture of his neck and shoulder, nosing his shirt collar out of the way. I could see the bed just a few steps away now, his room large around us in the darkness. "I told you," he gasped. "I wanted to see how you looked in my bed."

"Well, here we are. Bed."

After letting myself be lowered onto the duvet, I pushed up to my elbows to watch as Phel moved around the bed to grab condoms and lube and turn on a lamp. I got a better look at where he slept. Though not brightly lit, the room was industrial and cave-like with its exposed crossbeams, air ducts, and stone walls. The tops of the stained glass windows were visible just past the balcony.

"I feel like I've wandered onto the set of *The Hunchback of Notre Dame*," I said. It was easier to comment on that than the condoms and lube, which reminded me I was still undecided as to how things should proceed. I'd fucked a guy only once and was otherwise uninitiated. Thing was, I couldn't say the idea of Phelan taking me up the ass was remotely a turn-off. In fact, the thought made me shiver a little bit, my cock giving a sharp twitch of agreement.

Shedding his shirt and dress pants, which he then folded over the back of a chair, Phel lifted his eyebrows at me. "Come now, we're both far too attractive for that to be true," he quipped.

I chuckled at the remark, but it came out sounding like a dirty old man laugh as he stepped out of his underwear and turned to face me, completely naked. His body was better than I'd imagined, pale and wired with muscle, hips bisected by deep cut lines that begged to be tracked with a finger or tongue. Nestled in the bed of dark hair that trailed from his navel, his cock was still half-hard, magnificent, curving in a perfect *Playgirl* arc down over his balls.

He flexed his shoulders a little under my gaze. "You're still not undressed."

I didn't need to be told a third time. While I was shrugging out of my shirt, he came to help remove the rest of my clothing, and I felt my cock jump. Legs on either side of my knee, he unbuckled my pants and slid them down my legs, obligingly pulling my socks off as well. Phel took a step back to look at me. Under the scrutiny I felt both ridiculously exposed and like the hottest guy on the planet; his gaze was so appreciative that I burned all over.

Before I knew it, Phel had stepped closer again and was kneeling on the floor in front of me, pushing my legs apart with a hand on either of my thighs. His aggressive, businesslike manner excited me, and the mischievous look on his face fired me up even more. I tilted my hips toward him a little in invitation, and all the warning I got was an arched eyebrow and that same enigmatic smile from earlier. Not pausing for breath, he ducked and slipped his mouth over the head of my cock, holding me still, tongue immediately working to send me into overdrive as he swallowed me down. Some adult film actors had to work to make deep-throating seem like a breeze, and never quite managed to hide the instinctive cough or gag. Phel didn't have to try.

"Holy shit," I cried out, trying not to buck into his mouth or grab his hair.

The sight of my dick disappearing past those sinful lips was un-fucking-believable. I arched my back deliriously, head rolling loosely on my neck. He laved the underside of my cock with random patterns and swirls, and I swore I could feel every swipe and flick, but he could have written his name on my dick for all I wanted to him to stop. His hands cradling my balls and stroking up the base of my shaft brought me to the edge pretty quick, making short work of my already overexcited state.

If he was hoping to keep me in the game much longer, though, he was going to have to ease up fast. "I'm close, Phel, really close," I stuttered, and at a desperate yank of my hand in his hair, he pulled off. Nevertheless, the sudden absence of that crazy suction made me whine in complaint.

Coyly, he stopped lapping at the purple head of my cock long enough to observe, "Guess the tables are turned."

"You're driving me crazy, man."

He laughed, the most unguarded sound I'd heard him make all evening. At its most brilliant, his smile lit up his whole face and crinkled his nose in the sexiest fucking way imaginable.

After releasing me altogether, he climbed on top to straddle my hips, grunting when our cocks bumped off each other and slid a little in the cooling saliva he left behind on my skin. Phel was rock hard again. He kissed me once, fierce and dirty. "I want to feel you inside me," he whispered hotly against my lips, shimmying a little in my lap with what I guessed was impatience. It was a good look on him. "Do you… is that okay?"

Half-relieved at the request—there'd be more time later to admit I'd never had anything more than a couple of fingers up my ass—I nodded, carding my fingers through his hair and holding him still long enough for us to kiss deeply, tongues soft, teeth sharp. I felt Phel reaching up the bed for the bottle of lube and the condom, but when he pulled away, I only just caught him pouring a generous amount into his palm and reaching behind himself.

The thought of Phel opening himself up made me shudder right down to my toes, and with one arm about Phel's waist, holding him steady, I slid the other around to help. At the touch of my fingers, he arched his back and groaned, looking so ridiculously beautiful that my chest hurt. Together we pressed in until I felt my second knuckle slip past the taut muscle alongside Phelan's own. He was so tight, hot inside like an inferno. I couldn't hold back the whimper that escaped my throat, already lost to the thought of how amazing he'd feel around my dick.

Phel rocked onto our fingers, cock bobbing with the movement, and I leaned in to kiss his throat until he keened and gave another impatient shuffle.

"You ready?" I asked, breathless. At his furious nod, I withdrew my hand so I could fumble for the condom and get it unwrapped. Once it was on securely, Phel was there to smooth more of the lubricant onto my dick.

I barely had a moment to appreciate his thoroughness before he positioned himself above me and slid down in one long, torturous move, calling my name in a shout, wiggling his hips a little to take all of me in the first determined, if cautious, downstroke. I'm no Ron Jeremy, but I'm not small—that he did it with hardly a flinch was impressive, leaving no time for me to grab his hips or wish he'd go faster. Without jealousy or judgment, I considered this was obviously something Phel was experienced at. My eyes all but rolled back in their sockets from the squeeze.

He started slow at first, rocking his hips back and forth at a careful pace, adjusting, but after a short period, Phel settled his hands on my shoulders and used those amazing legs of his to move faster, pumping harder. Fuck, he was practically bouncing on my cock, content to do all the work while I clung to his hips and gasped against his neck. No one had ever ridden me like this before, never so sexy and in control, when the most I could contribute were weak thrusts in counterpoint. It'd never been like that with a woman, Emilia or otherwise. I could just manhandle them—Phel was too large and heavy in his own right for me to do anything without force. There wasn't much leverage with my ass still at the edge of the bed anyway, all of my strength and balance going to support the writhing body in my arms. The sounds that tumbled from his mouth, his voice deep and rough like chalk, shivered right down to my cock as his dick rubbed between us against my stomach, slicking my skin with wet. While the penetration of his body had made him go a bit soft, I felt him growing stiff again as he fucked against my abdomen.

"Fuck, oh fuck, Nate," he chanted, fingers digging into my shoulders, and sped up a bit more. All I could do was wrap my arms around him and hold on, shouting nonsense against his throat until he pulled my head back for a kiss, panting into my mouth.

Right then, I couldn't imagine doing anything else but this ever again, lost in the tightness of his body and the sweetness of his hips. All I could think was Phel looked like some kind of wild animal, rapt and delirious and in the most shameless abandon I'd ever seen. Like most guys in the throes of a mind-blowing fuck, I only wanted this for the rest of eternity and fell a little in predictable love. An orgasm was building with frightening speed deep in my gut, tingling so richly at the base of my spine I knew I wasn't going to last long at all.

"C'mon, baby," I gasped at him, "go harder," craving just that little bit more, needing to know he'd feel this for a week. I could feel him try to find the right leverage, shoulder blades flexing beneath my palms, legs shaking with effort, and Phel growled in frustration as the position found its limits.

That was all I needed. Taking a deep breath to brace myself, I grabbed Phel tight around the waist and lifted him, pressing up from my heels against the plush rug underfoot, and flipped him so he was on his back beneath me. I worked one knee up onto the bed so I could push him down a bit farther and get his legs onto my shoulders, a change of angle that made Phel jerk and howl with his head thrown back, his neck a long, flawless line. It was a rough, crude, cavemannish move, and Phel fucking loved it.

As I started to drive into him with more force and depth than he'd been able to achieve while on top, I felt the pressure build again in my belly, this time with more intensity, more fire. From up here I could aim for the place inside I knew would make Phel see stars, and sure enough he bucked into my thrusts with his back arched beneath me and his lips bitten almost bloody. No one's ever crooned my name that sweetly, not before Phel, not since. His hand went to his cock like a magnet and started to move up and down in firm strokes, more pornographic and gorgeous than anything I'd seen before. A second before he tensed and started to shoot, wet heat spattering between our stomachs, my knees buckled with the strength of my own orgasm and sent me pitching forward onto Phelan's chest. The aftershocks left us both twitching, breathing hard, and for a few minutes I was incredibly grateful he wasn't complaining about being crushed.

I rolled off and onto my side next to him, both of us gawking like newborns, sweaty and flushed and out of breath. Without saying a word, we reached out and pulled each other close, our mouths meeting with such a depth of emotion, overwhelmed and overwhelming, that I felt a sharp pain in my chest like I'd impaled myself on a piece of broken glass. Whatever had just happened, however irrevocably changed I was by the encounter, one thing I knew was I didn't want to move or get up or do anything that might constitute leaving Phel's side. So I didn't. I didn't leave his apartment that whole weekend; I didn't leave him for a year.

Sighing at the memory, I reach into my jeans to adjust myself—just thinking about Phel in the throes of ecstasy is enough to get me hard, and I'm already feeling light-headed thanks to his surprise appearance—and a slow shudder runs through me at the touch of my own hand. I pause, wishing to high hell it could be his fingers gripping me tight, his fist starting to slowly stroke me, adding the gradual intensity he knows I like. With my other hand, I pop the button on my jeans and then slide the zipper down to give myself more room. There's no one around to see, but I'm suddenly so desperate to come it wouldn't matter if there was. It's been so long since I last saw Phel or was able to touch or feel or smell him after a year of craving him like a drug. Whatever's happened, I still need him, still want him, still *love* him. If only I hadn't fucked it up, he could see what the thought of him alone does to me now.

I slouch back until my shoulders hit the wall, rolling my head against the warm brick of Hugh's house, feeling sunlight and sea air and the heat of my palm and fingers growing slick with precome, as wet as if Phel were standing in front of me, naked. Every ridge and curve of his body is clear to me as day, the smell of him lingering, the way his face and chest flush red when he gets close to orgasm. My own is within sight, within reach, and biting my lip, I increase the force and speed of my strokes, my breath ragged and loud in the quiet. I let my other hand slide beneath my T-shirt to drag across my stomach, imagining it's Phel pushing me to the brink the way I've imagined it a thousand times since he left.

The orgasm hits and I stagger into it with a grunt, half-startled by the spurt of come onto my hand and stomach, hot against my skin. For a few seconds I can do nothing but slump uselessly and ride out the aftershocks, face flushed with embarrassment that I let myself get so carried away. I get a glimpse of Phel for three freaking minutes and this is the result. I'm so fucked. It's worse than the state I was in after we first met, the frantic need that drove me back to Columbus a week later so I could sit on Phel's stoop like a homeless dog, waiting until he came home and I could see him again. I had it bad then, and I've got it bad now.

The scent of come hits my nose and I grimace slightly, retreating to the en suite bathroom so I can make myself presentable. I'm sure Hugh has already started to wonder what the hell is keeping me so long, why I'm acting like such a freak. I wish I could tell him, but I know he wouldn't understand. It's bad enough I already have no idea how to explain about Emilia and the divorce, the whole reason I'm in California to begin with.

After changing my clothes, just in case, and rummaging for the bottle of cologne I know is in my suitcase somewhere, I head downstairs to face Phel, face my brother. Part of me hopes they won't be able to smell any evidence of what I've just done, because, hey—I've had enough mortification for one day. All the same, a part of me hopes otherwise, hopes that Phel will figure it out. That he'll take one look at me and know.

3

Hugh

SOMETIMES I think my brother might be certifiably batshit insane. After an inexplicable delay, Nate slinks downstairs wearing a fresh set of clothes that aren't enough of an improvement on his previous ensemble to justify changing in the first place, reeking of cologne and looking more shifty-eyed than a kid with a pocket full of stolen baseball cards.

Meanwhile, Phel has been popping Xanax in front of me like he thinks I won't notice his shaking hands or quickened breathing. What the fuck? If that isn't bad enough, the way the two of them glower at each other across the kitchen island puts me in mind of how Nell's brother used to act around his ex-wife at family dinners, taciturn and silent and using their kids to deliver messages back and forth. There's not a single freaking explanation I can think of for why Nate and Phel are so frosty toward each other, but after five minutes I feel like I'm about to scream.

The sad thing is, most of it comes from Phel's end, which is unusual given the healthy interest he's shown in Nate before. Maybe it's because I was never really forthcoming with my answers, always putting them off out of some misguided paranoia that my blabbing would make its way back to Nate. I'd made a promise I felt bound to keep, that no matter how famous I got, I'd always leave Nate and his family out of it.

As with most things, I blame Stephenie Meyer. *Twilight* turned the young adult genre into such a gong show that the popularity of my own series went through the roof after a couple of short months on the market. Before I knew it, my books—which are about a couple of white-trash brothers who, in *Hardy Boys*-esque fashion, solve mysteries and occasionally fight crime—were being translated into dozens of languages and optioned for movie deal after movie deal. Insane.

Considering the books' origins, this success still feels pretty damn unprecedented; the series is based on the bedtime stories Nate used to make up about us when we were little. While we were hunkered down in bed, waiting for our dad to come home from a case sober and hopefully in one piece—both if we were lucky—he'd tell me all sorts of crazy tales about how when we grew up we'd travel the country and solve crimes, just like Dad used to do. I forgot all about those guys until I was in college and living away from Nate for the first time, at which point I started writing everything down and printing them as short stories in a local student-run mystery journal. Eventually a publisher noticed, and the rest is history. Now people go bananas for the Manderfeld twins and what kind of shit they'll get into next, and at the center of all this is me. Hugh Fessenden, regular guy with a dead girlfriend and a house with too many empty rooms.

I'm grateful for my blessings, but I don't deal so well with the media circus. When Nell died, shortly after the release of my second book, it was really bad—photographers and entertainment interviewers hounded me, desperate for a word about what the recent tragedy would mean for the Manderfeld brothers. Total lack of sensitivity. And then they turned to Nate, tracked him down in Ohio for the scoop. They were particularly invasive when I was in the midst of my... troubles. I don't mean like the Troubles in Ireland; I mean that Phel isn't the only person here who's been to rehab.

Not, of course, that I've told Phel any of this. I wouldn't know where to begin. He seems ignorant of the whole deal, anyway, and it really isn't his business. There are a lot of reasons I feel bad about that, knowing it's not how friends treat each other, but then again, it's not like I know all his secrets either.

Caroline did an excellent job of keeping most of the grisly details out of the papers, but for my first little while in Cardiff, I was enrolled in Palermo Springs' twenty-eight-day program. Not quite the same as what Phel is doing, since I wasn't allowed medication or intoxicants of any kind—hell, inpatients weren't even supposed to masturbate, since we were told it was common for addicts to transfer their dependencies to other things like coffee or cigarettes or sex. Since Nell passed, I'd developed a problem, you could say, with putting shit up my nose. In some ways I guess it could have been worse, could have been heroin or meth or something, but not much worse. I met this girl, Kristen, who in combination with the coke seemed to make the pain go away for a little while each time. She was into harder stuff too, got into trouble with the law often enough that I had to bail her out once or twice. To an outside observer, it was only a matter of time before I stumbled down the same path.

For me it's hard to tell how bad the problem actually got in the end, because Nate noticed and stepped in long before anything really bad happened. There were no money problems or arrests, and the public scenes were minimal. Couple of bar fights, some lost time. Nate's an amazing brother that way, always in tune with what's going on with me, and before I could say "ballin'," he was on a plane to Los Angeles, ready to intervene and send me packing to the first rehab program we found.

I didn't put up much of a fight. Kristen did, but I knew that if Nate was worried, I owed it to him to do what was needed. Stop freaking people out. I chose Palermo because of how much I'd enjoyed Cardiff before, and in less than a month, I was clean and ready, almost, to become a productive member of society again. Weird thing is, while high on blow I wrote this entire novel about the Manderfeld twins investigating a case entrenched in the methamphetamine industry—my most intense one yet. It was an instant best seller, even got some critical acclaim that surprised me as much as it did the reviewers. Nate would kill me for saying this, but maybe Hunter S. Thompson and all the rest were onto something with their writing methods, just as much as *on* something. Anyway.

My point is, some entertainment reporters caught wind of my little stint and harassed Nate and Emilia—even Liam at school—for the dish, until a crying Emilia called me up one day asking if they were going to have to move someplace more private. Nate was furious. After that, I promised I'd never disclose anything about them again. To anyone. People have big mouths, and Nate is protective of his family that way. It's not like I couldn't see his point. The fame is my bag, not his, but even so, I know he's equally tight-lipped about telling people we're related. Luckily, Emilia and Liam's names were never released to the press, upon pain of litigation, but as a result I started withholding as many details about him as possible, even to Phel. I trust Phelan with my life, but Nate... I don't trust his life with anyone. I don't even like giving his name anymore.

Turns out that wasn't such a bad thing, since the kind of looks Phel is giving Nate would turn a lesser man to stone. I know he has anxiety, but jeez—he seems ready to Hulk out at the wrong comment, or if Nate so much as looks at him funny. My brother, meanwhile, just takes it all in with uncharacteristic quiet, which might freak me out the most of anything. Considering he's the biggest loudmouth I know, it's about as serious as if Callie started hatching kittens.

I decide to help myself to a beer from the fridge, not caring if it's early in the day. Some would call it irresponsible to go within fifty feet of alcohol, given my past substance abuse, but my sponsor at the clinic trusts me to handle a couple of beers every so often, as long as I don't go about getting shitfaced. The line is as easy for me to spot these days as a neon sign that reads *DON'T FUCK UP AGAIN, ASSHOLE.*

"So, Nate," I say casually, popping off the bottle cap against the counter, "what's with the surprise visit? You know I never complain to have you here, but usually you, well… call first. How long did it take you to get here?"

Nate gives a nervous smile, and I don't miss the way his eyes flick over to Phel, like he's afraid to answer and is trying to choose his words as carefully as possible. "I left in kind of a hurry," he answers, and shrugs in too offhand a way to be natural. "Started out five days ago and didn't stop until I hit San Diego. I grabbed a shower before I got here, though, since I didn't think it'd be polite to turn up on your doorstep smelling like a truck stop."

"How considerate," murmurs Phel, and that's the first thing he's said so far this morning not in response to a direct question. The words make Nate's back go up—I can see his shoulders tighten—but he fails on the return volley. Definitely weird. And Phel… well, Phel can be a bit of a princess sometimes, but one thing he isn't is ill-mannered. I'm sure they saw to that in finishing school or wherever. At this point, I think, we're obligated to have a confrontation about this later. I moodily swig my beer.

Much to my annoyance, I'm equally unimpressed by Nate's explanation. This is exactly the type of nonanswer he likes to give when avoiding something major. It's probably impolite for me to pursue an interrogation in front of a complete stranger—strange to Nate, at least—but I'm compelled to take advantage of his sudden timidity. Brothers are like that, always exploiting weaknesses out of love.

"Didn't Emilia have anything to say about you taking off like that? Normally she'd have called to make sure you arrived in once piece by now." When Nate's face darkens, I fold my arms and grunt in displeasure. It's one of those uncontrollable responses of mine that remind me why Nate sometimes calls me a Neanderthal, but right now I'd rather get some answers than worry about my image. "Nate, is everything okay?"

"Yeah, everything's peachy; just needed a break," he tells me—too quickly—and that's about as much as I can stand of him lying to my face. It's 100 percent clear that's what he's doing, playing me off like I'm some fucking nitwit and not his only brother, not the person who knows him better than anyone else alive.

"Nate," I repeat. I catch the look in his eyes that begs me to drop the subject, let it go, but my hackles are up and I just *can't*. We aren't so different, Nate and I; the thought of there being something wrong with him makes me crazy. "Tell me what's going on, or I'll phone Emilia myself." Well, that's a bit extreme as far as strong-arm tactics go, but from the wild expression that flashes across his face, I know I've hit pay dirt. I don't know what to make of the fact that Nate is freaked out by the prospect of me speaking to his wife, especially since Emilia and I have always been on great terms.

"I should… go," Phel interjects, starting to rise from his stool. He and Nate both look like they're going to be sick, but I'm not letting Phel out of my sight just yet either.

I throw out my hand to grab his arm. "Stay," I tell him, and Callie makes a small noise of confusion, dancing on her paws in front of me. Clearly she thinks the order is for her, even though she hasn't moved since we got to the kitchen.

Still, both she and Phel obey, though he says, "Obviously you two have something to discuss," in a strangled voice. "It's not my place." The glance exchanged between him and Nate is one I have no hope of interpreting. "I wouldn't want an audience present for a conversation of this kind with *my* family."

I want to remind Phel that he doesn't even *talk* to his family, but the point is moot and it would be a dickish thing to bring up. So I roll my eyes and say, "According to Nate, it's nothing anyway. Right, Nate?" Both of them glare at me. "It's my house!" I add stubbornly. "I deserve to know why my married brother is suddenly showing up unattached on my doorstep."

Something about my phrasing makes Nate and Phel both flinch. "Who said anything about 'unattached'?" my brother demands, fingers tightening around his glass of water. For the first time since he got here, I realize his fingers are naked except for the silver ring he always wears on his right hand. His gold wedding band is gone, which wouldn't normally be such a big deal—he's always afraid of losing it at work somewhere—except for the look on his face when he sees me notice.

I take a step back from the table. When I was little, the best way to get Nate's attention or find out information was, if not outright bribery, to keep saying his name until he caved. I'm tempted to do that now, a steady line of *Nate, Nate, Nate, Nate, NATE*, but it's as much to satisfy the sudden flash of worry as it is concern he won't eventually tell me what's the matter. When your brother—who never goes anywhere without his family—suddenly shows up at your house at the other end of the country with a single suitcase and a stubborn refusal to call his wife, there's a really short list of explanations.

He must know me too well, because before I can start scrabbling for the one that's least likely—Emilia's mother wanted a quiet vacation with just her daughter and grandson, maybe—he sets his jaw and says, "Emilia and I are getting divorced," in a voice tight with *something*, and refuses to look away from the middle distance. Not at me and certainly not at Phel, and suddenly I feel like the biggest heel going for not letting Phelan make a break for it when he first tried. I swallow around the lump in my throat that threatens to choke me. "She and Liam are still in Mount Vernon, and she's going for full custody. I didn't know how to tell you this over the phone, so I just started driving. Okay? She threw me out." Phel is staring at him, hard, but Nate won't meet his eye and takes a swallow of his water instead. For a fraction of a second, our gazes collide.

"What happened?" I ask in a horrified whisper, but before Nate can respond, Phel pushes himself away from the counter with a deafening scrape of the chair against the kitchen tile. Both Nate and I jump. Phel says, "I'm leaving," in a tone of voice that clearly says, *That is fucking it.*

Nate nods to himself like the announcement surprises him not at all, lifting his glass in a sarcastic toast. "So long, Phel," he chirps.

"Don't move," I order Nate, and scramble after Phel in the direction of the front door, which he's managed to reach with surprising speed.

Maybe Nate's impending marital breakdown—my response to even thinking the words is an automatic *what the fuck?*—takes precedence, but I still promised myself I would get to the bottom of Phelan's sudden moodiness. We're at the point where we're blunt with each other pretty much all the time, or at least I am, and I kind of like what we have going. But I know I'll never get a straight answer out of him if he leaves now, since honesty with Phel is like spotting Halley's Comet: miss it, and chances are you won't see it again this lifetime.

"Phel, wait up," I say, trying once again to grab his wrist. This time he manages to evade me. "What's going on? I'm sorry you got pulled into the middle of that, but even before you seemed—"

"*What?*"

My eyebrows lift at the sharpness of his voice. "You seemed to really dislike Nate. I never gave much thought to the two of you meeting, but I guess I didn't expect you to actually hate the guy on sight." Baffled and not afraid to show it, I give a shrug. "Is there a problem?" I can't think of a single damn reason why Nate might have pissed Phelan off within seconds of meeting—if anything, he tends to charm his way past people's defenses so fast it gives me whiplash. Not Phel, though, and I want to know why. I could leave it alone and hope it'll change, but in my experience, Phel always responds best when given the chance to explain himself.

Unnervingly, Phelan looks at me really hard for a moment, and I get this creepy sense he's trying to decide whether or not to trust me. That stings a little bit, because I thought we were way past all that, but I can recognize the expression of someone who's deliberating whether or not to rescind my security clearance. But just when I expect him to blow me off, Phel sighs, and his eyes flutter shut like the weight of the world has attached itself to his eyelashes.

"I'm sorry," he says eventually. "I didn't intend to be so rude, but Nate just… he reminds me of you-know-who." I do know, though it's vaguely ridiculous that Phel still refuses to refer to his ex-boyfriend by name around me. "My back went up a bit and I didn't do a very good job of controlling the emotional response. Hence the pills. I'm sorry, Hugh."

His earnestness makes me laugh in surprise, then quiet when Phelan's shoulders stiffen a little. "That's kind of a relief," I admit, astounded it's so simple. In a way I pity Phelan for feeling haunted by his ex, to the point he's even seeing flashes of memory in my painfully straight big brother. Nate probably never looked twice at a guy in his life.

"Obviously there's some stuff going on with Nate and his wife, but I don't think you need to worry—he's a decent person and pretty much the straightest guy on the planet, if you don't count his weird obsession with Hugh Jackman." The reference either escapes Phelan or he isn't in the mood to joke around; an unimpressed muscle tics in his cheek. "Let me find out what's going on with him today, alright? We'll meet up for surfing tomorrow, promise. I hope you give Nate a chance, though, because he'll probably want to hang out. I'd really like it if the two of you got along. It'd be shitty if my brother and my best friend wound up hating each other."

Those wide blue eyes blink up at me as Phel chews his bottom lip for a moment, worrying the plump flesh red. "I'm your best friend?" he asks. The surprise is clear in his voice. What the hell did he think we were doing this whole time, hanging out every day like we're the only two people in Cardiff?

"Well, yeah," I retort. "You think I'd put up with your crazy otherwise?" This earns me a smile—I don't swing that way either, but I have to admit that Phel's smile is something special—and I can't help grinning, sagging a little at the respite in Phel's dark mood. "Go home, Phel. No way should you be trying to surf after all that Xanax you ate."

Reluctantly, Phel nods. For a brief second, his eyes flicker toward the kitchen, and seem to rest there as a single line of concern forms between his brows. Then it's gone just as suddenly, and he's sliding his feet into his sandals and pushing the front door open. "I'll talk to you tomorrow, Hugh," he says in farewell. "I hope... I hope everything works out with your brother."

"Me too."

With one last smile, I close the door behind his departing back and, sighing, have to lean against it for a moment to get my bearings. I've coached a few buddies through breakups before, not including Phel, but trying to help my brother come to grips with divorce seems another animal altogether. I know everyone says this, but I thought he and Emilia were going to stay together forever. Shows what I know.

Nate's still staring into space when I return to the kitchen, though I notice there are another couple of beers open on the counter, braced for the impending conversation as much as either of us. At my entrance, Nate looks up with a faint lopsided smile that doesn't reach his eyes.

"Sorry I scared off your buddy," he offers.

"Phel doesn't do well with emotional stuff," I answer. He's not the only one, far from it, but at least Phel is man enough to admit it. "If I'd known, I'd have never invited him inside."

"Where'd you meet him, anyway?" I know Nate's trying to change the subject and put us off talking about his divorce for as long as possible, but since I don't blame him, I let this one slide.

I shrug and play with the label of my beer. Beneath the table I can feel Callie breathing wetly on my bare toes, her quiet mood seeming to feed off the maudlin energy in the room. "We met at the beach a few months back," I explain. "I know he comes across as kind of intense, but he's a really good guy. He has his own shit to deal with as much as anyone else. Cardiff seems to be the place to be for emotional crises." Though I smile at the joke, Nate doesn't.

"He's having an emotional crisis?" he asks instead.

For a second I debate how much to tell him. I don't think it's kosher to let slip that Phel is being rehabilitated for his nervous breakdown, but the basics probably won't pose an issue. "Some guy back East really fucked him over—Phelan fell for him, hard, except the jerk turned out to be married with kids the whole time. The wife found out and the whole thing turned into a colossal mess, so Phel pretty much came out here to recoup and hide. The dude sounds like a classic douchebag, but Phel is still torn up." Maybe I said too much; Nate flinches. The tic reminds me to stay on topic. "What's going on with you and Em?"

The way Nate stares down at his beer makes it look like he really wants the beverage to up and speak for him. It doesn't, of course, so Nate gives a miserable grunt that curls his lip at the corner. "Hugh, I—" His voice breaks, which I don't think I've heard since Dad died. His hands come up to push through his hair roughly. "Fuck. I'm the classic douchebag, man. Emilia, she… she caught me messin' around with someone else."

The force of my jolt rocks my stool against the counter. "*What the fuck?*"

Nate grunts in response. My guess is he doesn't want to have to repeat himself. Nevertheless, he sighs and chooses to elaborate, which I suppose is one of the perks of being a brother—if I were anyone else, I'm sure he would have told me to eat a dick. I can tell he's not happy about it, though. "Yes, it was only one person, and no, I didn't mean for it to happen." He looks so damn tired when he says it and, if I can be honest, sad. I can count on one hand the number of times I've seen Nate look that worn-down.

This information is somewhat reassuring, though only moderately so. Nate's never been one for thinking ahead, and the spontaneity of his decision to cheat isn't totally surprising to me; that he cheated at all is what's shocking. My mind can't decide what it wants to know most, however, so it seems best to stick to the basics. "And Emilia filed for divorce once she found out?"

Unexpectedly, Nate laughs, a quiet snort through his nose. "Actually, no. Despite what happened, we tried to work it out—did couples therapy for a while, separate bedrooms, 'I feel' statements, the whole bit. But it wasn't helping, and eventually I just told her I'd gone as far as I could go, had the papers drawn up. *Then* she threw me out and announced she was applying for full custody of Liam."

"Wait, you're divorcing *her*?" I don't mean to suggest Nate could only ever be the one to get dumped, not at all, but he's always been first to admit Emilia is a perfect ten, not only gorgeous, but intelligent, sane, awesome, and a great mother to boot. Divorcing her is the equivalent of a homeless dude turning down a $50 million windfall. "Are you out of your mind? Why?" A horrible thought occurs to me: "Oh God, you aren't in love with this other woman, are you?"

That defeated sigh again. "Yeah, Hugh, I am." Our eyes meet, and he looks troubled, but not unsure; when I asked him the same thing about Emilia almost a decade ago, just after he found out about Liam, his answer wasn't half as confident. "It was totally unplanned. We just met and...." He hesitates. "She changed my whole life, man. Changed the way I think about myself, who I want to be. I couldn't stay with Emilia after that, not even for Liam. It'd be just as unhealthy for him to live in the same house as two parents who don't love each other and fight all the time, a father who regrets everything he never became. Hell, we grew up with a dad who hated himself, and look how much fun that was."

"So you would have left Emilia eventually, if she hadn't found you out first?" I have my doubts about that, but leave them unsaid. Nate, for all his bluster, isn't much of a risk-taker, especially when it comes to falling short of other people's expectations of him. It's for that reason I try not to ask too much of him, because I know he'll bend over backwards every time to try and come through, even if he kills himself in the process.

"I was thinking pretty seriously about it," Nate admits. "It never seemed like a real option, but after a year, it began to feel like the *only* one. I couldn't keep living a lie, and it wasn't fair to anyone."

It feels like my mind is running at half speed; much of what I should be extrapolating from this conversation is losing out to the bombshells Nate probably doesn't even realize are bombshells. "A year?!" Jesus, my voice is starting to screech worse than Gilbert Gottfried's. I knock it down a few decibels until I'm almost at a whisper, even though we're inside my own house. "You screwed around on your wife and kid for a whole *year*, Nate? Seriously? What the fuck?"

"It wasn't that simple, dude." The flush high in his cheeks hints that Nate is starting to get angry, defensive. "Both of us had something to lose by the relationship coming out." He gets flustered for no reason and adds, uselessly, "In the open, I mean. Out in the open. Trust me, the last thing she wanted was for it to become public knowledge she was dating some loser contractor from the middle of nowhere. Her family is super conservative and high-profile, and it just... trust me when I say the fallout was bad."

God, what is it with these people? I think. Like it wasn't bad enough Phel's parents kicked him to the curb and forgot his name when they found out he was gay; apparently there are still families out there pulling *Gone With the Wind* Scarlett O'Hara shit. "Where is she now?" I ask awkwardly. "Are you two still together at least?"

Nate clenches his jaw. "No. She pretty much told me to get herpes and die painfully when she found out I was married. I'd told her about Liam before that, but Emilia... I tried to play it off like we were no longer together." He must catch my look, because he adds, "I know, Hugh, I fucked up big time. You don't need to say it."

"Holy shit, Nate. You didn't just fuck up, you ruined three people's lives, not including your own!" The force of my own outburst surprises me, but goddamn—I've never known Nate to be so careless with other people. He's never been anything but overprotective of the people he loves, me and Emilia and Liam. If the shoe were on the other foot, he'd have killed someone for pulling a stunt like this. I feel like I don't know the person sitting in front of me, and I think maybe that comes out in the way I look at my brother across the countertop, because Nate bristles and visibly restrains himself from throwing something, either a fist or his beer bottle.

"I said I know, Hugh, okay?" he grates out. "I tried to do what I thought was best for everyone involved, but I didn't think it through—obviously. What I thought was the right thing to do turned out to be totally wrong, and I see that now. If I could do it all again, I'd—" He makes a hurt sound. "Maybe I would have never married Emilia in the first place, who knows? Maybe I would have tried to be a good father by keeping the hell away from them both."

"That's bullshit." I don't know where this sudden anger is coming from. I probably should feel bad about yelling at Nate when he's obviously in a rough place himself, but I just can't fight it. It all seems so... so *wasteful*, so callous in its carelessness. Sure, I don't know the whole story, but what I see in front of me makes a hard knot of nausea form in my stomach. "The only person you tried to do right by was yourself. I mean—Jesus Christ. Do you have any idea what I'd *do* for a family like yours, for a chance to have that kind of happiness? You've had your whole life just handed to you, and you don't even appreciate it!"

"Fuck you, man." Lurching out of his chair, Nate whips his half-empty bottle at the sink, where it clatters against the stainless steel with an awful noise but doesn't break.

Though the sound makes me want to flinch, I remain seated, remain still, staring Nate down even as I will my anger to get itself under control. Nate and I don't do this: we don't turn on each other. But there's a lot of stuff I've heard about this morning that I sure as hell never expected either. What hurts most of all is the tremor I notice in Nate's hands a second before he balls them into fists, trying to get a hold of himself. But I don't know how to respond to that any more than I knew what to say when our dad got drunk late at night and started to cry over our mom while I did my homework in the kitchen. I've never thought of myself as a particularly strong person, and it's a pretty big deal for the one person I look up to—Nate—to keep it together for both of us.

It seems I've fallen short of his expectations of me too, which I know without him saying anything. Still, it wouldn't be Nate if he let me off the hook easily—he's been lecturing me since he was six years old. "You know," he begins, "of everyone who's bothered to remind me what a piece of shit I am throughout all this, the one person I didn't expect to hear it from is you. My own fucking brother. We've both made mistakes in our lives, but apparently the door don't swing both ways like I thought it did." He goes quiet for a second and I can see his rage dying in front of me; he looks exhausted again. "Guess it's a good thing I didn't have time to unpack," he says grimly. "I'll grab my crap and be out of your hair if you don't want me here ruining your chance to play house with Phel."

This last part is too much to keep me from rolling my eyes—honestly, my brother is such a drama queen sometimes—but Nate stalks out of the kitchen before he can see, then clomps up the stairs like he's forgotten how to be the elder sibling and not some melodramatic little bitch. I don't belittle his angst, but where I'm concerned he'll have calmed down by the time I count to ten and make my way upstairs after him. The cool-down is as much for his benefit as my own, and as the seconds tick by, I can feel the anger slowly start to recede, replaced by what I know is sadness for Nate's situation and, if I'm honest, bitterness over my own. I don't have a right to start comparing his position to what I might have had with Nell, because they're very different, same as Nell and Emilia were very different women, and Nate and I are different men.

Upstairs, there's some shuffling around and the sound of various objects being slammed, hopefully nothing of mine, but then everything goes quiet and I recognize my cue. Tail thumping, Callie keeps one eye on the ceiling like it could start up again any minute, but I know it won't. Nate knows the two things he can always expect from me are tough love and someone to have his back, which might seem contradictory but really aren't. Right now he's railing against the fact that staying in my house means having to put up with my honest assessment of his idiocy. But he'll get over it, and together we'll figure out what's next.

Sure enough, Nate is sitting on the edge of his bed when I pause in the doorway of his bedroom—so named because he has a standing invitation here—and while his bag is indeed packed, it isn't zippered. Having arrived with just his bike, he packed light. Nate glances up at me without saying anything, waiting, and eventually I approach and take a seat next to him on the mattress. Busybody that she is, Callie leaps onto the bed and settles herself precisely in the middle, head nestled on her paws so she can watch us both by only twitching her eyes back and forth. I guess for her this is better than reality television.

"You know you're welcome to stay here as long as you want," I say grimly. "I didn't mean to upset you." It's not an apology, but I'm not going to say sorry for speaking the truth when Nate probably needs it most.

"That's totally what you intended," Nate says with a snort. He's right. Or at least I didn't try *not* to upset him. "It's, like, your God-given right to try and piss me off." He falls silent for a few seconds before adding, "I know you think I took my marriage for granted, Hugh, but it wasn't like what you had with Nell. You two chose each other, legitimately wanted to spend the rest of your lives together in a way I never got to think about with Emilia. Yeah, I love her, and God knows I love Liam more than I can say, but jumpin' into that marriage was just the first in a long line of shit I didn't really think through." He huffs, and I know he's ready to try to inject humor into the situation—Nate's special way of trying to regroup, not so much from me as the issue at hand. It's how he deals. "Well, that and not using a rubber. Woulda served me right if I'd gotten the syph or somethin'."

With a sigh, I reach out and pat his knee, registering that Nate is a bit thinner than when I saw him last, the tiredness coming through in the quiet slump of his shoulders and the way his flesh seems to cling to his bones with only purpose and no joy. Nate, when he's content, is the kind of person to let things slide and embrace a little happy weight; it occurs to me that, by those standards at least, he probably looked happier in the last year than I've seen him in a long time. Not that he'll ever be fat, because Nate works too hard for that to happen, but he certainly had the look of a man at ease in his life. I don't know whether to thank this other woman for that, whoever she is, or blame her.

"The fact that you asked for a divorce is a start," I tell Nate. "At least you're not leading Emilia on by pretending it's what you still want. A bit late, but better than never. I guess."

To my surprise, rather than accepting the olive branch for what it is, Nate grimaces. "Ironically, I think that's what pissed her off the most of anything," he admits. "Emilia was ready to sweep the whole thing under the rug—forget about my 'phase', as she called it—and couldn't believe I wasn't willing to do the same. But by that point it couldn't have gone any other way, man. You're right in that much."

I hesitate for a second, pitying Emilia and fretting about Liam, but also painfully sad for my brother, who is obviously shouldering a whole lot more than a pending divorce. "Are you going to try and find her?" I ask. "This woman? If you love her, maybe there's still a chance."

"I don't know." Nate rubs his hands against his thighs and stands up. He wanders over to the window to peer out at the ocean for a few minutes, brow furrowed. "Even if I bumped into her today, I'm pretty sure she wouldn't want to talk to me. Same as Emilia and Liam, she put a lot of trust in me, and I betrayed it. I didn't mean to, and I sure as fuck didn't want to, but there you have it. No changin' that fact now."

We are both quiet for a little while, there being not much else to say on the subject, but then Nate turns back around to face me with an inscrutable expression.

"How come you never mentioned Phel before this?" he asks.

The question stumps me for a few moments. There's no good answer to that. "I don't... I guess it just never occurred to me. He's pretty low-key, for one thing, and in a way... I didn't feel right burdening you with my problems. It's like Phel and I are each other's therapists sometimes, and it felt best to keep it private. In case I accidentally wound up talking about his issues as well as my own." I shrug at the ineffectiveness of this response, but Nate nods in a way that seems to indicate he gets it. That's one thing about Nate; it doesn't take a whole lot of explaining to get him on the same page.

"That's okay, dude," he says. "In all fairness, I kept a hell of a lot from you for a whole year." I snort, because Nate is the king of the motherfucking understatement, but in actual fact I wouldn't have it any other way. Especially when I tend toward overstating things a little myself. There are so many questions I have about that time, where Nate met this woman, how he knew she was different from Emilia, what about her could have changed his life so fundamentally, but there will be time for all that later on.

"Just... no more secrets, okay?" I plead. Nate looks down at his hands, which maybe isn't the response I want, but we've had enough awkwardness today to last us a lifetime. I can stand to let him off the hook just this once. "I can't be an awesome brother to you if I don't know what's going on."

"Fair enough." I think that's the end of it, until he blurts out, "So does he still love the guy?" Nate's also the king of the non sequitur, apparently. Sometimes his train of thought is more like one of those insane Shinkansen from Japan than your average locomotive.

"Who?"

Still not looking at me, though. Fuck, at the rate we're going, I'm going to need to brush up on my psych textbooks just to decipher my own brother. "Phel," he clarifies and, wow, that's pretty random, even for Nate. "Does he still love the guy who broke his heart?"

Since I can't think of a good way to hide my surprise, I don't. That Nate knows how wrecked Phel is feeling after one meeting might say something, but that doesn't mean I'm at liberty to start divulging secrets behind Phelan's back. I wouldn't do that to Nate if the shoe were on the other foot. "Why do you care about that?"

Nate shrugs and finally meets my eyes with a steadiness I don't expect. "I don't know, Hugh. I guess I just want to know if there's still hope for someone like me."

Because there's no better way to respond to someone who is hurting and lost and kind of alone except for the dubious comfort of your presence, sometimes the only thing you can offer is a hug. So I rise from the bed and go to put my arms around Nate, my broken, well-meaning brother who has nevertheless managed to make significant disasters of a bunch of people's lives. Try putting that on a Hallmark card. Instead Nate accepts the embrace for what it is, sort of awkwardly since we haven't done this in a while, and doesn't try so hard to hide the fact that he's leaning most of his weight into me.

"Phel's situation isn't the same," I tell him gently, "but it's not for you to worry about. You and Emilia and Liam... I'm sure everything will all work out. There's hope for you yet, you idiot."

Nate is wearing a brave smile when he pulls away, but it doesn't reach his eyes and he's gone back to not looking at me. I sigh and say nothing, because even though I'm just his brother, it's painfully clear how badly he wants to believe me, but doesn't.

4

Phel

THERE'S a moment, just before you're about to catch a wave, where the only sensation you're aware of is of pure force—not the burn in your arms of paddling out, the salt spray in your face, the anxiety of not popping up in time, not anything else in your life—just water and power and sheer exhilaration. It's like flying, hurtling along on your stomach at an incredible speed until that last second when you push yourself up, surfboard hopefully angled in the direction of the swell before it breaks. Suddenly you're on it, balanced between riding the wave and racing it, fighting every impulse of mind and nature to hurl yourself against that wall of water again and again, carving into it like your whole body's the knife.

It's probably stupid that I came out here alone, but as long as no one cuts into someone else's priority, aloha spirit dictates we all look out for each other while we're here. Though it's getting late in the afternoon and the tide is almost out, there are plenty of surfers doing the exact same thing as me, trying to squeeze in a few more waves before they call it a day. I'll stay out until the end, I think, surfing to make up for lost time. The past few days without it have felt... empty.

True to my word, I didn't go back to the beach that day after running into Nate, hopped up on Xanax to the point where I'm lucky I made it home in once piece. It started to rain on the way there, but I was so loopy and numb from the drugs I barely registered the wetness, or how cold it got with my clothes soaked through. Doesn't mean I didn't miss the waves, though.

When I first came to Palermo Springs and got set up in my little apartment here, Willa gave me a contact card listing what's considered to be the three most important pieces of information in the patient's arsenal: the number for emergency medical services (overdoses or self-injury), the number for client services (housekeeping, security, or not enough food in the fridge), and, finally, the assigned counselor's direct line for emergency therapy sessions. I know one of those things is not like the other, but if there's anything they take seriously here at Palermo, it's health, comfort, and mental well-being.

Before the front door was even closed, I started tearing through the drawers in my tiny kitchen, unmindful of the water I was tracking everywhere, looking for that damned card because I went ahead and listened when Willa asked that I not program her number into my phone. She wanted to discourage me from calling her direct every time crisis struck, a dubious luxury reserved for higher-maintenance patients. At the time, I kind of liked that there was a level of trust between us; she didn't think I needed her on speed dial, and counted on me not to abuse the system. I know Willa isn't a friend, but this is something that keeps me feeling like there is an element of reciprocity to our professional relationship. As she probably intended, it gave me a much-needed sense of control over my actions, confidence that I could rise above losing my shit over every little thing.

Yeah, right.

I couldn't find the damn card anywhere and got so frustrated that I contemplated calling emergency medical services and faking a suicide attempt or something; naturally, that was the number I'd memorized. Except that with Xanax, the feeling of frustration becomes abstract, conceptual, more like you're aware that you *should* feel upset about something, but don't. So while I likely couldn't have scratched my own ass right then, much less faked a convincing suicide attempt, dialing out to emergency services was an idea that came and went like a slow-moving tide.

Instead I flopped onto the couch and melted into the cushions for a few minutes—hours, maybe—coasting along on that feeling of nothingness unique to benzodiazepines. I felt like part of the air, completely insubstantial and weightless. For a while I considered going to sleep, which of course was when I spotted Willa's card in its usual spot in the middle of the coffee table. Independent living patients are given a "private" cell phone for the duration of their stay, reachable only by switchboard, and I fumbled it out of the pocket of my jeans, amazed it hadn't suffered water damage. My first few attempts to dial out were unsuccessful. On the fourth or fifth try, I managed to get Willa on the line.

"Phelan?" Since I never called her like this, she picked up right away. "Phel, is everything okay?"

Some people think drugs like Xanax and Valium turn you into a complete mess, and I'm sure in large enough doses they do, but I was perfectly coherent, if numb, capable of stating the facts without hyperbole. "I need to see you," I told her. "Can we set something up before our scheduled time this afternoon? Right now, maybe? I'd really appreciate it."

The thing about Willa is she makes each word sound like she's paused to think about it, a trait that usually gets on my nerves if I'm in a heightened state of anxiety. Right then, however, it was instrumental to my being able to follow along. "I'm sure we can," she answered, "but first, can you tell me why you feel this urgency?" A second later she added, "Phelan, have you taken anything?" She must have recognized something different in the cadence of my speech to indicate I was under the influence.

"I took Xanax for my panic attacks, just like you told me to do in an emergency," I explained.

"How many?"

That, I had to think about for a moment. "Just two. No more than that. Like you said. I read the label. But the Paxil wasn't cutting it."

She sighed a little with relief. "That's okay, Phel." Another pause. "Did you have alcohol with those?"

"No." When this seemed to meet with her approval, I said, "Remember that guy I told you about? Nate? The married man?" This seemed a pointless question, since I spoke of little else during our sessions. By her silence, I took it she found the clarification unnecessary as well. "Well, he's here."

"Here, as in... your house? He's with you now?"

"No, of course not. He's in *Cardiff*, staying with Hugh." It was time to prove my sarcastic streak could still function even when medicated. "He's Hugh's brother. Isn't that fantastic? This whole time, another mystery just waiting to be discovered. Are you surprised? I was surprised."

I thought I heard Willa murmur an *Oh dear*, but what she said to me was, "And you just found this out? That's why you had a panic attack?"

Although she couldn't see me, I nodded once.

The message must have gone through nevertheless, or Willa knew my habits too well. "Any thoughts of hurting yourself, or hurting someone else? Or are you just anxious?"

"Don't worry," I assured her. "I'm not going to do anything to fuck up my program. I just… I couldn't breathe and I had to take the Xanax, and then I left Hugh's and came here. But now I need to talk to you." That sounded entirely reasonable to me. This is why I've been here so long—three months ago, I doubt I'd have been able to keep myself from falling apart all over again. Now I have a better idea of how to act, how to hold it together until I can lose my shit in a controlled situation, like under Willa's supervision.

"Well, Phel," she began, "I'm happy to meet with you at any time, you know that. But if you've taken 0.5 mg of Xanax already, my concern is you might be in need of some sleep before we really get a chance to talk about this. You might feel more comfortable if you have a rest and let the effects wear off a little bit first. Then we can sit down and have a proper chat. What do you think?" This was something else Willa always did, asking me my opinion on matters in which I had little to no say.

"I could sleep," I answered neutrally, because neutral was about all I had in me right then. I'd only broken into my emergency stash of Xanax once before, only a single 0.25 mg dosage, but I could more or less remember being overcome by tiredness after a couple of hours, to the point I couldn't keep my eyes open. No doubt Willa had too many patients to see that day to deal with someone falling asleep on her in midconversation.

"Okay. That sounds like a good bet," she agreed. "How 'bout you drink some water and go lie down, and I'll come by in a few hours to check in, see how you're doing?"

For a minute I chewed my lip, considering. Then I said, "Alright. I'll leave the door unlocked." I was pretty sure she had a key anyway, but we're all about the appearance of normalcy here. Even though some patients aren't allowed cutlery in their rooms, or windows that open.

I suppose I must have slept through the rest of the day and all of that evening, because I didn't meet with Willa until the following morning, when she greeted me over breakfast with a smile. Despite my earlier urgency, this suited me fine. Thanks to the Xanax, I'd had no dreams, no opportunity to dwell upon what had happened the previous afternoon. What might still happen.

We remained in the quiet sanctuary of my apartment for almost three times our regular session length, and the threat of further anxiety attacks kept me inside the rest of the day—that, and the fear of whom I might run into. For three days I refused to leave the safety of the compound in spite of Willa's urging to carry on with my life as normal, but today's the day the hiding ends. We met again this morning for a couple of hours before I ventured outside and down to the beach, late enough that I could be reasonably sure of having missed Hugh. And Nate, of course, though I was doing a pretty good job of not thinking about that.

The difficulty is how to avoid thinking about him now, even as I concentrate on making my cutbacks and bottom turns on the wave as neat as possible. I'm getting pretty good at those, although my duck diving still needs some work. My progress across the face of the wave is swift and steady, a good amount of spray following in my wake. The day is so warm that I ditched the wetsuit in favor of board shorts, and the water feels amazing against my bare skin and between my toes. The tubes are beautiful and the weather is stunning, bright and sunny and clear, and yet all I can think about is Nate and what Willa had to say on the matter.

Naturally, she wanted to know how I felt about seeing him, not counting the panic attack and the terrified hiding, and I think my initial answer was something along the lines of "Angry and scared shitless and totally fucked." Her response? To ask if I still had feelings for him! Of course I responded in the negative, cheeks flaming.

This look came across Willa's face that was exasperated and knowing and sad all at once. "Do you really think you would still feel those things so intensely, if that were really the truth?" she challenged. "Furthermore, why do you feel it's necessary to eradicate your love for him completely?" Fucking therapists.

Do I still love Nate? I so desperately want not to, and yet, Willa's right. The past four months filled me with hope that I'd finally moved on and made real headway in putting him out of my mind once and for all, just as he was out of my life. But in the quiet moments of honesty I sometimes allow myself, I know this isn't true. Seeing him framed by Hugh's doorway brought that home for me in an instant, a rush of grief and loss and *need* sweeping across me like, well, a tidal wave. The subsequent panic attack had as much to do with being face to face with him as my realizations to this end.

Pretty much from the beginning, Willa has been a strong proponent of the idea that I get attached too easily; she blames it on my perceived lack of approval from my parents growing up, approval I thought I'd lose if I ever came clean about my sexuality. According to her, the person I fell in love with wasn't Nate Fessenden as he existed in reality, but my vision of him and how he saw me. In his eyes, I was someone strong and successful and desirable, and that—that person who so valued me—was who I wanted to be with.

Perhaps this has merit, but I've never considered myself particularly fond of attachments, and I've always tried to avoid them. I can honestly say Nate is the only person I wanted to be with for real, and even then, I bucked the relationship at first, thinking him no more than a weekend fling. I suppose Willa's idea comes from the fact that I let myself love someone who hid so much of himself from me, loved him in spite of the warning signs that presented themselves. What I think she sometimes fails to consider, though, is I hid an awful lot of myself from him too, out of wariness and sheer force of habit—at least at the beginning.

Despite my thorough enjoyment of our first weekend together— after two days with Nate, I could barely walk, let alone drive to Chicago—I deleted his number from my phone as soon as he left. That he gave me his contact information at all seemed charming, naïve, and I reciprocated with a kiss good-bye and a vague promise to call. Clearly he didn't do one-night stands often. Although I felt bad for leading him on in that respect, it was difficult to rob him of the charade that we'd see each other again. We just… couldn't. That wasn't me. He didn't even live in Columbus. Sure, I spent a few days thinking about him afterward, feeling both aroused and wistful at the memory of our time together; Nate left an impression, to be sure. But that was supposed to be the end of it.

Two weeks later, I found him waiting on my doorstep as I returned from a dinner with the account people from my firm. The sleek black motorcycle was the first thing I noticed when I rounded the corner. Then Nate swung himself off the driver's seat and rounded the bike to lean against the front handlebars, hands pushed deep into the pockets of his jeans. I stopped dead at the sight of him, right there in the middle of the sidewalk. As with most things too beautiful to be real, I thought he was a mirage. That is, until he said my name.

"Hey, Phel," he greeted with some awkwardness. "Remember me?"

He seemed to be playing it cool, or trying to. After a second his mouth twitched and broke out in a huge grin, but, appearing self-conscious, then ducked his head to try and hide it. I'm not prone to smiling like that myself, but the moment I saw Nate lit up with such happiness—happiness over seeing *me*, wonder of wonders—I caught myself beaming back, my arguments about flings and relationships forgotten. I never really found them again.

We started seeing each other almost weekly, work permitting and when Nate could make the trip down to Columbus. Sometimes he came on his own, sometimes for business. I kept telling myself it was a convenient arrangement, a reliable source of sex with someone whose smile sent shivers down my spine, but… maybe Willa has a point, and I was more of a goner than I thought. Long gone, in fact, before I realized it.

Our encounters became about much more than sex and hiding out in my apartment or Nate's hotel room. Like two wary animals circling each other in the woods, we seemed unwilling to acknowledge that, more often than not, we each spent weekdays and lonely nights thinking about our next time together, both of us playing at some ridiculous pretense that each meeting might be our last.

Quietly, almost too imperceptibly to notice at first, the nights became longer and bled into days, shifted to include dinner and coffee and breakfast in bed, or the occasional movie where we made out or groped in the back row like teenagers. Novel as the concept seemed at the time, eventually I had to concede we were dating. Personal details grounded our conversations, secrets we had no one else to tell. We started to learn things about each other beyond what we enjoyed in bed, though there was plenty of that. Almost as if by accident, Nate stopped being a regular fuck buddy and started to feel like something else entirely: a friend and a confidant. A lover.

We talked about his job and the smallness of Mount Vernon, how much Nate sometimes longed to take Lucy out on the road and do nothing but drive around the country; he confessed his real name was Fessenden and not Smith, though this surprised me almost not at all. Smith never suited him. Nate admitted he often felt like he wasn't doing enough good in the world, or that he wasn't smart enough in comparison to his brother, about whom he spoke little but with overwhelming affection when the subject came up. I told him about my family and the pressure of hiding myself from everyone but Aurelia. With more passion than I knew I possessed, I told him how I often daydreamed about storming into my father's office in Manhattan and announcing, "I'm a fag: love me or leave me." Nate said he knew the feeling, though both his parents had died before he had a chance to come clean. He thought his mother would have accepted him without hesitation.

The first sign of trouble was when Nate shyly kissed me in line at my neighborhood café, a quiet response to my having remembered his order without prompting. While not a particularly romantic or demonstrative person—actually, I sensed bouts of anxiety over what was developing between us, nervousness not so different from my own—that small expression of gratitude, the way he blushed furiously but gripped my hand afterward, said more about his feelings than words could have. Nate wasn't one for big speeches; that's not how he would confess himself to me, I knew. Sure enough, later that day, when he took me to bed, I started to understand the palpable difference between fucking and making love.

Nate, by then, had already expressed the opinion that I was the only person around whom he truly felt he could be himself. This terrified me, but not so much as the realization I felt the same way: I couldn't fathom being like this with anyone else. I didn't know what it was about Nate, who wasn't cultured or educated or terribly sensitive, but nevertheless always seemed to understand how I felt and thought. He changed how I interpreted the world, how I interpreted myself.

I first entertained the idea I might be falling in love one afternoon a few months after we met—September maybe, or late August—and we were in bed doing what we did best. Although when we first started up together I could tell Nate was a little inexperienced with men, before long his technique was so magnificent he could render me speechless with a single touch. That is, when I didn't think he was trying to suck my brain out through my cock. I'd barely recovered from his mouth and was reaching for the lube when he closed his hand around mine, stopping me.

"What?" I asked in surprise. "Don't you want to—?"

He swallowed a little and pulled me on top of him, hands firm against my ass so I was nestled between his legs and unable to go very far. The press of his cock against mine made me squirm and gasp. "I know we haven't talked about this yet," he began, "but I think I'd like you to fuck me instead."

Not that he sounded hesitant, but the request alone made me pause. Nate was right—we *hadn't* ever talked about it, since I was all too happy to bottom and he'd never expressed the desire to change it up. Topping was rare for me, but certainly not a pleasure to which I'd object. I'd never quite worked out Nate's feelings on the subject. It seemed to make him shy. A finger up the ass while I went down on him was something he loved, no doubt about it, but until that point I assumed he was one of those gay men who never bottomed for anyone. I guess it's true what they say, that every top secretly wants to bottom.

"Why the sudden change of heart?" I asked, sliding a hand into his hair. "In no way is this an objection, but I didn't realize it was even on the menu."

Nate shrugged. "I've been thinking about it a lot—for a while, actually. Things have been unbelievably good and it's not really a big deal, but this is something I want to try. And obviously I want you to be the one to do it."

The words made me push myself up on my elbows to look down at him, eyebrows raised in alarm. "Wait, you mean you've never—"

"No." Nate shook his head. The flush in his cheeks deepened. "I wasn't exaggerating when I said that Mount Vernon is a small town, man. My opportunities to experiment have been kind of limited. Before you, there weren't really a lot of guys; almost none, actually." He flashed the kind of smile usually reserved for getting himself out of trouble, but I caught the edge of anxiety in his expression, fear of rejection or something else. "Call me a late bloomer."

That was the first time it really occurred to me to ask what kind of history Nate had behind him—had he only recently started to question his sexuality? Was I a phase?—but the urge was largely overridden by the warmth I felt. Not only did Nate trust me to be his first, but I was a pioneer for him in other ways as well. We both had that in common, it seemed. I was determined not to let him down, surprising myself with how much I wanted to be the one to stay with him forever in memory.

"I had no idea."

Nate smirked up at me and wrapped a hand around the back of my neck so he could pull me in for a kiss. The stubble around his mouth teased at my lips so deliciously that I groaned; I'd felt that electric scrape against my thighs not moments ago. "Not all gay men are as slutty as you," he teased.

"Says the late bloomer," I shot back. I gave a small thrust of my hips, rubbing our cocks together until Nate's eyes rolled back and he moaned. So easy. "Besides, you always *seemed* to know just what you're doing."

He gasped as my tongue found the pulse point in his throat. "What I lack in experience I make up for in imagination," he mumbled. Braver now, he asked, "So are you gonna fuck me or not?"

"It'd be my pleasure, obviously."

I realized I was working my way down his body before the words were even out of my mouth. Finding my lips level with his nipple, I closed my teeth around the small nub and tugged until Nate's hips bucked and he cursed. He had the most sensitive nipples of anyone I'd ever met, the pair of them like a couple of on/on switches and just fleshy enough for biting.

I laughed at his response. "I can make it so you won't know why you waited so long. Is that what you want?"

"No, I'd rather talk about it some more," he gritted out. I felt his fingers weave into my hair and gently press down, encouraging me to make the rest of the journey without delay.

Maybe this was a first for him, but I'd been on the receiving end so many times that he had to know what was coming; I took it as a personal challenge to exceed the talent of Nate's fingers and the cleverness of his mouth, sliding down his torso until I was able to press kiss after kiss to the crease of skin where thigh met groin. Mouthing at the sensitive area with the occasional nip of teeth, I got my hands on the bottle of lube again. This time I poured a generous amount into my palm with the intention of using it on Nate instead of myself.

Obligingly, he lifted a leg toward his chest when I nudged at his flank, his eyes fluttering to meet mine with complete trust and only a hint of nervousness. The expression on his face made my mouth go dry. With a sharp inhale at the sight of him exposed to me so unquestioningly, so *eagerly*, I rose up to brush my lips against the back of his knee, a quick flash of encouragement as I let my hands settle lower.

The first touch of my slick fingers against his hole made Nate gasp and twitch, not, as I saw it, with apprehension, but anticipation of my circling gently and pressing inside to the first knuckle, then the second. In a split-second decision, I leaned in to flicker my tongue over the same spot, licking and teasing, tasting lube and traces of soap from his recent shower. Nate gave a moan so loud I smiled against his skin. So it went for the next several minutes, me working him loose to the point of incoherence with my tongue and fingers, tapping against his prostate to wring delirious cries from his throat while my other hand pumped his cock. I could feel how close to the edge he came, and exulted in his responses. It's quite something to see a man reduced to that point, especially one as masculine as Nate, and the sound of my name shouted in that deep voice made my own cock leak without any help from my hand.

"You've made your point, Phel," he chastised hoarsely when I got up to three fingers. Strangely enough, my mind wandered to all the times my father had preached the evils of homosexuality and sodomy; but how could a body hunger so much for something supposedly so wrong? Nate was excited to the point that practically all the work was done for me, so hot for it that his muscles were nothing but responsive and relaxed. Not, of course, that it stopped me from enjoying myself.

And I did, immensely. The first time someone ever did this for me, I was sixteen and with a much older lover; despite my trepidation, those fingers of his were so skilled that I begged to be fucked by the time he was done. I very much wanted Nate to have that experience, to feel that same zeal each time we broached the subject of who would be on top. This yearning I felt for someone to desire me that way, with equal intensity, was something else I'd yet to experience with a partner before Nate.

"Be patient," I told him. "You're always in such a hurry."

"I'm sorry I waited, and I'm sorry for all those times I made you come with my dick up your ass instead," he goaded. Nate knew just how to push my buttons.

This earned him a sharp slap to the fleshy part of his ass, which in turn received a hiss from him. It made me wonder whether he might not enjoy a little roughness under different circumstances, but that was for another time. "There's no reason to get testy about it," I said archly. Nate groaned as I withdrew my fingers, but had the wherewithal to hand me a condom. I rolled it on and crawled back up his body to kiss him once, deeply, and tried to shift him onto his stomach while I grabbed at a pillow to place beneath his hips for leverage.

The whole process would be less painful this way, but he stopped me, cupping his hands against the back of my neck so I couldn't get very far. "Hey," he said, "I've heard it's supposed to be easier from behind and all, but I'd kind of like to look at you. If that's okay."

I actually felt my face soften, and thought again of how completely gone I was on this man. "Of course it's okay," I told him. I bent to brush another quick kiss against his mouth. "If you're sure."

At his nod, I placed the pillow under his ass instead and then scooped up his legs, giving a sigh when his knees settled over the crooks of my elbows. The skin there felt warm and clammy—both of us were nervous. Despite my earlier chagrin for Nate's tendency to rush through everything, I decided it was best to stop dawdling and get the anticipation over with. I worked one of my hands between our bodies to line myself up, slicking more lube over my cock, and I shook with the intensity of my desire for the man beneath me, breathtaking and overpowering like a force of nature.

The way he bit his lip at me, all nerves, made my mood shift from jovial to serious; he looked like a man about to jump off a cliff, terrified of what might lie below. "Are you alright?" I asked quietly.

Nate seemed to shake himself out of it before he nodded and rubbed his face against mine like a cat, back arching at the prod of my cock against his ass. "Just go slow," he murmured. "Okay?"

We kissed again. "Whatever you need, Nate," I swore. "This will be good for you, I promise."

Still, I bit my lip at his initial grimace. It always hurts a little bit, no matter the care or love that goes into the preparations. A shudder wracked through him as I started to ease inside. "Push out against me,"

I suggested weakly. "Relax and let me in, I won't hurt you." That was all I could manage. I had to press my mouth against his neck to keep from crying out or giving in to the impulse to shove myself inside that soft heat. He was like an oven on the inside and gripped me like a silken fist.

Each inch forward seemed to make Nate's cries grow louder, his breath more ragged. His responsiveness, his vocalness, made all the hairs on my arms and legs stand up. "God, Phel, I want you so bad," he keened into my ear. His arms encircled my shoulders to hold us together, as if in anticipation of when I finally slid home. It was close, so close, and I felt Nate's cock jerking between our bellies in similar excitement, its hardness unaffected by the burn he must have felt, that beautiful, torturous stretch. "You ever feel anything like this before?" he gasped. "Anything this fuckin' good, this *right*?"

I hadn't, not in the way he meant, though I had a pretty good idea how overwhelmed he must have felt right then. My breath hitched as I shook my head, and he pulled me down so our lips could meet, not a kiss so much as the opportunity for us to pant into each other's mouths. With that, I seated myself fully inside him and shivered at his warmth and tightness, shivered at how badly I wanted to say I'd never felt anything like what I felt for Nate, period.

Details of what happened after escape me. We fucked—made love—of course. If possible, Nate came even more alive beneath me, his voice loud in my ear as I started to thrust into him, first with gentleness and then increasing force as he bucked and cursed and demanded I go harder, faster, demanded I make him feel it. Each time my cock skirted his prostate, he moaned and writhed in ecstasy. He gripped my face so I couldn't look away from him, and the intensity of those green eyes is a memory I'll always have, no matter how bad things get. No matter how bad they *are*.

From that moment on, if I'm not being overly generous with my restraint, I wanted so badly to make Nate my own; I never imagined he wasn't mine to keep. The look on his face when he came in my hand could only be described as wondrous, like he never knew it could be this way, like his whole life changed in that moment. Maybe it did. Knowing what I do now, I realize for Nate that was probably the point at which he started to really think of himself as a gay man—started to embrace his desires. Not that it changed anything, since he was more closeted than I ever was. He probably never let his wife put anything up his ass for fear she'd suspect something.

Later, as we lay in bed with nothing left to us but our sweat and the dwindling willpower to stay awake, Nate rolled onto his side to face me and laid a palm on my cheek. I turned my head against the pillow to look at him, so close I could almost count his freckles, his eyes nothing but blurs of mossy green. The weight of the happiness I felt made me sigh and bump our noses together with what had to be the goofiest smile on my face.

I was about to make a smartass remark about how disgustingly romantic and unmanly it all was, but then he said to me—and this I'll never forget: "I feel like you're the only thing I've gotten right my whole life, Phel."

The comment sobered me right away. I can only imagine how much it cost for Nate to say that, averse as he is to emotional scenes, and I saw the flush that rose to his cheeks the minute the words left his mouth. There seemed no correct reply other than to bundle him into my arms and hold him close—cuddling so aggressive I know Nate secretly enjoyed it. Every part of me agreed with him at that moment, and I had no idea—none—that, months later, he would come to feel like the single greatest mistake I'd ever made.

Feeling lower than low, I coast my board into the surf before dismounting and treading the twenty or so remaining feet to the beach, my feet slipping a little in the soft bed of sand. The salt that stings my eyes is, I know, not seawater. No matter how many times I remind myself not to get frustrated over these emotional responses, which everyone from Willa to Doctor fucking Phil would say are perfectly acceptable, I can't help but feel a little more angry each time a memory of Nate makes me cry.

At this point it's not even sadness but sheer *outrage* over how much a blind fool I acted—for a whole damn year, feeling like I was finally doing right for once, living some impossible fantasy where I got the guy and a shot at happiness. Aurelia warned me of what I was getting myself into, trying to hide my relationship from our parents in plain sight, dismissing her suggestion for a background check on Nate. I wrote off her concerns as jealousy of my fairy tale coming true, my queer Cinderella story. What a laugh.

Instead of riding off into the sunset with the proverbial Prince Charming, I destroyed a family, ruined a child's life, and let everyone down, most of all myself. What would Hugh feel if he had even the slightest inkling I'm the man responsible for breaking apart what little family he has left in the world? Like it isn't bad enough I've avoided his calls all week, I can't even be upfront about why. Furious as I am, I couldn't do that to Nate, couldn't knowingly out someone when it's a secret he so obviously isn't ready to tell.

Willa constantly has to remind me of the value of forgiveness, not just for other people, but for myself; right now all I feel is ashamed and broken and crazy.

Months ago, Hugh and I discovered this little inlet up the beach from where the good waves are, a bit of a trek but quiet and ideal for stashing our stuff without fear of having things stolen. I head there now, desperate for a towel and a change of dry clothes. When I reach the little pile of my belongings obscured behind a large piece of driftwood, though, I notice someone else's things are there too, an assortment of clothing and a portable cooler. Hugh. It has to be—he's the only other person who regularly throws his stuff down behind the log, and after a second of dumb staring, I recognize his towel and thong sandals.

I contemplate throwing on my T-shirt and hightailing it out of there, but I need a moment to recover from my surfing and impromptu emotional turmoil. Besides, I can't avoid Hugh forever. It wouldn't be right to hold his relationship with Nate against him, and anyway, I realize I have no desire to forfeit our friendship because of that. Surely Nate won't be in Cardiff forever, and if I make up some excuse about how I'm too emotionally fragile to assimilate new people into my life right now, maybe I can get out of hanging out with him. This, I know, will upset Hugh and his plans for us to become some happy band of misfits, but I have to look after myself first. Nate, no matter how badly I might want to see him, is detrimental to my progress, though glibly I think Willa would no doubt suggest couples therapy for us.

After digging out a pair of sunglasses and my secondhand copy of *Goodbye to Berlin* from the pocket of my bag, I settle in with my back against the driftwood to read and wait for Hugh, enjoying the feel of the ocean breeze drying the water from my bare shoulders. For a gay man, I'm rather late in discovering Christopher Isherwood; I was always paranoid my parents would catch on if I left copies of his books about my bedroom, back when I still lived with them. Cardiff, however, has a few bookstores from which I've amassed a decent collection of his writing. I all but devoured *A Single Man* and *Christopher and His Kind*. That beautiful line "I am a camera with its shutter open, recording, not thinking," felt so representative of my years in the closet that I wept the first time I read it.

I like to think I'm stronger these days, but when the crunch of footsteps approaching across the sand forces me to glance up, I lose faith in this notion entirely. Even with the rays of the sinking sun haloing his head from behind, I recognize the height and bulk of Nate's body coming toward me, the familiar breadth of his shoulders and long legs. My first instinct is to fling myself behind the log and cower with my arms over my head like a frightened child. He might be the first man to make me feel love, but damned if he isn't also the first to make me feel like a total pussy as well.

"Phel," he says in surprise. He's carrying a shortboard under one arm and is similarly attired in surf shorts and a tan that hasn't yet darkened to California bronze. As he quickens his steps, it's not joy I see on his face, but apprehension. In that much, at least, we're on the same page.

I'm on my feet and backing away before he can get too close, holding Christopher Isherwood in front of me like a shield of flimsy paper. I wish I knew where this scared-animal routine comes from, or how to control it. A year ago, I knew when to be calm and when to display aggression if necessary. These days it seems all I do is react and run away, react and run away. Now isn't the time to start trying to modify my behavior, though, because I can feel the stirrings of an anxiety attack building in my chest like a leaden weight, and the slight edge of nausea that always follows. I'm pretty sure I left the Xanax back at the apartment.

Seeing me frantically starting to stuff my belongings back into my bag, Nate quickens his pace and drops his own board on the sand with a dull *thunk*. He tries to grab me and manages, just barely, to get his fingers around my wrist before there's time for me to jerk away.

"Come on, Phel," he says in a mix of desperation and impatience. The glance I sneak at his face before trying to wrench myself away confirms he is no less stricken. "Don't go running away, man, this is stupid. We need to—"

I finally succeed in snatching my wrist back, although there's a faint band of red on my skin from where Nate's fingers dug into me. "What, *talk?*" I spit. I back up a little more and somehow avoid tripping over my own bag. It would be so like me to fall and break my hip and have to hear him out. "What are you doing here, Nate?" I ask, and the catch in my voice disgusts me. I sound fucking terrified. Hating myself for it, I attempt to straighten my shoulders and steady myself. I tear off my sunglasses so I can look him in the eye. "I have no interest in talking to you," I say. "I was waiting for Hugh." Though I think I sound confident enough, I know this constant barrage of rhetorical questions, practically babbling, indicates otherwise.

"Hugh?" To my surprise, Nate's expression goes from uncertain to furious. This time the few steps he advances are definitely more threatening, aggressive, the way you know a man of Nate's size has the potential to be. He gestures back in the direction of the ocean, which I'm to assume means Hugh is still out there on the waves. "As in my brother Hugh? The kid you've been avoiding for fucking *days?*" Nate gives an angry shake of his head and comes close enough that it takes all my willpower not to stagger back farther. "I can't begin to tell you, Phel, how seriously *fucked up* it is that you're here, but don't you be taking that stuff out on him, do you hear me? He considers you a friend, and right now he thinks you hate his guts. I almost came right out and told him everything just to convince him otherwise, because he has no freaking idea why you've suddenly gone cold on him."

A part of me has to admire how Nate hasn't bothered with pleasantries and small talk, as if to pretend this chance meeting of ours is anything less than what he said—fucked up—but I think it has far more to do with his defense of Hugh than anything. Before I knew who Hugh was, I always got the sense Nate was fiercely protective of his little brother; there was something in the way Nate spoke about him, or *didn't* speak about him, combined with his reluctance to share identifying details, that suggested that to come between them would be a mistake. It's good to know my read of the situation wasn't completely off, even then.

That doesn't mean I'm deaf to the one very important piece of information Nate has accidentally let slip. "You *almost* came out and told him?" I shoot back. For a moment I'm glad my own anger seems to have finally overridden my instinct to curl up and have a panic attack in the sand. "Why the hell didn't you, then? If Hugh and his emotional well-being are so damned important to you, why didn't you just lay everything down so he can know exactly how it is? Exactly why you're *here*?"

As I knew he would be, Nate is cowed by my challenge; he tilts his head back and looks at me from down his nose like an animal on the defensive, trying to protect its face from harm while still maintaining eye contact. "He doesn't deserve to be dragged into the middle of this," he grates out.

"And I did?" I don't meant to shout, but it feels good, weirdly, to be launching into this outburst without preamble, without being allowed to think of all the whys and wherefores and whether or not this is what Willa would recommend. "Like I deserved any of the shit you heaped in my lap, Nate? A year of lies and deception and broken promises? Your *marriage*?" My throat closes off around the last word and I look away, pressing the heels of my palms into my eyes to block out his face.

Nate, damn him, catches it right away. "Phel," he says again, and his voice is gentler now, pleading. He doesn't say anything else until I look at him. Whatever I'm feeling must show on my face like a tragic mask, judging by how he frowns and rocks abortively onto the balls of his feet like he wants to come closer. "This isn't how I wanted to do any of this. I never thought I'd see you again, but even so, this isn't what—" The tension lines around his eyes and mouth seem to have deepened dramatically over the last minute. Those green eyes meet mine with all the force of what we left unsaid between us. And, I see now, he is miserable with it. *Good*, I think.

Nate's voice grows more insistent, but thankfully he doesn't try to touch me again. "For months I've been thinking about what I'd say to you if I had the chance, man, and now you're here? We *do* need to talk. Fuck knows how any of this happened, how we wound up in the same place, but that don't matter. Don't storm off again, not before we've had a chance to figure things out."

The anger that bubbles up inside me is, I find, more than a match for Nate's own, catching like a spark to gunpowder at the suggestion there's anything left to figure out, anything that hasn't already been destroyed. Our relationship is a razed landscape. It should be clear that Nate and I are finished, washed up like seaweed on the beach. He seems, mysteriously, to feel otherwise, but I've no choice but to disabuse us both of the notion before either of us can get any ideas. Same as at Hugh's house, I'm too petrified to keep looking at him and too petrified to look away.

A laugh bordering on the hysterical breaks from my throat, and I remind him, "You had a year to speak to me, Nate. A whole year with just us, alone, when I would have listened to anything you had to say if you'd only been honest. But all you did was bullshit me. And not just me, either—your wife, your son, your brother. Everyone. What interest could I possibly have in what you have to say now? It's done. Whatever cosmic joke brought us here doesn't entitle you to a second chance. It doesn't even entitle you to this conversation."

Much as I'm convinced of this, I'm both surprised and confused we've gotten this far at all. Nate might be the one with the temper, but we're equally stubborn and, to top it all off, I am hopeless when it comes to confrontation. While I'd never known Nate to welcome an emotional discussion about anything—it truly was like pulling teeth—he was always the one ready to stick it out to the end and see a conversation through. I, on the other hand, couldn't wait to run at the first sign I might lose an argument. Nate liked to call this habit "drive-by fighting," wherein I'd say the most unconscionable thing to come to mind, then immediately flee the scene. It's how my last conversation ended with my parents, how Nate and I broke up without ever talking about it—I just ran and ran and didn't look back. Shows how well that worked out for me.

To his credit, Nate must anticipate I'm planning my exit, despite the limited options available; either I fling myself into the sea or dig myself a hole in the sand. He advances a few steps and makes like he wants to take my arm again before thinking better of it, but is close enough to block my escape with his body. I inhale at the proximity, the subtle smell of sweat and sea salt on him, and hope to high hell he doesn't notice the flare of my nostrils and my tongue darting out to wet my lips the same way he notices every other one of my tells.

"Do you hear me denying any of that stuff, Phel?" he asks with a shake of the head. "I'm not—I know I fucked up royally. But just... I never meant—"

My hands tighten into painful fists of their own accord. "So help me, Nate, if you say you didn't mean to hurt me—"

His eyes drift shut in resignation, because we both know my guess is correct. With Nate, they always are, just as I'm not dense enough to believe he doesn't know me equally well. It's been months, and I don't doubt we could still carry on a conversation with just our eyes like we've been doing since Day One. That's part of the problem with feeling you know someone so well—it's all the more devastating when the farce is revealed.

Nate has to know how far he's pushing me out of my comfort zone, but still, he insists, "I didn't. Fuck, Phel, I lo—"

Without warning, my first flies out and catches him on the chin, close enough to his mouth that I feel my knuckles split against his teeth, the painful collision with bone. The whole thing happens so quickly. I wonder if I haven't blacked out, seconds lost between thinking, *Please don't say those words, anything but that*, and finding both of us bleeding, Nate from the lip and myself from the hand. I have never punched someone in my life, and it shows. Belatedly, I remember Hugh commenting, in the midst of some shitty action movie we found on Netflix, that only amateurs go for the face, since the stomach is an equally effective target and far kinder to an assailant's fists. At the time, I dismissed this information as useless, but apparently there is a point where even an adamant pacifist will resort to physical violence to shut someone up.

Appearing as shocked as I feel, Nate stumbles back with a curse and reaches up to touch his split lip. He glances between his blood-smeared fingers and my face with an expression of utter bewilderment, but the sight of him hunched over and breathing hard, face flushed, doesn't move me to pity or regret. Instead it inspires the only real reaction of which I'm capable—the one thing I've been trying to suppress since Nate hurtled back into my life with all the subtlety of an apocalyptic disaster.

Sometimes I think my mind isn't my own. Judging from the speed with which I can go from in control to the grips of a panic attack, this more or less is consistent with how I've come to view my body when adrenaline floods my system and the fight-or-flight instinct kicks in: a vessel occasionally at my disposal, but with significant override functions to which I do not hold the key. Over the past few months, I've come to accept these feelings of helplessness, since I do not, after all, have much say in the hormonal revolt my body might display in the face of anxiety. Other behavior, however, escapes even my considerable powers of rationalization—the only explanation is that I simply don't know what the fuck I'm doing.

Striking faster than a fist, I lurch forward and collide with Nate's body as I grab at that startled face, pulling him forward until there are a dozen surprise points of connection leading up from our hips and ending at our mouths. At first Nate is too stunned to do anything but grunt, the sound immediately swallowed by my kiss, lapped up like his blood upon my tongue. But then his hands are moving, gripping at my hair, my waist, everywhere they can reach, bruising, possessive, greedy. Familiar. Nate's grip is hot in contrast to the clamminess of our sea-chilled skin; I push myself into the touch, pressing our bodies together, his chest as smooth and muscular as I remember.

Teeth and tongues dominate the kiss, my lips burning from the force with which we fight one another, and take and take and take. A groan of frustration, barely recognizable as my own, wrenches from my throat at a bite of particular violence from Nate. While this bit of roughness in all likelihood splits my lip, the tang of my blood is impossible to distinguish from Nate's own. He moans into me, a guttural sound deep in his chest, and the sting of his nails in my back punches a noise of similar urgency from me.

Moving on autopilot, I shove once, hard, against his chest, and then again. We both make surprised sounds when Nate's heel catches on the piece of driftwood and sends him careening backwards, arms flailing for a moment before he grabs back onto me and takes me down with him. The sand barely cushions the landing. My weight crashes on top of Nate and forces the air from his lungs in a huff, warm against my lips, but hardly a second passes before we're mauling each other's mouths again with me perched heavily across his lap, straddling his hips.

Though neither of us are strangers to passionate lovemaking, Nate and I have never been rough to the point of discomfort. As such, my fingers surprise me by tightening in his hair to what is surely a painful extent, tugging as far as my grip will allow until his head is jerked backwards at an angle. I continue kissing him in a fury, and it elicits a sound of such open need from Nate's throat that I feel my cock harden in my shorts, twitching against his erection. I realize I want more. I want that rush of fear and adrenaline and uncertainty flooding through *his* veins for once instead of mine.

I find his wrists and pin them above his head in the sand. Nate is the larger man, but all the time I've spent surfing, paddling out through rough water and building the muscles in my back and arms—I've gotten strong, strong enough to hold him down so he will have to struggle to free himself. If he so chooses. He doesn't, not really, bucking against me for a moment before he gasps into my mouth and arches his whole body instead, letting me savor the thrust of his pelvis and the bump his ribs against mine, sharp protrusions from the awkward angle of his arms.

The feeling is powerful, heady. In fact, I haven't felt this way since the night I met Nate in the bar, when anything I did would surprise him, draw him in, keep him off-balance. I so badly want to feel that way again, and I dig my nails into his skin a little harder, pressing into ligament and bone. My mouth detaches from Nate's long enough to find the pulse in his throat and bite down until he cries out, distinctly, with my name. The flash of his eyes shows only want, surrender, and that's what I need to keep the balance in check. I'm too afraid to give anything of my own, unsure if that side of me still exists.

"Phel," he says over and over, "Phel, please." I want to ask him what he's begging for, since I've never known Nate to beg, but then he rolls his hips and arches against me again and moans, "Baby, yes."

Something in my chest snaps so hard at the word and the need in his voice that my ears ring. I shove him back into the sand with all the force I can muster, then push myself upright and off him altogether, as if an invisible hand has yanked me back by the scruff of the neck. Whatever sense of power I felt recoils like a rubber band that's been stretched too far and then released, cracking back against my skin with a sting I can feel all through my insides.

"What?" Panting, Nate struggles into a half-sitting position with his elbows dug into the sand. I watch his chest heaving for a few seconds and follow the intense flush that travels down from his face, proof of the same rapturous burn I felt not a moment ago. "What was that?" he asks in a gruff voice. He licks his lips and I see his tongue emerge to prod at where the flesh is torn.

To distract myself, I waffle a moment before I begin to shove the rest of my belongings into my bag, not bothering to check if it is all mine or if I've forgotten something. My plan to wait around for Hugh is a thing of the past, because right now I want to be as far away from

Nate and my recurring insanity as possible. I need to go back to where it's safe and I don't fear my own behavior so much. Obviously I'm not to be trusted.

Nate sits up a bit further. "Where the hell are you going?" he demands.

I ignore him, but all this does is make him try harder—of course. He's pursued me every other time I've tried to run away; it'd make no sense for him to stop now. But when that word comes again, "Phel, *baby*," the fog dissipates completely and I stumble back farther, finding myself more or less where I began when he showed up. The only difference is I'm through trying to shield myself from him; I just need to *go*.

"I am *not* your baby," I spit. His face crumples in surprise at the vehemence of my words, but I want so much more than that. I want him to feel as deeply shaken as I've felt the past few months, like nothing will ever be right again. I want this so badly, I worry it'll never be enough. "I'm not your anything."

With that, I start to jog back across the beach, away from him, and I don't look back despite the several times he calls out to me in that heartbreaker's voice. He sounds pretty heartbroken himself. I can't look; it's all I can do to keep going before something gives out and I can't run any more.

5

Nate

EVERYTHING is broken.

It's hard to feel otherwise when the cut on my lip scabs over and my jaw bruises a gross purple from Phel's fist, harsh reminders each time I look in the mirror or see worry written across my brother's face in response to my injuries. He looks at me like a concerned parent whose kid has fallen in with the wrong crowd, so fraught and tense that I could scream, like I really need another layer of stress added to what I'm already feeling. The pain itself is no big deal, little more than a twinge when I talk or chew, but that isn't what I mean, not what freaks me out. I feel disaster closing in each time one of Hugh's sideways glances shows doubt in the lies, suddenly numbering in the double digits, that I've been forced to tell. Since I found Phelan living here in Cardiff, they seem to be multiplying with terrifying speed; damned if each one doesn't hurt more than a hundred of Phel's punches or a thousand of his kisses.

But what's the alternative? Do I tell Hugh, *Hey, buddy, sorry for the recent weirdness but—your best friend? I've been fucking him this whole time and single-handedly ruined his life, along with my family's?* I don't think so. Something tells me Phel wouldn't be down with this course of action either.

I write off my injuries as an accident with the surfboard—amateur's misfortune, blah, blah—but aside from feeling like Hugh sees straight through the bullshit, I can't believe I'm back here. The reason I came to Cardiff is because I was sick of secrets, sick of feeling my whole life was a lie. I'm supposed to be rebuilding, escaping the shit that piled up past the rafters in Ohio, finding a way to set things right with my family—and if I'm lucky, myself. Instead it seems to be happening all over again, like I'm stuck in a budget remake of *Groundhog Day* or some shit.

For days I can think of nothing but Phelan's mouth, the way it burned into me so hotly my lips felt branded after. I wish I knew why he did that, why he turned so suddenly and took off like the freaking hounds of hell were on his tail. Maybe I shouldn't have yelled at him. Maybe I shouldn't have kissed him back or tried to say *I love you*, but even if I regret the method of delivery, I don't feel guilty for saying what needed to be said. Phel ripped himself free of my life before I could tell him any of that stuff. I guess I didn't want to miss out on the opportunity a second time, and desperation does funny things to people.

Weirdly enough, I find a strange source of preoccupation in wishing he'd honor my request to talk to Hugh. Knowing Phel, he'll come around on his own eventually—my brother is difficult to ignore for long, and pretty irresistible once he's decided he likes having you around, the spoiled brat—but in the meantime I can tell the radio silence is getting to Hugh. Maybe getting to them both. Phel never had many friends to begin with, not even in Chicago, and I think it would be good for both of them to get over this hump and pick up where they left off. Even with the limited amount of time I've seen them together, I can tell they fit. They *like* each other, probably even more than Hugh and I would if we weren't related. Easy friendships like that are hard to find. I won't say I'm not jealous, because I am, but I'm not so much of an asshole I can't see how good the friendship is for them both. I want them to have that, but haven't got a clue how to help. My own life could stand some fixing first.

An answer of a sort comes about a week after the incident at the beach. I'm out walking Callie, watching her run back and forth across the sand after the stick I've been throwing, over and over, until my arm starts to hurt. Much like my brother, she is completely inexhaustible—despite the fact that I seem to have taken over her walks, the only time I've seen either of them tire is around each other, the pair as well matched as it's possible for dog and human to be. She seems dismayed I don't share Hugh's boundless energy, but humors me as long as I keep throwing the stick. It's a good specimen, as sticks go, heavy enough not to blow away in the strong coastal winds, but even with a dog of her size, it looks comically huge in her mouth. I've taken to throwing it like a javelin to conserve my strength for the next round.

My phone trills from the pocket of my cargo shorts as a crab or some other sea critter lures Callie into the surf. With one eye on the dog and the other on the caller ID, I almost drop the phone when I see Emilia's name flash across the screen. For a moment my mind whirrs like a turntable with no record on it, around and around while nothing plays. We haven't spoken in weeks, my wife and I, not since I announced I wanted a divorce. Although I've tried to call Liam plenty of times, needing to hear his voice as desperately as I want to see his face, Emilia has managed to intercept every call, making it perfectly clear she doesn't want me talking to our son while the divorce proceedings are still being worked out. Does she think I'm gonna brainwash him or something? I'm sure I could push legal action over that, but the thought of dragging Liam even further into this mess makes me sadder than anything. I've already disrupted his life. Am I supposed to make him miserable too?

I plop down onto the sand when my knees start to feel a bit wobbly. Hands shaking, I answer the call. "Hello?"

"Dad?" Speak of the devil. The sound of that small, uncertain voice makes my heart clench so hard in my chest that I wince, fighting the knee-jerk urge to either drop the phone again or slam it shut in surprise, like I'm being punk'd in the cruelest way possible.

Thankfully, I do neither of these things, though I do take a moment to compose myself, easing the shakiness out of my voice as I reply, "Liam? Is that you?"

"Yeah." Anticipating my question, he explains, "She went to the store. I know I'm not supposed to be calling you, but... I miss you a lot, Dad. Mom won't tell me anything about what's going on or why you won't come home."

So much for small talk. The sheer confusion in his voice makes my chest hurt more than if he'd accused me of abandonment. He wouldn't be wrong, not really, but the thought of him alone, ignorant of why his home is in tatters, makes me angry and so, so guilty I can't be there to make it better. Add to this the knowledge it's my fault to begin with, and a watery grave starts to look pretty damn attractive.

Thing is, I have no idea what to say. Emilia and I aren't getting divorced because we can't stand each other—in fact, my opinion of her is pretty hard to beat. She's protective, is all, the same way I'd be if our roles were reversed, and it's not like there's a road map for this one, at least not a good one. It would probably be a lot easier to take a page straight out of the annals of divorce court and say something disparaging, but I hate when couples turn ugly. The last thing I want is to say something out of line, make Emilia look like the bad person. She isn't. I am. Liam deserves to know that.

But first things first. The phone might prevent me from giving my son the hug he so obviously needs, but I can still reassure him he's not alone in feeling, well… alone. "I miss you too, kid," I say gently. "I've been thinking about you every day I'm out here. Sorry I can't be there right now."

"Where are you? When are you coming back?"

"California. I took a drive out here to spend some time with your Uncle Hugh." Realizing I'm putting off the inevitable, I take another deep breath and shift the phone to rest between my ear and shoulder so my hands are free. Needing something to hold on to, I push all ten fingers into the soft, beautiful sand, warm and silky between my knuckles, digging in deep until my bones ache from the pressure. "As it stands, I don't know when I'll be back, Liam. If I had it my way I'd be there now, but there's some stuff I gotta work out with your mom before I can do that." There's an awkward pause. "How much has she told you?"

I hear Liam's guilty, conflicted sigh. "I asked her if you guys are getting a divorce, since my friend Matt says it's normal for dads to take off when parents split up." By the time Liam has reached the end of his sentence, I can't decide who I want to punch more—myself, or Matt. "Mom started crying when I said that, but she didn't deny it." Now I kind of want to smack Liam too, because seriously? Sometimes my kid acts like his sensitivity chip short-circuited in the bath. I know for a fact Emilia and I raised him not to go saying shit like that, even when angry, but I guess it's not like we planned for this eventuality. He might be entitled to a free pass right now, but not if he's going to start upsetting everyone in the process, or heeding bullshit at school he knows better than to listen to.

"Hey, hey," I reassure him, gently chastising, "no one said anything about me not coming back, okay? This isn't a permanent thing, believe me. Your uncle and I would kill each other eventually."

Wincing at the empty promise, because who the hell knows what *this* is, I attempt to man up for real and tell it straight, talk to Liam like an equal and not a little kid. He deserves that much, not that I blame Emilia for trying to buy herself some time or not knowing what to say. Hell, it's possible I'm about to screw the pooch myself, if my guess is wrong; I tend to overestimate people a lot, myself most of all.

"Listen, Liam," I begin. "I'm not gonna lie and tell you this isn't happening, because you're old enough to understand relationships don't always work out. People get divorced when the problems pile up too high, even if they still love one another. Your mom and I—we still care about each other a lot, but we've got issues that aren't going to fix themselves, no matter how we go about trying to find a solution. The reason I left is because we both needed some time to accept that it's over." Breathless from saying so much all at once, I sigh, pausing to find out whether Liam is following along. I clench my hands a bit harder into the sand like it's an impromptu stress ball. "Believe me when I say it has nothing to do with you. If I didn't think it would make your life a living hell, I'd be there right now trying to patch things up. You know that, right?"

From the silence on the other end of the line, I know Liam is trying his best to parse what I've told him before he lets himself get angry. A fast temper is a trait we both share, but Liam has enough of his mother's patience to make up for it. He's been working through meltdowns on his own since the age of five. Maybe he'll go off on his own later and rip something to shreds, but I can count on him to stay civilized until that point. Just in case, though, I prompt, "Liam?"

Finally I hear his voice emerge, small and tightly controlled. I almost don't hear it over the crashing surf where Callie continues to play, oblivious. "Are you going to go live in another house?"

"I don't know," I admit, meaning, *Probably.*

He grunts angrily. "So what makes you think my life isn't going to suck from now on anyway?"

"I'm not saying it'll be easy for any of us, buddy," I sigh. "You're right: it'll probably suck like crazy for a while, but it'd be worse if you had to listen to your mom and I fight all the time. Remember what happened with your cousin Nick?" I ask, referring to Emilia's sister's kid. "He had to come stay with us before your aunt and uncle split up, 'cause the arguing was so bad. You know how much it used to upset him. Eventually we'll find a way to live with the decision and help you live with it too. I know I speak for your mom when I say you're our main priority, making you happy."

"I'd be happy if you just stopped being stupid and got back together!" There it is, that first shout, the sound of tears harsh in his voice. My own eyes sting in sympathetic response, and even Callie looks up from where she's digging in the wet sand, like she senses a change in the air. She starts to trot back toward me, making me swipe at my eyes in embarrassment before I remember she's just a dog, and not much in the habit of judging grown men who cry in public.

"We can't do that, Liam," I tell him firmly.

He makes a frustrated noise like a wounded animal. I see Callie's ears perk at the sound as she crawls forward on her belly, knowing someone is upset and trying not to be intrusive. She's a good dog, and I'm kind of glad she's here, so I won't have to sit on the beach and cry by myself. A stupid friggin' thought if there ever was one, but there it is.

"Why not?" he demands. "What's such a big deal that you had to go all the way to California and leave us here, huh? If you still love Mom, you should be able to come back and *be here*. If you were around, you'd find a way to fix stuff again. I know it."

Biting my lip, I stare down into Callie's worried brown eyes—what I assume is worry, anyway—and stay silent for a long minute, trying, and failing, not to picture Liam crying over the phone. I don't know what decides me in the end, but I realize I've made up my mind about what to say next even before my brain can catch up with my mouth. "Liam, can I tell you something secret?"

"Is it bad?" He sounds so afraid. My poor, terrified kid. I am officially the worst goddamn father on the planet.

"It's...." I hesitate again. "No, it's not bad. But it's a lot of information, so I need you to listen closely and tell me if there's something you don't understand, all right? It's okay if you don't, so don't feel embarrassed if you have to ask a few questions."

"Okay."

"The reason your mom and I are splitting up, Liam, and why we don't have much hope of working things out, is because"—here my throat closes up like an allergic reaction to what I'm about to say— "I'm gay." There is silence on the other end: deep, confused silence, and it occurs to me I have taken a step that cannot be undone, ever. Not for myself, not for Emilia, and certainly not for Liam. It makes me want to throw up. "Liam?"

"Uh-huh."

God, what does that mean? I have a sudden vision of my kid failing to respond because he's trying to drive a sharpened pencil into his neck. "Do you know what I mean by that?" I don't intend to patronize him, because I know Emilia has covered an abridged version of the sex talk before—the look on Liam's face was priceless—but his sudden calmness is freaking me the fuck out. Not wanting to leave anything to chance, I decide to elaborate, since I'm probably fucked either way as soon as this gets back to Emilia. "It means that I like men more than I like women."

"I know what 'gay' means, Dad," snaps Liam, with an edge of bitterness to his voice I'm not prepared for.

"Okay, well… that's good. So you know it means I can't stay married to your mom, because she isn't a dude." Deciding to go all in, I swallow so heavily I know he'll hear it on the other end. "I'm gonna be honest, Liam. There's someone else—a man—I've been in love with for a really long time."

The strangled sound that emerges makes me cringe. I'm not sure what's pissed him off more: the fact that I've come out of the closet, or that I've more or less admitted to messing around on his mom. Probably both. "Does this mean you're with this new guy now?" he demands. "Is that why you left?"

"No!" The word comes out sharper than intended, but at least it's not total bullshit. "I told your mom the same thing, okay? Trust me when I say there's no chance in hell of fixing things with him. But my answer would be the same either way." Realizing I might be harping on about the wrong thing, I hurry to add, "It's totally my fault I wasn't honest with Mom from the beginning, okay? Full blame there—I had no excuse for keeping things from her, which is another reason why we probably shouldn't be together. A good husband wouldn't have lied for so long."

"So why did you?"

Scrambling for a good answer—good luck, Nate—I venture, "Same reason why you didn't like to admit you broke your mom's favorite bowl last Christmas. I was scared to admit the truth and what she'd say. Don't make it right."

"I don't get it," Liam interjects. Good, a question—hopefully something I can work with. "If this is something you can't change, which Mom told me gay people can't, why don't you just come back and... I don't know... talk to her about it? Why you gotta be all the way on the other side of the country? She said herself that being gay is nothing to be ashamed of."

"She's right." That Emilia covered this part of The Talk so effectively—Liam doesn't remotely appear to be struggling to sympathize with or understand homosexuality—makes me want to bash my head open for how much of a tool I am by comparison. "It isn't shameful, and that's not why I left. But the situation is kind of different when the person you're married to suddenly announces he likes dick." I immediately cringe at my choice of words.

Apparently, Liam does too. "Dad, gross!"

"Sorry. But my point is, your mom has a right to be upset at the information, because it kind of affects her in a big way."

"Can't you just talk to her about it and say you're sorry?"

Oh, to be ten again, when apologies solve almost everything. "I have. And maybe eventually she'll listen, but right now I think she needs a bit of time to let it sink in." I wrack my brain for an analogy that will explain exactly what I mean, that will communicate the depth of what Emilia is going through to Liam as much as myself, but smooth marketing pitches were always much more Phelan's forte. Even Hugh could probably explain this better.

"Look." I take another deep breath on the windup; at this rate I'm going to start getting light-headed from too much oxygen intake. "It's like... it'd be like if Babe Ruth had left the Yankees in the middle of his career to go play hockey in Canada or something." An awful start, but when Liam doesn't object, I forge ahead. "It's not that hockey is any less of a respectable sport than baseball, but a lot of people would feel betrayed and disappointed because they had all these expectations of him as a great ball player, right?"

Liam says, "I guess...," and I wait to hear if there's anything else before I continue. There isn't.

"I'm sure there would be some people out there who would have been encouraging and supportive of the choice, because in the end Ruth has to do what makes him the most happy, but there'd still be a lot of resentment, a lot of shattered hopes." This is either the worst analogy of all times, or I deserve a Pulitzer. "You see what I mean? I've changed teams, and sports, kind of, and there's nothing that could convince me that hockey is less awesome, but I'm not gonna delude myself everyone is thrilled with the decision. Like your mom."

"Is that why she won't let me talk to you?" asks Liam.

"No!" Not that it feels counterintuitive to defend my soon-to-be-ex-wife's honor, but a little part of me wonders whether she'd do the same if Liam asked her about me. "She's pissed 'cause I went about it the wrong way, quit the league without telling anyone first, started dabbling in hockey before I said I was through with baseball. That's the real problem here, the real reason I fucked up—it's not being gay, it's that I was an asshole about it. Okay? So while I'm sure you're gonna hear plenty of stuff at school about how being gay is bad or wrong, if you haven't already, whenever you've got questions or doubts, you just think about me, or better yet pick up the phone and ask me yourself. Even ask your mom, because despite the fact that she's pretty upset with me right now, she isn't a bigot. She'll never try to convince you that being gay is a bad thing. Like you said."

I'm running out of things to say. Despite the rampant stereotypes out there about homosexuality, talking about my feelings isn't one of my strong points. Just ask Hugh or, Christ, Phel. The number of times that guy accused me of "not sharing" exceeds that of even Emilia, though in all fairness there's no question of who's more uptight. Phel got away with it by virtue of being Phel, a fact he didn't often overlook. No word of a lie, I would have walked out on anyone else. He once accused me of withholding so much the relationship felt one-sided—this not even to do with my infidelity, and I remember how that fight wound up being not so different from the conversation I'm now having with Liam.

Phel and I reached a point, several months into the affair, where a system fell into place to establish when and where we spent time together. Meaning, I was the one imposing all the rules. This was both intentional and not: to me, it was pretty cut and dry why I couldn't be cavalier about the whole thing, but I guess I never stopped to think how this came across to Phel. Not until he brought it up, anyway, which he did one night over baseball.

Now, Phel is obviously a guy, and he isn't stupid, so I knew right away he was making a point by raising a touchy subject at a time most likely to rile me up. Emilia would try to start Important Conversations all the time when there was a ball game on TV, and later wouldn't understand why I was distracted or annoyed about missing the last inning. With Phel, it was purely strategic. It wasn't even that he was looking for a way to get out of watching sports, because I'd been getting him into the Rangers and he was on his way to being a knowledgeable fan.

I knew something was up the second he said, casually, "We should watch the next game in Mount Vernon so you don't have to drive home after," in this tone that dared me to contradict him. The words were clipped and calm, practiced. "Or you could come to Chicago."

Freezing with my beer halfway to my mouth, I slid a sidelong glance at him. As he was curled against me under a blanket, the most I could see of his face was a fuzzy profile and that shock of dark hair. "You know your TV here is about a million times better than anything I can afford at home," I pointed out, "so what's that actually supposed to mean?"

Phel sighed and guiltily chewed the inside of his lip. "Can I mute this?" he asked in answer. "The Rangers obviously won't be winning this game."

Though I bristled at his lack of good faith in my team—*our* team, I thought—I didn't protest when he grabbed the remote and switched off the television altogether, like he knew one or both of us had the propensity to become distracted under fire. He also divested me of my beer, which he set down on a coaster atop the glass coffee table.

"I can't believe I'm about to say this," he began, "but I'm starting to feel a bit *put out* by the fact that we've been dating for months, and I've yet to see the inside of your house." His nose wrinkled in a way I tried not to find adorable. "Maybe I'm new at this relationship thing"—here, he made air quotes—"but that seems odd to me. Isn't it? Considering you live less than an hour away?"

"Is your question about whether it's weird, or why you haven't seen the inside of my house?" It was a long shot and kind of a cheap one as well, but this seemed like one of those conversations where any opportunity to prevaricate was best taken advantage of. I was good at avoidance when I wanted to be. Emilia hated it, but Phel, thankfully, detested talking about this shit almost as much as me. I figured I was doing us both a favor by dragging it out, like easing a Band-Aid off a sensitive patch of skin.

Scowling, Phel folded his arms and turned his body a bit more to face me. "Fine," he grumbled. "I'm asking why I've never been to your house."

Shit. I tried again. "Is that, like… a deal breaker or something? Dual residence or nothing? You want a new space to decorate?"

"You're being a jackass," he told me firmly. Maybe joking about gay stereotypes wasn't the way to go here. "Obviously it's not a deal breaker, and I pay people to decorate." I snorted. Phel punched me in the arm. "Quit it, Nate. It's bad enough having to hide you from my friends and family, or feeling half the time like I missed the class on relationship 'dos' and 'don'ts'. But whenever I try to show an interest in your home life or suggest going to Mount Vernon, you brush it off without much explanation or become cagey. I don't appreciate being made to feel like *you're* hiding something as well. Like there's a reason you don't want me to see where you live."

My whole body went still, mind racing from *Does he suspect? Did he follow me home?* to *Does his ridiculously rich family have spies on my tail?* Even though I knew it was a stupid thing to think, by that point I was on such high alert for any sign of suspicion from either end—Emilia, too, had started to wonder why I was taking so many business trips lately—I didn't feel comfortable brushing off these kinds of questions. Until I laid each and every one to rest, I could barely sleep at night. Half the time I lay awake wracked with anxiety anyway, clutching Phel to me the way Liam used to cling to his battered stuffed elephant as a toddler.

They say fear is proportionate to guilt, and I was one hell of a guilty, terrified motherfucker. I thought about Phel all the time, thought about how I was lying not just to him, but to Emilia and Liam too. I'd started thinking a bit about the D-word, and whether it was feasible to stick around in a marriage that was coming apart at the seams. Whether it was feasible to pretend I didn't leave a massive part of myself behind in Columbus each time I left. Emilia and I barely touched each other anymore, or at least I did a pretty good job of finding excuses to put off having sex whenever she came to bed wearing new lingerie or tried to pack Liam off for a sleepover. It killed me to carry on with something that would end worse for everyone the longer I kept it hidden. I just hadn't figured out the logistics yet—not about how to broach the subject with my wife, and certainly not with my boyfriend. At that stage, the only thing I was clear on was who I wanted to be with, and currently he was staring at me and interpreting my silence as proof I was about to break his heart.

"Is this not working out for you, Nate?" Phelan asked quietly. He smoothed his fingers down my cheek, then withdrew. "Maybe that's not something I'm supposed to say, I don't know. I hate to ask where we stand, but if this isn't what you want, it's probably better to get it out in the open now."

I sighed. While Phel might have been 100 percent wrong about me wanting to end the relationship, I knew this was what he was most afraid of: getting unexpectedly shit-canned from a relationship he'd tried to resist in the first place. There was no denying that neither of us expected to end up here after that first weekend. But he was also offering me an out, an opportunity to make a clean break without weeks—if not months—of lying and waiting for the right time to spring the bad news.

It wasn't going to happen, though. That much I could deny with a clean conscience. Even my dysfunctional male brain knew I was in love with him, the feelings sincere, though I hadn't yet worked up the nerve to say it out loud. Still, it was equally clear he needed a show of good faith to make him believe it, to reassure him of the crazy risk he'd taken on me with his heart. That, more than anything, made me want to step up and start thinking about taking a risk of my own. I wanted to prove Phel wrong, show him I was worthy. Maybe I still didn't believe it myself, not while I was married to Emilia, but I was determined to give him as much as I could. Hell, if my wife and son's feelings hadn't been on the line, I'd have given him everything already.

I found Phel's hand beneath the blanket and gave it a squeeze, lacing our fingers together in a way I'd long stopped feeling self-conscious about. "You're amazing," I told him, trying not to chastise him for thinking otherwise. "But there *is* something I haven't told you. It's got nothing to do with how I feel or how much I want to be here, okay? Because we're good. I love being with you." I wished I could have done away with the "being with" part, but dropping the L-bomb right then would have looked suspicious, like I was trying to divert him from the topic at hand or buy him off. Instead I took a deep breath and wound up for the pitch. "Fact is, Phel, the reason I haven't felt comfortable bringing you to my home is because I don't live there by myself. I've got a son—Liam. He's nine, and he has no idea I like men."

For a few seconds Phel just blinked at me, which I guess I should have anticipated, but what freaked me out was the total lack of expression on his face. Usually this meant he was trying to throw me off of how he really felt about something—Christ, that face could have made it to the finals in the World Series of Poker—but in this case I think he was just trying to decide how to react, and coming up empty.

"You have a son," he eventually repeated.

"Yeah."

"Are you... joking?"

I frowned. "Why the hell would I joke about something like that?" I dug out my wallet and threw it to him so he could see the photo of Liam I kept there. It was one of my favorite pictures of him, taken about a year ago. In it, he was scowling at the camera in my dad's old leather jacket, which was comically huge on him.

When Phel said, "You have a son," a second time, his tone was very different. He gazed at the photo for a few minutes and then looked at me with his eyes slightly narrowed, mouth opening and closing like he couldn't figure out where to start. It would have been amusing if there'd been anything funny about the conversation. "Were you... were you planning on telling me at any point?"

"Aside from now?"

He grimaced. "No, I asked you point-blank; you didn't volunteer the information. There's a difference. And it's not like this is the same thing as telling me you keep sixteen ferrets in your basement, Nate. Not the same thing at all." Christ, with semantics like that, Phel could have been a lawyer. But something in his expression softened, and I caught an edge of hurt in the twist of his mouth, like it was only just occurring to him what I'd said. "This is... big, Nate. A big part of your life."

It went without saying: Phel was offended I hadn't told him sooner, hadn't unlocked this part of my life as readily as he'd unlocked himself to me. But when I considered whether I'd have done differently, even without Emilia in the picture, I realized the answer was no. Liam sometimes reacted badly if we gave him the wrong thing for lunch without sufficient warning, and this seemed the kind of thing you didn't spring on a kid. Significant others... that was a big fucking step, not one to be taken lightly. Not that Phel was the clingy type, but it wouldn't have surprised me if he started to express an interest in meeting the kid, now that he was aware of Liam's existence. In all fairness, my son was pretty irresistible.

"You're right," I answered. "He *is* a big part of my life—huge—and I guess I felt protective about sharing too soon. It's not that I don't trust you, or else I wouldn't be telling you now, but...." I shrugged helplessly. "I wanted to be sure, you know? Before I went and introduced him to something this major. Or vice versa." Funny how it came so naturally to tell Phel he was something major in my life, and mean every word.

Another few minutes crept by while Phel considered my confession and continued to gaze at the photo. Much to my relief, he nodded and handed the wallet back to me with a brave smile. "This is significant. Sorry for being so surprised, I just...." He swallowed heavily. "This is significant," he said again.

It was my turn to hesitate, to swallow around a cold stone of fear. "'Let's talk about it' significant, or 'Get the fuck away from me' significant?" Suddenly I realized I had no idea how I'd expected Phel to take the news. He'd never expressed any particular dislike of kids, but it's not like he'd ever claimed to want one either, what with his jet-setting lifestyle and apartment full of valuable, breakable things.

He frowned. "I don't know what to make of the fact that you thought I'd kick you to the curb."

Fair point, but I'm sure plenty of legitimately single parents go through this dilemma all the time. "Does that mean you're not?"

I felt his hand squeeze mine. "Nothing that dramatic, Nate. I can't say I saw this coming, but... I want to accept all parts of you, even your son, and I suppose I understand your hesitation. Your guardedness. The boy's had no say about who you involve yourself with, and you have to make the right choices on his behalf."

Sensing Phel's approval, not just of Liam, but also the fact that I'd taken a big step in a positive direction, I shifted around until I could crawl over his body and bear him back against the soft leather of the sofa. "You know that means you're my right choice, right?" I asked, voice muffled as I pressed a kiss to the corner of his mouth.

"I think you're trying to butter me up," he corrected. Despite being half-trapped in the tangled blanket, Phelan's arms came up to wrap around my neck. "But I'm glad you told me. I didn't mean to push." Smile growing, he added, "I hope you'll tell me all about him. He looks just like you."

I grinned, unable to stop myself. "Handsome little bastard, isn't he? His mom's quite the looker too." The words slipped out before I could hold them back.

Not surprisingly, Phelan's face darkened and he started to withdraw his hands. "His mother... where is she?"

A nervous lump choked me up for a moment. I prayed Phel wouldn't notice, or wouldn't interpret the pause for what it was, and I fought not to withdraw myself from his embrace. "She's around," I explained. This lie was much harder, when it came. "We're divorced, but Emilia's a big part of Liam's life. And mine. Raising him without both of us being involved wasn't an option, so she's in my life too. She doesn't know I'm gay, though. Not yet." I watched his face carefully. "I'm sorry if that complicates stuff."

Phel hesitated and then slowly nodded. "It does, but... it's just how things go, I guess. You don't have to explain what it's like to hide this from your family, Nate. It's a freedom I don't enjoy either. So there's no judgment on my end. I often think about telling them too, just to put an end to all the lies, but I know what a huge disaster it'd be. Protecting yourself is nothing to be ashamed of, even if it's from your own family."

I smiled sadly at how Phelan's voice hardened when he talked about his family, the way even his words became more tight and formal. Now that I knew who the Prices were, I knew he wasn't exaggerating about how they'd react to this information about him. Phel's father was not only one of the wealthiest and most successful ad men in the United States, but one of staunch Catholic values. His support and endorsement could make or break a brand, and to hear Phelan tell it, he felt a responsibility to promote only those companies that upheld the proper, God-fearing attitude of the Midwest. That didn't include much room for a gay son, even if Phel had a stronger sense of morality than most. At least to me, he did.

"I'm not just protecting me," I said, though that was certainly part of it. "Sometimes you gotta protect your family from yourself too." Did I mean about being gay? No. Even then, I think I knew Liam would have handled it well if I eased him into it, if there hadn't been other factors to consider. What he needed the most protection from was the lies building up around him and his mom, without their knowledge.

The memory, in retrospect, is no happier now that I know its resolution. Phel and Liam went on to become friends, the few times he was able to meet his dad's "nerdy pal from Columbus," but I never quite shook the desire to come clean to them both, never felt it was a whole victory. It feels damn good to have told Liam the truth at last, since, as it turns out, he needed even less protection from my sexual preferences than I thought. I guess I'm more of a "nature over nurture" kind of guy, because I don't think being attracted to men is something I've got a choice over. Much as I've tried to fight it over the years, anyway. What's left to account for is the fact that I lied my face off to him the whole time, which is the real reason he should be upset. Maybe he doesn't understand, or maybe he's just that much better than me as a person, I don't know, but even as I end the conversation with a promise that he's my number-one priority, as well as his mom's, I know there's still a long, hard way to go before Liam will feel like he's got his dad back for real.

HUGH is locked away in his study by the time I get home. He's either writing or jerking off, two things he's always done with the door closed, but I've got no desire to interrupt him in either case. I settle for some aimless channel surfing instead, both impressed and repulsed by the ungodly large television and accompanying surround sound. It's bigger and flatter than the one he had last time, and I can picture Liam going crazy over it, since like most kids his age, he seems to have a direct link between his brain and his Xbox.

Thinking about Liam sucks the mindless enjoyment from watching TV, though, and reminds me of how badly I want to be there to curl his small body into mine. Not just to make all the pain and confusion go away, but to thank him for being so awesome that he took the news of my being gay on the chin like a champ. No one could think that's easy, finding out everything you knew about a parent is wrong. Coming out to Liam did to my brain what the Vulcans did to Romulus, and if his world is only slightly less shattered right now, it's a friggin' miracle.

What I don't expect is the sense of freedom that comes with it, like a weight's been lifted off my shoulders after years doing the Atlas routine. For that alone I could latch on to him and not let go. One aspect of parenthood no one ever warned me about is how seriously addictive it is to hug your kid; I could do it forever. My own father was never much inclined toward tactile affection, not like my mom, and the tendency to be physical with my family probably comes from her. It's how I was with Hugh growing up, and Liam and Emilia—even Phel, who always squirmed and protested but, I could tell, secretly loved it. I don't think he came from a very affectionate family either.

Having no such physical outlet here makes me feel out of sorts and even more alone, almost as much as having no one to talk to about how my kid is the greatest human being on Earth. How his mom's levelheadedness rubbed off on him, despite my fuckups. I can't tell Hugh, because that might raise one of his massive eyebrows, though if I'm honest with myself, the one person I want to call the hell up and boast to is Phel, because he'd get it. Once upon a time, he was always the one to tell me not to worry about my kid so much. Liam made it obvious to everyone he met, Phel included, that he would grow up to be a really outstanding guy. If I called Phel now to say he was right, he wouldn't be surprised to hear about Liam. Okay, he wouldn't pick up the phone to begin with, not with my number on the caller ID, but if he did, I know he wouldn't have anticipated a different outcome for my son. The kicker is that I wouldn't know what to say to him, even if I did manage to reach him outside of Hugh.

I don't believe in God, but the second I notice Hugh's Android phone sitting there on the coffee table, the realization is so sharp I might as well have asked for a sign. Guilt tightens my throat before my fingers close all the way around it, my hands suddenly clammy against the rubberized skin of the casing. My gaze ticks instinctively down the hall in the direction of Hugh's office, senses on the alert for any sign he might be about to find me out. Even through the paranoia, the thought occurs to me I haven't quite decided what I plan to do. Except that as far as my hands are concerned, I have. It's nothing to click into the address book and scroll down through the alphabet until I see Phelan's name there in front of me like the Holy fucking Grail—well, almost nothing, since with this futuristic phone of the future, I barely know which buttons I'm tapping at first.

I don't recognize Phel's number, which makes sense considering he had them all disconnected at the same time he changed the locks at his apartment, but I can see the area code is local. The call connects with a click of my thumb, so fast I could call it an accident, had I the stomach for it. Speaking of which, that pansy-ass organ is slowly sinking to my feet as I listen to the pregnant *ring, ring* on the other end. My breath hitches when someone picks up. Every muscle in my body tenses.

"Palermo Springs Rehabilitation Centre, how can I direct your call?"

Wait. What?

Except for a slight choking sound in the back of my throat, I'm silent for long enough on the other end that the receptionist sighs in a huff and repeats, "Palermo Springs, hello?"

"Uh, sorry," I blurt out. "I think I've got the wrong number or… something." I end the call immediately and sit staring at the phone.

Wrong number. Has to be. It makes no sense that Hugh would still have this number kicking around in his phone, because it's been ages since he set foot in a rehab facility—and yet it dawns on me I haven't exactly been around to know for sure, one way or another. But Hugh hasn't touched more than a couple of beers around me the whole time I've been here, and, well—I would know if he were using again. Wouldn't I? He was a whole other person on blow. No way that's the case, I tell myself. Hugh's way too much of a dick on drugs for any backsliding to have escaped my notice.

Besides which, I don't even remember having seen "Palermo" in his address book entries to have dialed the facility by mistake. It's possible I hit a speed dial button or something, but…. Only one way to be sure.

I glance down at the phone again and, very deliberately, hit the call button to dial Phelan's number, my earlier nervousness almost forgotten in the confusion and sudden slap of fear about my brother. I'm practically *eager* to hear Phel's voice on the other line, and pray for him to pick up as the phone rings a few times.

Rationally, I know what's going to happen before it does; a few theories about Phel are already starting to come together in my mind. But denial has always been one of my strong suits. The idea of Phel on drugs is kind of absurd, I tell myself, considering the guy barely drinks.

I'm sure there must have been a bender or two after we broke up, but he's like Hugh—I've never seen him drink much around here. Following Hugh's lead, most likely. Still, he's been acting totally different, nervous and withdrawn compared to the sharp, confident cat who picked me up at a bar like he ate man-shaped people for lunch. I wouldn't have recognized him if not for his face. Drugs can do that, if Hugh's Dr. Jekyll routine was anything to go by, and I find myself holding my breath again until the line clicks and I hear that chipper voice again.

"Palermo Springs Rehabilitation Centre, how can I direct your call?"

Fuck. Mind still racing, I stutter a greeting in response and tentatively say, "This is Hugh Fessenden calling," in the hopes that, if he's a patient there, the receptionist will recognize him. I remember Palermo—not only is it small, but staff members are so expertly trained that they're on a first-name basis with everyone, especially celebrity guests. It's kind of creepy.

"Hi, Mr. Fessenden," chirps the receptionist. Definite recognition in her voice, and warmth like she's plenty used to him calling. Huh. "Did you need me to direct your call?"

"Uh...." Though I'm conflicted, the receptionist's gentle *hmm?* of encouragement settles the issue. I've come this far already. If I'm going to steal my brother's phone and stalk his friends, I might as well go all in. Just in case, I lighten my voice to sound more like my brother's, which is noticeably less gruff than mine. "I'm looking for Phelan Price," I say shakily.

"You usually are," she replies with a laugh. "Should I connect you through, or did you just need to leave a message for him?"

No to both—it'd do me no good to be ignored *and* have my name placed on a blacklist or something. "I misplaced his info," I answer. "Can I get his room number off you again? I'm thinking of visiting this afternoon."

"He's in cabin number four." Wracking my brain, I recall at the last second that Palermo has a bunch of small cottage-type places for patients with less severe issues, or who are starting to regain their independence. Well, "small" is a bit inaccurate: Hugh stayed in one for a week near the end of his program, and at the time I remember thinking it was bigger than some of the apartments we'd lived in growing up.

"Right, of course. Silly me." I clear my throat a little and decide to wrap this up before I can blow my cover. "Well, thanks for your help, I'll be coming by in a little while." I hang up.

Sucker-punch nausea is a normal response to discovering that your ex-lover is in rehab, right? I don't even know where to begin trying to wrap my head around that, because—Phel. This guy I love, who is quite possibly the biggest square on the planet, apart from my memories of him in bed that can still make me blush, is camped out in some fucking facility?

My brain can barely compute, but what Hugh said about Phel's "issues" is starting to make a hell of a lot more sense. Between my dad and my brother, it's safe to say I come from a family of addicts; I've hit the sauce too hard enough times in my own life to know how destructive it can be, though thankfully never around Emilia or Liam. The thought of Phel being caught up in drugs or alcohol, *because of me*, sends me pitching forward to sit with my head between my knees so I don't vomit all over Hugh's bazillion-dollar carpet. It should be enough that Phel is getting help, clearly near the end of his program if he's living unsupervised, but now more than ever, I feel how important it is to go talk to him, to just… apologize for everything, right up to yelling at him on the beach last week. For all the good it'll do.

In the process of trying to convince myself I don't have every intention of going to Palermo to see Phel, I spend a fair bit of time wandering around the house, no less aimless than before. As I shower, I wonder if Phel showers a million times a day to contend with the heat I know he must hate, and afterwards I spend so much time pondering the selection of clothing from my open suitcase, I'm both embarrassed and tempted to announce this sartorial dilemma to Hugh and say, "See? Gay." Although Emilia threw out all of my flannel and jeans with rips in the ass during the first year we were married, even she was a little puzzled by some of the outfits that started showing up in my wardrobe under Phel's influence. I distinctly remember the way her eyebrows went up the first time I wore a scarf when it wasn't cold outside.

Eventually I settle on tightest pair of jeans I own and a gray V-neck I must confess looks damn good. Still with no clear picture of what I hope to achieve by going there, I figure it can't hurt to look presentable. Phel used to use this tactic liberally, dressing in clothes that perfectly matched his eyes or strategically ruffling his hair whenever he had something touchy to bring up, and me being an average twentysomething dude, I fell for it every time, oblivious and distracted by his mouth or the open V of his shirt while he went on about the opera tickets he'd purchased for that evening, or the toilet that needed to be fixed. Hell, it's an art women have perfected for ages, right up there with asking for a new living room set during sex. If Phel is going to slam the door in my face, I at least want him to stare at my package and hesitate first.

"Hugh, I'm going out!" I yell at the closed door of his office, and in response I get something that sounds like a grunt of acknowledgement. He doesn't ask where I'm going or when I'll be back, which suits me just fine, since that way I won't have to lie about it. Already I contemplate signing his name in the Palermo guestbook, which I should feel shitty about, but regard as sheer necessity. Desperate times and all that, and I'm pretty goddamn desperate right now.

Years have passed, but I still know the way to Palermo without a map. Although it's within walking distance of Hugh's house, I take Lucy in case I'm forced to beat a hasty retreat. The compound looks just as I remember it, serene and cookie-cutter neat and not unlike a gated community you'd see in Newport or other überwealthy parts of California—parts of Cardiff, in fact, which is why Palermo fits in so well. The damaged wealthy feel at home here. Hugh used to complain more about feeling pampered and coddled than he did working the steps, but Phel…. This is probably not much different than the conditions under which he grew up, him being the product of old money and a truly intimidating empire. Even cut off from his family's resources, he no doubt found a way to hold on to some of it, some way to keep himself in the creature comforts he once enjoyed freely. Phel always was one for planning ahead.

The visitation policy for unsupervised patients is pretty relaxed, considering they are clients, not inmates, and can come and go as they please. The guard at the front gate waves me through before I finish giving a name. By comparison, arranging face time with inpatients in the main facility is a whole other song and dance, regulated by strict hours and pat-downs for the more severe cases, just in case a visitor gets the bright idea to smuggle something in. This reassures me somewhat. I would submit to eighty fucking cavity checks for Phel—not the fun kind either—but I doubt he'd feel the same, fiercely private to the end. I wonder how much Hugh knows about Phel's issues, though I imagine he has filled in most of the blanks already. He was the one who spent time here, after all; I was nothing more than a lousy commuter.

The compound really is beautiful, green and pristine, inviting, obviously a place of meditation and relaxation. I have to park Lucy near the main building and walk the rest of the way, since most of the compound is accessible only on foot. Other people, be they patients or staff, walk the grounds with far less of a sense of purpose than me, seemingly happy to be out and about, enjoying the cool breeze and sweet sea air. I trace the hedged-off paths that lead the way, bypassing a quiet pond and several meditation areas, and try not to reminisce about all my other visits here that were filled with fear for my brother. More than anything, I pray it won't be the same with Phel.

Christ, I hope he's okay. He's done such a damn good job of hiding all this, he could be in deep shit and I wouldn't know it—wouldn't be able to do a damn thing to help. He must hate it here. I can almost picture him forcing himself to relax in this environment, pretending like he belongs, but I know he must miss his old digs, that ridiculously opulent condo in the steeple of a church or his second home in Chicago, which could have gotten Oprah's nod of approval. Hell, she probably bought it off him when he moved. I'd buy them back myself if I could, for him, but all I've got to offer is a weak apology and a plea for him to look me in the eye again. It'd be nice if he looked at me *that* way again, too, and kissed me with the same need as on the beach, but that's nothing but a stupid fantasy on my part. No hopes or expectations to that end. I don't deserve it, but then, I've always asked too much of Phel.

There are six independent-living cottages on the compound, arranged around a leafy outdoor pond and a little cul-de-sac. It looks not unlike a fancy overnight camp, with a decent illusion of freedom and normalcy. Each has its own small porch and sitting area out back, partially fenced off for privacy. Not unlike the first time Phelan took me home, my hand is shaking slightly when I stop in front of the cottage with the 4 on the door. There's no doorbell I can press and get it over with, no touch of a button to seal my fate; I've got to reach out and knock, feeling each rap of my knuckles against the wood like a fucking new nail in my coffin.

I try to stand as far back from the peephole as possible—cheap of me, I know, but my objective here is to get Phel to open the door, not take one look and call for security before I even catch a glimpse of his face. In some small way, seeing him will make it better. Whenever things used to get really bad with Emilia and I had no clue how to carry on, seeing Phel's face reminded me I was fighting for something important, even if the only person I was fighting was myself.

At first there's no answer, no hint of life within, but then I remember this is Phel we're talking about, not my brother, and not everything he does sounds like an army rushing into battle. Still, the sudden rattle of the doorknob surprises me. I wonder if they still leave everything unlocked around here? I suck in a thick breath when the door swings open and Phel is *there*, sleep rumpled and dressed in sweats that make him look unbearably young and carefree. My stomach flips when I realize they're an old pair of mine.

"Nate," he says in alarm, voice rough with disuse, and takes a step back like he's discovered a tiger on his doorstep. His eyes track over me in a rush and then to our surroundings, probably a knee-jerk reflex to the past couple of weeks of secrecy and suspicion. Much to my relief, his desire to keep me hidden overrides his impulse to chase me away, and he drags me inside by the wrist so he can shut the door behind us. "What the hell are you doing here?"

"Obviously I came to see you," I answer tersely. "What the hell are *you* doing here? At Palermo?" Before we can launch into a frantic back and forth, because I know he'll want to know how I found this place, I say, "I got your number off Hugh's phone, okay? I had no idea you were in fucking *rehab*, for crissakes, I was just… I was just going to call you, but then I find out you're here fighting a goddamn addiction?" I remember at the last minute I'm supposed to be here to apologize, not give him the fifth degree, and add, "Sorry. I had to come see if it was true for myself."

Phel scrunches up his face like he doesn't know which part is more ridiculous. "Oh, great," he retorts. "So now you're going and stealing private information off your brother's phone. Glad to see nothing's changed." He shakes his head angrily. "Can't you see you aren't wanted here, Nate? I've kept this information personal for a reason—it's none of your business."

Unable to help it, I snort. "Right, none of my business. We break up, you take off, and when you're suddenly locked away in a rehab facility, I'm expected to believe I had nothing to do with it." It's one hell of a thing to try to lay claim to, but I'm not here to weasel out of my responsibility or haggle for a smaller share of the blame. I deserve all of it, and that's exactly how much I'm here to take. "Phel, the thought of you hurting yourself with something, I just—" I muffle a strangled sound of pain and have to look away from his face, allowing myself to observe my surroundings for the first time. His temporary home is exactly as bland and unoriginal as I expected of Palermo, decorated in soothing blues and whites, with inspirational paintings of sailboats on the walls. Fresh flowers and a river-stone fireplace attempt to cheer things up. "I'm not worth it."

Phelan's expression hardens at me, and he moves back to lean against the wall near the entrance to the kitchen. On the table next to a steaming cup of coffee—he takes it with three sugars and so much milk it's nearly white—I can see a crisp newspaper that must have been left by the maid. Stories of a world all but inaccessible to most of the patients here. I can feel Phel watching me for a second, observing my curiosity. Then he says, "You're right, you're not."

I can't be upset at what's true. "Then why all this?" I ask, gesturing around me.

By his sigh, I can tell Phel is deciding how much he wants to commit to this conversation, how much he wants to tell me. That I've yet to be hauled away by Palermo's intimidating security team is heartening. "I'm not here for drug or alcohol abuse," he eventually says. "Believe it or not, my life has kind of fallen apart recently. I needed to recoup, and I needed a place to live. Considering I had enough of my own money saved, this seemed a logical way to achieve both." I watch as one of his shoulders lifts, a gesture that makes my throat close up with its unspoken pain. "I needed help."

"And it's my fault."

His eyes lift to meet mine, and there's no hostility or reproach in them, just tiredness and heartbroken acknowledgement that what I've said is the absolute truth, and a flickering resolve to not contradict me.

That's painful, but good. Phel doesn't need anything more on his plate right now, from the looks of it, including trying to protect my ego.

I advance slowly toward him, anticipating being pushed away at any second, but he lets me get closer than arm's reach before he flinches and presses himself back against the wall. Frozen, I maintain my distance.

"I'm sorry I yelled at you last week," I murmur. "It was a shitty thing to do and I knew it at the time, I just… lost it. You didn't deserve that." At his jerky nod, I risk coming an inch closer. "Tell me what I can do to help, if there's some way to…."

Phelan's mouth gives an ugly twist as he straightens. He sets his shoulders in a tense, angry line that means business as much as the warning flash in his eyes. "What? Some way to make it better, Nate? Take back the lies and get my family speaking to me again? Change the fact that I've lost everything because of you?"

"Don't you think I'd fix that if I could? Hell, I'd leave and go back to Ohio if that's what you wanted. If it'd make things easier." This isn't what I'm ready for at all, but once the words are out, I realize I really would do that for him. Hugh wouldn't understand, of course, but knowing Phel might be more at ease with me gone is worth my brother's confusion and my own mileage. My own heartbreak, too, though that goes without saying. I'd move to freaking Antarctica for him. "I'll go if you ask me to. Even though I might not be able to fix things myself, I won't stick around and watch you hurting, not if leaving can change that."

"Out of sight, out of mind, right?" he snaps.

"You know that's not what I mean."

Recognizing the muscle that tics in his jaw as disgruntled agreement, I give in to the desire to touch, pressing our bodies lightly together so he can feel I'm here. Last thing I want is for him to go off someplace else in his mind to escape the conversation. He shivers against me, hard enough that I feel it, and I dip my head to meet his gaze since he's staring pointedly at the floor. The only way to snap Phel out of his withdrawn moods is to be direct, so there's no way out of the conversation except through it. I don't want a repeat of last time, and my face sure as hell would appreciate not getting punched again, but something about Phel makes me want to push and push until he shoves back—until he gives me some spark of anger, of the old, passionate him. But let the record show I have no fucking idea what I'm doing.

"Phel. Do you want me to leave?" I repeat.

He looks at me again, finally, chewing the inside of his lip, then counters, "What do you want from *me*, Nate?"

Well, that's simple enough, at least. "I don't want to see you acting like some goddamn zombie all the time," I say. "I'd like you to be happy again and not… this."

"And what if that man doesn't exist anymore? What if this is all there's left?"

Shit, he looks ready to lose it, face pinched and upset in a way that could mean he's about to go mental at me or just start bawling. Since I've never seen the latter and have no desire to, I'd happily settle for outrage if it gets us somewhere, gets me more of that Phel from the other day. Like I said, I'm in no hurry to get pummeled again, but I'll take that over strained silence. Therapists always say anger is useful, right? That's what I want. He can beat me to a bloody pulp in the name of progress. Not knowing what this new Phel is capable of, however, I don't say that out loud.

"I don't believe that," I tell him. "But maybe you do, and that's why I'm willing to do what I can to change it. Anything, Phel. If you want me to go, I'll go. But if you want me to stay…." I let that hang there for a second, aching with hope, and dare to think his silence can be read as acceptance. "Tell me what you need, man."

The request is pointless; we both know the answer already. Phel needs nothing less than what he took for himself on the beach that day, something hard and hungry and brutal, the desire to exact punishment for wrongs done to him. And hell, every part of me is willing to give it to him if it'll help. From the way it made me feel, it might help me too. His fist made me feel like I was atoning for something unspoken.

"What motivation could you possibly have to stay?" he asks me, and one of his hands fists the fabric of my T-shirt before he reaches to touch the place where my lip is still a bit swollen, the cut fading. At first the pressure is tentative, distracted, but as I open my mouth in invitation, he presses harder, seemingly fascinated by what his fist left behind. It stings a little and I hiss.

"I'm not here to talk about me," I remind him, fighting the impulse to lick at the pads of his fingers, or else take the digits into my mouth altogether.

He seems to anticipate what I want, eyes going stormy indigo with sudden heat, dark as angry thunderclouds. "You don't particularly want to know what I want to do to you, Nate," he spits. "I have never wanted to treat anyone that way, much less you, and I don't like it. I don't even want to talk about it with my therapist, and she's paid to listen to that crap. It's just that you make me so...."

"What?"

"*Angry.*" A quick shift occurs, too subtle for me to decipher, and I feel his other hand sneak out to curl around my hip. His fingers dig into the bone. This time there's no hesitation—the sharp pressure is hard enough to leave a bruise. I push myself into it and watch with satisfaction as his nostrils flare. "Are you telling me that's what you want?"

The lowness of his voice sends a shiver up my spine. Shifting my weight forward, I press our chests together to show how much I'd welcome a glimpse inside his head right now, even if it's something he's afraid to let me see. I'm not afraid to go there, though maybe I should be—I don't know. I keep thinking there's got to be something simmering beneath the surface, waiting to boil over; something he's done a bang-up job of hiding from Hugh and the people here at Palermo—even from himself. I want that part of him for my own, want all of that pain and resentment and whatever else lurks down there. If it'll let *Phel* finally think he's not the only one who's hurt, so be it. He isn't, and I could probably spend a few days unpacking every ugly thought that's crossed my mind since he left, but I'm slowly starting to realize he won't believe it unless he sees it for himself, feels like he's giving back a little of what I did to him.

With a shiver, I realize I want that for him, no matter what it takes. It's like that line about not knowing how deep the rabbit hole goes—I don't think the point is that it's deep, but that it's impossible to resist finding out for yourself once you've been invited to look. Phel has already led me down pretty far, since I'd hardly be here if I hadn't met him. Even if I'm starting to suspect we're wandering into seriously uncharted fucking territory, I trust him all the same, like I wouldn't trust anyone else.

"I want you." My voice comes out hoarse, words cracking around everything I don't know how to say out loud, but my hands are weirdly steady as I reach out to him, bracketing the edges of his slim hips with my hands. He's breathing hard into me, a flush creeping up his neck to stain his cheeks, and I feel the length of his cock begin to harden against my leg. The loose sweatpants do nothing to disguise his growing arousal. Thing is, he doesn't seem to give a shit if I notice. "I want to feel you kiss me again like you did at the beach," I say. "Honestly, Phel, I don't care what I have to do to get you to make me yours again, how fucking low I have to stoop. I'll do anything, just… let me."

To prove it, I slide down to my knees, wincing at the hard impact against the wood floor, and lean in to nuzzle his erection through the soft cotton until he gasps. As his hand creeps into my hair and tightens almost right away, I release the soft moan that's been building since I walked in the door. I haven't had a cock in my face since the last time I was with Phelan. I'm not ashamed to admit having both of these things in front of me is enough to make my mouth water. Meanwhile, the tight jeans that seemed such a great idea an hour ago are hot and constricting, trapping the boner that suddenly presses against the fly. I could unbutton myself—would be grateful for the relief, actually—but get the idea Phel might have something to say if I go off script now. Especially after I've all but offered myself to him in slavery or some shit.

He smells so unbelievably good, though, a combination of soap and the musky sleep scent I remember. It drives me wild, breath quickening, sweat springing up at my temples, heart beating hard against my chest. I press my face in closer, parting my lips to mouth at the head of his cock and the fabric growing damp with excitement. The sting of protest from my lip makes it better. A long glance at Phelan's face shows him watching me with an expression gone slack, and his grip tugs a bit harder now, sending a sharp tingle through my scalp. The gesture would be rude if I didn't want it so bad. I obey his hand and let him pull my mouth away so he can press against my lower lip with his thumb. This time I *do* flicker my tongue out to taste, and can't hold back a deep groan of gratitude.

"Please," I say. Phel murmurs assent and pets at my hair a little, absently, then draws back from my lips and slides the sweatpants down over his hips. His cock bobs toward me, thick and glorious as ever, and I chase after him to take his length onto my tongue.

The taste is hot and bitter and sweet all at once, and the low cry that escapes Phelan's throat isn't human enough to resemble language. He's all need, shoving himself into my mouth insistently, so I give up trying to stroke along the vein that bisects the spine of his cock and hollow my cheeks, closing my lips around the crown as he fucks my face and keeps my head steady with that hand in my hair. I'm so turned on I can't stop to think about the power I'm giving him here, something he's never asked of me in this way.

For all the months I've been out of the game—it never seemed right to make it with another guy, not after what happened with Phel—my throat remembers how to take his girth. My gag reflex relaxes so he can slide all the way in, Phel easing up as I near the base so as not to choke me. I use my hands to cradle his balls and work his pants down the rest of the way until he can kick them right off. Needing to feel him around me, I nudge at his leg; he gets the hint and hooks his knee over my shoulder, heel bumping against my back and drawing me in closer. The soft hair on the inside of his thigh tickles my face while the coarser pubes around the base of his shaft brush my nose, little teases of sensation that make me suck harder out of frustration that I'm not also touching myself, despite my hands being busy. A quiet rustle of fabric from above lets me know Phel has stripped off his T-shirt, and I swallow another soft moan around his cock. Having him naked against me while I'm still fully clothed is all kinds of hot, like I could walk out of here right now and no one would be the wiser. Except maybe for the fact I'm so horny I could die.

"Nate." A rough yank at my hair pulls me off him with an unexpected whine from my own throat, so plaintive it makes me blush in embarrassment. It soon fades when I see the state of him, flushed halfway down his chest and breathing like he just came off the biggest wave of his life. "I'm going to fuck you," he informs me in that dark honey voice. "Stand up."

I do, legs shaky, and I'm barely vertical before he drags my shirt up over my head. He attacks my belt next, working my jeans open with a look of determination on his face that's almost venomous. As he crouches to shove them down my legs along with my briefs, he noses against my hipbone before he bites down, so hard I buck and holler obscenities into the quiet of his house. I feel his relentless nails scrape lines of fire down my torso, and then the fingers of one hand slide into the crease of my ass to press against my hole. It's a miracle I don't shove myself back onto them, I want it so bad. The smile he shoots me is raw with hunger and knowing at the way I push myself into his touch.

"This is what you want," he says. It's not a question. Off the jerk of my head, which I suppose passes for a nod, he draws himself back up to full height and takes a step back.

He hasn't once touched my cock, which is so hard it judders, purple and leaking, against my stomach. The realization he isn't going to hits hard. I don't know why, but I can tell from the flintiness of his eyes I'm on my own for this one. Unsure how I feel about that, I start to take a small step away, but the slow stroke he gives his cock, mouth twitching at the look on my face, makes me shudder in anticipation. He was right: this isn't a Phel I recognize, not one I'm used to, but I can neither figure out what he's thinking nor walk away, since I'm the one who asked for it.

Recognizing the moment understanding dawns on me, he gestures to the couch. "If you want it so bad, go lie down and spread yourself open for me."

The words make me gasp like I've been slapped across the face. My feet move of their own volition, carrying me to where he's indicated. Kneeling tentatively on the soft leather, I look at him over my shoulder, suddenly unsure. "You got condoms and lube?"

He laughs at me. "Nate, you're the last person I was with. Since you're the one who was fucking around, tell me: do I need one?"

I could flinch in surprise at the words, but the answer is still no. Although I can think of nothing I'd like more than his naked cock sliding inside me, it seemed like too much to hope it was something I'd ever feel again. So I jerk my head once in the negative, and he stalks forward to snatch up a bottle of hand cream from the side table, then tosses it in my direction.

"Lie down," he repeats.

I do, squirming at the brush of my nipples against the leather sofa, and a moment later I feel his broad, warm hand grip the flesh of one of my asscheeks, pulling me firmly apart. Squirming, I moan softly and he says, reproachfully, "Show me."

It should be impossible to feel this naked around Phel, who has literally seen every inch of me up close, but spreading myself like this makes my face go hot, my mouth dry. I can only imagine what the hell I must look like, holding my ass open to him like a goddamned whore, but the want is so powerful I don't so much as utter a sound of protest. I think he knows how badly I need it, because he strokes a finger over where I've exposed myself to him and makes a desperate noise of his own. "Let me see your face, Nate," he murmurs, and when I glance over my shoulder at him, he looks as wrecked as I've ever seen him.

He fumbles with the lotion but holds my eyes as he presses his finger inside. Every ounce of me that wants to screw my face up and bury it in the cushions fights against my will to maintain eye contact. It feels important somehow. The latter wins out, and I'm rewarded with a glimpse of how Phel bites down on his bottom lip when he adds another digit, then another. I spread my legs wider and rock back against his hand despite the burn—after this long, it's practically like getting drilled for the first time—and the gradual force with which he fucks into me makes my throat clench, a broken, keening noise emerging from me as if from a dying animal. Phel knows where and how deep to work his fingers, massaging my prostate on the first try, and he curls them against that spot again and again until the muscles in my legs shake in involuntary response.

"C'mon, Phel, you dick," I growl at him. The words emerge sounding ambiguously like "your dick," both an order and a plea. Christ, this is more than I can take, this relentless *toying*, and he knows it. What I'm less sure of is whether he cares, because this is a side of Phel I've never seen, not even when he's been angry. But he must be getting impatient himself, judging from the speed with which he withdraws his fingers and slicks himself up.

I have to look away for this part, not from squeamishness or anything, but because my senses go into overload as he plants my right leg on the floor so I'm good and open for him. A gentle stroke of his cockhead over my entrance is all the warning I get before he guides himself inside, pressing in as relentless as anything. The stretch of him splitting me open is so goddamn good that I groan his name, long and low, arching my hips so he's got a perfect angle at my ass. He takes advantage of it a split second before I'm ready, starts to move when he knows it'll still burn. Unlike the first time he topped—and every time after, for that matter—he doesn't wait to ask if I'm okay, just reads off my impatient shifts against him to start fucking me.

A thought occurs to me: we haven't kissed once since I got here.

The impact of Phelan's cock against my prostate makes me yell his name, over and over again, and when my voice gets too hoarse, I lose myself in his heavy breathing and stuttered moans, savor the slap of his pelvis against my ass as he fucks in and in and in. My hands clutch at the sofa cushions until my knuckles ache. It's rhythmic, a pounding drumbeat I feel down to a molecular level, and I catch myself grinding my hips back and forth in counterpoint, building the friction against my own erection in addition to the unbelievable pleasure of Phel's dick inside me. When he fists a hand into my hair, pulling tight to the point of pain, I arch against him even more, taking everything, offering everything. I'm so close to the edge, my whole body is a flayed nerve.

Phel falls forward to bite and kiss at the skin of my shoulders, muttering nonsense in my ears about how good I feel, how much he's missed being inside me. I expect him to work his way around to my mouth, a kiss I need so badly, but what I get instead is his two hands around my neck, index and middle fingers pressing against my throat and Adam's apple hard enough to make me think twice. Never in my life have I felt anything like that. I expect to panic at my dwindling air supply, but all I feel is an unbelievable calm at the trust I have in Phel. It's a trust he hasn't asked for, but has all the same.

My heart hammers, blood pounding straight to my dick as he continues to thrust and slide his chest against my back, both of us slippery with sweat. The undulations of his body feel as graceful as ever. Not quite knowing why his chokehold excites me—my mind keeps flashing between the need to fight for breath and the mental picture of how I must look, being used this way—I'm so surprised by the pressure that I suck in a labored gasp and spurt all over the couch cushions. I think it's the sound of me coming that knocks Phel over the edge too, which he does with a choked-off shout, flooding me with slick.

"Fuck," I whisper, breathing hard. My insides feel painted and raw, and all I can smell around us is sweat and sex. I feel Phelan heaving against my back and wish I knew what the hell just happened.

Though I wince and groan a little as he pulls out, I continue to lie facedown on the couch and make no effort to move. I take a minute to figure out why I feel so weird, and it turns out to be the sensation of Phel's spunk leaking from my abused hole. That's got to be one the most unlikely phrases I've thought of in this lifetime, and I want to laugh about it to Phel but can't summon the energy even for that. The rest is probably best not to think about right now, because that way lies sheer fucking madness. He warned me, I remind myself, and I couldn't leave it well enough alone. A part of me is conscious, in a vague sort of way, of having been punished. Used, at the very least. I get no further than that before I shut the whole ugly train of thought down. This was for him.

I do manage to turn my head when I feel Phelan's weight withdraw from the couch. He stumbles down the hallway—headed for the bathroom, is my guess—and sure enough returns with a damp towel that he flings at my head. Taking the hint, I struggle onto my back and wipe myself down, trying not to notice the stony expression on Phelan's face as he does the same. I don't like it, even less the fact that he won't look at me, and when he grimaces and starts to pull on his sweatpants, I guess he isn't going to invite me to stay for lunch. My legs are rubber as I retrieve my own clothing.

I'm halfway dressed when I glance up from the buckle of my belt and see Phelan staring off into space, shoulders tense. He's barely in the same solar system right now, let alone the same room, and for some reason the only thing I can think of to do is clear my throat and say, "I won't tell Hugh."

Those saucer-blue eyes swivel toward me, this freaky habit Phel sometimes has of looking at me without turning the rest of his head. "I wouldn't imagine you would, no."

"He's been wondering where you are." Catching the barely perceptible slump of his shoulders, I sigh. "Cut this bullshit out and go talk to him, okay? You and me—he's got nothing to do with any of this. Call your friend. He's worried. And don't say you don't want to, 'cause I know that's bullshit too." There's an imperceptible nod. "Good."

Hesitantly, Phel says, "Are you going to come back here?" not like he's shy, but like he doesn't trust himself to ask any more than he trusts my response.

"Are you asking me to?" By the muscle that leaps in his cheek, I know I'm not going to get an answer to that, so I go into the kitchen and grab a pen off the table, then scribble my cell number on top of the cover story of the newspaper. "I meant what I said, Phel. This is—whatever you want. If you want me to leave, I'll leave. But if you want…." Thought unfinished, I leave that hanging there and shift the newspaper closer toward the edge of the table so he's sure to see it. My message is pretty clear: *day or night.*

"You should go," he says, finally.

"Okay."

I'm still shirtless, but since I find my boots before I find my shirt, I put those on first, not bothering with laces, letting the tongues hang out of them like the wannabe gangsters we sometimes see down at the beach at night, teenagers with rich parents and aspirations to the 'hood. Phel watches me dress, staring almost, the way someone'll stare you down when they're waiting for you to take the goddamn hint and *leave*, though there's no animosity behind it for once. That he wants me to fuck off is clear. That he wants me to stop talking, doubly so. But it's like he's just too tired to ask again.

Hoping this indicates a momentary weakness in his defenses, I say, "I came out to Liam this afternoon."

Phel makes a sound between a grunt and a snort. He says, "Congratulations," in the most deadpan tone imaginable, and I guess I misjudged his magnanimity just now, considering the iciness of his voice.

I frown. "'Congratulations'? Seriously?" Not like I expected a parade, but that one word seems so inappropriate for the experience, I'm of half a mind to demand a do-over. Then again, I could have kept my mouth shut and walked out of here with, if maybe not dignity, composure. Instead it's gonna be another fight, I can feel it.

"What else do you expect me to say?"

Growing angry—it's so much easier to get angry about an offhand comment than it is to think too hard about what just went down, the sudden, painful pull of damn near every muscle in my body—I shuffle over to the kitchen entrance and snatch up my T-shirt where it lies discarded on the wood floor. Although I inch toward the door to let Phel know the change of subject doesn't indicate I'm planning to stick around, I realize from the returning stiffness of his posture how desperate he is for me to GTFO. The look on his face makes it seems like my presence in his home is sheer fucking torture. Son of a bitch.

"Just thought you'd appreciate it, man," I say, my voice steady as I can make it. "Seein' as how you always longed to share yourself with your family and all."

Phel steps closer to the front door, which he pulls open, and he stands there with his hand on the doorknob, glowering. That's that, then. I get the message and walk past the threshold, though not before turning to him to say, "I'm trying to fix things. Make them right."

With a hard twist of his lips, Phel shakes his head. "You're trying to fix things for yourself, Nate. At least you can still do that." He starts to close the door. "But don't talk about it like it could possibly make a difference to me, because I've got nothing left. There's nothing for you to make right here, okay? Understand that."

He shuts the door in my face without another word, but I don't knock again or try to get him to open up. He's right, in a way. After that, there's not a whole lot else to be said.

6

Hugh

WHAT'S the opposite of déjà vu? Is there a word for that? Because I feel like I might have it. I'm not trying to be thick or anything—I've experienced, many times, the feeling that I'm someplace I've already been, or that I'm doing something I've done before. This happens pretty frequently on drugs, as a matter of fact, so... I would know. But it's far less often that I've felt like I've spaced out and come back while sober, only to realize a lot seems to have happened without my noticing. Kind of like how spring sometimes creeps up in climates with distinct seasons, the trees bare and depressing one moment and suddenly covered in fresh green foliage the next, like everything decided to bloom all at once while your back was turned. Except that California doesn't have seasons like that, and I'm pretty sure my back *hasn't* been turned. Still, I feel there's a bunch of stuff I missed.

Part of it has to do with finding out about Nate's divorce, the shock and unexpectedness of it, the realization that there was this life-changing event taking place in Nate's world, something I didn't know about or even anticipate until he showed up on my doorstep. That got to me, I admit. But I was beginning to adjust when Phel up and disappeared on me too, shut me out like a complete stranger for bordering on two weeks.

There's no doubt in my mind there are a lot of explanations for where he went and why: obviously he's got issues he's still working on at Palermo, and that—that's good, that's as it should be. He needs to take care. After how he reacted to meeting Nate, even if I've yet to figure out the source of the problem, it shouldn't have come as a surprise that he might need some time to himself. It's none of my business, and besides, it doesn't matter. Really doesn't. But it would have been nice, when Phel suddenly appeared on my doorstep again, if he'd treated me to just a little insight, so I might have a better idea of what the hell goes through his head in times like these. None came.

For my part, I couldn't help but feel surprised at how *happy* I was to see him when he turned up for surfing one day without warning. He had the good grace to look sheepish, like he knew he'd done something wrong but couldn't quite talk about it yet, and I almost grabbed him into a hug before I realized that's not something we *do*. Phel isn't an affectionate person that way, but the sight of his rumpled hair and crooked smile made me want it all the same.

Instead I asked, "Did something happen?" the way my dad always used to do if I went too long without calling, immediately assuming something was wrong. I pulled him into the kitchen, where Nate was drinking a coffee and reading the paper. "I was worried."

"No, nothing happened," sighed Phel. My attention was momentarily distracted when Nate clattered his dishes down in the sink and stalked out of the room. Phel made an unimpressed face and settled his hands on his hips before his gaze flicked back to me. "I had a lot on my mind. Sorry I didn't call you."

I lifted my eyebrows at him like he could volunteer more information at any time, but he just continued looking at me like, *No, this conversation is done, Hugh. Drop it.*

I think I made the face Nate tells me not to make, the one that makes me look like I'm constipated. "I thought you were dead or something, man!" I exclaimed. We both knew how much of an exaggeration that was, and for a second Phel let that sink in before he gave a tiny eye roll.

"Had something serious happened, you would have received a phone call," he said. "You're my emergency contact." While I was busy trying to process that information and the weird sense of warmth it gave me, Phel gestured vaguely. "Okay, well, if that's settled, I'm going to hit the restroom and then we'll go surf." I nodded dumbly.

Phel wandered off down the hall just as Nate walked back into the kitchen. "You sound like a needy girlfriend, man," he informed me, voice more sour than usual. "I'm sure Phel wasn't half as concerned about what you were up to while he was off doing his own thing."

There seemed to be no justifiable reason for this sudden peevishness on my brother's part, except that these waspy comments would become par for the course when Phel was around, and Nate's mood swings all the more frequent. At the time I didn't think much of it, because Nate has always been a moody guy, and slow to trust; I was too glad Phel was back to think much of it. His reappearance made me relieved and happy, and gave me something to look forward to again each day, like when you meet a cool girl and can't help but wonder when you'll hang out again.

So we're back to spending time together, Phel and I, acting for all intents and purposes like nothing has changed. We talk, we surf, we hang out and argue about *Battlestar Galactica* or *Doctor Who* until Nate looks ready to pull his hair out. Aside from my quiet fear Phel will up and disappear on me again, the sudden addition of my brother's presence is the biggest change. Nate refers to himself as an intruder in the clubhouse whenever he feels he's interrupting something or doesn't know how to join my conversations with Phel.

Surprisingly, this happens way more often than I would have expected from him, because Nate doesn't *do* socially awkward. Socially boorish, maybe, but never awkward—he's been charming crowds since the age of five. Nate should be able to manage one gay ex-socialite, especially with those dimples, but if I'm honest, Phel doesn't seem all that receptive, nor interested in changing that fact.

As if he's aware of this hostile climate, Nate makes a habit of steering clear, taking timely walks with Callie or runs around the neighborhood, anything to get out of the house and whatever line of fire he seems to think exists. He jokes about how he doesn't want to walk in on Phel and me playing *Dungeons & Dragons* in full costume—an absurd thought, because Nate is and always has been the biggest geek in the family, especially if his obsession with *Star Trek* is anything to go by—but to an observer it seems to run much deeper than that. For reasons I can't begin to figure out, Nate and Phel don't like each other.

So why does it feel like the two of them have this private conversation going on all the time?

I don't have anything to qualify why I feel this way, except for the weird atmosphere that seems to fill a room when they're both in it, the drawn-out looks that sometimes pass between them like I'm not even there. There's no animosity to it, though, nothing abrasive to reinforce the pervasive sense of underlying hostility; rather, it's how different they become around each other, Phel sharper somehow, coolly confident, Nate withdrawn until he's sullen and silent and unsure like I've never before seen him. If there's an explanation for that, I can't find one, and Nate isn't talking. Maybe I'm just imagining it all, though, and they're not really spiteful of one another, but best buds when I'm not around.

If it's not obvious, I've spent a lot of time thinking about it. With Phel AWOL, I couldn't help but dwell on how empty my life started to feel without him. What is it about me that makes me place such weight on friendships and family relationships, however few? I think back to the time I spent at Palermo myself, weeks of struggling to understand my weaknesses and how to get strong again, how to make choices that would lead me down a different path than the one I was currently travelling.

When I first enrolled at Palermo as a patient, I remember thinking it didn't quite hold up to my idea of what rehabilitation facilities were supposed to be, the kind referenced in gritty cop dramas or stories about down-and-out folk overcoming their personal demons. Sure, you hear about celebrities entering rehab all the time, but that's not real life, right? Since Nate was the one who staged the intervention and set everything up, I hadn't exactly researched the digs that would become my home for twenty-eight days. I was surprised by how much like a luxury resort it was, and how the majority of people there were average folks with above-average incomes: housewives addicted to prescription meds and stockbrokers with drinking problems, teenagers with eating disorders and trust-fund kids who partied a bit too hard in college. There were a few people there who struggled with the harder stuff, like me, but I think I only ever saw one person with a heroin problem, an aging rock star who in my mind automatically resembled Keith Richards. No crack, no crystal, nothing like that. I guess I had it easy—I doubt I would have been able to handle the horror stories you get wind of from state-run facilities or jails, tales that haunt you forever. Call me selfish, but I'm not cut out for that.

There was one girl in particular, Eleanor, who struggled to control her own coke addition. Maybe I took a shine to her because of the similarity of our experiences, but what touched me from the beginning was her determination and the fact that she was there on her own steam. She was an artist who'd had numerous shows in LA and New York, whose work was once so in demand you stood a better chance of landing one of Picasso's sketches. In fact, I attended one of her shows when I lived in Los Angeles, though of course I refrained from sharing this fact with the rest of the group. Anonymity and all that. But I remembered her face—even the violence and vibrancy of her art—and couldn't help but feel betrayed to know how much she depended on drugs to create, to help her withstand the pressure of her own success. No doubt people would have felt the same way about me if they knew. Perhaps it was for the best, but Eleanor's name had all but faded into obscurity ever since that slip of control started to take its toll on her ability to satisfy clients and wow critics.

What saddened me was how all those people, the ones who crowded around her when she was famous, were nowhere to be seen. With no living family, Eleanor often talked about feeling totally cut off from her life before—so-called friends who wouldn't return her calls, a manager who dropped her as soon as the cracks started to show in the veneer of success. I knew the story well: everyone loves to watch a train wreck, but no one wants to stick around to clean up the damage.

"I tried to get clean a few times before," she told us one day in Group, with her kind of soft-spoken sincerity that made everyone lean in to listen. "Figured I might be able to do it on my own and without anyone knowing. But with no one to help, it was practically impossible. I would have had to seal myself up in a basement for two months and cut off all contact with the outside world. I couldn't think about anything but how much coke defined my life. The people around me, the lifestyle in Hollywood, it's like there was this gate that locked down in front of me and kept me from getting through to the other side. To being my own person again." She glanced at me with a small smile, then at a couple of the other group members with whom she'd become close over the last couple of weeks. "When people found out what a mess I was, it wasn't any better. They basically ran as fast as they could in the opposite direction, which just made me feel even more alone and less capable of sorting myself out."

"Everyone?" I asked.

She shrugged. "Pretty much. I had one close friend from high school, someone who stuck with me even when I was a nobody, but when I really started struggling, I think he gave up. It was too much for him to handle on his own, and I don't blame him. This is the first time I've actually felt like I have a shot at getting clean, because I know there's a support system behind me here, and I don't have to dump all of it onto one person."

I thought about Nate and how utterly lost I would have been without him behind me, without the well-wishing and support of Emilia and Liam behind him. "Are you worried about what will happen after you leave?" While this might sound like a douchey thing to ask, the one thing I learned in Group was to ask the hard questions people were sometimes afraid to admit to themselves. Our fears get a lot smaller once they're out in the open.

"I'm terrified," answered Eleanor, blue eyes fixed on me. "I don't want to walk out of here and realize I'm still alone." She was a beautiful girl with long strawberry-blonde hair and a heart-shaped face, huge eyes the color of seawater. I didn't spend all my time thinking about that stuff, to be clear, but there was something so striking and unusual about her features, her whole expression echoing whatever sadness or uncertainty she might be harboring on the inside. Without looking like a wreck, Eleanor appeared exactly as broken as the rest of us felt, and it wrenched my heart a little to look at her.

"You aren't alone," said Patricia, another woman in the group. "We'll still be here for each other after we finish the program, whenever we need the support."

Eleanor gave a brittle laugh and immediately looked abashed. "That's what we all say now," she responded. "But who knows what will happen once we go back to our lives?" She gave a gentle shake of her head. "No, it's better to build lasting relationships you know you can count on. I wish I'd taken the time to do that in my old life instead of just breezing through surface friendships that collapsed at the first sign of trouble. I wish I hadn't killed the friendships I had. Because now I have no one, and even *I* wouldn't want to be friends with me."

This statement stuck with me for a long time, all through the rest of the session and into that night, into the following days and eventually months past my own recovery. It's a pretty obvious concept even now, one I've stopped to consider a lot over the last little while—I know a thing or two about isolation, which is why meeting Phel was such a big deal. As for Eleanor, I heard she was clean for a little while, but got back on the powder when she couldn't keep working the steps. She OD'd at a party and had a well-attended funeral of people she probably hadn't spoken to in years. Her artwork is now prohibitively expensive to come by. And shit, when I heard that, all I could think about was how much I didn't want to be her. How I needed to stay close to people who wouldn't ever let that happen. Now, with Phel, I have faith that if something bad happened, if some ugly truth came out down the line, we'd still be there for each other. Plus I still have Nate, and he'll always be there too.

But can Nate and Phel say the same thing for themselves? Obviously I'll never turn my back on either of them, but I have to stop and wonder—who else, besides me, have they got in their lives that will have their backs in good times and bad? Eleanor is totally right—one person isn't enough to keep an entire life from collapsing.

I wish we could be each other's support systems without me having to worry about this unspoken animosity between my brother and my best friend. How great would that be? Aside from the obvious reasons, I mean. I've been back at work on a new book and slightly less available than I was before, and I like the idea of Nate and Phel hanging out together in my stead, maybe forming the kind of bond I share with both of them. It would be awesome to feel like we all belong in this place together, three people that are kind of mismatched, each of us outcasts in our own way, proving that a family needn't be a big or elaborate unit to work or care about each other. Nate is blood, obviously, and I've come to think of Phel as a brother as well, but the whole thing will fall apart if they can't stand each other or can't find a way to communicate except through weird glances. Call me selfish, but I don't want it to fall apart.

I try to run the idea by Nate, a quiet suggestion to patch up his issues with Phel and become friends, and I admit his response isn't quite as I imagined it. That the conversation happened at all was because he wandered into my office one day with questions about my new book, his loneliness or boredom—or both—thinly disguised as curiosity about my work.

I know Nate has read all the previous books in the series and is a fan of the Manderfeld twins; why shouldn't he be? He's the one who made up the original bedtime stories that inspired me. When I was six or seven and terrified of our house being broken into or robbed in the night, probably around the same time I first learned about the kinds of people my dad locked away, Nate was the one who deliberately checked all the locks on our doors and windows with me before tucking me into bed. He even invented a safe word I could use in the night if I ever got scared: "Benny," after the stuffed rabbit I carried around everywhere.

"So I'll always know to come when you call," he'd said solemnly, and promised he would keep me safe even when we grew up and Dad wasn't always around to look after us. I blush to think about it now, what a needy kid I was, but it's something Nate never teased me for, even when he made fun of me for plenty else, the way big brothers do.

So naturally, this was a detail I included in my books, the Manderfeld twins' childhood safe word one could always use to let the other know he was in real trouble. Like characters in any good suspense novel, they seemed to get into trouble a lot. Nate *did* tease me about bringing this sliver of our childhood to life in the series, especially whenever Nell cooed about how adorable we were, but I could see how secretly touched he was by it, by the fact that I remembered.

But for years I've been stuck in what I now see as a rut, writing books about a self-enclosed family of two that had a hard time letting other people in. The Manderfeld twins remind me of Nate and myself, of course, and all the years we spent fending for ourselves as kids, cut off from other family besides our dad, who wasn't around much. But that changed when Nate and Emilia started a family and I met Nell. We learned that life, just like a story, needs the introduction of new characters to develop and grow. Just because Nell died doesn't mean I want to remain alone for the rest of my life, which is largely why meeting Phel was such a big deal for me. I don't want that for the Manderfeld brothers either, and so in my recent work, I decided to expand their little family unit by one: I gave them an ally.

"His name's Jacob," I tell Nate, who sits on the sofa holding my manuscript draft in one hand, a beer in the other. From the perplexed look on his face, I can tell he's either confused or not keen on a new character, so I decide to explain and sell him on the idea in one fell swoop. "Ever since the last book, it's been obvious to me how badly the guys need someone else to have their backs, someone on the inside." The last book had seen Chris and Alex, my two main characters, wanted by the FBI after being falsely accused of murder.

"So I thought it'd be neat if at first Jacob was trying to stop them, or maybe manipulating them toward turning themselves in or something, but instead ends up becoming a friend, even working with them against other cops when he sees how corrupt his superiors have become, how much the FBI wants to close the case and be done with it, even if they put two innocent people away." Nate continues to look at me blankly, so I add, "And he's the one who got Alex off the meth, right?"

That was another story in and of itself, certainly one of the more ambitious and drug-influenced plot twists I'd attempted. Surprisingly enough, I pulled it off to decent critical response, and not too many comments about the book being semiautobiographical. Still no idea how that happened, but apparently readers loved the plot twist of Alex getting caught up in drugs to infiltrate the cartel they were trying to investigate, and saving his brother's life in the process. Not semiautobiographical at all. "So they have this, I don't know... this *special bond* between them as a result."

Shifting in visible discomfort, Nate chews the inside of his lip and then takes a swig of beer. "So what about Chris?" he asks. "He's just a reject, now that Alex has a super special FBI agent buddy?"

His question, or rather its vehemence, throws me off. "What? No!" I struggle to recall if I included anything resembling this dynamic in the text, but nothing comes to me. Still, Nate seems wary of the development. He's far more protective of Chris and Alex's brotherhood than I expected. "Jacob is supposed to be a friend to them both; there's no third wheel in this arrangement. Don't you think things were becoming a bit... claustrophobic? With just the two of them?"

With a shrug, Nate sets my manuscript down in front of him on the coffee table and presses his palm flat against the paper in contemplative silence. I can't begin to guess what he's thinking. Eventually he says, "Chris has given up everything for Alex, man. His childhood, his shot at a happy life and a family, his whole future. Even almost his life a few times, just so Alex could be normal and not follow in his footsteps. No wonder he was so pissed Alex tried to throw away his life to save him. Yeah, it's a big deal Alex got mixed up on drugs to take the heat off his brother, but... Christ. Throw the guy a fucking bone, would you? He's totally alone, and now it's like he doesn't even have his brother anymore."

The bitterness in Nate's voice makes me recoil. "Nate, that's... that isn't the point of this at all. Just that it's hard to recreate the same circumstances surrounding Chris and Jacob as with Alex and the agent who saved his ass from gang-style execution. There's a history there Chris isn't a part of, but that doesn't mean he can't become friends with Jacob in his own time."

Before Nate answers, his phone beeps from the pocket of his jeans, and he pauses to fish it out and read whichever message awaits him. Though he offers no indication as to whom it's from, his whole face darkens and a flush rises in his cheeks. He shoves the phone back into his pocket and pushes himself up from the sofa, in a worse temper than I've seen him in a long time. "Maybe you should just let Chris have something of his own once in a while, instead of Alex hoarding everything like a goddamned child," he snaps. "Even if he'd just fuck it up eventually, Chris deserves that much."

Whoa. As he's about to storm off, I reach out to snag Nate's wrist, the one not holding the beer bottle. For a second he glares at me so hard, I almost expect him to hit me with it. "Hey," I say gently. This whole conversation has come out of left field for me, even though I'm the one who started it. "We *are* still talking about the books, right?"

He shakes off my hand. "Yeah, Hugh." And then—"I'm going for a run, I'll see you later."

HOURS later, he comes back smelling inexplicably of sex. I see faint scratches against his skin, pale bruises that might still darken into hickeys. I have no idea how Nate has the capacity to go out and find a girl when he's out for a run, of all things, but he's certainly capable enough—or was, before he got married. Our old house hosted a veritable parade of women, sometimes a different one every night, sometimes more than one. I often wondered what the hell he was trying to prove. I have every certainty that's what he's done now, and the thought that he'd do so because of some stupid character in a book makes me want to grab my brother by the shoulders and shake him until some common sense rattles loose.

I catch him on his way up to bed from the kitchen, cornering him at the bottom of the stairs like a parent who's just nailed their kid breaking curfew. "Nate," I say gently, and the eyes he turns on me aren't angry or annoyed, just tired and maybe a little shifty, like he's been busted doing the walk of shame back up to his room. "Everything okay?"

He shifts his weight from foot to foot and scratches the back of his neck before answering. "Yeah, Hugh, I'm fine." Sounding reluctant, he adds, "Sorry for storming out on you before, guess it must be that time of the month of something."

The quip makes me wince, but it's such typical, politically incorrect Nate I can't help but chuckle. "I appreciate the apology, but I think I might have been acting a bit insensitive myself." Despite how much my brother hates talking about feelings, it seems like all our major conversations lately are about that. Still, this is a period of adjustment for both of us, and even if that has to do with very different things, there's enough overlap to compel me to get on with it and make sure our relationship isn't another source of friction. "Does it piss you off that I'm friends with Phel?" I ask. "I know you don't like him all that much." Fighting the urge to inquire why, I stop myself there and wait for Nate to answer.

The response is slow in coming as he stares down at his hands and chews the inside of his lip. I brace myself for the full barrage of reasons why my big brother can't stand my best friend, maybe with a demand or two that we stop hanging out, but Nate surprises me by speaking in that soft voice he uses when he wants to say something important. "I don't hate Phel," he begins, "and no, it doesn't piss me off that you're friends with him. I just… I guess I'm going through some stuff right now that makes me realize I'm not doing so hot at the family thing. Pretty shitty, actually, and that's kind of a lonely feeling." Nate gestures vaguely. "That hurts, no lie, and then I see you and Phel together, the way the two of you click, and it makes me realize how isolated I really am."

I shift uncomfortably, knowing how petty my next statement will sound before it's even out of my mouth. "That's not how it looks from my end," I tell him. "Maybe I hang out with Phel more, but sometimes I get this creepy feeling like the two of you have this… this *mind meld* or something. This conversation going on that doesn't include me."

Nate looks at me, a hard, stony look. "That's retarded," he answers curtly. "I barely know the guy."

Shrugging, I fold my arms. "Since we're sharing, I figured I'd just put that out there."

"Trust me," says Nate, "I don't know the first fucking thing about what goes through that guy's head. Half the time he looks like if he clenches any harder, he'll pass out. So, no, there's no 'mind meld'. You and Phel, on the other hand… you understand each other, even if some of your conversations together could out-geek an astrophysicist. I don't have that with anyone anymore." For a second he looks like he wants to say more, but then he tightens his jaw and comes to a full stop, glancing up at me hopelessly.

With Nate being so serious, I'm for some reason compelled to fill the void of inappropriate humor that's usually his forte. "You want to have geeky conversations with people?" I ask glibly. Off his unimpressed look, I offer, "You have that with me, man; we can talk about anything."

He dismisses the thought with a wave. "That's not what I'm talking about, Hugh. You're my brother—it's different. I wouldn't give that up for anything, but you said so yourself—it gets a little claustrophobic without other people."

"I was talking about my book," I point out.

Nate snorts. "No, you weren't."

Okay, point taken. "That doesn't mean you can't also be friends with Phel," I suggest. "I know he seems kind of uptight, and, well... he is. But he's a really interesting guy once you get to know him and he starts to relax. He could probably use someone like you to help him loosen up too."

Grimacing, Nate mutters, "I'll say," and then, louder, "You trying to set us up, Hugh?"

I shrug. The wording isn't exactly right, but Nate's not far off the mark. "Not the way you're implying, but yeah. I think it'd be great if you started spending time together without me. It might be good for both of you, especially now I'm going to be spending a lot more time writing. This might sound stupid, but...."

Nate lifts his eyebrows at me. "What?"

My cheeks flush. "I kind of feel like we have to stick together, you know? You and me and Phel are kind of like outcasts around here. We should have each other's backs."

Nate rolls his eyes. "Christ, Hugh, this isn't Robin Hood and his band of merry men. It won't solve anything to have three codependent assholes instead of two." I glare, and he sighs. "Is it really that big of a deal to you that Phel and I hang out?"

"Is it really that much of a hardship that you *do*?" I shoot back. Great, what was supposed to be an adult conversation is quickly dissolving into bickering, and we're still facing off at the bottom of the stairs, no less. "You're a big boy, Nate—do whatever you want. I just thought it'd be less awkward if we all got along with one another."

It shouldn't delight me so much that his resigned sigh signals my victory over the argument. Nate knows it too, and shoots me a pained glance. "Okay, okay. Don't get all passive-aggressive on me." Leaning back up against the wall of the stairwell, he quirks a smile. "Suppose it makes a certain amount of sense, though, since I'll probably be sticking around for a while."

This catches me off guard. "Sticking around? Here?" He nods, and I furrow my brow. "You mean… you aren't going back to Ohio?" I don't mean to sound like I don't want him around, because my house feels so much more *full* with Nate here, so much like old times, but this is a development I didn't expect, given the circumstances and the people he has waiting for him in the Midwest.

With a shrug, he makes a vague gesture. "Eventually, yeah, but for now it seems kind of moot. Emilia and I are through, and I might not even get joint custody of Liam. There's nothing for me out there besides him, and until I know for sure how much I'll even be allowed in his life, it makes sense to start thinking about the kind of life I could have out here."

"I guess…."

"Nothing's definite," he assures me. "I understand if you don't want me in your hair forever, so I've been looking around at apartments in the area. Even San Diego would be okay, if I can't afford anything here." Apparently my silence and hesitant expression must be getting to him, because his face darkens. "Try not to act too excited about the prospect of me coming to live nearby."

Unable to stop myself, I scoff. "Come on, Nate, you know that's not what this is about. You aren't exactly a free agent, that you can just go moving across the country on a whim."

"It's not a whim!" he protests.

"Okay, well, what about your job? Suddenly you no longer need to work?"

There's a dramatic eye roll, the kind Nate often employs when he thinks I'm being thick. Which—I get that eye roll a lot. "You honestly think I still had a job after word got out I cheated on the boss's sister-in-law? Craig's wife would have had his balls if I'd stayed on. I left as much for his sake as mine." Apparently Nate hears the defensiveness in his own voice, and huffs gently before trying to get his temper under control and stave off another of our legendary spats. "Look. This time of year, there's never a shortage of construction jobs, that's for sure. Hell, you could probably even pay me to mow your lawn and I'd make a decent living of it. Work is just about the one thing I'm *not* worried about right now."

From anyone else, the talk about finding alternate living arrangements would be a way of blowing smoke up my ass, a thinly veiled guilt trip before I dismiss the idea as stupid and offer a place to stay in my own house. But from Nate, I know it's genuine—he doesn't mooch off anyone and never accepts handouts. He has to know I'd never force him to go off and live in a shitty studio apartment somewhere, though, especially not with all he's done for me, and the four extra bedrooms I have at my disposal. Plus, having Nate around makes me happier than almost anything. At least that's a better alternative to how much I tend to worry about him when he's out of my sight, and there's a lot to worry about these days. Really, all this points to me as the asshole, the one who should shut up and drop it. I guess a little part of me still wants to teach Nate a lesson, make sure he understands what he's gotten himself into. But that's stupid, I realize. It's been clear for weeks Nate doesn't think about much else.

"You don't have to move out," I sigh, still a bit sullen. "I want you to stay here. And you don't need to worry about finding a job, unless you really want to. It's not like we're short on cash."

"I know I don't *need* to," Nate scoffs, flashing a smile that's both grateful and annoyed by the suggestion. "But you know how I feel about pulling my own weight." He scratches idly at his wrist. "You sure you don't mind me staying here?"

"*No*, Nate," I say. "I might not totally approve of your decision not to go back to Ohio, but as long as you're here, my home is yours. Plus, someone needs to keep you out of trouble."

Nate's look turns sad and a bit wistful. "I coulda used you before," he says, the statement less an accusation about my lack of involvement in his life and more recognition that the responsibility for his fuckups is entirely on his shoulders. That might seem like a heavy thing to take for granted, given that the human condition is to reject accountability whenever possible, but Nate is the kind of person who needs to be reminded he can't take fault for everything. He assumes the blame for all of my mistakes but none of my successes, and if you sing his kid's praises, he'll say he owes it all to Liam's mother. As far as Nate's concerned, the only good he's ever done in his life was getting Emilia pregnant by accident.

I'm struck, suddenly, by such a wave of sadness and loneliness on my brother's behalf. I can't help but go up to him and put my arms around in him a hug. He tenses at first, then relaxes into me, clutching at my shoulder for a second before trying to withdraw. I don't let him. "Everything's gonna be okay, Nate," I promise him. "We'll get you through this. I'm sure even Phel is rooting for you."

"Yeah, I'm sure he is," says Nate in a flat voice, and I think that's probably about as much as I'm going to get out of him tonight before he starts to feel I'm pushing too hard. But that's okay. I think we're as much on the same page now as we'll ever be, even considering the unusual circumstances that have brought us together this time around.

DETERMINED not to leave Nate in the lurch, I broach the subject with Phel as we're out surfing the next day, waiting until we're both tired and sunburned and loading up the Land Rover for home. Phelan looks so happy, his thick hair madly tousled from the sea, and he beams at me in a way I've never seen, but reminds me why we're friends all the same. Nate begged off from the excursion, claiming a headache like a put-upon housewife trying to escape her marital duty. I wish he could see Phel like this, excited and carefree and alive. Maybe this should give me pause, because Phel has always been a bit subdued from the Paxil, kind of like a muffled bell; but it's so *nice* to see him full of life like this. I can't help but imagine this is what he was like before his dreams came crashing down around his ears. In a way, I'm enchanted by it, dazzled even. We could be meeting for the first time. There's no way Nate couldn't like this person as much as I do.

"You seem a lot better, man," I tell him, sure my grin must match his own as we load his surfboard into the back of the Rover and slam the hatch closed. At his smile of confusion, I add, "Happy. It's a good look on you."

"I guess I have a lot to be happy about," he answers with a shrug. "I'm almost at the end of my program, and for the first time in a while,

I feel like things are finally back to the way they were. It's a great feeling."

"Did you get in touch with your family or something?" He swore never to talk to his ex-boyfriend again, but for a while he spoke really wistfully about convincing his parents to come around, getting them to show the same level of respect and acceptance as his sister, Aurelia. That's another relationship he hoped to patch up, since he knew estrangement from the rest of the family would take its toll on her too. Perhaps he's made headway in this regard, but a swift shake of his head disabuses me of the notion.

"No," he answers. "I've kind of given up on them.... Maybe if they make the first move in contacting me, I'll consider it, but right now I'm concentrating on myself, on feeling like I'm in control. Doing things I never would have done before, standing up to my fears."

"Like what?"

Much to my surprise, Phel shrugs tentatively, nothing more than a lift of one reddish-bronze shoulder. "I've been seeing someone."

The words make my stomach clench unpleasantly; I have no idea why. I immediately want to blame it on some bad food I might have eaten at breakfast, but remember all I had was a couple of slices of toast and some jam. Some other reason, then. Frowning, I answer, "You have? Where the heck did you find time to start dating?"

Phel grimaces as though something I've said offends him deeply. "I didn't say 'dating', Hugh, I said 'seeing'. There's a distinct difference."

Touchy. "Okay, so you're 'seeing' someone. Did you meet this person at Palermo?"

Another shrug. "Sort of. I don't want to rehash all of it," he says. Plastering that look of happiness back on his face, he comes around to the other side of the truck to clap me on the shoulder. His hand moves down to squeeze my arm reassuringly. "But trust me, I feel great. I'm really happy you're here to share that with me."

"Of course, Phel. I'm happy too." Man, he's like a kid in a candy store. Right now, I could ask him to do just about anything and he'd probably giggle, while here I am fretting over a casual suggestion that he spend some time with my brother. My weird response to this information about his love life makes me feel like the aged aunt who's a bit stingy with her change and won't spring for the gum tape or something. "Speaking of sharing stuff," I begin, "I've been doing some thinking lately—a lot of thinking, actually."

"You?" he quips, and I scowl.

Trying to hide my expression as we go around the car to our respective doors, I ask, "Who taught you sarcasm, man? Nate? Or this new lover boy of yours?"

The jibe makes his face darken slightly as he climbs into the passenger seat and shuts the door, using a bit more force than is necessary. I wince, because—hey. It's not like Land Rovers come cheap. "Why the hell would I have learned it from Nate?" He sounds so baffled and bitter at the suggestion that I begin to see shades of what Nate was talking about. His hesitation to chummy up to Phel makes sense when both of them seem to flit from good mood to foul in the span of a blink.

I close my own door a bit more gently, twisting my body so I can prop my knee up on the seat under me. It's not the most comfortable position, but comfort is a pipe dream once you exceed six feet tall. I need to look at him, and the cramped space of the car isn't ideal for that. "It was just a joke," I inform him with a roll of the eyes, "but it actually ties in to what I wanted to ask you. Nate and I had a chat a couple days ago and, well, I thought it might be a good idea if the two of you started spending some time together. I've been so busy with the book that I haven't had much time for either of you. No offense—because this applies to all three of us—but we aren't exactly known for our vast and diverse social circle. I feel shitty about ditching you guys, and I'd be really happy if you got to know each other a bit better instead. The best friend and the brother should get along, right?"

To my surprise, Phel doesn't get upset, not like the time he and Nate first met, but he does level me with a look that's both disbelieving and pissy. "Hugh, your brother and I have absolutely nothing in common. I appreciate you trying to look out for me, but I think that's a horrible idea. We'd kill each other after ten minutes."

Gesturing wildly, I feel my voice go up a couple of decibels before I can stop myself. "But that's what he said to me, and I don't get it, man! I don't think that's the case at all. Sure, maybe it doesn't look like you have a lot in common at first glance, but Nate has *really* diverse interests, and...." I waver, but only just. "You're both kind of going through the same things right now. Being separated from your families and all that. And you both like the Rangers."

Phel sighs and pinches the bridge of his nose. Luckily he doesn't bother to acknowledge the weakness of my last argument. "Except that we're at totally opposite ends of the issue. It's not the same at all. Nate *hurt* people. You have no idea what that's like, Hugh, to look at him and know the full extent of the damage he's caused. None. All I see there is someone who didn't give a shit about anything except getting his dick wet, okay? At the expense of his family and someone he claimed to love."

Once again I open my mouth, prepared to argue, but Phel cuts me off with a wave of his hand. "But it doesn't matter anyway, Hugh. I'm going to be finished my program really soon, and after that I won't even be around. This whole discussion is moot."

I try to keep myself from physically recoiling from the news, and fail. "What do you mean, you're not going to be around? I-I thought—"

"What? That I'd be in rehab forever?"

"Of course not," I snap. "But I figured you'd at least be sticking around Cardiff after." Hesitating, because what I'm about to say next still isn't a fully formed thought, even for me. I say, "I was going to suggest you move in with me, man. After you leave Palermo." Afterwards I need something to distract me from the sudden train wreck of this conversation, and swivel back toward the steering wheel and start the ignition.

As we begin the drive back to my house, Phel is silent. But then he offers, "I'm really touched you would think of me. I just… when I came here, I never gave too much thought to sticking around after. The idea was to try and get myself sorted out, and then get on with my life."

The statement, though not meant to offend, pisses me off. "And what, you don't have a life here? Nothing worth sticking around for?" I shoot a glare at him. "What about this guy you've been seeing, huh? You were just planning on walking away from that too?"

Phelan furrows his brow and gives a little snort. "I'd hardly allow for some guy I'm just fucking to alter my plans," he retorts. Then, more gently, "The fact that you'd prefer for me to stay has much greater bearing, Hugh."

"Then stay!" Hell, my hands are so tight around the steering wheel, my knuckles are starting to cramp. "From the sounds of it, you hated the Midwest. California suits you."

Head tilted, Phel considers. "California isn't without its own problems."

I grunt. "Such as?" At his silence, I growl lightly to myself. "Jesus, Phel. We should be past this crap about keeping secrets from each other, but obviously there's still plenty of stuff you don't trust me with." This is wildly hypocritical of me to say, since I've never told Phel about my own time at Palermo, but all that bullshit is in the past anyway—I don't keep stuff from him regarding what's going on in the here and now, not unless it's something sensitive about Nate I'm expected to keep to myself. I do the same for Phel, obviously, because his business is his own, but I'm—different. Or so I thought. Apparently that was a huge assumption on my part.

"Trust has nothing to do with it," he tells me bluntly. "Of course I trust you. But there's a difference between trusting someone with information and being ready to share it. There are things I don't even talk to my therapist about, and supposedly I can tell her anything."

"You can tell me anything too," I remind him petulantly, feeling as left out as the last kid picked for the team. "I'm your best friend, for crying out loud. It's not like I'm going to sit here and judge you."

I can feel Phelan's eyes on me from the passenger side of the car. "How can I expect you not to judge me negatively when there are things I still judge myself for?"

Since he doesn't seem prepared to offer anything further, I catch myself sighing, again, and feeling like if I keep at it enough, I'll start to sound like a dying moose. "Well, will you at least *think* about it? I mean, you haven't made any definite plans yet, right?"

Phel hesitates. "No, I haven't."

"Okay, then. Just think about it. You can do that, can't you?" I refuse to beg Phel to stay, but it's surprisingly hard not to. Any more of this stonewalling act, and I just might. This development is one I never could have banked on, even more than finding out Nate wouldn't be going back home. But the thought of the three of us sharing a living space, however unexpected, isn't unattractive. Even the—minor—issue of Phel and Nate's unspoken drama seems easily enough resolved if I wear them down, and so I find myself offering up my home a second time in as many days. "My house is yours, Phel. I'd want you to stick around where you know people, not move off someplace where you're alone again. Besides, you need someone who'll keep you from calling your ex in a moment of weakness, right?"

I'd hoped this little quip would brighten the mood, but instead it makes his jaw tighten until I see a muscle ticking frantically in his cheek, and he glares out the window with his arms folded. Oh, well... okay. Not the right thing to say, then, and so much for the earlier good mood. Phel is silent again for a really long time, staring out at the passing scenery until we're practically on my doorstep, the tension so thick I can picture myself choking on it. Not even the group of half-dressed young surfers we pass on the way is enough to get him to perk up, and Phel has always had time to admire a strong set of shoulders.

I expect that to be the end of the conversation, but before we pull into my driveway, he bunches his fist in the fabric of his shorts. "I'll think about it," he tells me, still not looking in my direction. "But I make no promises."

The lingering note of hesitation at the end of Phelan's sentence is, I know, as far as I'm likely to get with him today. He might have a bit of a soft spot for me, and from this conversation I know he still does, but at the end of the day he's a stubborn bastard rivaled only by Nate. It might not look like it, but this could be a small victory if I keep working at it, not pushing, just coaxing him round. Phel would forever deny being anything like a scared animal, but that's how he's always seemed to me. Wounded and weary, but nothing's irreparable.

I park the car and turn off the ignition. We sit there in the quiet for a few minutes, listening to the engine tick. "Don't promise anything," I tell him gently, and he sighs, probably able to guess what I'm about to say. "Just stay."

7

Phel

His hands are bound to the iron rails of the headboard, sweaty skin tanned and sweet against the glistening satin of my neckties, one red and one blue. I no longer have an office job to go to, so they've no purpose now but this. Long fingers grasp and twist around the metal, clenching and releasing as he gasps and murmurs my name in prayer, lashes on those beautiful green eyes fluttering, lips sucked and bitten raw red. I want to answer those pleas with an Amen *or a wry* Hallelujah, *but all I can manage is a long, low note of surrender at the sparks building at the base of my spine, fire coiling with each slick slide of his cock into my body. Gentle nudges of his pelvis lift into the aching rhythm of my hips as I raise and lower myself on his length, my hands braced against his ribs for balance, skimming the abundance of freckles scattered across his shoulders and chest and belly like I'm mapping constellations and he's the whole fathomless sky.*

I think Nate begs me because he's scared I won't let him come, or that I won't agree to see him again after he drives away and leaves me exhausted and wrung out in bed. Much as I love to hear those words coming out of his mouth, *Please, Phel, baby—please*, his fear makes me feel heartless, makes me give Nate what he wants—an orgasm, a kiss, another opportunity to plead for forgiveness—not because he's earned it or deserves it, but because I don't like to think of myself as someone who might refuse. I'm not heartless: quite the contrary. Too much heart is what got me here in the first place. If Nate's responsible for making me feel too much, well, I'm hoping to build up immunity the second time around.

"Phel, how was your evening?" Willa repeats her question, the one that got me thinking about Nate in the first place. The reminder in her voice snaps me out of my reverie long enough to flash her an apologetic smile and a slight shrug.

"It was... relaxing," I say, folding my hands in my lap. We're seated on one of the many private patios scattered across the Palermo compound, shielded by a white wooden gazebo just like in all the full-color brochures. "I stayed in."

She nods and treats me to one of the thoughtful silences that normally precede her more loaded questions. "And did you see Nate?" There it is.

"I did."

After the minor breakdown that led me to confess to Willa that Nate was in Cardiff, I'd briefly considered withholding the truth about the recent developments in our relationship out of a misdirected sense of... I don't know, exactly. Shame, perhaps, because I (correctly) anticipated her disapproval, but also fear that outside interference would somehow ruin it. As it turns out, I'm not a wonderful liar; after the first time I took Nate back into my bed—or my couch, as the case happened to be at the time—she knew what had happened almost immediately. I've no doubt Willa would feel relieved if I put a stop to things here and now, but that isn't going to happen, and we both know it. Instead she's attempted to acknowledge my honesty by including me in the process of dissecting this latest psychological development, appealing to my sense of reason the way only a therapist can.

I have a great deal more to share, however, than the details of last night's meeting with Nate. In the interest of full disclosure, I'm compelled to be upfront about this information before we can go any further. I want Willa to know I'm not hiding anything.

"I've stopped taking my meds," I tell her evenly, meeting her eyes as if, through this act alone, I can convince her this is the best possible course of action I could have taken. I believe it is, of course, but in this day and age of pharmaceutical dependency, I'm prepared for an uphill battle in trying to talk my shrink into seeing eye to eye with me on the matter. "It's been nearly two weeks now, but I didn't want to say anything until the drugs had had a chance to leave my system, to see what it was like first."

"The Paxil or the Xanax?" she asks. Naturally there could be no great outpouring of emotion over this news, but I'm impressed, yet again, by how calmly Willa is able to accept information and deal with the facts one at a time.

"Both. The Xanax I've not had a need for recently, not since that last big panic attack when I saw Nate." I shrug and cross my leg over my knee so I can pick at the frayed hem of my jeans, now more the result of wear and tear than fashionable distressing. "Actually, I'm still prepared to make use of the Xanax if the situation calls for it—the Paxil is what I really wanted to cut myself off from." Unable to decipher her silence, I ask, "Does that bother you? It was you, after all, who prescribed it in the first place. I don't mean to second-guess your medical wisdom." That comes out a bit more smugly than I intended, but I don't bother to correct myself. I want to appear firm on the decision, even if it means sounding like a bit of an arrogant shit. Then again, if the shoe fits....

Willa pauses to consider the question, pushing a lock of shoulder-length dark hair back behind her ear. Her hazel eyes show no hesitation in their dead-on stare. "No, it doesn't... bother me," she says eventually. "You're not an inpatient, Phel, and it's not like I prescribed you with medication meant to correct a significant or harmful mental imbalance. The decision to cooperate with the program we outlined together is, and has always been, yours. Our sessions aren't about making me happy—they're about making you feel like you're in a better place in your life."

"Thank you," I say with a nod.

But she isn't done. "That being said, I do wish you'd consulted with me before choosing to discontinue the medication, since there could have been unexpected side effects. Luckily, that wasn't the case. But that concerns me less than how this decision is a continuation of a series of worrisome behavior." Although she pauses, perhaps in anticipation of a protest of some sort, or for me to ask for clarification, I don't interrupt. So she continues, "We can get to that. First I'd like for you to explain why you arrived at this decision, why you felt it was the best step forward."

I resist the urge to shrug—why does this seem to be the primary response in the patient's vocabulary?—and stop fidgeting with the hem of my jeans when I realize this does not add an air of confidence to my demeanor. Instead, I sigh. "The Paxil felt both unnecessary and counterproductive to achieving a feeling of control over my emotions,"

I explain. "In the last couple weeks I've been feeling remarkably more assertive over my feelings—not panicked or overwhelmed or afraid, but... empowered."

"You mean since you started re-engaging in sexual relations with Nate," she supplies.

Hardball. Fine, I get it. "Yes. Since then." Feeling, for a moment, undeniably petty, I add, "Plus it wasn't doing me any favors in the libido department. So it seemed prudent to stop on both counts."

"How have you been sleeping without it?" Willa asks, changing tack unexpectedly. "Any nightmares or insomnia?"

"When I've been sleeping, you mean?" I allow myself a quick smirk and a lift of eyebrows before I shake my head. "No, none. I've been sleeping like a baby."

"And your mood? Any abrupt changes, any periods of extreme highs or lows?"

"No." I choose—for Willa's own benefit, I tell myself—to refrain from adding that my emotional extremes tend to occur precisely when I'm having sex with Nate. Not that I'm bipolar or anything, not even with him, but I'm definitely in a pretty good mood most of the day after I've worked off some of my aggression with him between the sheets.

Willa nods again and jots something down in her notebook. "I'd like to go back, if we can, to the association you seem to be making between a feeling of empowerment and your sexual relationship with Nate. We've touched on it before, briefly, but this is the first time you've come out and worded it in this way. What about your involvement compels you to describe it as a matter of control, rather than love or desire?"

Unable to help myself, I snort. "I'm compelled to describe it that way because I don't *love* Nate. I desire him, yeah, same as he still desires me... but after what he did? Love is a nonissue. It isn't even on the table."

"No?"

I glare at Willa. "No." It's hard to explain to another person what I've had a hard time explaining to myself, but I know she won't let this go until I've at least tried to articulate why I feel things are different this time. "Look, what have I been saying the whole time I've been here? That if I could go back and do the whole relationship over again,

I'd take charge of how things unrolled instead of just going along for the ride. I'd make myself feel like less of a victim. I'm sure if I'd been a little more assertive with Nate the first time around...." I trail off, recognizing the fault in my reasoning before it's even out of my mouth.

Willa, of course, catches it. "What, maybe you wouldn't have gotten hurt?" She shakes her head. "That you got your heart broken has nothing to do, ultimately, with anything you did or didn't do," she reminds me. "Yes, we've discussed the idea that you let go of your reservations more quickly than was healthy, or that you were too accommodating—but you were an autonomous part of the partnership, same as Nate. You've said yourself that he wasn't pushing you around." She pauses to let this sink in, though she's probably aware this is one of those topics I'm still resistant to. I start to shake my head in refusal of what she's saying, but Willa presses on. "What makes you think control is an issue that has any bearing now?"

"Because he's fucking learning what it feels like to be totally powerless!" I don't mean to shout. Not because it startles Willa—it doesn't—but because these little displays of emotion never quite sit well with me. Especially when I know I'm on the defensive.

"And what's more important to you?" asks Willa. "That he feels powerless, or that you feel powerful?" Mulishly silent, I fold my arms. "Describe the power dynamic in your current relationship," she suggests instead. "As far as you see it, who calls the shots?"

"I'm the one who sets the terms, if that's what you mean," I answer reluctantly.

"Which means what?"

I shrug. "I decide when we meet and where, and I decide what we do. It's not like Nate can't refuse, he just... doesn't."

Willa meets my eyes. "Why not? From what you've told me about him, Nate doesn't seem like a particularly meek individual. Open to suggestion, perhaps, but you've never described him as someone incapable of asserting himself."

This is harder. "Because he knows I'd end it otherwise. He was the one who said he was willing to do this my way—I'm not the one who initiated it. He said he'd do whatever I wanted, to make it up to me. To get me to stop turning him away."

"He's afraid of losing you again," Willa concludes. "He's forfeited his power in your arrangement out of fear. Is that correct?" At my eventual shrug, which she correctly reads as agreement, Willa folds her hands across the pad of paper in her lap. "Do you want him to feel powerless?"

"Of course I do." No point hiding it. "It's how I felt for months. He gave up his power so I could have it for once. It was an... an exchange."

Willa shakes her head. "Phelan, that isn't how it works. It seems like it should be a straightforward transfer of power from one person to another in a relationship, but the dynamic is rarely, if ever, that simple. In a relationship of true Dominance and submission, the sub still possesses power in the arrangement because he possesses the ability to say no at any time. The Dom knows this, and those are the terms under which he has to abide, what keeps the power balance in check."

"I don't want a Dom/sub relationship with Nate," I point out. Not even with the experimenting we've been doing lately, with the tying up and the rough sex and even the occasional bout of orgasm refusal—his, of course. I'm not stupid enough to consider the things Willa is describing. "That's not what we're playing at. Sure, maybe there's a bit more power play than we had before, but Nate isn't the one who decides yes or no. I am. He said—he said giving me that choice, that power, is his way of trying to prove how sorry he is."

Still staring at me, Willa twirls her pen once before setting it down. "And what will you do if Nate no longer wants part of this game? If he wakes up tomorrow morning and decides he's through with being punished and no longer cares if you forgive him?"

I meet her eyes steadily, refusing to allow myself to swallow nervously. Willa doesn't know Nate from Adam—doesn't know that's not how he works. "He wouldn't. And even so, I wouldn't care."

Smiling without malice, Willa sighs. "I find that difficult to believe, Phel. If you truly didn't care, you would have turned him away the first time he came to you. But you didn't, because even after weeks of our sessions together, you still don't identify a difference between taking the control others give you and taking control for yourself. The whole point of you coming to Palermo was to learn that a healthy partnership can't take root until you have a healthy relationship with yourself—you have to learn how to assert yourself without feeling dependent upon the permission or approval of others, be it Nate or your father or anyone else."

Anger floods my system and makes my face heat up, blood rushing to my cheeks. Even against the tan I've developed here in California, I know it must be stark against my skin. "Just because I'm not turning him away doesn't mean I *can't*," I grit out. "I choose not to. Why would I? Obviously there are benefits to this arrangement, the least of which is the sex."

"You aren't doing it for the sex, Phel," Willa tells me gently. "In fact, I think your reasons for going back to him—or letting him come back to you; that distinction matters little—are no different from Nate's." Her tone holds such calm assurance that I want to storm right out of there and prove just how much I'm doing it for the sex—to bend Nate over the nearest flat surface and have my way with him. Remind him—*everyone*—that he's nothing more to me than an easy fuck with a pretty face and the willingness to do whatever I should desire, no matter how depraved it is.

"Our motivations are *nothing* alike," I spit. "Nate and I are nothing alike."

"How so? Surely you wouldn't have lasted more than a year together if you had nothing in common with the man."

"Nate hurt people," I point out, exasperation loud in my voice. God, how many times do I have to explain this? "He did what he did knowing people would be hurt by his actions, his wife and his son and—me."

Willa's pen taps. "And you're hurting no one?"

"No one who didn't hurt me first."

Tap, tap. "And what about Hugh? Would he agree with that assessment if he were to learn the truth of your history with his brother?"

My growl should more than suffice as a response, but in the interest of playing along, I say, "Hugh has nothing to do with this. He wasn't involved before, and it's none of his business now."

Wisely, Willa recognizes when she's hit upon a point I'm not willing to concede, and the woman isn't one for arguing lost causes. No, she's all about changing tactics, finding a new route into what she perceives to be the heart of the argument. "You're right about one thing," she tells me, seemingly through with the topic of Hugh for the time being. "This isn't a Dom/sub relationship you've got going, because those relationships, at the end of the day, are still about love.

They might involve pain and an element of punishment and reward, but they aren't, fundamentally, about a desire for one person to hurt the other. Nate hurt you while you were together, yes, but even his motives were free of the kind of vengefulness—maliciousness, even—you're describing to me now."

I drum my fingers against my leg angrily. "If you're saying I should walk away from Nate right now," I tell her petulantly, "I'll damn well do it. I'll go back on the bloody Paxil and go back to being an emotionless zombie."

"I'm not telling you to do anything," answers Willa quietly. "But what I'm saying is, if your completion of this program was dependent upon my approval or a pass/fail grade based on your progress—you wouldn't get it."

Utterly finished with this conversation, despite the fact that our hour isn't up, I get to my feet and walk purposefully to the entrance of the gazebo. All of a sudden I want nothing more than to be back in the sea and losing myself in the biggest wave I can find. Not losing myself literally—still no latent fantasies of suicide—but anything to keep myself from wasting another fucking thought on this subject.

"Good thing I've only got another few days here," I snap, and Willa, predictably, frowns. "After that, I'm not your problem anymore."

I LET myself into Hugh's house through the back door, which is always—though I've told him a million times this isn't the Midwest—unlocked, just in case I should happen to stop by. It's getting on in the afternoon, around the time Hugh is usually barricaded inside his study to work on his book.

Although I'll never understand what compels him to ensconce himself in his office during the nicest time of day, especially when the California days are sweet indeed, I have to admire how methodical and regimented Hugh is as an author, setting himself a specific schedule from which to work. Not the creative type myself, I always saw writing as something spontaneous and undisciplined, to be completed whenever inspiration strikes, not according to set hours of the day. But Hugh insists this is the only way his novels get written, and who am I to argue? We surf in the mornings; then I leave him to his work each afternoon. Which is why, I suppose, he was in such a rush to get Nate and me to spend some time together during his off-limits writing periods. His concern for our respective well-being is touching, but I sometimes wonder how Hugh thinks I or his brother got along without him before. Before we were actually together, I mean.

I can hear two different sets of music emerging from separate locations in the house, each trying to drown the other out: classical music from Hugh's study, and classic rock from the living room, where Nate is likely reading or taking a nap. Since I already know where I'm not welcome, I wander into the living room and discover, instead, that Nate is busy in the kitchen, where he beckons to me in response to my tentative "Hello?"

Upon entering, I see Nate, shirtless, bent over at the fridge, digging around in the crisper and cradling a pile of vegetables in the crook of his elbow. He glances over his shoulder and flashes me a grin, and I have to wonder at how happy he always is to see me when I'm not quick enough to spoil the mood.

"I made you a cheeseburger," he says in greeting, and withdraws a head of lettuce before he kicks the fridge door closed with his heel. Sure enough, there are two burgers set out on the kitchen island, fresh off the barbecue. Faint smokiness still lingers in the air, and I notice Nate has even gone to the trouble of toasting the buns on the grill. A stickler for detail, Nate is, when it comes to food.

"How did you even know I'd stop by?" I wonder. I have the good grace to feel abashed that my first response is suspicion, rather than a smile or even thanks for this show of thoughtfulness; especially when I catch the hurt twist to his mouth, but it seems too late to backpedal now. I'm trying to break him of the habit of expecting displays of friendliness from me when I've never given him cause to do so. At least, not since he arrived in California.

"I hate to break it to you, Phel, but there's not a whole lot of inconsistency to your routine," he points out gruffly, then sets down the lettuce, tomatoes, and onion on the cutting board to be chopped up for burger dressings. "You stop by most days around this time, so I figured we could expect you. Maybe you're a bit earlier today than normal. There a reason for that? Hugh won't be coming up for air for a while yet."

"I finished my session with Willa early," I answer, trying to hide my annoyance that Nate fancies himself such an expert on how I spend my time. Luckily, Callie wanders inside through the dog flap to greet me, giving me an excuse to divert my knee-jerk sense of snippiness. I was raised to be polite enough not to start an argument in payment for free food just because I've had a bad morning. Not even with Nate. "I came to collect my surfboard, since I thought I'd get a bit more time in at the beach today."

Ripping off leaves of lettuce to rinse beneath the tap, Nate nods. "Fair enough. The surf report for this afternoon ain't anything spectacular, but I was thinking of hitting the waves for a while myself." He lets that hang there a moment, and with nothing else to do, I go to the sink to wash my hands. I begin to help slice up the tomatoes and onions. Nate watches me without comment before going back to his own task. Then he says, "Do you want company?"

"It's not a private beach," I answer, voice neutral. We don't have to talk to each other out in the water anyway. I remind myself there's no harm in going down together. "I doubt it'll be very crowded on a Wednesday. No competing for waves."

"Gee, thanks," snorts Nate. "If it offends you that badly to be seen in public with me, you could just say so."

With a shake of his head, he leaves us to finish our tasks in silence, handing me a plate to fill half with sliced tomato and half with onion once I'm done. His own pile of washed and shredded lettuce goes on a separate plate before he returns to the fridge for a jar of mayonnaise, along with the ketchup, relish, and mustard he likes on his own burger. He sets them down on the counter with a bit more force than is necessary, a hard twist to his mouth as he refuses to meet my gaze. It brings me straight back to the morning's conversation with Willa, and I just—I refuse to be drawn back into it.

Ignoring Nate's arched eyebrow, I wipe my hands off on a dishtowel and go to turn the stereo up, inching the volume nearly to the point that would lure Hugh out of his study to complain about the noise level. He'll not be bothered for this, though, and so when I return to the kitchen, I've no designs on being disturbed. I snatch the bottle of Heinz out of Nate's hand to press him back up against the kitchen island.

"What the—" he starts, expression one of surprise, but his protests end there as I shove our bodies together and take his mouth in a kiss, my hands going tight around the warm, bare skin of his hips.

"How long ago did Hugh go into his study?" I ask, gauging the limits of our privacy. Nate always seems to require some acknowledgement of the risk involved in our dalliances, but after a year of hiding from his wife and son, I should think anything less than an Amber Alert would barely register as a blip on the radar. I get tired of him glancing around like we're about to be interrupted, but old habits die hard, I guess.

Nate worries his lip for a moment, then slides his arms around my waist, palms broad and hot against my back. "Less than an hour ago," he answers. "He won't be leaving that room at least until dinner."

"Fine." Releasing him first, I then pull my T-shirt over my head and let it fall at my feet, my lips curling at the quick flush that suffuses Nate's cheeks, his pupils dilating with arousal as his eyes skim over my exposed chest and down to my low-slung board shorts. "Turn around," I order.

"What? Why?"

Exasperated, I roll my eyes and grip Nate by the shoulders to spin him around myself, giving him a light shove against the counter for good measure.

The hiss of excitement in response to my little displays of aggression—however unnaturally they come—makes it all worthwhile. "Phel, what are you—"

Growling a terse "Shut up," I sink to my knees behind him and pull his jeans down at the same time. The denim is loose on his hips, enough that a sharp tug puddles them around his ankles, button and zip untouched. A large part of Nate's California attitude seems to worship at the altar of comfort and relaxation from the typical constraints of everyday life, which apparently includes underwear; his bare ass is exposed to my gaze before I can blink, as easy as wishing.

Nate gasps in surprise, the sound turning to a low groan as I reach out to squeeze a handful of that firm muscle. All I can think is he must be sunning himself naked on the private balcony of his bedroom, because there's hardly any tan line below the belt. He's so exquisite I can scarcely believe it some days, and he's mine to do with as I please.

I've never wanted a sex slave, but Nate at times makes me understand the appeal.

Right now it pleases me to grip the other cheek in my hand and spread him open, leaning in to bury my face in the warm softness of his crease, my mouth open against the perfect dark pink of his opening. This behavior isn't contradictory, I think. Willa is wrong. I never desired retribution to the exclusion of all else, and I quickly grew bored satisfying my own needs at Nate's expense, especially not when he yields so beautifully to the pleasure it's within my power to give. True to form, Nate curses and jerks above me, a surprised noise dragging from his throat almost the instant he feels my tongue on him, and he pushes instinctively into the kiss. He's been a glutton for this kind of attention ever since his first rim job, and I lavish it upon him like no time at all has passed, tasting his musk and the clean scent of an all-too-recent shower.

The response is symphonic, Nate nearly collapsing forward onto the island with his back arched in a bow, arms tensed, low cries and moans building in crescendo as I lave and tease and press into him with my tongue. The flesh is still loose and open from last night, when I fucked him with four fingers before riding us both to completion. I reach between his legs for his erection, already wet for me, and point his length toward the floor as I stroke and work him closer to orgasm. A grin splits my face when his hips jerk, trying to fuck my hand and my mouth simultaneously like they don't know in which direction to thrust. Nate's so near the brink already. I can feel his muscles shuddering around my tongue in spasms, flutterings as gentle as a kiss, and his prick swells in my hand. Almost there. I try not to think about how desperately I still want to please him sometimes.

Impatient for more, I let go and maneuver Nate back around so I can capture his cock between my lips, allowing his hands, for once, to grip my hair and direct the pace, hard and fast just the way he likes. I take him as deep as my throat will allow, pressing in toward the base and swallowing around the head so he can feel every suck and constriction, every swirl of my tongue against the underside of his shaft. The tug of my hand at his heavy balls is what does it, constant pressure until he stiffens and comes with a shout, spending hard and slippery down my throat. I close my eyes to accept it, but I can picture the very expression on his face: eyes rolled back, red lips slack and gorgeous as he croons my name and his release.

I pull away and sit back on my heels to watch him recover, wiping absently at my mouth while Nate slumps against the island and opens his eyes to barely more than slits staring down at me. "Phel—" he begins, but I cut him off by rising to my feet and giving him a swift kiss. Willa can say what she wants; I might make it very clear to Nate what the terms of our arrangement are, may be at times harsh when my anger is scarcely able to contain itself, but after that first day, I don't think I've ever been malicious or cruel. Just because I'm confident Nate wouldn't walk away from me, even at my most punishing, doesn't mean I'm compelled to be a total dick to him. Not all the time. Not even if I still think he deserves it.

"I'm going surfing," I tell him, and stoop to snatch my T-shirt up off the floor. "Come if you want, I don't care."

MUCH to my chagrin, surfing proves something of a wasted endeavor, and not the cathartic release I've craved since my disastrous session with Willa. The waves are meek and unfulfilling, acceptable but not great—decent enough for someone like Nate, who is still getting back into the sport, but not nearly enough for someone looking for a challenge or to blow off some steam. I can sense the frustration of the other more seasoned surfers in the water, and in unspoken conference, a few of us paddle out to the Suckouts on the other side of the reef, hoping for better sport there. I know Hugh would kill me if he knew, because this is a dangerous stretch of water he's yet to let me attempt. But the thought of the challenge alone makes up my mind.

No one says anything to me at first, but I watch the other surfers for signs of the local vibe. As much as Hugh explained to me about the caliber of surfer out here in Cardiff, I've seen for myself the elitism in some of the experienced athletes who ride these waves. The locals guard this spot jealously, displaying keen hostility toward fumbling shortboarders who waste the waves out here—a longboarder would get laughed out of the Suckouts as soon as look at it—but to my relief, my presence goes unremarked upon, four of us paddling out in relative silence except for the odd greeting or comment on the weather.

I quickly see the Suckouts is a waiting game—at first there's nothing, no sign of the famed tubes that crest out over these low tides, but after maybe twenty minutes of watching, one of the other surfers sends up the alert, nodding in the direction of a swell just beginning to take shape. Pack-like, we advance upon the wave, me bringing up the rear so as not to get in the way. I'm a little nervous about making the drop, to be honest, knowing I might as well go home if I blow it. Hugh's warnings about notoriously low water levels ring in my ears as we get into position along the wave's trajectory. This, he said, was a bombora.

The sound of the wave advancing is almost as powerful as the feeling of it, four of us paddling furiously to stay ahead of the whitewater as it begins to break. Then I'm pushing myself up and being thrown down one of the sharpest drops I've ever experienced, a thick, grinding tube of water that shoves me along at breakneck speed. I hear the whoops and hollers of the other surfers as they hurtle down the length of the barrel, prismatic water encircling us from all sides like multifaceted blue glass. It's incredible, a perfect wave that pushes all my troubles so firmly to the back of my mind that I actually laugh out loud, dragging my hand through the water on the inside of the tube for balance as much as the sensation of it.

I see the other surfers kick out of the barrel, attacking the nice, steep wall of water at the end of the wave, turning neat carves and breaks for several yards before they hit the channel where the Suckouts empties into the mouth of the river. I concentrate on where best to position myself, calculating how to maintain my speed and enjoy the rest of the wave after I exit the surrounding crash of whitewater, but instead of a smooth glide, I hit an unexpected step in the water that catches the rails of my board and sends me plowing head over feet into the base of the wave. I land shoulders first in the surf.

Even through the shock of finding myself unceremoniously unseated from my board, I am aware of the sudden real danger of bashing my skull open against the reef due to the low water level. I brace for the worst, except that, somehow, my board ends up back underneath me. Instead of sharp rocks and coral, I collide with fiberglass-covered foam. Pain explodes in my back—that will be a spectacular bruise later—and the crash of so many tons of water over my head is a feeling I will never come to enjoy, but relief floods my system as I consider how much worse it could be. I feel the surfboard snap under the impact; the nose shoots up to the surface and is carried away with the rushing waves, and the other half, still tethered to my ankle, jerks free and drags me a short distance. After that is a tumble of water and air bubbles as I'm tossed along like a feather in the surf, never ceasing to try and fight my way to the surface.

The other surfers have already kicked out of the wave and are waiting for me in calmer waters, perched on their boards in a loose circle. Floating nearby is the broken half of my board. One of the surfers, a lanky brunette, extends a hand in my direction, indicating I should swim over and grab hold so I'm not treading water by myself.

"All right, bro?" he asks. Gripping me by the arm, he helps pull me on his board so I'm straddling it alongside him. "Rough ride—that tube was one steppy bastard."

"I'm fine, thank you," I answer, smiling at him in gratitude. "Can't say the same about my board, though. Looks like it won't be joining me on the Suckouts again."

"That's a bummer," agrees one of the other surfers. "Lucky you weren't hurt, though. You should visit Logan and Max's shop when you get back to the beach—they can set you up with a new ride straight away. They do good work."

I nod, recalling a wooden hut on the beach that looks more like a shantytown shack than a surf shop, but I'd trust a local recommendation more than a four-star rating on Yelp. "I think I've passed by it before," I answer. "I'll take a look on my way home." It occurs to me that I will receive an epic lecture from Hugh once he hears of this incident from Nate, who will no doubt kick up a small fuss of his own. Considering I'm the better surfer—not to mention a grown-ass man, as Nate would say—he still treats me like a china doll sometimes.

In a display of chivalrousness I scarcely expect, the brown-haired surfer—Ian, as he introduces himself—offers to paddle me back to shore where Nate and I stashed our gear on the beach. Much to my surprise, Nate is already waiting for me. He stands when he sees me carrying half a surfboard, sporting what Ian calls an "impressive palette" of bruises along my back and shoulders from my impromptu introduction to the reef. From the feel of things, there will probably be a few more on my neck as well, if not my face. Already my back is beginning to ache from the pummeling I took in the surf.

"What the hell happened?" demands Nate, placing a warm hand against my bicep so he can turn me around to inspect the damage. His suspicious gaze immediately turns to Ian, who backs away with his hands up. Since Nate has a generous foot and at least fifty pounds on the guy, I don't blame him.

"I just paddled him in, man," Ian says defensively. "His board is toast." To me he adds, "Hope to see you out on the Suckouts again, dude. You handled yourself pretty well out there for a first-timer. Guess I'll leave you in the capable hands of your boyfriend, but check out Logan's work before you leave; tell him I sent you, and he and Max'll hook you up with a deal for sure."

Neither Nate nor I bother to correct him on the use of "boyfriend," since it seems more trouble than it's worth, and after Ian heads back into the ocean, I turn to my lover—"fuck buddy" doesn't have the same ring to it—with a sigh. "Hit a rough wave," I tell Nate sharply before he can start with the questioning. "It's nothing, just a few bruises. I'm ready to go home if you're done, but if you planned to do more surfing I'll just… see you."

Nate rolls his eyes. "Don't be stupid, Phel," he chides. "You may not like me, but I can still escort your broken ass back home." I open my mouth to protest, because going to face Hugh was *not* in the evening's plans, but Nate cuts me off with a dark look. "No way am I letting you go back to Palermo in that state, man," he says.

His earnestness makes me snort; on his face is the same worried expression he gets whenever Hugh so much as stubs his toe or gets a paper cut, however quickly concealed with laughter or an obnoxious joke. "I'm not your responsibility, Nate."

There's no disguising the flash of hurt in Nate's eyes, nor the way his hand briefly tightens around my arm in reproach. "Can you stop being a dick for five seconds and let me help?"

"Why?" I counter. "What's the point?"

Wisely, Nate foregoes any pretty statements about his concern for me, sticking to the realm of the practical. "The point is: you need to ice that shit before you wake up tomorrow unable to move."

I roll my eyes. "Will you drag me back kicking and screaming if I refuse?"

Nate quirks his mouth, knowing I'm only at my most exasperated before I'm about to cave. Suddenly tired, I can't be bothered to get worked up that he still knows my tells. "Sounds about right, since I'm the one who got tied up last night."

"Let's just get on with it," I grumble, flushing.

We're halfway back to where the car is parked when we cross what I realize is the beach shack/surf shop Ian described to me earlier. Despite being sore and undeniably bone tired from sun exposure and the culmination of the day's excitement, I catch Nate's arm, the one not wrapped around his surfboard and my half of one, and pull him to a halt. It's the only explanation I can think of for what proves to be a series of dubious flashes of genius to follow. "Wait."

"What?"

"I'd like to go in here," I say, indicating the surf shop with a nod of my head. "Ian mentioned this place earlier, said the owners produce excellent gear." With a shrug, I add, "I need a new board anyway."

Nate cocks an eyebrow. "You need one right this minute?"

"I did say you could go about your own business if you wanted," I remind him peevishly. "You don't have to come with me."

Another eye roll, as if Nate has chosen this as his default response for the afternoon. Curious that he never just says no. "Christ, you're such a little bitch sometimes. Worse than Hugh."

"Is that a yes, or a 'fuck off'?" And then, before he can beat me to it: "If you're just going to roll your eyes *again*, I'd rather you left."

"This better be good."

The inside of the shack is hardly a surprise, given its exterior, though it is quite a bit larger than I expect. Rough-hewn wood and bamboo thatching give a cozy, rustic appearance both outside and in. There aren't many frills beyond a few basic work surfaces along the walls and trestle tables that vertically bisect the main floor space. Near the back of the shop, a man wearing a protective mask is in the process of sanding down a board, his tools and materials strewn about the workspace. The "storefront" is nothing more than a simple if cheery front desk decorated with the requisite hula figures and swaths of long grass that look to have once belonged to a Hawaiian skirt. Examples of surfboards produced by the shop hang from the walls, and I don't have to try very hard to be impressed by the intricate and colorful graphics that decorate the surface of each one, ranging from standard shortboards to longboards and even a few wooden boards. Nate, too, gives a low whistle and a muttered "Sweet," and I turn to look at him with a smile.

Before I can comment, a tall man with a ponytail and painted nails abandons his seat in front of the shortboard he's airbrushing and comes to meet us at the desk. "Afternoon, gents," he says cheerfully, and I immediately pick up on a Southern accent and the scent of beer on his breath. "What can I do you for?"

"I'm, er… looking for Logan or Max," I answer slowly, taking in his ragged cut-off shorts—inexplicably paired with the most battered set of cowboy boots I've ever seen—and faded red wifebeater. "A group of surfers at the Suckouts suggested I come here for a new board."

"And right they are," he says jovially. "I'm Logan, and the handsome devil out back is Max—he's the boss man of our humble operation, but he lets me handle the customers because I'm prettier."

Ignoring Nate's snort of laughter from behind me—leave it to him to be charmed by anyone with '70s hair and a taste for PBR—I nod and try not to let my disbelief show. "It's just the two of you?"

"Yep." Logan spreads his arms and gestures at their shop. "It don't look like much, but the Maxster and I know our product, and our customers always come back with their friends. You're kind of living proof of that, eh, hermano?" To Nate, he asks, "You looking for a board too, bro?"

Nate holds up his hands. "Just checkin' out your wares at the moment, man, but thanks." I absolutely don't miss the proprietary way his free hand curls about the bare skin of my hip, and I resist the urge kick my heel into his shin in retaliation. "Some nice work you got here, though. I'll definitely come back with my brother whenever we're in need of new gear. Hell, he might come back on his own, since he collects enough of the damn things."

"Man after my own heart," says Logan, approval clear in his voice. "Would I know him?"

For a moment Nate hesitates, clearly considering the matter of his brother's minor celebrity around town, but then he says, "Maybe. His name's Hugh Fessenden. Big guy, stupid hair."

Logan pauses to consider, muttering, "Hugh Fessenden… Fessenden…," to himself as he tries to place the name. Then his face brightens. "Hey, you wouldn't mean Hugh Dorian by any chance, wouldja? The author? He's bought a couple custom jobs from us. Designed 'em myself."

"That's Hugh all right," Nate answers, huffing a laugh. "More money than brains sometimes."

"No way," Logan answers with a quirky smile. "Dude that big, gotta go custom. Nice guy, though, your brother. What do they call you?"

"I'm Nate, and this here is Phel," says Nate, still clutching my hip like his fingers have any right to be there. I twitch away from his touch hard enough that he gets the point, and his hand falls uselessly to his side.

Logan nods. "You lookin' for something off the rack, Phel, or a custom job?"

"You do custom work on a regular basis?" I ask, stunned. I've seen plenty of small businesses before, but that two men are capable of running a beachfront operation, as well as producing custom orders, is a little astounding, even to the grandson of a self-made man. My father was fond of regaling my sister and me with tales of how the Price business grew from a small marketing firm of just five people and one secretary to a true behemoth of the industry. All the same, the idea of two men such as Logan and Max holding down the fort on their own fills me with moderate anxiety. If Max is anything like the average business owner, he experiences more than his fair share of panic on a regular basis too, especially during these harsh economic times.

"Well, much as we can," says Logan. "Hard to keep up with the big companies sometimes, which is sort of why we depend on customers like Hugh to keep us in work. Not enough to keep Max from thinking of selling the place, though."

This confirms my suspicions, though I'm not happy to hear it. "You're selling?" A note of curiosity creeps into my voice, enough to get Nate casting a sidelong look in my direction. Like I said, sunstroke has probably addled my brain.

Before Logan can answer, the man he indicated as Max comes to the front of the shop, through with sanding his surfboard for the time being. He's shorter than me by a couple of inches, middle-aged, and once he pulls the protective mask from his face, I can tell from his shaggy, graying hair and unshaven chin that he's pure old-school hippie. "These fellas in need of something, Logan?" he asks. With a nod at Nate and me, he adds, "I'm Max. Logan helping you out all right?"

"Yes, sir," answers Nate, surprising me with his formality. Apparently he, too, picks up on the note of authority in Max's voice, aided by a steady gaze and an accent similar to Logan's, the kind that suggests he's no stranger to settling disagreements with shotguns when necessary, despite his appearance. It gives him a distinct "don't fuck with me" air, though his tone is friendly enough and Nate's voice is suitably respectful. Aloha spirit only goes so far out here, is my guess. "We were just discussing surfboards for my friend here; haven't gotten into too many details yet."

"You own this place?" I ask Max, wincing internally at the abruptness of the question. I can't help my sudden fascination with the operation, despite the modest presentation and my inexplicable disappointment that it might go under. I suppose getting kicked out of the family corporation didn't quite kill the businessman in me.

Max shifts and turns his sharp, gray-eyed stare on me. "Yeah," he says slowly. "What's it to you?"

I feel Nate hiss in disapproval, clearly wondering why I'm not just chatting about surfboards like any other normal customer. "I mean nothing by it," I say, as much to Nate as to Max. "I'm impressed you've grown such a solid reputation from the local surfing crowd, despite the size of your business. I imagine your work must really blow everyone else out of the water, so to speak, to go up against companies like Billabong. Especially since they sponsor half the professionals in the area."

"Don't remind me," Max mutters, folding his arms. "Word of mouth keeps us afloat most months, but rent's goin' up all the time; so's the cost of materials. Hard to compete with the big outfits when you're just tryin' to break even."

"Logan mentioned you're considering selling the business," I tell him, trying to sound as free of judgment as possible. Unfortunately, repeating this bit of information makes Logan go pale and stutter something about having work to do out back before he slinks away with a nervous glance at his boss. Nate shoots me a look like he thinks I've lost my mind, combined with suitable wariness of what he used to call my "scheming" moods.

"Logan needs to learn to keep his damn mouth shut," Max replies, loud enough for his voice to carry to the back of the shop. Grimacing, he hesitates to answer my prompt, but eventually concedes. "Yeah, maybe. Who am I kiddin'? But nothing's finalized yet, and it isn't affecting whether or not we take new commissions, if that's what's got you worried. We can still do the job, and Logan's a bit of a genius when it comes to new designs. You should see the hollow wood boards he engineers. Can make you a board you won't find the likes of anywhere else."

"The last thing I am is worried," I answer, taking a step toward Max like he needs convincing of my intent. "Do you have a card or anything? I'd really love to talk to you some more about the business, if you have the time."

"Phel?" Nate looks utterly baffled now. "I thought you wanted to buy a surfboard?"

Max and I both ignore him. "I don't know you from Adam, son," he points out. "Part of the reason I've only got one employee is that I keep to myself, and he's hard enough to keep quiet as it is. Done well enough on my own all these years, though we've had our fair share of potential investors come knockin'."

Plastering on my most winning smile—Nate once said it was such a disturbing sight, I could probably lure the Pope into bed with it before he knew what happened—I extend my hand with the invitation to shake. "But you're thinking of selling," I remind him cheerfully, "and I don't know you either. Sounds like a friendly beer might solve that problem, if you're willing. I'm just curious to know more; no harm intended."

"Make it a whiskey, and we'll talk." Though he accepts my hand in a wary shake, Max shifts his attention back to Nate. "This guy for real?" he asks. His voice is only half-joking.

Face solemn, Nate continues to stare at me with an expression that suggests he just realized I'm from another planet. Considering that's how I feel around him most days, I'm surprised it's taken so long. "I have no idea," he says seriously. "But you better do as he says."

LESS than two hours later, we're back sitting in the living room of Hugh's house, Nate holding a bundle of ice wrapped in a towel against the bruises on my back and shoulders that are probably lost causes by now.

The television plays in the background, a football game to which neither of us is paying much attention. Having yelled at us upon our return to shut the fuck up and leave him alone, Hugh is still hard at work in his study, leaving Nate and I to our own devices for dinner, as well as our entertainment for the evening. Well fed on barbequed cowboy steaks and free from his brother's curious gaze, Nate sits much closer than he would otherwise. His body accommodates mine like it's second nature, but he looks nervous for reasons I can only assume have to do with his wariness of Hugh walking in on us and my own tendency to snap if Nate gets too familiar.

I must admit I brace for it too, expecting my stomach to lurch unpleasantly at Nate's proximity under nonsexual circumstances—circumstances that resemble our old intimacy entirely too much to be good. My body aches all over, though, and I find myself too exhausted to put up a fight, even when Nate's legs shift to bracket my hips on either side and he encourages me to lie back against him and into the ice wedged between our bodies. Part of me admires him for putting up with my snippiness with such saintly patience—astounding enough for someone with a quick temper—and recognizing I'm on edge with discomfort that extends to the mental as well as physical. At one point I opened my mouth to tell him to fuck off and play nursemaid to someone else, but Nate cut me off at the pass with a gentle "Please."

Apparently there are some things even I can't fight against, but for the first time in a couple of weeks, I find myself wishing for a Xanax to wash the rest of my uncertainties away and numb me the hell out.

"What was all that back at the beach, at Max's shop?" Nate finally asks. I'm impressed by his restraint for not having asked about it until now. "You thinkin' of buyin' into the business or something?"

Or something; my own thoughts on the matter are still far from clear, just a jumble of ideas and inspiration I haven't felt for a while. But there's definitely a spark of interest I can't deny, smacks of the same drive that had me off investing in property and obscure stock options from a young age—the very things that have more or less kept me afloat since being cut off from my family. It might not be much compared to what I was once promised, the decimal point having moved some, but selling off my real estate in Ohio and Chicago, not to mention some of my shares, has padded my bank account nicely enough. I'll never have to work again, if I play my cards right. Deep down, I know one of those cards is Hugh's offer to move in, the sheer generosity of the suggestion appealing to my good sense as well as my affection for my friend. Without quite meaning to, I've started looking at his home a bit differently, weighing the ways in which it's already felt like my own for months.

Where Nate fits into the picture, I don't know. I remind myself he's probably headed back to Ohio in good time.

I'm silent for a little while, considering Nate's question and how much I want to answer. To my surprise, it comes much easier than I expect. "Something about that shop appealed to me," I tell him quietly. "It just felt so home-grown and authentic in there, you know? And I was really impressed by how highly regarded they are around here; I'm sure if I asked around some more, most of the locals would say the same thing. Obviously Logan and Max do quality work."

I feel Nate nod. I also feel what could be fingertips skimming my bare shoulder, and I shrug it off as imagination, knowing Nate is too smart to start getting overly familiar when I'm in a snit.

"The whole thing is probably crazy, but I saw that place and thought, 'Hey, maybe this is something I could invest in.'"

Hesitating more now, I add, "It's pretty stupid. I haven't even gotten myself back on my feet yet, and I'm already starting to think about what it'd be like to set up shop here for good and just... rebuild. Start over. I do like California, and surfing feels so... me."

"That doesn't sound stupid," Nate answers, voice low. "You've got a good head for business, better than almost anyone. I've seen that brain of yours in action, man; almost puts Hugh's massive gray matter to shame."

"Well, that's a relief," I answer sarcastically. "Good thing I've got some good business sense, since I obviously don't have much for anything else."

Nate shoves at me lightly. "Don't be retarded, Phel. You make good choices."

Christ, when was the last time he said that to me? I wish I could say I didn't remember, but that'd be a lie. It was at a baseball game we went to with Liam late last spring, the Rangers against the White Sox. Such a big deal on multiple counts—not the first time I'd met Nate's son, not by then, but certainly the first trip the three of us took together, a special treat courtesy of my company's box seats in Chicago.

I'd never seen a little kid so happy in my whole life, his face split in half by a grin that didn't budge from the second I greeted them at the airport. His father was practically over the moon too. I wasn't doing so bad that weekend either, considering the rare treat of having Nate in Chicago and the son who was gradually becoming a part of my life. Although I'd never been one for kids, I had to admit I was crazy about Liam, who was, like Nate, as smart and cocky and funny and generous as anyone I'd ever met. Weirder still, he seemed to like me, even if it sometimes meant I had to withstand being teased about the stick up my ass by father and son at the same time. I didn't mind in the least, and I... I admit I started to dream big.

As far as I can tell, the misunderstanding started when Nate took my hand during the game, right there with Liam between us, snacking on popcorn and having the time of his life as he cheered on his team. Granted, our entwined fingers stayed hidden behind Liam's back where he couldn't see, but I think I somehow assumed it meant everything was okay, that Liam's being here and his father's openness with me were signs that he *knew*. Obviously that wasn't the case, as I quickly learned when Liam went to call the score in to his mother between innings, and I leaned over to give Nate a kiss.

He jerked away like I'd spat in his face. "What the hell are you doing?" he hissed, putting so much space between us so quickly that I was surprised he didn't jump out of our private box altogether. "Liam's right there!"

Something lodged painfully in my throat. It took a few moments for me to answer. "I'm sorry," I stammered, and backed away with my hands up. "I thought... I thought you'd told him. About us."

Nate was watching his son with alarm written clear as day across his features, staring so hard he might have willed the kid to turn around and start hurling accusations our way. With his back to us, on the phone, Liam was completely oblivious to our exchange and to the fact that I'd tried to kiss Nate, but Nate seemed equally oblivious to Liam's ignorance. "Jesus Christ, Phel," he said, voice like gravel. "Of course he doesn't know. He's nine fucking years old. Don't be retarded."

I think Nate knew the gravity of what he said the moment the words left his mouth; he started backpedaling immediately, apologizing so many times I eventually had to ask him to stop. "I think I'm done with this conversation," I told him quietly. "Let's just finish watching the game."

"We can talk about this after Liam's gone to sleep," Nate suggested raggedly, whispering. "I'm sorry, baby, you know I didn't mean that. You just—I freaked out, okay."

"Shut up about it," I snapped, then sat back down in my seat to indicate my refusal to listen to any more. "And don't call me 'baby' like it changes anything. You made your point."

The fight that ensued didn't actually happen until several days later—Liam's presence prevented it, and when the weekend was over and we flew back to Ohio, Nate took him home after giving me a hug and a promise to call that I didn't acknowledge or return. He made a special trip back out to Columbus to see me the next day, though, and that I knew he was sorry didn't make me feel much better about anything. Nor did it change the few harsh realizations I'd made since seeing Nate and Liam off.

I tried not to be too hard on myself about it, or so I kept telling myself—my space, after all, had become shared space with Nate, as he'd been staying with me in Columbus for so long that his presence was visible everywhere in the apartment. His clothes were in my dressers, his beer in my fridge, his life *my* life. Little things that made me happy every time I was reminded of Nate's place in my world, his place in my heart. Corny, I know, but I was at the point I'd started considering making a space for Liam, an adjustment I'd never anticipated but was willing to make for Nate.

When Nate came to visit after the Chicago trip, I told him as much. Not because I wanted to make him feel guiltier, but because I thought it necessary for him to know. "I put my place up for sale in Chicago," I told him once the silence across the dinner table that night became too much to bear. "I'm never there anymore, and I have three bedrooms here: I was going to start living here permanently. Maybe even buy a house."

"But you fucking love Chicago," Nate said, puzzled. "Why move?"

"Because I fucking love you more," I snapped. We both fell silent for a moment. After taking a deep breath to collect myself, I continued, "I wanted—want—you to move in with me. And Liam. I was going to ask you to move in." The expression that crumbled over Nate's face almost shattered my own resolve not to cry. Aside from a slight quiver of my lip, I think I managed.

"You *were going* to ask me," he repeated.

Without meaning to, I barked a laugh that sounded twisted even to my ears. "Obviously the answer's no, isn't it?"

Nate made a face. "The answer isn't *no*, Phel," he forced out. "Jesus Christ—it's 'I can't.'" Apparently feeling useless unless he was touching me, Nate pushed back his chair with a loud screech across the tile and came around to my side of the table. He dropped to one knee in front of me, taking my hands. Pleading with me with his whole body and the scared set of his eyes. Perversely, it looked like he was about to propose marriage. "Liam doesn't know about all this—and even if he did, I wouldn't be able to disrupt his whole life and move him somewhere else, move him away from his mom. No way is he ready for that, and neither am I. But it doesn't mean I wouldn't, in a heartbeat, if things were different. You know that, right?"

I wrenched my hands away. "Yeah, Nate, I know." Unable to look at his face any longer, I pushed myself up from my own chair and grabbed my plate, still bearing the dinner I'd hardly touched. "But let me ask you something," I began, going over to the kitchen island to clatter my dishes down into the sink. "We've been together for a year. I would marry you tomorrow if I could, and yet you won't even tell your son what I am to you. You won't come out to your family, and you won't move in with me. So when the fuck are things ever going to be different? If not now, *when*? You gonna tell Liam the truth and sign a joint lease with me from your goddamn deathbed in sixty years?"

Nate's arms folded across his chest, a sure sign all hope for a civil discussion had just flown out the window. But I didn't care. I didn't think "civil" was a word I even knew right then. "Don't give me the guilt trip bullshit, Phel," he growled. "I'm here, and I'm with you. I'm sorry things aren't moving along according to your personal schedule, but I got a son I have to think about too."

"Oh, are things actually going somewhere?" I asked with incredulity. I hated to voice that fear out loud, but the thought had stuck in my head sometime over the weekend, and I hadn't been able to unstick it. "From where I'm standing, it doesn't look like this fucking relationship is moving anywhere at the moment. We're in almost the exact same spot we were that first night we came back here to fuck, except then I still thought I'd have my common sense left in the morning—not some terrified asshole who's afraid to be seen with his faggot boyfriend within fifty yards of his 'real' family." I gave another sharp laugh, watching Nate's face darken with each word that left my mouth. Fuck him. "What's the problem, Nate? Are you still in love with that ex-wife of yours? Scared I might ruin your chances if she sees us together?"

I think I expected Nate to pick up the nearest plate and smash it, or maybe throw a punch at my head. That's not what happened. Instead he left the room and came back carrying his jacket, motorcycle keys in hand. I stared at them mutely and then up at his face, unsure what to say because I knew it would sound like a challenge for him to leave. But I also couldn't say I didn't want him to, the words catching on my tongue like lead.

In the end, my silence probably pushed him halfway out the door as much as another cruel taunt would have. Nate walked to the exit and wouldn't look at me at first. He fiddled with his keys, twisting them over and over in his hands. "Tell you what, Phel," he said, and I knew from the tears in his voice this was going to hurt. "I'll come out to my kid when you come out to your father, okay? You criticize my priorities, but from where I'm standing? The only reason you haven't done it already is because you're more attached to your trust fund than anything else. Whatever you say, you'd rather he give you a pat on the head for a lie than be true to yourself, when that's something I wish for every day."

From his key ring came the key to my home, which he flung at me across the floor. His eyes flickered up to meet mine for a second, and then he was gone. The door slammed after him.

Once I'd roused myself enough to throw the deadbolt behind him, I picked up Nate's key from the tile, I thought it was the last time I'd ever see him. I maybe even prayed for it a little.

But here we are, nearly two years after we first met. Nate telling me I make good choices when his very presence is irrefutable proof I absolutely *don't*. He makes me, to use his word, retarded, a fact over which I always end up hating myself, no matter my best intentions. Right now I can't seem to decide whether I feel more wretched for being able to look at him at all, or that I for a moment chose to share with him something of my private hopes for my future. *Stupid Phelan.*

That future doesn't exist, not with Nate in it. Can't stay with him here, can't ask him to go—Hugh will never give him up for you.

This conversation is over, and he doesn't even know it yet. It shocks me, really, how easily the words to push him away come to me.

"I've been wondering about something lately," I begin, and I lean back a little into Nate's loose embrace, the one he's trying to pretend isn't happening on purpose.

Predictably, he rests a hand against my forearm to indicate he's listening, gives a gentle squeeze. "Yeah?" I can actually hear the hope in his voice, the tightening of his groin against my lower back as he responds to the tenor of my voice like an invitation.

"Is this what it was like for you the first time around?" I ask. "It's kind of like we're carrying on an illicit affair all over again, doesn't it? There's risk, excitement.... We could get caught at any time. Did cheating on Emilia and sneaking around fill you with the same sense of exhilaration as throwing yourself at me now?"

Nate stiffens against me in an entirely different way, muscles rigid, and on my lips there's a smile that won't come, no matter how hard I try. Silence crawls over us in what feels like an endless haze, cloying, but then Nate shifts backwards into the cushions, trying to put space between us without shoving me out of his lap altogether.

"Well?"

He clears his throat. When he speaks, I can barely hear him even from a few inches away. "Lemme make something clear," he murmurs, but we both know I'm listening. I asked, after all. "Every time I cheated on Emilia was the saddest I'd ever been in my life. Much as I wanted to lose myself in how happy it made me to be around you, I never forgot what I was doing to my family without them knowing. Not a day went by that I didn't dream about coming clean to Em and ending the whole charade, but I was fucking weak."

To my horror, I try to speak, but nothing comes out; something grips my throat so hard I have to stop and wonder if it's a panic attack, here out of the blue, but I know it's not. No, this is something else, and I fight against it until I find my voice again and ruthlessly suppress Willa's words surfacing in my head. Still, it penetrates that I do not, in this moment, feel proud. "We agree on that much, at least," I force out.

"Phel." However reluctantly, I turn to look at Nate, then immediately away when I see tracks of moisture on his cheeks, wiped hastily away. "I wasn't sure whether or not I should say anything to you about it, but I'm thinking of coming clean to Hugh."

The non sequitur makes my body go cold, and I pull myself up off the couch to face him. "That's kind of petty given the circumstances, isn't it? You might think you're upset at me, but telling your brother we've been fucking on his good leather sofa isn't the right way to express your anger."

Nate shrugs, hands curling around his ankles as he pulls his knees in to his chest. His eyes glitter in the low light of the room, and I realize, too late, that the look on his face isn't the same need for blood I've found in my own reflection of late. He looks tired, which is perhaps most frightening of all. "Tired" often means "done." But the flash disappears quickly, shoved beneath the surface as Nate's mouth quirks in a sad smile that's just for me.

"I wasn't gonna tell him about us," he explains. "Just that I'm gay. It's time, and the way I figure, only fair. Liam knows, and Emilia knows—Hugh should know too. But I can see how you'd be worried it might give the rest away." He pauses. Then he suggests, "You could just tell him yourself."

"No." It would break Hugh's heart; I know this. Nate knows it. He loves his brother, but he's not volunteering to be the bearer of that information either. But it does, for the briefest of seconds, make me wonder why it would be so bad if Hugh knew, before I remember how much I actually care. The thought of Hugh ending our friendship makes my stomach twist, but that isn't what terrifies me so much.

It shouldn't surprise me that Nate's thoughts are running along similar lines. "It'd be over if he knew. All this, what we've been doing." Meeting my eyes, he asks the one thing I could stand here all night wishing he wouldn't, begging him with my silence, willing it with every fiber I possess: "Do you not want it to be over?"

Suddenly my blood is pumping fast, a sharp surge past my ears like the knee-jerk response to a hand placed on a hot element, contradictory desires striking through me to flee, to scream and lash out and *hurt*. I refuse to run, legs sore and lungs exhausted from how far I've fled already. This isn't like that time on the beach, when I was still so petrified and weak. "Fuck you," I choke out and launch myself at him. Seemingly of its own accord, a fist swings out that nearly catches him in the jaw before he grabs my hand in midair.

"Phel, what the fuck?"

As I've proven before, I'm not much of a fighter, and this time I don't have the element of surprise; Nate's body shifts to simultaneously avoid the blow and curl itself around mine, his arms and legs snaking around my limbs as he rolls me onto my back. The ice pack rattles between us and then falls to the carpet. I land with all the grace of a sack of potatoes, grunting with indignant, impotent anger despite the thrill of excitement that rushes through me. Our bodies press flush, heavy and breathing hard.

Nate feels it, too, his cheeks going scarlet, and his mouth drops open in a near gasp. "Stop it," he orders, hands tightening painfully around my wrists. "Stop fucking doing this, you're like a goddamn child—hitting me because you don't know what to say."

I fight the urge to spit at him. "I have nothing *to* say," I growl. My voice comes out breathy and choked from his weight on top of me. "I've been telling you, Nate, there's nothing left to this goddamned conversation you insist on trying to drag out. Why can't we just fuck and have it not mean anything?"

Nate's jaw clenches. "Because that's what you want, not me—even if it's like trying to put a square fucking peg in a round hole, but who am I to tell you otherwise? You obviously don't give a shit what I have to say, or if it means anything to someone other than yourself. I'm trying to make things right."

"You *can't*."

"I didn't just say for you." Hesitating, Nate lets go of my wrists and sits back a little. "I'm coming out to Hugh for *me*, because it's the right goddamn thing to do."

I reach out to grab him before he can withdraw too far and wrap my arms around his torso. "Nate, leave it alone," I beg him, disgusted by the tremor in my own voice and the fact that I'm proving him right the more I try to fight against him, answering his question with a "no" so resounding I might as well shout it out loud. I *don't* want it to be over, damn it, but neither do I want him to know how badly the thought shakes me. "Just leave it alone. Fuck me and stop trying to ruin it."

I snake my fingers into his hair and pull him to me. Our lips crash together as I kiss silent whatever he might have said in response, licking the denial right out of his mouth. Tumbling us over so he's once again on his back, I drag my hand down to the crotch of his jeans and squeeze at his half-hard cock, making him moan into me and reluctantly arch for more. With us it's always more and more until we're scraping the bone with nothing left to give. I flick the button fly open and work my fingers inside, grasping at skin and the first few drops of wetness from the tip of his shaft.

"Fuck me," I say again, hopefully this time. I pull away and hold his eyes as I skin out of my shorts and turn my body on the couch, laying myself out on my stomach beneath his gaze. Glancing back over my shoulder from where I've pushed up onto my elbows, I let my legs fall open in blatant invitation. I close my eyes and moan softly at the audible hitch in Nate's breath as he looks at me, then push my tongue out to lick at lips that have suddenly gone dry. "I want you to. I want it so badly."

"Phel," Nate chastises. I can hear the resistance in his tone, but he crawls toward me, crouches on his hands and knees over my legs and dips his head to nuzzle into the small of my back. It's a bit forceful—he knows what I'm trying to do, and doesn't like being manipulated. Nor does he like his own acquiescence to so obvious a play for his silence.

"Come on." I arch and shift back onto my knees, pushing my ass into him so he's forced to take my hips to avoid being shoved off-balance. The feel of his palms grabbing hot and rough against my skin makes me groan in genuine need, and I drop to my chest against the sofa, hips still thrust in the air. My actions are a bit selfishly motivated, I admit—I'm essentially trying to buy Nate's obedience and an end to this topic of conversation, but the hot flush of desire for him is never forced, never reluctant. If anything it's like a brush fire, whooshing out of control if I so much as bring a match within sparking distance, devastation just waiting to catch.

Two fingers slip down the crease between my buttocks, dragging hard over my opening—they're wet, Nate seemingly having slipped them into his mouth when I glanced away, and one presses inside me so easily we both cry out, me perhaps the more raggedly. A soft "*Oh, oh, oh*" falls from my lips as he works in and out, the second finger joining the first and making me sob when he presses into my prostate, rushes of fireworks licking through my whole body. He withdraws. Nate unfastens his jeans the rest of the way and pushes them to midthigh; I feel the brush of his erection like velvet against my exposed hole as he rocks into me, rides my crease for a second and sighs.

"Baby," he says and presses against my body until his hips are flush against my ass and I'm groaning nonsense, trying to rock into him. He keens, "Baby," again, and I'm not even coherent or sane enough anymore to reject the endearment.

"Isn't it so much better this way?" I gasp. Nate's teeth bite down on the flesh between my neck and shoulder, and I feel him shaking, tremors that match the ones in my arms. I rub my face into the smooth leather beneath my cheek. "So much better this way, Nate, when you fuck me." Echoing my thought from earlier, almost deliriously at this stage, I tell him, "Don't spoil it, please don't spoil it again."

The movement stalls, Nate's whole body going tense and still above me while I try to arch and thrust back into him, a deep whine pulling from my throat. Just when I expect him to stop teasing and fuck me deep, or think maybe he's just getting a hold of himself, Nate, impossibly, withdraws, pushing himself up and off me.

"What are you doing?" I demand. My stomach churns with unpleasantness as I roll to my side and see Nate rise from the couch on unsteady legs, pulling up his jeans. The flagging erection he tucks away with trembling fingers, wincing in discomfort, but for a moment he doesn't say anything, doesn't even look at me from the spot on the carpet he's studying so intently. "Nate! Come back here."

Green eyes drag up to meet mine, and I know that look, Nate's soft, broken little-boy face that says he might be dying on the inside, but isn't going to budge an inch.

Body still thrumming with arousal like an overwarm engine, I shiver and swing my legs underneath me, sitting up but not trusting myself to stand. Sudden pressure against the place Nate's fingers so recently vacated makes me squirm, makes me ache and want to pull him to me, my mouth already open to beg him back. How can I beg, though, when he promised to do whatever I ask? How the hell can he get up and leave when for once I am trying to give something to *him*?

With shocking coldness, I shudder at the thought that Willa's prediction is coming true, and Nate is starting to realize he's not so powerless against me after all, not even if he wants to be. He can say no; he *is* saying no.

"You're leaving," I splutter. Scooting closer, I catch his hand before he can back away. "I don't—I don't understand. I'm not the one who—you *said* you would do—"

"What, whatever it took? Yeah." Nate curls his fingers around mine briefly but ultimately withdraws, looking no happier for it. "I'm sorry, Phel. You don't even know what you're asking, but turns out I can't do *that*."

"You can't fuck me all of a sudden?"

Brow furrowed, he shakes his head. "No—hide. 'Cause when it comes down to it, that's what this is about. Hiding. I'm finally ready to come out of the closet to my brother, tell him the whole reason I left Emilia and Liam in the first place, and here you wanna drag me back in there with you because it's safe. You're fucking scared, Phel, but I don't have that problem. I'm not afraid of who the hell I am, not like you are. Not anymore."

"Hugh knows who I am," I answer, pulling back. Miraculously, I keep my voice steady despite feeling like my insides are crumbling. "He's known all along. What you and I do in private has nothing to do with him."

"Nah, he doesn't have the first clue." Nate skims his knuckles across my cheekbone in a gesture that's far gentler than his words, even though I can't find any malice in his voice. "But I don't think you do either, baby."

At this, I snap, "I told you not to call me that."

"Yeah, okay, Phel." A brief touch to my lips and then the hand is curling around the back of my neck like Nate wants to pull me up for a kiss. I can't deal with him when he's being tender like this, because I know it takes infinitely more certainty on Nate's part to show affection over anger. "I—I guess I get it. Believe me. It's not my place to drag you into this when you obviously aren't ready to admit it, which is why this ain't about you. I'd like your support, but I know I pretty much squandered it the first time I had my chance."

With a snort, I bat his hand away. "You don't think Hugh's going to put two and two together if you come out to him, Nate?" Finding my legs again is easier now, and I stand up so I can look him in the face, press in close and warm so he is sure to feel me, sure to meet my eyes when I turn his head toward me with my hands against his cheeks. "Everything you said about wanting me back? Well, don't expect there to be much chance of that if everything's out in the open. Look what happened the last time."

He smiles and leans in to kiss me, so soft I almost lean away from it in confusion, the way Nate sometimes doesn't know how to respond to my smiles. "There wasn't much chance even now, man. I knew that going in. But if you were always gonna walk away again, doing things exactly the same way as last time wouldn't change that."

With that, Nate retrieves the bag of half-melted ice from the floor and hands it back to me, pressing it into my hands like I might still sit here babying my bruises. The room feels much quieter once he leaves, even the sounds from the television going mute as I try and fail to herd my thoughts into something resembling coherence. Tomorrow—or whenever Nate decides to talk to Hugh—everything will be completely changed, and I suppose I ought to feel relief I've already begun to think about where I'll go after I leave Cardiff. Impossible to stay here now, with everything poised to shatter at a mere touch. We might as well have broken it ourselves.

The classical music from Hugh's study continues to waft toward my ears as he writes on, oblivious for now, but not much longer.

8

Hugh

NATE dropped out of high school the year I started ninth grade. Not right away, mind you, but a couple of months before he was all set to graduate, he up and quit without any warning and no explanation except to say he had no intention of ever going back.

His GED arrived in the mail not long afterward, something else he did without telling me or our dad, and after that Nate kind of changed. Maybe not in so fundamental a way that I no longer recognized him after—he was still as cocky and carefree as ever—but little things were different.

He was more protective in some ways, more guarded in others, and it was around this time the womanizing and the drinking started in earnest. Nate was a little wild, but our dad was a cop and ran a strict household; anything major would have gotten Nate kicked out, and he once said that if that happened, there'd be no one left to look after me the way I needed. So he always watched himself and never did anything so crazy that it would land him in serious hot water. Even I was old enough to recognize that the stuff he started doing after that point wasn't a danger to anyone but himself. Though he didn't know it then, it's absolutely what led to Emilia getting pregnant. Maybe everything would have gone differently if he'd never left school—it might have been a miracle that things eventually worked out, but it sure as hell wasn't chance that made things fall apart. To this day, I never understood why he left when he was so close to the finish line.

When I say "to this day," I literally mean until today. Because I think I get it now. But I'm getting ahead of myself.

About a month after Nate turned eighteen, I witnessed something that made so little sense at the time that the only logical explanation was I'd confused it for something else. Now, I know I wasn't mistaken, but I also know I wasn't meant to see what I did. I never spoke a word of it to anyone, not even Nate, which in retrospect was the smartest thing I could have done. Kids are easily confused at that age, or so I always thought, though as it turns out they're a lot more perceptive than they're given credit for—not by others, and certainly not by themselves.

There was this teacher at the school, Jay Garrett, who started teaching English at Sidney Lanier High in Montgomery, Alabama, the same year I started there. I never had him because he taught mostly the upper-year students, but I know Nate was in a couple of his classes and complained about them far less than he did some others. Mr. Garrett was young: barely twenty-five and newly certified as a teacher, with shaggy dark hair and exotic eyes Nate said came from Japanese blood on his mother's side. In retrospect, his inexperience and good looks probably should have gotten him eaten alive, but he was so easygoing and cool that he hardly got any trouble, not even from the kids like my brother who prided themselves on causing it on a regular basis. Word was, Garrett was funny and smart and had a knack for making his classes fun. Apart from the requisite number of crushes that developed almost immediately, he was well liked by everyone, faculty and student body alike. More importantly, he was well liked by Nate.

That day, I was waiting around after school for Nate to show up and drive us home. Over thirty minutes had passed without any sign of my brother. Usually he was pretty good about being punctual, or would let me know ahead of time if he had to stay behind in class for detention or to speak with a teacher. But he hadn't said anything to me that morning other than "Meet you after school." All my other friends had already gone home, picked up by their parents or the bus, and suffice to say I was getting a little impatient and cranky with hunger, the way only a fourteen-year-old can.

Nate's last class of the day was English, so I got it into my head that maybe he'd stayed behind to talk to Mr. Garrett about something. He once introduced us on a similar occasion, calling me his "brat kid brother," and the teacher seemed to like me enough; it didn't seem like a big deal to stop by the classroom to see whether Nate was there. The only other thing I could think of was maybe he was off smoking behind the auditorium or something, but in the event I was wrong, I didn't want to risk getting harassed by the older kids who also frequented the spot. Garrett's class, it was.

By then all the hallways were deserted, and all the classrooms I passed on the way were dark and had their doors closed, teachers having packed up and gone home for the day. As I rounded the corner to Mr. Garrett's room, the first thing I saw was that the light inside was on, even though the door was closed. I barely made it up onto my tiptoes—I hadn't hit puberty yet—to peer through the door's single porthole before I stopped dead, my throat closing up so abruptly I made a choked noise.

There inside the class was Nate and someone who looked a great deal like Mr. Garrett, judging by the trademark suede patches on his tweed jacket. Except instead of deep in conversation like I expected, they were pressed up against the chalkboard, my brother's shoulders, familiar in his football jacket, bent toward Mr. Garrett, who was a few inches shorter than Nate's six-foot-three-inch frame. The teacher's hands were in Nate's hair, clutching at those dark-blond strands, and even though their faces were mostly turned away from me, they were either having some kind of quiet argument or making out, or else Nate had turned into a vampire. I could see the pale strip of skin on Mr. Garrett's side where Nate's hands had bunched up his jacket and shirt, the shiny flash of tongue between their mouths, an image I later did a damn good job of forgetting.

After that, I didn't stick around; I ran home, although I paused for a while in the park to talk myself out of whatever I thought I saw. Due to my tarrying, I turned up late for dinner, to furious reprimands from both my father and Nate, who had arrived not long before me. Apologizing for a quickly invented homework study session at a friend's house, I begged off from the rest of dinner with the excuse that I had a project to finish. Smartly, or so I thought, I tried to put that afternoon as far from my mind as possible. Even though I desperately wanted to figure out why the hell someone like my brother would be kissing another dude—Nate was popular with the senior girls and never without a Saturday-night date—it seemed easier and ultimately wiser to forget I was ever there.

For a while, I managed okay, even when Nate started having to stay behind after his English class most afternoons, during which time I did my homework in the empty cafeteria until he was done. I successfully ignored the few whispered phone conversations I heard late at night, convinced Nate was talking to one of his girlfriends even in the absence of his typical endearments of "baby" and "sweetheart" to whoever was on the other end of the line. I pretended the gray sedan that sometimes dropped him off after midnight—always when our dad was on duty, of course—belonged to a buddy from school. Much as I was able, I forgot anything out of the ordinary had ever happened. I even started to believe I had truly misunderstood what I'd seen that day.

That is, until a few weeks later, when a special news story came on while I was eating dinner with Nate and my father. We always left the TV tuned to the news during meals, which my dad said was the one time of the day he actually had a chance to catch up with the outside world. In a place like Montgomery, most of the news was comprised of human-interest stories or reports from Birmingham, but that night they interrupted the regular broadcast to update us on a scandal that had broken out right here in town.

Two men had been arrested for sodomy and acts of public indecency in Hayneville Road Park, one of them a local high school teacher. The news anchor made it seem like this one occurrence made Hayneville Road Park a "hotbed of homosexual activity" in Montgomery, and explained that, while men elsewhere were regularly arrested for engaging in sex or soliciting undercover cops, the involvement of a local teacher made this breaking news. The accused was none other than Mr. Garrett, who was described as "young, likeable, and popular with many of the local students, and assistant coach of the boys' basketball team," as though these things had any bearing upon what he was currently being held for at the local jail.

"Oh my God, Nate, that's Mr. Garrett!" I said stupidly, but neither my father nor my brother responded. Back then, I was still too young to fully understand what the big deal was, but I'd heard about Proust and knew what sodomy was. Even though the law's interpretation of the crime was fairly broad in those days, I also knew that, in God-fearing Alabama, it meant nothing good. For the first time in weeks, my stomach sank as I realized what I'd seen that day between Nate and Mr. Garrett implied Nate had a pretty clear understanding of the word as well. Thankfully he'd been home last night.

Casting a glance at Nate from the corner of my eye, I saw he'd gone white as a sheet, knife and fork gripped so tightly in his hands that his knuckles were completely bloodless. All three of us watched the broadcast in silence until the anchor moved on to the next story, and for a few minutes, no one said anything until my dad got up and turned off the TV. It was obvious he hadn't heard the news until now, the arrest most likely having taken place while he was off duty. Our dad was a big man, gruff and stern on a good day, but as he glanced over and his hazel eyes met mine, it was the first time he actually made me nervous.

Although he returned to the table, he didn't pick up his utensils right away, staring hard at Nate while my brother refused to look at him. Then Dad asked, "He's one of your teachers, isn't he? Garrett? I recognize him from parent-teacher interviews."

"He teaches English," I supplied, only realizing my mistake when Nate jerked up from the table with his plate in his hands and went to dump it in the sink.

"I'd like to be excused," he said gruffly. "I got homework."

"Nathaniel." The sharp bark of his name from Dad's mouth made both of us go still as statues, Nate already on his way out of the kitchen, me with my fork halfway to my mouth. "Sit your ass back down, boy."

Because our dad wasn't the kind of person you disobeyed when he spoke in a tone like that, not without a death wish, Nate's expression darkened, but he did as he was told. I noticed he was sitting on the edge of his chair like he needed to be ready to bolt again at any second. It was weird, seeing Nate so discomfited and nervous, but a part of me was obscenely curious to find out how things were going to unfold. To be honest, I had no idea.

Watching Nate's face the way I always imagined he looked at criminals from across the interrogation room, our dad the cop leaned forward and his voice got really soft. "Son, I hate to ask this, but you gotta tell me the truth. That teacher ever try anything funny with you, or any of the other boys in your class?"

Nate's palms slammed the tabletop so sharply that I jumped. Dad didn't bat an eye as Nate shouted, "For fuck's sake, Dad!"

"You watch your language," he warned. "I asked you a question and I'd appreciate an answer. This is important."

"How the *fuck* is it important?" raged Nate. To my eternal surprise, I saw my brother's face was red, fresh tears making his eyes glossy and wild. I knew if he let them fall, it would open up a whole other round of questions from our father, but Nate composed himself after a second. Though he trembled, the tears didn't budge. "He's a good teacher—a good guy—and it's bullshit he got arrested for something like this. Who the fuck cares who he screws so long as he ain't hurting anyone? Hell, it's not like he's the only fag in Montgomery."

"It's important, Nate, because I care whether or not that pervert's been pulling shit with my kids!" With a screech of his chair, Dad pushed himself up from the table and pointed furiously at the now silent television, the voices from which still echoed through our small kitchen like a ghostly whisper. Breathing hard, Dad let that same pointer finger jab at the surface of the table with a hard *thud* to punctuate each word. "*I* care, since it turns my goddamned stomach to think that faggot was allowed within twenty feet of my boys!"

I watched Nate, whose arms were now folded, visibly try to get himself back under control, to not respond to our father's words. They didn't make much sense to me either, because it's not like unmarried women teachers routinely go throwing themselves at teenage boys, but this was obviously something our dad cared about a great deal, and it's possible there was something I had missed. What it was, I didn't know, because despite what I'd seen that day, Nate was technically an adult, and far from helpless. I'd seen him kick the shit out of someone twice his size in a scuffle, and he was the one player the other teams knew to avoid on the football field.

"He's a good guy," Nate said again. "I like him a lot, and he isn't a pervert. Not like you're saying, and not just because he got caught fucking—"

"Nate." I saw Dad's eyes flicker over to me, unspoken caution to watch what he said in my presence, and Nate capitulated with a huff. Gentling his voice, Dad said, "What he does in private is his own business, you're right, but if that's the kind of lifestyle he wants to lead, then he should be out in California with all the other queers. Those faggots got no right showing their face in a school. Teaching *basketball*, for crissakes, where they're around young boys in a locker room. Where boys go lookin' to him for advice and guidance." His expression went tragic, and Nate swallowed in response. "Would you be sticking up for the man if he'd been coaching your little brother, huh? If he was watching Hugh here change into his uniform each day after school?"

"Jesus, Dad," Nate cried, eyes rolling. At the same time I protested, "But I'm too short for basketball!"

Nate shot me a look that meant, *Hugh, shut the fuck up and stay out of this.* "They didn't say he got caught with a little kid!"

Dad shrugged. "In my experience, there ain't much separating a man who'll lay down with another man, and one who'll lay down with a young boy. Mark my words, it'd only be a matter of time before this teacher was coming on to his students, or better yet confusing someone young and impressionable about what's right and what's decent in these parts." Reaching across the table to cover Nate's hand, which was quickly snatched away, Dad sighed. "I'm just trying to look out for you kids," he said unhappily, seeming genuinely saddened that Nate couldn't see it. "You don't know half of what's out there, the stuff I've seen."

Nate laughed. "Last time I checked, I'm an adult," he retorted. "Don't need you looking out for me anymore. But it's good to know what kind of a household you've got going here. Real inclusive. Real open-minded."

Eyebrows lifted, my dad rocked back like Nate had just hit him, expression going from surprised to inscrutable. "What in the hell is that supposed to mean, son?" At Nate's silence, he said, "Are you sayin' that—"

"No." The conversation had become a mystery to me; I no longer had any idea what either of them was talking about, except that Nate looked miserable and my dad looked afraid. "All I'm sayin' is it's a good thing, because I'd seriously hate to see what kind of response I'd get if I ever came out with something like that. Or even Hugh."

"What the hell are you guys talking about?" I asked, voice shrill with confusion.

Typically, Nate ignored me, lost in the staring contest currently going down between him and our dad. Amazingly, it was Nate who lost, his gaze skittering away to somewhere in the middle distance when Dad sat back down in his chair. What followed was a pregnant pause if there ever was one, though I couldn't for the life of me figure out what would result.

Then, from my father: "I'll tell you one thing, if I ever catch wind of either one of you boys carryin' on like that queer, you best not come home. Do I make that much clear?"

I wanted to say, *What?* but decided it was better to stay quiet. Some hidden meaning was playing out between Nate and Dad I wasn't yet equipped to interpret. Nate clearly understood, however, since he got up from the table again without waiting for permission to do so.

"Sure thing, Dad," he spat, and gave the kind of mock salute which our father, as a Nam veteran, couldn't help but find offensive. "You don't ever have to worry about finding one of your boys eating dick."

Considering it was a promise made out of spite, it's ironic, in a way, that Nate never broke it. I don't think our dad was ever too impressed by his womanizing ways, and Nate certainly got an earful when the news broke that he had a son, but Dad loved Liam like crazy and, true to Nate's word, there was never another discussion about sexual orientation in the Fessenden household. Although Mr. Garrett went to jail and was eventually released, he was mostly forgotten about in the excitement of Nate dropping out of school. Despite my suspicions about why he did it, I mostly put it out of my mind in favor of concentrating on my own future and, to be honest, forgetting a secret from Nate's past I never really understood or wanted to know in the first place.

Not, like I said, until now.

I knew something was up the second Nate asked to talk to me in the kitchen bright and early on a Saturday. Because Nate at times still resembles an overgrown twelve-year-old, Saturday mornings, for him, are always reserved for cereal and cartoons in the living room; instead I found him at the table and fully dressed in jeans and a T-shirt when I wandered downstairs in my pajamas. A cup of coffee sat cupped between his hands, which after a second I noticed was no longer steaming, a sign it had probably not been touched in a while.

"Morning," I said, pausing in the doorway to cast a wary eye over what looked suspiciously like a setup. A paranoid conclusion to jump to, perhaps, except that I'd encountered this very tableau when Nate staged his intervention to pack me off to rehab. "What are you doing dressed? You got somewhere to be?"

Nate smiled, a grim sight if there ever was one, and nudged a chair away from the table with his foot. I saw he was also wearing his boots. "Maybe. Have a seat, Hugh, there's something I gotta talk to you about."

I did, and that's when my brother told me, in surprisingly few words, that he was gay. For the first time in over a decade, I thought about Mr. Garrett and what I'd been so determined to deny having seen between them in that classroom. How I let it fade from memory because the alternative scared me too much and made me question everything I knew about my world.

Very little time has passed since Nate opened his mouth to say, "Hugh, I'm queer," and, when I failed to respond, "I left Emilia because I'm in love with a dude." I still haven't said anything, caught between not knowing where the fuck to begin and thinking I haven't seen a look this beatific and calm on Nate's face since the day he met Liam and said, *I'm a dad.*

Suddenly I wish I had a coffee or a beer or—hell—a bottle of Jack in my hands so I'd feel less like a big speechless, useless lump. Nate is still looking at me expectantly, expression growing a little worried now, as the seconds tick by and I try and try and try to come up with something better than "Um."

"Hugh?" Nate's eyebrows shoot up and he leans back in his chair, nervousness bleeding into a quirked smile that, to a brother's eye, is as powerful as a look of complete terror. That's the smile Nate gives when he's so worried about something that he can't even let himself see it, let alone anyone else. Not surprisingly, it doesn't reach his eyes, which are bleak and creased with pain. "C'mon, man, you're killin' me here," he pleads. "Say something."

There is a note of such pleading in Nate's voice that it actually makes me afraid. Of what, I don't know, but the knot that springs up in my stomach makes me bypass every last outpost of reason and spring right into fight-or-flight territory, sweat breaking out on my palms and lower back like he told me I've got five minutes left to live. "You're gay," I repeat.

My throat feels like it's closed up. Instead of feeling knotted, my stomach has suddenly transformed into what feels like a birdcage with some wild thing beating itself against the bars inside, fighting to get out with everything it's got. There's no surprise television crew, no twinkle in Nate's eye or cocky smile to let me know he's had me going, gullible Hugh to the very end. All I've got is my brother sitting in front of me with a look that's somewhere between terrified and utterly fucking serene.

"Okay," I choke out. "I'm here. I'm listening."

"So it's like I said," he tells me. "I'm gay. I won't pretend that isn't outta left field for you, because as much as I'd love to be glib about it, I know what you're saying is true. The whole ladies' man thing is something I worked pretty hard to establish for a long time, right up until I met Emilia. And it's not like I mind women, 'cause I don't. I like 'em okay. But that's not...." He sighs, glancing away briefly. "That's not who I am. I don't want to be involved with a woman, and I've pretty much known it forever, so it's about time I started owning up to the fact and not hiding it from everyone. Especially you."

Considering my brain has started doing this thing where it only picks up maybe one word out of every three to come out of Nate's mouth, I'm pretty proud to have followed along with at least half of that. "So you're bi," I clarify, for some reason seizing upon the part where Nate said he still likes women. Call it petty, but it's like I need to start there, start with something familiar. The rest of that speech could have been delivered entirely in Swahili for all it resonated.

Nate shakes his head. "No, man, that's not what I'm saying."

"But—"

"I'm *gay*." Nate leans on this extra hard, like he's figured out my brain is only running at half speed right now. "I know it'd be a helluva lot easier if I agreed with you, said something about how I'll never get tired of tits, but—that's not what I'm saying. Women don't turn me off, but to me they're like forcing myself to eat salad when what I really want is a burger." There's a flash of something in Nate's face, a twitch of his lips. "Or a hot dog."

"Oh God," I groan, appalled in equal parts by the untimely humor and the inappropriateness of the image, in about a million ways.

"Too soon? Sorry."

I shake my head. Starting to feel a bit trapped even in the airy white brightness of my kitchen, I push away from the table and stand up, needing to pace. "Nate, this is...." I trail off helplessly. "I don't even know what to make of this, man. This is like...."

From the corner of my eye, I catch an oddly bittersweet smile from his lips. "I know, Hugh. It's like I just told you Santa Claus isn't real. Liam more or less responded the same way when I told him, except I used a lot more baseball analogies there. But... I get it. You won't catch me pretending like this is easy for anyone."

At the mention of Liam's name, I turn to face my brother, wondering if he's even conscious of the whole other layer he opened up in this conversation. "Wait, you told *Liam?*"

Nate lifts one shoulder. "Yeah. A couple weeks ago. I knew he'd be having a hard time with me bein' out here and all, and I figured I owed the kid a full explanation since his mom didn't exactly give him the whole story." Chewing the inside of his cheek, Nate stares down at his hands for a couple of minutes, then wipes at his eyes before looking back up to me. "I don't know what he makes of the whole thing. He said he understands, but... I could tell he was confused, and I haven't been able to talk to him about it since then either. I think he's scared."

No shit, I want to say, but for one thing, that wouldn't be helpful, and for another, the tears beading at the corners of Nate's eyes tell me he knows perfectly well this isn't a picnic for anyone. "So Emilia knows too, then?"

"Of course she knows, Hugh," says Nate. I see his throat constrict and the rough swallow that immediately follows. I know from Nate's voice gone thick this won't be good. "She's the one who found me out. Caught me in the middle of the fucking act. Obviously it was pretty clear where my interests lay after that, but I came out and told her point-blank before I left Ohio too. When I told her we needed a divorce once and for all, I said there was no changing the fact I had no business being married to a woman, ever. That it was my own fault for not accepting it sooner."

"Holy fuck, Nate." I sit back down heavily, rocking both the chair and the table with the force of my weight collapsing into the seat. "So this whole time you've been saying you had an affair with a woman, when—"

"There was no woman." Somehow I manage to lift my eyes to find Nate staring back at me. "I'm so sorry, Hugh," he says. "Lying to you hurt most of all, but I just... I didn't know how to say it."

"Mr. Garrett," I say dumbly, then smooth my hair back from my face. I can feel my damn forehead sweating now too. "You've known since Mr. Garret, back in high school."

Nate huffs. "There's a name I ain't heard in a while." A brief silence descends as we both ponder that. "How the hell did you know about Mr. Garrett? I never—"

"I saw you." He obviously needs more from me than that, and I add, "One day when you were late picking me up after school, I went to his classroom to find you since I knew you sometimes stayed late for homework help, or for—" Here, my voice breaks. "I saw you. I think you were kissing, but ever since then I just... I just told myself I never saw what I saw. That it couldn't possibly have been right." Nate is still staring at me with his eyes focused and hard with this revelation. "You knew since then," I say again.

"I probably knew since a while before then," Nate corrects. "Not much happened before he—you know. But he was the first person who really made it stop being easy to pretend I didn't want what I did. He was—he was a good man. Didn't push me into anything. Actually, I'm kinda the one who pushed him. No way he deserved to go to jail for some fucking blowjob in the park."

"You got scared after that," I supply. The pieces are starting to come together so quickly now, it's like I'd already put half the puzzle together years ago but chose instead to bury it in the attic and forgot about it when the jigsaw got too difficult or confusing. When I realized the picture was a lot more frightening than the one I'd anticipated. "That's why you dropped out, isn't it? Why you started up with that stupid Casanova shit?"

"Pretty much." Although I didn't realize my vision had gone out of focus with the force of my memories—which now feel like discoveries all over again—the image of Nate crying at the other end of the table makes the present come back to me with a clarity that's pretty dizzying. "I didn't want to end up like him, Hugh. I thought about what you or Dad would do if I ever got caught like Jay did, went to jail because of something I couldn't fix about myself. It seemed easier to try and change it, or at least make it so that no one would ever question otherwise."

"You've been lying to me for twelve fucking years," I whisper. "Longer, even. I'm your goddamned brother, and this whole time—" Nate cuts me off with something that sounds like *don't start that*, but I ignore him and force the rest out like a bitter pill coming up instead of going down, and each word emerges progressively louder until I'm all but shouting. I know I'm being unfair, I know it. But for a second I'm seven years old again, a kid whose only brother is all the family he's got, and is terrified of losing that too. "This whole damn time I haven't had the first clue who you even *are*. Like I don't fucking know you at all."

Whatever Nate could possibly say in response is cut off by Callie rushing up from under the table—somehow I managed not to notice her under there this whole time—and running to the front door with her tail going a mile a minute. Sitting with his back to the door, Nate turns to look in that direction, too, since apparently neither one of us heard it close. A second later, Phel is standing in the kitchen doorway with sleepless rings dark as bruises beneath his eyes. Aside from that, he looks nice today, like he took extra care in dressing himself in a neat waistcoat buttoned over a crisp striped shirt and dark jeans. Planning went into that outfit, and I think about how Nate was already fully dressed when I came down this morning too, none of it accidental.

Phel looks at Nate for a long second before his gaze flicks over to me. Whatever tension is floating around in this room must be strong enough that he feels it, since he doesn't even say hello.

"Phel," I say instead, voice like gravel. "This isn't a good time, man, sorry. Nate and I are kind of in the—"

"I already told him," Nate interrupts, the startling iciness in his voice directed not at me, but at Phel. He has to tilt his head back a little to look up at Phelan's face, but it doesn't diminish the authority in his posture. I realize, with a jolt, that Phel is getting *told*. "If that's why you showed up here, then Hugh's right—you might as well just go back home, because it's already done. Nothing you can say to change that now." That Phel registers the words with hardly more than a blink makes my eyebrows climb my forehead all over again; I may have a hard time coaxing them back down to their normal place if there are any more surprises this morning.

Nodding, Phelan lets that—whatever *that* is—sink in before he casts a ponderous look down at his feet, which are scuffing at the kitchen tile like he's an embarrassed teenager. "That's not why I came," he says eventually, to Nate.

Nate's jaw clenches. "Then what?"

"I thought you could use a little moral support." Phel hesitates, which is a lot reminiscent of how he was when I first met him, but startling all the same because I feel like it's been weeks since I've seen that guy. He seems to be winding up to something really big, though after the bombshells that have been dropped so far in this kitchen, I haven't a clue what the hell that could be. "I realized something important last night," he begins, "that, a year ago, I never would have condoned the idea of forcing someone to hide who they are because of what another person might think. Considering I've had to hide my sexuality for most of my life, I know firsthand how awful that feeling is." As I look between him and Nate, I can see their gazes are locked and holding steady. "I should have never tried to stop you from speaking up, Nate, on account of how Hugh might react. That was wrong of me, and I apologize. You're not the coward I thought you were." Awkwardly, he reaches out to pat Nate on the shoulder. "I suppose that dubious honor belongs to me."

In a weird turn of events, at least for me, Nate's hand comes up to cover the one Phelan has resting on his shoulder. Though Nate doesn't say anything, the expression that flits over his features is one of relief, then gratitude. They both withdraw their hands after a moment, still silent, but I don't miss the way Nate catches Phel's wrist when it falls to his side, fingers encircling that slender joint and resting there, a little more manly than holding hands, I suppose, but with a similar effect. Phel glances down at it, too, as a slow blush spreads across his cheeks. There are probably a million different explanations for this little display, and I can't figure out a single one of them.

"Thanks," Nate says eventually, voice leagues softer than when Phel first wandered into the kitchen, but also rough, like he's about to start crying again. Nate is an emotional man, a fact I know in theory but right now still manages to catch me off guard, but the one person it doesn't seem to affect is Phel, who looks at Nate like he knew exactly what his presence here would do to my brother. I file that away under "More Shit I Don't Understand." Offering a faint smile, Nate murmurs, "Coming from you, that means pretty much the most ever."

"It shouldn't."

"Yeah, well." Nate gives an offhand shrug. "I ain't too bright. But I do know the fact you're here proves you aren't a coward either."

I can tell Nate and Phel could go on staring at each other for a while longer, playing out one of those interminable, silent conversations of theirs that is starting to make a hell of a lot more sense right now. So before that can happen, I catch myself spluttering something along the lines of "Whoa, whoa, whoa," spreading my hands out like the presses need to come to a stop right the fuck now. Not unlike before Phel walked in, stuff is beginning to click into place so quickly that it agitates me. If this were a movie, I'd have missed the pivotal scene because the subtitles were moving too fast for me to read. "You seriously mean to tell me *everyone* knew about this before me? I'm the last schmuck on your list of people to call?"

Looking away from Phel, Nate gives me a complicated look and swallows, which is pretty much a yes. "I came out to California to tell you," he says. "You were supposed to be the *first*, after Emilia. But some overwhelming stuff was going on. I... lost my nerve." Even though it's partially hidden by the table, I know Nate's grip just tightened on Phel's wrist. "I'm telling you now, Hugh."

"I'm your fucking *brother*," I remind him needlessly. My voice is too loud, but I can't get it under control even when I see Callie's little face take on that wide-eyed look common to dogs and children who aren't sure whether they've done something wrong. Her tail goes between her legs and she glances nervously at Nate and Phel from over her shoulder, then starts dancing on her front paws like I either need to put her outside or shut the fuck up. I don't do either one. "Phel is—you've been telling me this whole time how you guys can't stand each other, but somehow you managed to spill your guts to him instead of me?"

Naturally, Nate's mouth opens to refute this statement, but to both our surprise it's Phel who speaks. "Hugh," he says quietly, but with unbreakable calm, "I know about Nate's sexuality crisis because it's something we have in common, if nothing else. I advocated *against* telling you because I thought you would take it badly, and that was a huge mistake on my part. Personal feelings aside, I should have put myself in his shoes and considered how difficult this step would be without added drama. But this isn't the issue here, and nor is who Nate did or did not tell before you. That he trusts you enough to tell you at all should be enough, so don't make this out to be about you."

A strange kind of choking noise comes from Nate, as though Phel's words have startled him and he's only just remembered it's his brother Phel is talking about. "Phel—" he starts, but Phelan just shakes his head.

"No. He either supports you or he doesn't." Phel meets my gaze, gesturing apologetically, and the look in his eyes is both conflicted and vehement. I know his stubborn streak well enough by now not to expect that to sway him away from his beliefs. "I'm sorry, Hugh, but this isn't some deal your brother's failed to follow through on, and it's not a collaborative effort. Since it's something that doesn't affect or involve your life, not really, it shouldn't even be up for discussion."

"Phel," Nate says again, gently chastising. "This isn't like your parents, okay?" He tugs on Phel's wrist, pulls him closer so his shoulder nudges up against Phelan's side.

My stomach drops when I see that, and I can't quite begin to understand why it would, or why it clenches when Nate's hand slides up Phelan's arm to the elbow and then back down, lower, so they're now actually grasping hands, albeit loosely. Nate is a tactile person: he touches and clutches at people he trusts during emotional periods, I guess to remind himself there's someone else there, and maybe now that he's gay it's perfectly normal for him to grab a dude's hand, to let his fingers catch against another's in a way that looks stark and intimate. But it's Phelan letting him that throws me off most of all.

My eyes rest on their touching hands as Nate speaks. "No one's threatening to kick me out of the house or send me off to Bible camp, okay? I don't question that Hugh will accept who I am, warts and all—it just needs time to sink in before I start marchin' in any parades in a sparkly thong. Right, Hugh?"

Still staring at their hands, my mind turns over and over and over like an engine about to catch. Nate reaches out across the table to grab my attention, nudging my shoulder once. "Hey," he says. I drag my focus back up to his face. "You accept this, don't you? My bein' gay isn't actually the issue here, right? You went to Berkeley, for crissakes."

"Nate...." One more turn, and I can feel the spark is going to catch. Sorting through months of information and vagaries ever since Phel showed up in California with a bad case of a broken heart and a duplicitous ex-boyfriend. Then Nate turned up not much later with all his secret skeletons in tow. Turning and turning, almost there.

From his end, all Nate can see is my silence and none of my thoughts. He doesn't know where I've drifted off to. "Listen, Hugh," he begins, "the order in which I told people has absolutely nothing to do with anything, except maybe it got more difficult as I went." He shakes his head, trying to meet my eyes as I stare off into space. "In one way or another, I've been wanting to tell you since I was eighteen years old, and it's because of my personal hang-ups that I didn't, not a reflection of how much I love you, or how you've been as a brother. Because you're the best there ever was, and I mean that."

I look up at Phel. When he sees me watching their hands, he frowns and withdraws.

Just like that. Ignition. It's always in the act of pulling away that we see what's really there, isn't it? "You're sleeping together," I blurt. It all makes perfect sense. The overlap in their stories is so thick it almost makes me sick to realize how much I've failed to pick up on until now. "You and Phel—"

Nate looks confused, but Phel is on the ball, his frown deepening at me as he takes a step forward. "No, Hugh," he says, grave as ever.

I think his tone clues Nate in to the sudden shift in conversation, because all of a sudden my brother is up and moving away from the table too, putting space between himself and my best friend. "Dude, what? Are you kidding me?" He sounds a lot less composed than Phel, which, right now, seems pretty damning to me.

"Where in the Midwest did you say you're from again, Phel?" I ask, trying to keep my voice steady. Getting it now, Nate curses, trying to move in before Phel catches his arm and stops him. "You said it was the Midwest, right? Like Ohio, maybe?"

"Chicago," he corrects stiffly. I catch an edge of impatience from him, but he holds himself together, even seems to keep Nate from blowing a gasket at me with that hand on his arm. "Hugh, you've had a big shock today. But just because Nate and I are both gay doesn't automatically mean—"

Unable to help myself, I snort. "No, what means something is the fact that Nate cheated on his wife with a man for a year, while you were recently duped by a married guy. Same timeline, same part of the country—what are the odds? And how come you never told me his name, Phel?"

"Because it was never your business," answers Phel at the same time Nate says, "That's called a fucking coincidence, man," like it's every day this kind of drama unfolds independently in the lives of people I happen to know.

Both Phel and I ignore him, since for some reason I feel like this conversation is between us, not between me and Nate. Maybe because Nate has already admitted to lying to me once today, I know if I try to take his word for anything right now, it might not stick. Heeding what Phel said earlier, about how his sexuality doesn't involve me, I do my best to maintain a sense of goodwill toward him. It's hard, and obviously a large part of why I'm so riled up right now, but I think even if I'd known he was queer all along, the thought of him and Phel going behind my back this whole time would still make me crazy.

Like he knows it, Phel softens a little, tries to pull back on his obvious irritation for the sake of... I don't know. Putting himself in my shoes, maybe, which Phel was always pretty good at. Never quick to anger or judge, always ready to take a breath and think something through before flying off the handle. Not like Nate; hell, not even like me, not really. Ever genteel, that's our Phel. Do I feel bad, knowing I'm testing him? Of course I do—but I also want to draw it out, see what it'll take to crumble that restraint and make him *mad*. I've never witnessed it personally, but something tells me an angry Phelan is a pretty fearsome thing to behold, wrathful in the manner of someone not used to giving his emotions free rein. "I told you when Nate came here, Hugh, that your brother's situation was reminiscent of my own," he reminds me. "That's why his presence upset me at first, because I saw the similarities of what we'd been through even from opposite ends of the spectrum. It's not because—"

I cut him off with a grunt. "What, not because you're the one he was fucking behind Emilia's back?"

At this, Nate starts forward but is once again halted by Phel's hand on his arm. When Phel first showed up here this morning, it was as Nate's bulldog, but now it starts to look like it's the other way around: Nate agitated and ready to attack his own brother, Phel pulling him back with a firm, gentle hand on the collar.

And yeah, okay, I know I'm talking in pretty crude terms here, but I get this really awful sense that isn't even the worst of it, the stuff I'm accusing them of. In my mind it all seems to click into place: why I've sensed something else going on since Nate got here; why, instead of bringing us closer, Nate's arrival made me feel shut out of both my relationship with my best friend and my relationship with my brother, as if there was something between them that didn't and would never include me—like the family I'd wanted to build with the three of us was over before it ever started. It tightens my chest to think that, an indescribable dark feeling that eats away at my insides like a cancer, a tight knot of fear I get over the thought of them leaving me alone again. Now I've latched on to it, I can't seem to let go, not even at the expense of this thin veneer of patience Phelan has scraped together for my benefit; and I can see, from the hard glint in his eye, a veneer is all it is, easily shattered.

Kind of like a house of cards, it'll only take one hard nudge to shake those flimsy foundations loose, and I'll have my answer. So I go for it. "Have you been fucking behind my back this whole time too?"

Phel drops his hand from Nate's arm, not even looking over at my brother, who's gone mysteriously silent except for the expression on his face that screams, *Who the fuck are you?* I know that look, having seen it a few times before I went to rehab, sure as I know what it means when Phel makes that pinched face like he's just been slapped and he stares at me without blinking. Part of me expects him to launch into a panic attack any second now. He's holding it together remarkably well, though the rigidity of his spine lets me know this façade of control doesn't come to him easily—he's genuinely furious and struggling to get a grip. He was almost in the clear before I went and pushed him over the edge like the caveman Nate frequently accuses me of being.

"I don't need to listen to this," Phel bites out. He brushes off his waistcoat in a clear sign he's done with this conversation—brushing *me* off, I suppose—and the hardness of his eyes is startling. I've never been on the receiving end of a look that venomous, not from Phel or anyone. It… doesn't feel great. "This bullshit, Hugh," he says, "this pettiness? It's beneath you. Be upset at yourself for failing to recognize who your brother's really been all these years, but don't take it out on me or turn it into something it's not. While you're at it, though, you can go fuck yourself."

With that, he leaves the kitchen, and a second later the front door slams, hard enough that we not only hear it, but we three who remain—me, Nate, and Callie—flinch.

Ears burning, I look toward Nate, who still hasn't said anything since Phel and I stole the floor from him. I wouldn't say his expression is outraged, exactly, but he looks as though someone kicked his dog, and then kicked him in the nuts too for good measure: pained, but also shocked. I can't begin to figure out what it means, and whether it's in response to my words or Phel's reaction or both. Somehow, though, I know enough to feel embarrassed and mortified and deeply ashamed.

"Well?" I ask him lowly. "You got any choice words for me too?"

Spreading his hands, Nate struggles to say anything for a moment, his lips eventually closing and pressing into a thin, disapproving line. Then he asks, "What the hell would be the point, man? You seem to think you've got it all figured out."

"I just want you to tell me the fucking truth!" I shoot back.

"And is that more important than letting your best friend walk out that door?" challenges Nate. "Jesus, Hugh, but you're a fucking idiot sometimes." He starts to leave too.

"Where the hell are you going?" I demand, rising to go after him. I reach out and grab his shoulder. "Why is what Phel thinks suddenly so important to you, if I'm totally off the mark?"

Slapping my hand away, Nate then grabs the front of my T-shirt and tugs me forward so our faces are close, pulling hard enough that I have to lean forward or risk ripping the shirt altogether. "I'm not the one who expects anything from Phel," Nate growls at me. "*You* are. Even I'm not so fucking stupid not to realize you're way out of line, and if I don't speak up for your ass now, you can sure as hell count on him not coming back here. Ever."

Then he's gone, running out the door to try to catch Phelan before he gets too far, probably.

It occurs to me my brother had his boots on this whole time, maybe because he expected to have to get up and leave at any point during this conversation. Get up and walk out of his own house like he was no longer welcome.

It also occurs to me, hard enough that I stumble back into my chair, that he wound up being right.

NATE comes back a short while later. I hear the beep of the security system as the front door opens and closes behind him, but otherwise

I'm not really around to see what state he's in, having grabbed a fifty of Jack and locked myself in my study. After how our conversation ended and the way I left things with Phel, it seemed an attractive prospect, so inappropriate and wonderful, to get stinking drunk before noon and let the rest of the day bleed out like a severed artery until I passed out or it was time for bed.

Before I snuck away to hide—yes, hide, because there's no other word for what I'm now doing—I caught a glimpse of Nate and Phel arguing out in the street from the front window of my house, which I ran to in the hopes of seeing whether Nate managed to catch him up. He did, as it turns out, and maybe "arguing" is a bit strong; certainly there was some kind of an intense discussion going on, and Nate gripped Phel's shoulders hard as if to keep him from running away again. I admit Phel has a talent for exiting stage left after he's said something particularly wounding, a sniper with deadly sharp aim who doesn't stick around to see whether or not he's hit his mark. So I stood there at the window, shadowed by the curtain, waiting for them to hug or kiss each other or *something*, because that's obviously what lovers do in a quarrel with no negative outcome. I guess I was still waiting for proof there was truly something else going on, having not sufficiently learned my lesson in the preceding argument. But the kiss never happened, not even the hug. Nate just cupped the back of Phelan's head and stared at him until eventually Phel nodded and they parted ways.

That's it.

I felt like I might be sick.

No way could I face Nate when he came back inside, so I disappeared myself in the hopes he'd assume I'd gone to write. He didn't come to find me either, his own escape upstairs evidenced by the slamming door I heard from within the safety of my cave. The sound made me sigh, because—fuck. I'd really gone and screwed the pooch, hadn't I? This whole time I've wanted my best friend and brother to forge a bond, and instead I basically drove them to forge one that didn't include me, even if it wasn't the sordid affair I got around to envisioning in the heat of what I admit was a very stupid, very illogical moment on my part.

I break open the Jack. The first sip of whiskey has a pleasant burn but ultimately doesn't do much more than make me feel guilty and even more ashamed of myself. This isn't how I handle stressful situations anymore, I remind myself sharply, especially not ones of my own devising. I was always supposed to be the responsible one, the levelheaded brother, according to Nate and my dad and just about everyone else who ever met us standing side by side. Yet I'm not the one who manned the fuck up and decided to come walking out of the closet with my head held high. No, I'm the one who turned that courage into an absolute nightmare for my brother, offering not support or love or even a shred of human fucking decency, but the petty, wounded offensive you'd expect from the kid picked last for the team. Phel was right about that much. Even if drinking this whole bottle of Jack didn't mean backsliding from the steps I fought so hard to master, I don't deserve anything that will let me forget the colossal mess I've made.

Surprisingly, I do manage to accomplish some writing today, banging out a couple of chapters that may or may not prove useable when I go back to edit later. It helps get my mind off things a little, calm me down. The few trips out to the bathroom or kitchen I risk during the day are miraculously Nate-free, a blessing as I try to pull myself together and figure out what to say to the guy. *I'm sorry* will be a start, but after that I keep coming up empty. It's hard to admit to someone how scared of being alone you are, especially when that person has been doing nothing but trying to get closer this whole time. By this I mean Nate, of course. I love Phel, but ours is the closeness of two solar systems that, while once totally separate, have bumped up against each other for a long period of time and eventually merged; unlike Nate, who has always been more like one of Jupiter's ancient moons, sometimes distant but always faithful. I've no doubt he won't hesitate to point out how determined I seemed to drive both him and Phel away this morning, though, so a lot of my anxiety has to do with feeling ashamed.

Sometime before midnight I wander out into the living room. I find Nate settled on the couch with Callie sprawled on top of him in her usual ladylike fashion. Nate flips through channels with the distracted air of someone who's not paying attention to any of it. I don't blame him. As I enter the room, Callie immediately jumps up and comes to say hello, but Nate just glances at me once and doesn't say anything, though his jaw tightens some. We could sit here in silence and he wouldn't try to leave or give me a hard time, but I know it's up to me to get this conversation going, if I want it to happen.

"Hey," I begin, hesitation strong in my voice. "I guess there's no point beating around the bush here, so I'll just come right out and say I'm sorry for this morning."

Nate grunts.

Right. "And I'm sorry I was such a dickbag about how I handled your coming out to me. It wasn't very mature, and I knew it at the time, I just...." I let my uncertainty hang there. "Something got hold of me and I lost my mind a little bit."

"A little bit," repeats Nate. He nods to himself like this is pure bullshit. "Okay."

"Fine, a lot," I clarify. All of a sudden I sound like I'm ten again, and Nate's caught me messing around with our dad's cop gear. Petulant, even though I know better. "I'm not proud of that."

"Nor should you be," Nate says. That muscle continues to go crazy in his jaw, and part of me wants to tell him to stop choosing his words carefully and just have out with whatever the hell he's really thinking. I don't, though, and he continues to struggle for the right words. "I'm sad to say I was fucking embarrassed for you today," he eventually tells me. "I ain't never felt that before, not even when I was showing up on your doorstep ready to cart you off to rehab."

Ouch. But also, yeah, if the shoe fits, I guess. I can tell he's winding up for a speech—maybe he's been working on it all day too— and to give himself some time, he reaches over for the remote and turns off the TV, swinging his legs around so he's sitting up to talk to me. As the television screen crackles a little with residual energy in the background, our eyes meet. I'm glad to see no anger in his, but he looks plenty exasperated.

"Honestly, though, I'm not the one you should be apologizing to. I'm prepared to accept your temporary insanity as an unfortunate reaction to finding out I'm gay—I know it's because you were upset about hearing it so late, not the fact I like dick. So as far as I'm concerned, you've had your hissy fit now and that conversation is over; we're good." I nod, having no desire to reprise the topic either, but Nate's not done. Far from it. "Hell," he continues, getting wound up now, "I'll even go so far as to accept that shit you said about me going behind Emilia's back, because after all, that's what I did. You won't get no argument from me on that one. But Phel... he didn't deserve that from you, Hugh. Even if you weren't totally fucking off base in what you said, Phel never purposely set out to trouble anyone, not from the beginning. All he got was a world of hurt he never asked for. Despite all that, he's been your friend, much as he can be with everything else going on, and today you went and flung that in his face."

I can't help but bristle at the undertone of condescension in his voice. "Nate, I *know*. I feel like shit, okay?"

As if anticipating my lip, Nate's already glaring at me with all the force he can muster. "So what the hell came over you, man?" he demands. "A couple weeks ago you were going on about how important it was that Phel and I stay in California—far as I can tell, we were both seriously considering it too. And now... I don't even know what Phel is gonna do, but this morning he didn't seem too keen on sticking around. Not that I blame the guy."

"I wouldn't blame him either. But I don't want him to leave."

Nate snorts. "Then don't you think you should do something about it?"

We let the conversation go there; there's not much else left to say, and we both know it.

Giving my arm a squeeze that suggests he knows it's time to let me start doing my soul-searching thing, Nate says, "I'm going to bed. Night, Hugh," and leaves to do just that.

It's hard for me to sleep that night. Almost like a kid on Christmas morning, I toss and turn all night long, continuously checking the clock like it'll make morning come faster. Maybe not in anticipation of anything good, but it's anticipation nonetheless, and I know that the sooner the sun comes up, the sooner I can haul ass down to Palermo and try to make things right with Phel. The not knowing is killing me.

Having taken Nate's words to heart, I feel guilty and stupid and ashamed that I wasted a whole day not apologizing to Phel, so even sleeping feels like a reckless, selfish waste compared to what I could be doing. I'd knock on his door right now if I didn't think that would hurt my cause. Although I can't shake the feeling that a face-to-face conversation would be best, Nate also has a point when he says Phel might feel crowded if I show up at his house and bang down his door. He's probably right, but I want to be able to see Phel's eyes and know for sure he's forgiven me. Phel's face can be doing a million contradictory things at once, each one a red herring as to what's really on his mind, but I can always tell what he's thinking from his eyes.

When morning comes and I'm all but bounding down the stairs with Callie at my side, I barely catch Nate on his way out. "Going for a run," he tells me, holding the door open with his shoulder. "Might be a couple hours."

"You want Callie?" I ask, and sure enough she's wagging her tail and panting at Nate in eager anticipation, knowing exactly what his running shoes and old gym shorts mean.

He doesn't really stop to consider. "Nah. I got some stuff to think about, so I'd rather fly solo today." To Callie, he says, "Maybe tomorrow, girl," and with that, he's off.

Left to wonder how my brother has suddenly started to make me feel like the unmotivated slugabed in the family, I shrug and lead Callie to the kitchen so I can fix us some breakfast. It actually isn't that early at all—nearly nine thirty, since I think I fell back asleep somewhere before dawn and caught up on the rest I'd missed while worrying about Phel. I know he'll be up and about himself right about now, since ten or ten thirty is usually when we head down to the beach to get a head start on the crowd. With that in mind, I decide it's probably safe to call him and put myself out of my misery. Hopefully he'll look at the clock and know I couldn't wait to call him.

Once I've filled Callie's food bowls with water and kibble, I pop a couple of slices of bread into the toaster for myself and grab a mug of the still hot coffee Nate must have made before taking off. As I'm waiting for the bread to toast, I grab my phone off the kitchen counter and dial Phel's number, then go through the rigmarole of requesting his mobile line after some polite chat with the switchboard operator at Palermo.

At first the phone rings long enough to make me worry he won't pick up, but after maybe seven or so seconds of no answer, the phone switches over and I hear Phelan's voice on the other end, gruff from a night of disuse. "Hello?"

"Phel," I answer, and then throw in a bright "How's it going?" before he can think better of it and hang up. "Glad I caught you still at home."

From the silence on the other end, I can tell Phel isn't necessarily in agreement. Eventually he says, "Hugh. What can I do for you?" in a tone that sounds more tired than antagonistic, but whose staid politeness still cuts like a knife.

"Look, man," I say, "there's no point pretending like yesterday didn't happen, so I'll just cut to the chase. I'm sorry. I was a dick, and I said some really unfair stuff to you and Nate. I won't even try to justify why I said what I did, because there's no excuse for how I treated you."

There's another pause. "I appreciate your calling, Hugh, but it isn't that simple. You really…." Phel makes a waffling sound I can hear on my end. "You really betrayed my trust."

"I know."

Phel keeps going like I haven't spoken. "I realize there's a lot about my past life I haven't been forthcoming about, but I always thought our friendship was about something other than knowing the trivialities of our individual situations. I don't know everything about you, and I kind of prefer it that way; I was happy with you not knowing everything about me too."

At first, I don't know what to say to that. I know what he means, and obviously we've both kept up our ends of the bargain by not sharing everything or demanding anything, but… I didn't realize it was an actual *pact* we'd entered into by unspoken agreement. "I would have told you everything if you'd asked," I say tentatively. "And I would never have objected to knowing everything about you either." I just never felt welcome to ask, exactly.

Sure enough, Phel says, "I didn't want you to." More gently, he adds, "There seemed to be greater trust required to satisfy ourselves with *not* knowing everything than there was sharing all our secrets." He hesitates. "That's what I always liked best about our friendship, Hugh. The trust."

"Which I broke," I supply for him. Even though I realize I'm not totally happy with how he's defined our friendship, it hits me that I've probably known this for a while and never spoke up. I assumed things would change, maybe? Who knows? I was wrong, anyway. Pretty damn wrong.

"Yes, which you broke," he agrees. Pause. "But you had just undergone a significant shock from your brother that made you begin to question what you knew about everything else. I know a thing or two about losing your worldview. It's challenging for even the most patient of people."

Surprised by how reasonable this sounds, I blurt out, "I'm not using that as an excuse."

Phel chuckles. "I know. And I'm not giving you one. For what it's worth, though... I think I would have explained everything to you at one point. Things just... changed. I got confused and started to wonder how much I could even trust myself. That wasn't your fault."

Another silence stretches out so long I begin to wonder if he's still there. I ask, "Phel?" and his grunt is, I guess, a form of acknowledgement. "So where does that leave us?"

Phel's hesitation is so profound that I can practically hear it. Then: "Would it really have been so terrible? If Nate and I had been lovers?"

Whoa. What a mental picture. I think if circumstances were totally different—if Nate wasn't married, for one—and had introduced Phel as his boyfriend, after getting over the sudden fact of my brother's gayness, I would have had no issue with the relationship. Of course not; Phel is a good man. Beyond thinking they have nothing in common, which even I know to be untrue, I would have been happy for them both. Probably even if they'd hooked up while in Cardiff, provided I'd known about it, I'd have eventually gotten over the initial weirdness of seeing my brother and best friend together. But I don't really want to say any of those things to Phel. Phrased like it was, though, there's no real way for me to dodge the question, which I suppose is Phel's point.

"It wouldn't have been terrible," I answer slowly. "Not that in and of itself. But if you *lied* about it the whole time...." I let that hang there, but something about Phel's answering pause seems to change.

"Yes. That is about what I expected you to say. The lies are always so much more damaging than the reality, aren't they?" Before I can think I have no idea what the hell to say to that either, Phel moves on. "I suppose, after what happened back East, I let myself believe that refusing to know everything about a person, and refusing to let them know everything about me, would prevent lies from ever becoming necessary." He pauses. The sound of his throat clicking in a swallow reaches me from down the line. "I was wrong."

What the hell does that even mean? Hoping to prevent further confusion, I just come out with it. "What does that mean?"

Phel sighs. "It means, Hugh, that I'm still angry at you, but I'm trying not to be."

"Okay...."

"It was wrong of me to leave you in the dark too. Were the circumstances reversed, suffice it to say, I'd have reacted the same." That little pause again, and it occurs to me that Phel is picking his words really, really carefully. "It would... bother me to think that the important people in my life were in collusion against me."

"But you're not, right?" Fuck. The second the words are out of my mouth—even before I hear Phel's sharp intake of breath—I feel impossibly guilty and start trying to backpedal like crazy. "Jesus. I'm sorry, Phel. I said the same thing to Nate and he almost flipped at me again. I didn't mean that."

Luckily for me, he ignores the comment altogether. "I'm sorry I told you to go fuck yourself," he says.

Even in the emptiness of my kitchen, I shrug. "I deserved it."

Chuckling, Phel replies, "In retrospect, I don't think you did. But it was too late to take it back, and I felt like being sore at you a while longer."

Sounds like Phel, all right. Whoever he *really* had that affair with, I can picture them running into each other ten years from now and Phel still wanting to punch him out, eyes narrowed and jaw set in that way of his I secretly think is more endearing than scary. Still, I'd rather someone else be on the receiving end of it. "Was it too soon for me to call?" I ask tentatively.

"No, it wasn't," he tells me. I think I can hear exhausted honesty in his voice. "I'm glad you called."

"So... are we good?"

I picture Phel nodding on the other end. He's probably sitting at his kitchen table with a cup of coffee, or curled up on his sofa. The normalcy of the image is almost as reassuring as the knowledge he's not still furious at me. "Yes, if you accept my apology too. For going behind your back. But I hope you understand I couldn't out Nate to you without also betraying his confidence." His voice is gentle but firm.

"Despite my reservations towards your brother, that wasn't something I would ever feel justified in doing. Do you understand?"

"Yeah, of course," I answer, surprised in spite of myself to be hearing such an overt demonstration of loyalty to Nate. If possible, it makes me respect Phel even more. "I probably would have been pissed if you had. So I guess we're good."

"I'm glad," sighs Phel.

Letting slip another self-conscious laugh, I ask, "Do you want to come surfing, then? Looks like it's gonna rain later; you know the waves are always the best before a storm."

But instead of him answering with an enthusiastic—if relieved—yes, there's more hesitation, unexpected this time despite being hot on the tail of one very uncertain conversation. "I wish I could, Hugh," Phel says with genuine reluctance. "But I'm afraid… I'm not feeling well. I planned to stay close to home this afternoon and… rest."

"What's wrong?"

"Nothing serious," he assures me. "Probably just a bug. I'll be fine."

"Do you want me to stop by?"

"No!" He tries to recover quickly, I can tell. "No. I'd prefer if you didn't—no sense getting you sick too if I really am coming down with something. It's a bad time of year for colds."

"I guess…." In the interest of being completely honest, I deny myself the impulse to let it go when I'm not really confident of what I'm being told. "You're sure you're not still pissed off at me?"

"I'm truly not angry at you, Hugh," he says. "Just unwell. We can go surfing tomorrow, if I'm feeling better. Or perhaps just spend some time together."

"Okay. As long as you aren't avoiding me."

"I wouldn't do that. I promise."

Because there's little else to say, we end the conversation there. I thank Phel again for being awesome, which makes him chuckle awkwardly, and when I hang up the phone, I realize my toast has long gone cold and charred in the toaster, since Nate is forever turning it up to the highest setting. It takes the wind out of my sails for some reason, and this thought occurs to me out of the blue, like it'd be even worse if

I were cooped up at home after a near-fatal fight with my best friend, too unwell even to go and surf my troubles away. And I decide, right then, it's unacceptable to let the conversation go there. Knowing Phel, he probably won't feel good about it until we see each other face to face either. For someone raised in such a strict Catholic family, he doesn't have much by way of faith in people.

Mind made up, I grab a few things from the pantry: an unopened carton of orange juice and a couple of boxes of this gourmet soup they sell at the local market. It's not as good as the kind made from scratch, but it's close enough that Phel probably won't turn his nose up at it. Soup is a pretty clichéd remedy for someone who's feeling unwell, but I know it always made me feel better as a kid, or when Nell made it for me, and that should suffice. The point isn't even to cure Phel of whatever ails him—it's just to be *there*, remind him he's still got friends who care about him.

Considering it's such a short drive to Palermo from my house, I arrive at the compound less than thirty minutes after I hang up with Phel. I don't know whether it's because I'm a former patient or because I'm there all the damn time, but the security guard at the gate rarely makes me sign in anymore, since he recognizes me on sight. Steph was there even when I was enrolled in their twenty-eight-day program, a huge Greek man with a shining pate and one of the most carefully groomed beards I've ever seen.

"Phel is a popular guy today," says Steph. He waves me on before I have a chance to ask what the hell that means. Having not seen the guest book, I can't pinpoint who might have already signed in this morning, but to be honest, the second the words are out of his mouth, I sort of don't have to.

There's really only one other person in Cardiff I can think of who'd be here.

As I learned all those years ago after seeing Nate and Mr. Garrett together in that classroom, the human capacity for denial is so strong that, in some people, it's practically a superpower. I guess for me it must be higher than average, since I make use of it so often. During the walk to Phel's, I tell myself Nate has as much right to be here as me, especially since it's clear he and Phel bonded a little bit over Nate being gay. Maybe Nate wanted to check up on him after yesterday's fight, though the little voice in the back of my head reminds me Nate knew I planned on calling Phel this morning to apologize. Then again, Phel did mention he was fooling around with someone; maybe Nate isn't there at all.

Still, all the hairs on the back of my neck stand on end as I climb the couple of steps to Phel's front door. As usual, it's unlocked. Although I always, *always* knock before entering someone else's home, regardless of whether or not there's a standing invitation—Phel has a free pass in my house because honestly, it's so big I don't hear him knocking half the time—today I give free rein to the tingling of whatever Spidey-sense I seem to have developed in the last ten minutes, hefting my little bag of groceries in one elbow as I silently push the door open with my free hand.

But here's the thing about intuition: it's only good if you let yourself pay attention to it. I constantly amaze myself with how perceptive I can be without realizing it. Quiet observations have served me pretty well in my writing and in developing characters. Maybe that's my psych background coming through; who knows. In real life, though, I might as well be as dense as a sack of bricks for all I trust what my gut tells me. And my gut, if I level with myself for even a second, has been giving some pretty strong hints for weeks about the quiet developments taking place below the radar in my own life, within the small circle of people I call family. I knew something wasn't quite right all along, and ignored it with every excuse I could find, like *I* was the one imagining things, my unfounded paranoia getting the better of me.

I think I knew, the second Nate met Phelan on my doorstep, I wasn't imagining a damn thing. And my paranoia? Maybe not so unfounded after all.

I enter the cottage and immediately hear music playing from Phel's bedroom at the back—it's only a four-room dwelling, so it's not difficult to pick out. I set my groceries down on the kitchen table and walk through to the bedroom in a daze.

I nudge open the half-closed door and stop there, throat choking off whatever surprised noise I might have made. They're on the bed. With curtains still drawn, the room is shadowy but still bright enough for me to make out Nate and Phel's faces. Good lighting isn't necessary, since I'd probably recognize them anyway, by body type or even how they move. It's a strange thing, really, to see two people so familiar to you in a completely unfamiliar situation, and I realize in that moment that I never really had a clear picture of this in my mind the whole time I accused them of sleeping together. First of all, gross—but secondly, I was a lot more clueless than I ever thought.

From the way their two bodies are angled sideways across the mattress, I can see Nate has Phel beneath him, body twisted half on his side and half on his back. One of Phel's legs is tucked up to his chest, knee supported over the crook of Nate's elbow, and this bizarre thought occurs to me that it's a good thing Phel does all that yoga, or else it would probably be an uncomfortable position to maintain for very long.

More significant than how their bodies are arranged, however, or even the fact that Nate is obviously thrusting into him—even in a stupor, my eyes know to avoid settling on that whole area—is the way they're looking at each other, the way their faces are so close, their lips almost touching. They each have a hand fisted in each other's hair so they're making eye contact and holding, and holding, and holding. The quick glance I get of Phelan's expression shows a man who's all but delirious, mouth slack and spilling obscene noises, but he doesn't look away. Nate doesn't either, whispering words I can't quite make out, and what I can see of his face shows a look of sheer amazement. As surely as I knew what I'd find when I walked into the house, I see confirmation of another thing I've known all along: that Phel, for all his denials, never stopped being in love with the man who betrayed him, the same love Nate admitted to having for the person who compelled him to step outside his marriage. They're expressions I haven't seen on a person's face since the last time I made love to Nell—the look of someone so totally in love that they're transported.

It could be that the sound that escapes me is borne of shock as much as jealousy and anguish for what I've lost; shock that the two people I have left and love most in the world have been lying to my fucking face for *ages*; renewed jealousy and anguish that I'm never going to look at Nell that way again. I don't think it truly matters, because the gut punch would feel the same, whatever the cause. Either way, it's enough that my presence is revealed as reality reasserts itself and the surprise begins to ebb, startling me back to earth so violently that Nate and Phel can't help but notice as well.

Very distinctly, I hear Phel's cry go from feverish to alarmed, sharpening around my name, both heads swiveling toward me as Nate gasps, "Oh fuck!" There's a tussle, the two of them scrambling to separate and cover themselves, but I don't stick around longer than that to see what happens. I turn and slam my way past both the bedroom door and the entrance to Phel's house. I don't stop until my shaking hands close around the rails of a surfboard and I find my way into the churning sea.

9

Nate

FOR a couple of weeks following the fight we had after our trip to Chicago with Liam, Phel and I didn't talk at all. Not a damn word. I begged my boss, Craig, not to send me on any business trips to Columbus, scared that I would break down and show up on Phelan's doorstep like I did after that first weekend, as helpless to him now as on Day freaking One. It's not that I avoided him because I was still angry (though I was), but because I knew Phel was right about everything. Whether or not my own accusations held any merit was unimportant; Phel wasn't the one destroying our relationship from the inside out with lies and secrecy. No matter how much of a little bitch he acted like— and yeah, I didn't have such hearts in my eyes that I couldn't see Phel had the capacity to be one sometimes—I couldn't help but feel all our problems came back to the elephant in the room, the one only I was aware of. The revelation that he wanted us to live together rocked me to my foundations. No one had ever *asked* me that before, and it made me realize we couldn't keep moving forward if I kept on as I'd been doing.

Phel, on the other hand… he was beautiful. Golden. Blameless. On the drive home after that fight, it hit me that he'd intended some pretty powerful subtext along with his invitation to move in: he was prepared to come out to his family for me. Since the Prices had more money than God, there was no conceivable reason for Phel to share a living space with someone who wasn't a partner. A lover. His family would have done the math eventually, and saying he wanted me there anyway was Phel's way of saying he was willing to take the plunge, damn the consequences.

And I fucked it up.

If it's any consolation, for those two weeks I was nothing but miserable. Couldn't sleep, could barely eat, dodged the concerned questions of friends and family who could tell something was wrong. I'm sure Emilia thought I'd been diagnosed with a terminal illness, if the looks she kept shooting me across the dinner table and the constant inquiries about how I was feeling were anything to go by. In a sense, I *was* ill. Heartsick, even. Not only did it nauseate me to think about where things stood with my lover, I was sick with knowing what I had to do, the extent to which I'd started to seriously hate my own existence. I wanted to talk to my brother like crazy. I wanted to tell him everything, but I was a coward and didn't know where to start. Hugh, having lost Nell not so long ago, would struggle to understand. I wanted to talk to Emilia even more, but couldn't do that either. In other words, I was fucked.

The one person I did end up talking to was a divorce lawyer. Drastic, I know. I could have gone to Columbus and found some high-powered terrier to talk me up about how easy it would be to dissolve my marriage, but I realized I needed the advice of someone close to home, someone who knew who I was and, more importantly, knew Emilia and my family. What I needed was compassion and familiarity with my situation, sympathy to the fact that I didn't want money or a generous settlement, that I was willing to pay any amount in alimony or child support to ensure Liam and Emilia were provided for.

I didn't want to be an asshole, but neither did I want to embody the cliché of the married man who never ends up making a change. I always feel sorry for those poor schmucks as much as their spouses, because no matter how hard they try to pretend everything's shiny, you can tell how unhappy everyone is. Emilia would be better off free of me than tangled up in that kind of mess for the rest of her life. At least she could finally find someone who could give her a proper marriage, and Liam wouldn't have to watch his parents grow to hate each other. And me? My expectations for myself were pretty low. I just wanted to own up to the life I really wanted and do away with the bullshit charade that I was anything but a gay man and in love with someone incredible. Even if that was someone I probably didn't deserve.

"Not to alarm you," the lawyer had said, "but a lot of men in your position make it to the very point you're at now, and no further. Perhaps it's a smaller percentage seek to dissolve their marriage due to a sexuality crisis, but in essence, the problem remains the same: the marriage is no longer feasible. I suggest, therefore, that you sit down and have a conversation with your family first, and call me back once you're ready to proceed from there. Divorce doesn't have to be a nasty set of affairs, but it has to start somewhere. I don't think you want Emilia to learn of your intentions as she's being served papers."

Obviously that was sound advice. But I knew I wasn't ready for that yet, not before I had a chance to talk to Phel and tell him everything first. Maybe it was selfish of me to want a soft landing and assurances he'd still be around—I'm sure some people would have said it was closer to an air-to-air transfer than a soft landing, but that was unintentional on my part. Whatever the case, I didn't think I had it in me to make the leap without knowing Phel would be there at the end of it all. Startling though it was, I realized I could envision my life without Emilia without much difficulty, whereas the thought of losing Phel practically sent me into fits of anxiety. I got the same way when I thought about not having Liam or Hugh around, which I suppose was my brain's way of letting me know what was most important to me. Quite frankly, I realized I'd rather die than lose what I had, though a part of me knew it might already be too late.

I couldn't not try, though. The week Liam went off to summer camp and Emilia allowed herself to spend a bit more time at the dance studio, teaching extra classes and giving her business a little TLC (she didn't say anything, but I think she needed a break from the tension between us too), I threw back a few beers and picked up the phone. When my hand stopped shaking enough, I dialed the Columbus area code.

To my surprise, Phel picked up right away, his voice guarded but with an undertone of relief that, to me, sounded clear as a bell. The conversation itself was simple enough: I told Phel how much I'd missed him, how badly I wanted to apologize in person. I guess it's a testament to how much he wanted to make things right between us that it took almost no convincing to get him to agree to drive to Mount Vernon. After all, our fight hadn't erased his desire to see the side of my life he felt had been denied him. For my part, I was through denying him anything.

We made plans for him to visit a couple of days after that. I had the day off work and knew it'd be no trouble for Phel to get the time off as well; since he said he'd drive up in the morning, there was no chance of Emilia being around. Although it made me feel like scum to consider it—even more like scum, I mean—I would need no more than twenty minutes or so to hide away the wedding photos and anything that might point to me still being married, including odds and ends of Emilia's left around the house. For whatever reason, I decided to call the master bedroom off limits; some belated attempt, maybe, to respect my wife's place in our home, even as I was planning to bring my lover onto Emilia's turf.

Like I said, I couldn't keep this up much longer. The lies had to stop that day.

In one way or another, they did.

Right on time, Phel pulled up in front of the house driving the sleek Audi convertible I often liked to razz him about, though secretly I thought it was a pretty sexy car. Kind of like its owner. I could see the small smile he wore from the minute I opened the front door to him as he came up the walk, looking incredible even in old jeans and a thin gray sweater. He must have seen the longing on my face; the first thing Phel did when I closed the front door behind him was throw himself into my embrace and bury his face in my neck, muttering about how shitty he'd felt since our fight. Having his body there against mine felt so right that my knees almost buckled, and while I managed not to fall to the floor in a heap, I did have to collapse back against the wall as I held him and murmured my own apologies into his hair, breathing in the scent of him like I was a man deprived of oxygen. When he kissed me, I didn't think I'd ever be able to let him go, and for once I didn't stop to think about how the hell I'd turned into such a sap. Like everything else, it didn't seem to matter if it meant hanging on to what was here in my arms.

"I shouldn't have pushed you," Phel told me, sounding frustrated and angry with himself. I wondered if he'd been beating himself up the whole time we weren't talking to each other, the same way I'd been doing, albeit for completely opposite reasons. "I got this idea in my head about us living together," he said miserably, "and didn't stop to think about the reality. Liam is your priority; I can't—and don't—want to force you to disrupt your son's life because I'm impatient and greedy."

Unable to keep from smiling, I kissed his forehead. "I like that you're impatient and greedy," I told him. "Trust me, Phel, you're not the one in the wrong here. I just didn't know how to deal with what you were offering. Fuck, at first I didn't even realize exactly *what* that was."

Phel pulled back to look at me, eyes hilariously narrowed like he didn't trust me to have correctly translated his vagueness. Oh, how little faith he had in my awesome powers of deduction. "And just what was I offering?" he asked.

With a shrug, I said, "Same thing I wanna offer you, baby: no more hiding, not from anyone. I'm so sick of only letting people see half of me or less because of what they might think. Fuck that. If anything, you make me way more respectable by association—there's a reason they call you my 'better half', right?"

If I can be really corny here for a second, that's honestly how I felt—feel—about Phel: he's the better side of me. Like Plato talked about in that book about love, we're two parts of a whole. Without him, I was hardly better than a dumb hick fuckup, and a pretty significant source of disappointment to myself and the people around me. That I'd found Phel at all was a miracle, and one for the fucking books, at that. You could give me a million years to try to catch up, and I'd never be the kind of person Phel was back then. But being around him… it made me feel like I could at least try, right? Now that I knew what I was reaching for, I had something to aspire to, and more importantly, someone who acted as if he didn't care if I ever changed. The way Phel treated me, like he loved me just the way I was, made me want to be better for him.

Who the hell ever gets that lucky, huh? I was freaking *honored*, every day of my life, that Phel could let someone like me near him. And not just near him—inside him. I don't mean that in a dirty way… but obviously that too (I can picture his eye roll now). For some reason, Phel actually loved me, and if that thought never ceased to amaze me, it'd be too fucking soon. More than that, he somehow seemed to understand everything about me without my ever having to say it out loud. I might have ruined Emilia's life, which I was genuinely sorry for and still hoped to fix, but Phel was my chance to do it right. And I really, *really* wanted to do right by him. Maybe then I could start doing right by myself and everyone else too.

Lofty fucking ideas, I know, but that's the kind of guy Phel was. He had a knack for getting me to let myself think big just by loving him. He had a knack for making me want to love myself while I was at it, impossible though it sometimes seemed.

I must have been silent a really long time, judging by the way Phel was staring at me. He looked confused, but there was something like amazement in his eyes that made me think the expression on my face wasn't much different. I said, "What?"

Though he watched me a while longer, Phel eventually chuckled and shook his head. "I never know what to do when you look at me like that," he said.

"Like what?"

His slow head tilt made me squeeze him tighter as he said, "Like you're trying to figure something out, and can't." He hesitated, and I could feel tension creep into his posture. "It makes me wonder whether it's *me* you're unsure about."

I sharply inhaled. "Jesus Christ, no," I told him, pushing him back to arm's length so I could look right at him, into those eyes that didn't seem to know whether to look rueful or wary. "Listen to me," I said and gripped his shoulders tight. "I love you, Phel, okay? More than I've ever loved anyone I'm not related to, and sometimes even more than my brother, which you'd understand if you knew him." At that, his lips quirked and got me thinking that maybe it was time to think about introducing him to Hugh. "I don't ever want you to doubt that, because I'm in this for the long haul. As long as you'll have me. *That's* the only thing I sometimes wonder about, that you're gonna wake up one day and realize you're too good for my shit. Losing you is just about the scariest thing I can think of, right up there with something happening to Liam or my kid brother."

"You deserve good things, Nate," Phel said, brow furrowed. His hands came up to touch my face, one tracing my cheekbone and the other crawling through my hair the way he knew I liked, as much as I liked having his hands anywhere on me. After two weeks apart, the touch made me shiver. From his smile, he noticed. "And you won't lose me. I'm not going anywhere."

Would Phelan still say that when he knew the whole truth? I didn't know, but it was time to stop being a spineless asshole and start trusting him like I did with everything else. Unable to resist any longer, I leaned in and kissed him so hard it made my lips tingle, his mouth opening around a gasp while his whole body sagged against mine.

Almost immediately, I felt his tongue flicker out and dart into my mouth, trying to deepen the kiss. But no—it had to be now.

"There's some stuff I gotta talk to you about," I murmured, breaking away slightly. "It's important."

"It can wait, goddamn it," Phel growled, and then he was pressing me back into the wall, his hands going for my belt as if drawn there by magnetic traction. "Two fucking weeks, Nate," he hissed, and my eyes rolled back at the first determined stroke of his fingers against my crotch. He gave this laugh that was low and dirty and made me feel a bit lightheaded. With the kind of expert touch that only comes from shitloads of sex with the same person, he started to massage my cock through my jeans. My eyes slitted open. He didn't have to look so goddamned gleeful about it. "Whatever it is, it can wait until after I fuck you senseless."

Christ, that voice. I shuddered again when he worked open my jeans and slid his hand inside. Meanwhile, his mouth slammed back against mine with a thousand times more force than a minute ago, and just like that, all thoughts of waiting to fuck until after I told him about Emilia flew out the window. So much for willpower. By then I was so hard, having barely touched myself for two weeks, that the lightest brush of fingers made me moan and clutch him to me, slide my hands down the back of his faded old jeans, the fabric so worn and soft it clung to his ass as if they were jogging pants. Phel let me grind us together just for a moment, tongue-fucking my mouth until we were both breathless, and then he pulled away.

"Bed," he ordered. To say I all but fell over myself to usher us into the guest room is a severe fucking understatement.

After that, I think we were both too desperate and impatient to worry about gentleness or finesse or, hell, anything resembling foreplay or condoms or lube. We rolled around on that bed until our clothes were gone and I was panting and cursing at the slide of his skin against mine, the way he manhandled me just how he wanted, despite being the smaller guy. I loved it when Phel got all toppy and aggressive like that, bossy and demanding and fully aware I'd do anything he could ever want, up to and including letting him tie me down six ways from Sunday or take a crop to my ass. This wasn't the time or place for the first, and he'd never expressed an interest in the latter, but let's just say I'm lucky if two whole seconds passed between him rolling me on top of him and spitting into his hand, and me taking that hard, slicked-up dick of his and sticking it inside me so fast it gave me a head rush. It hurt a bit, no lie, because it'd been at least three weeks since I had anything up me bigger than a finger, but one look at Phel all slack-jawed and dumb with pleasure made my stomach flip and the familiar burn start to tingle in a way that was decidedly not painful.

That was my favorite moment of all, the point at which pain became pleasure—not just because of how it felt, but because Phel always seemed to know when the change happened, when he could pull me down to him for a sloppy kiss and start rocking into me like there was something he wanted to touch deep in my chest, hidden back behind my ribs. He made it so good, memorized angles more diligently than a champion pool player, aiming to brush against that place that made me arch my back and moan and moan and moan, voice rough and breaking and threading between the wet sounds of my ass slapping into his pelvis. Phel found my hip with his palm, guiding, and I felt the fingers of his other hand catching my hair as we fucked together and the room started to lurch like a Tilt-a-Whirl.

"You'll never lose me," Phel whispered in my ear, breath juddering. "You're mine, Nate, and no one else's. I love you."

I'd heard him say those words so many times before, but it's as though they reopened a splintering dam inside I couldn't and didn't want to stopper back up again.

"I love you, I love you," I echoed, telling him the same thing over and over like I never wanted him to forget it. It didn't matter if it was an easy thing to say during sex; I knew he knew how hard I meant it, how I could feel my love for him down to the marrow.

Then, next thing I knew, Emilia was screaming at us from the bedroom door and everything became a blur. I couldn't say what happened after that if I tried, not even for a fucking police statement, except sometime between Emilia finding us and me and Phel separating at a speed that could have made my eyes cross, I know Phel's heart broke and never really healed properly. In the confusion of Emilia's shrieks and me crying and Phel looking so stony faced I wanted to vomit, he had his clothes back on and was out the door. He slipped through my fingers before I could beg him not to.

One thing I do remember is how relieved I felt. It swept over me like a wave, hard enough to steal the breath right out of my lungs. What quickly followed was the realization I was a lot more worried for Phel than myself or even Emilia. Either way, I was too late to stop him, and the rest is history.

Do I feel relief that Hugh walked in and discovered us pretty much the same way? Funny that Phel and I didn't learn our lesson the first time around. But I don't know. Maybe I do feel better, just from knowing I can put a stop to all the lies and betrayal and sneaking around. I'm sure even murderers must feel a certain sense of relief when they're caught. Not that I've ever murdered anyone, or that lying to my brother about loving Phel is remotely on par. Bad analogy. Either way, I've wanted to be free of the bullshit ever since coming to Cardiff, and for one reason or another, it kept getting put off until the situation was barely any different than the one I'd left behind.

I know there'll be plenty of explaining to do to Hugh when I manage to get him in the same room without him freaking out. In fact, for once my concern about what he'll say—what he thinks—far exceeds my mortification that he saw my junk in action, not to mention more of Phel than my typical jealous male brain can allow without getting inappropriately possessive. Relieved or not, I know things are bad here. They were rocky when Hugh found out I'd been lying to him about my affair for a whole year, and then, after I went and promised him not to lie to his face again, he found out I never actually stopped. Maybe that wasn't my intention, but given the speed with which Hugh hauled ass out of Phelan's house, I'm guessing he's not thinking too much about the what-ifs right now. I can only hope his first reaction wasn't to hit up a liquor store or, God forbid, exchange a knowing look with the bartender down at the Shanty on Chesterfield Ave., who I'm pretty sure deals prescription meds—or worse—on the side. The thought is almost more than I can entertain right now.

The only good part is that Phel chose to stick around this time. After Hugh ran off, a few minutes went by where neither of us did anything, both too paralyzed with shock to move. Then I crawled to the edge of the mattress to sit there with my head in my hands. A little while after that, Phel joined me. He looks the same as I feel—disbelieving and mortified and ashamed—but it gives me a small measure of comfort that he hasn't tried to leave or kick me out. Instead he sits slightly behind to me, body pressed along the length of my back, lips against my shoulder. He's quiet for a real long time before a sigh bubbles up from deep within his chest.

"Fuck," I say.

"Fuck," he agrees. There doesn't seem to be a better way to put it.

Truth is, I was surprised when Phel called me this morning, same way I was surprised when he turned up at the house yesterday in the middle of me telling Hugh I'm gay. Considering how Phel and I left things last time, I didn't expect to hear from him again except for the rudimentary "fuck you" we all knew was coming. He was so mad at me for wanting to disrupt whatever arrangement we had going, I was barely hopeful I'd get even that. But instead, Phel, ever full of contradictions, turned out to be the guy who had my back, and stuck up for me in a remarkably unselfish way that made perfect sense at the time he was saying it, but flabbergasted the fuck out of me all the same. Weirder still, he stood there and let me hold his hand the whole time Hugh accused us of going behind his back, squeezing against my fingers every time he felt me starting to lose my nerve. He had to know how much harder I fell for him at that moment. Bad enough that he was already the love of my life, he had to go and be my hero too.

So when he called, I came, and remembered the time he came to find me in Mount Vernon. For all intents and purposes, that was one hell of a perfect day, at least before Emilia caught us doing the dirty deed and it all went tits up. In the present, though, I don't think either of us said a damn word when I turned up at his door all sweaty and hot from my run; he just pulled me inside and kissed away anything it wouldn't have occurred to me to say anyhow. Clothes, few of them though there were, came off between the front door and the bedroom, and then it was all naked skin and joy.

There was a bit more foreplay this time, me sucking Phel so deep into my mouth that I wanted to smile at the noisy gasp he made, his head tipping back against the mattress as he tried to rein in the bucking of his hips. His hands were tight in my hair, but to hold on, not to control, and I made him come like that, taking my time and making him writhe around like a live wire. I still didn't know whether we were at a place where I could go further without Phel getting uptight about it—the rules on this thing kept changing—and I considered bringing myself off with my hand until he drew me closer for a long kiss.

"Please fuck me," he whispered, and he kept alternately locking eyes with me and letting his gaze flit away like he was embarrassed. The words made me go quiet, confused, but of course I didn't say no.

The only struggle was when he wriggled onto his stomach when I would have preferred him on his back and looking up at me. In the end, we settled on a kind of compromise; as I slowed my thrusts into him, I twisted Phel around so his torso was mostly turned toward me, and by then I could tell he was too far gone to argue or resist holding eye contact. In fact, he was clutching his hand in my hair again so *I* couldn't look away. He was so goddamn beautiful when he let me see his pleasure and the need in his eyes. Though it'd been months since I'd seen him like that, I shuddered at the familiar way it made my stomach drop and my chest clench tight. When Hugh broke in on us, I couldn't say whether I was more upset to have that connection ruined or my orgasm swept out from under my feet.

Lost again in that moment, which seems a million years ago now, I miss part of what Phel is saying to me, his voice low and worried close to my hear. "Huh?" I ask, then flush guiltily when he gives me a pissy look. "Sorry, man, thirty seconds ago I was inside you. Give me a minute."

Phel sighs. "You need to focus, Nate."

Trying hard not to roll my eyes, I say, "Thanks, Phel, but unless you can tell me what part of this I should be focusing *on*, no deal. I'm pretty sure we're fucked either way."

He shifts to sit beside me and levels me with a stare. "I lied to your brother point-blank over the phone this morning."

"I know. I was there."

His expression pinches. "I wish I hadn't done that."

Deciding to risk it, I reach out and take Phel's hand, which he allows, to my continuing shock. I hide it pretty well. "Trust me, Phel, right now Hugh is busy calculating exactly how long we've both been lying to cover this up. He's thinking of all the possible opportunities we could have had to sneak around under his nose, and wondering how the hell he didn't see it. One more lie you told him over the phone ain't gonna be much more than a drop in the bucket at this stage."

"You seem awfully sure of that."

Well, I am. Kind of. "I know how my brother thinks. Hell, I don't think much differently myself."

I want to add that I went through this exact process when I figured it out about Hugh's year making friends with Colombian snow, putting all the pieces together in painful hindsight. By the same token, I know Hugh won't let his righteous indignation run away on him before he realizes the similarities between our two predicaments, the Fessenden tendency to lie to each other as much as ourselves about the stuff that's staring us in the eyes. We think it's because we're protecting each other, when really we're just trying to pretend we aren't covering our own asses.

But I know Phel isn't in the loop about that slice of Hugh's past, so I don't mention it, though I'm sure he could use some reassurance right about now. Hugh is an honest guy when it comes to taking stock of his own faults and failures, which Phel gets. It'll have to be enough. Not that I'm thinking about how I can use this as a bargaining chip to take the focus off what we've done, or use it to excuse my own behavior; we aren't that kind of family. Instead I think it'll be relatively easy to skip the blame game portion of today's events and get right at what's really bothering Hugh: the lies he'll see as symptomatic of something bigger.

Namely, his fear that Phel and I will fuck off and leave him alone. Sure, it's an awfully codependent way to think, but that's the kind of childhood we had, waiting for one person after another to leave until there was no one left. Anyone would have abandonment issues with that kind of background. I can't sit here and say the same fears haven't occurred to me from time to time over the years, especially after Hugh went off to school and got himself a new life. Having Emilia and Liam, and then Phel, helped with that for a long time. But I'd seen for myself how fast it could all be taken away.

"What are you thinking?" Phel asks me. Guess I let the silence stretch out too long again.

I shrug. "Hugh's gonna be hurt and pissed and probably inclined to say some not-so-nice things to both of us," I answer. "Totally deserved, yeah. But if I know that kid, mostly he's going to push and push until one of us announces the bad news."

"Which is?"

"That we're gonna leave him here by himself."

"How do you know?"

I release Phel's hand and get off the bed, looking down at him for a moment. He seems small and taut with worry, a mouse caught between darting for freedom and trying to make itself disappear. That makes me nervous. Rather than letting myself evaluate the odds of Phel running out on me again—is Hugh finding us out enough to erase whatever headway we've made towards reconciliation?—I force my mind back to the subject of my brother. "Because it's what I would do. To him, the fact that we lied about all this only means we were trying to put off the inevitability of telling him."

Phel wrinkles his nose, but pauses. Slowly, he says, "But that's not why. The lie was because I thought *he* might want me to leave—"

"—when he found out," I finish for him. "I know." Swallowing, I then add, "He's a bright kid, but he obviously don't see it that way. It's the same reason I never told you 'bout Emilia. Same reason we were both afraid of coming out to our families. The people who fuck up are rarely the ones who leave by choice."

Phel meets my eyes and doesn't say anything. From that look alone, I know he doesn't agree, but for once I don't stop and think maybe he's right and I'm wrong. Not that Phel is a hypocrite, but sometimes he holds his own actions in such a different light from everything else that he genuinely believes the forces that govern other people's decisions don't touch him. In this case, it's fear. I know that in Phel's head, his fear of telling Hugh about us is different from me not telling him about Emilia in a million ways.

Sure enough, he says, "It's not quite the same."

I grunt. "Yeah, it is. But we aren't here to argue about that; we're here to figure out what the hell to do next." Silently, I promise myself the next step is to make sure Hugh doesn't do anything stupid. It's hard not to run after him right this second, but when he finished rehab and I spent a few months hovering over him like a suspicious prison warden, he made me promise to try to trust him to keep working the steps, keep himself from falling off the wagon. I do trust him, but then again, we haven't had something this fucked up to deal with since he finished his twenty-eight days in this very institution.

Since there seems no end to the surprises this morning, Phel makes a weak attempt at a joke. "I don't suppose we could brainwash him so he forgets this ever happened?"

"Be my guest," I reply, snorting. "I'm sure Hugh would be just as happy to forget he ever laid eyes on us fucking." He smiles weakly at that, and my heart breaks a little to see how afraid Phel still looks, his whole body drawn up tight even though he's doing his best to remain seated normally on the bed. It hasn't been my place for a while, but I think back to how he was there for me yesterday at the house, standing by my side and letting our skin touch in constant reminder of his presence.

All of a sudden, my mind's decided for me: I don't give a fuck what happened between us and how we're supposed to act now. It's clear what I have to do.

Offering a smile, I reach out and pull him against me, then turn gently so I'm pressing him back against the bed, crawling on top so he can't escape. "Hey," I tell him gently, "it'll be okay. It's a mess now, but things will work out."

Phel glares at my placating tone, and it's like he deepens his own in response just to prove his point. "Okay for whom?"

"Don't pull that James Earl Jones shit with me," I warn him. "I know you scream like a girl around centipedes or when I do that thing you like with my tongue." Ignoring his scowl, I reach up and stroke his hair, amazed by how noncombative he's being, even though I don't know what it means. Unlike most people, I lack the instinct to respond to the unknown with uncertainty or fear; instead it makes me brave and stupid. "We'll go talk to Hugh and we'll explain why we didn't tell him the truth, which I think is pretty straightforward. He'll come around eventually, you'll see. We were too surprised at findin' each other here to do anything about it right away, especially since we both knew it would have meant one of us packing up and leaving. And he wouldn't have wanted that, not any more than us."

Eyes remarkably steady, Phel looks up at me and takes his time answering, as if mulling the thought over in his head. Despite his outward appearance of calm, the muscle in his cheek gives him away; I can see it jumping with all the intensity of a wild bird trying to escape a cage. "And what about now?"

"Now...." I find myself thinking about that quaint little fantasy Hugh managed to get us all in on, the idea of the three of us living together under one roof as friends and family. Christ, Phel let himself fall for it too, formulating ideas about that little surf shop on the beach, putting out tentative feelers in the hopes they might someday become roots. The most uncertain one out of all of us was me, since I've obviously got my kid back in Ohio, but as I told Hugh, that hasn't stopped me from wanting to make the California dream work. Liam loves it here as much as I do. I still want it, as much as I want the guy lying in my arms. It's been a rough road to get to this point, but for the first time in a long time, I think we're finally getting back on track, back to where we're supposed to be.

I lean in and kiss Phelan slowly, starting softly and hesitantly but getting deeper when he opens his mouth to me and lets our tongues flicker and touch. He moans in the back of his throat, a quiet sound that makes my cock twitch against his thigh, and from the answering jerk of his hips, I know he's been on the knife's edge of arousal since we were interrupted, no different than me. It can be so difficult to know what's going through his mind, but in the absence of everything else, I know I can always trust this, the hot and violent electricity sparking between us when we so much as look at each other.

Although absolutely nothing has changed about our surroundings in the past hour, the whole act of pushing my body up against his, shifting until our cocks find that perfect angle to rub alongside each other, feels completely different. I try to put a finger on what it could be when the thought occurs to me I no longer have something to hide or act like I'm ashamed of, because the secret's out, no taking it back. For the first time, I'm kissing Phel as a free man, and there isn't a damned thing anyone can do to stop it.

"Hugh doesn't have to worry about one of us leaving, baby," I murmur against Phel's mouth, then turn my face so I can bite into the hard bone of his jaw before working down to the sensitive skin of his throat. "It might take some time for him to trust us again, and I know that, but if he's worried about us going somewhere... we don't have to. We can just stay here and things will be just like this."

I take one of my hands and reach between us to wrap around Phel's dick. His legs open for me in a lazy sprawl so I can start stroking him in long, easy movements that make him pant and buck, my fingers tightening beneath the head of his cock on each upstroke and finding all his sweet spots. He keens unintelligibly.

"No more hiding, Phel," I whisper in his ear, half promise, half revelation. "It'll be perfect—what we've always wanted. We can be together and not give a fuck who knows or who sees. I love you, you asshole, and I'm not letting you go again."

To my horror, Phel goes totally stiff beneath me and stays frozen for a second. Then he seems to think better of it and pushes against my chest. It's not gentle, and as if to prove the point further, his dick starts to soften in my hand. "Get off," he says, voice tight, and keeps shoving at me with increasing force until I let him go completely and back away.

Maybe calling him an asshole wasn't the best move, whatever the affection behind it. "What?"

"Fuck you, Nate," he spits, and the vehemence of the words manages to startle me good even if the sentiment is nothing new. Whatever anxiety was there before is gone, replaced by sheer fury and what to me looks like deep injury. My throat clenches at the sight, and I start to wonder whether the softness I saw in him earlier was a complete mirage or the product of wishful thinking. Phel seems to believe so.

"Nothing about this is perfect," he grates out, sliding off the bed so he can start collecting clothing. I want to beg him to stop, but I can't, watching a scene I've seen before and still don't know how to stop from playing out. "We can't be together because *I* still give a fuck, okay? This"—and he gestures between us with sharp movements of his hands—"is not what I always wanted. In fact, it's about a million times worse, because at least before, I knew my best friend didn't hate my guts. But what else is new? History really *has* repeated itself, because once again, you fuck up, and I'm the one who loses everything."

For a moment I'm speechless as Phel makes moves to storm out of the bedroom, up and casting about for his pants, but then a stuttering protest finds its way past my lips. "You're not the only one who's lost everything." Halfway to the exit already, he glares at me. As the door slams, I shout belatedly after him, "And I'm not the only one who's fucked up around here these past few weeks either!"

I'm left alone with my cheeks flaming and my stomach somewhere in the vicinity of my knees, while the rest of my organs try to force their way up into my throat. Another drive-by argument brought to you courtesy of Phelan Montague Price.

For a while I continue to sit there, apprehensive of what I'll face when I finally emerge from the bedroom, though I know Phel is probably no less afraid of having to look at me. I used to think he became so adept at running away midargument because he loved me and was scared I might say something true or hurtful that he was powerless to refute, like *I'm leaving* or *I don't love you anymore*. He never realized I probably spent a fair bit of time terrified of hearing the same things from him, because a part of being in love is caring, more than you've ever cared about anything, what that other person thinks of you, and the possibility they might not always be around.

But now I'm not so sure. Phel sure doesn't seem too worried about my leaving; in fact, he seems hell-bent on proving that's what he's wanted since the second I showed up in Cardiff. He might have slammed the first door in my face, but I'm pretty sure I'll find him holding the next one open for me on the other side, ready to dead bolt it behind me after I'm gone.

MIRACULOUSLY—or not, depending on how you look at it—I don't have to confront Phel on my way out of the house. He's already gone. I doubt he made it very far in such a short time, but the message is clear that he doesn't want me going after him or trying to resolve what we left unfinished in the bedroom. For once I'm not much inclined to try. Just how many damn people am I supposed to chase down this morning, huh? I gotta say, though, this is the first time I never felt it necessary to go after him with a million apologies at the ready. This is a fact that hits me with all the subtlety of a sack of bricks. As I was sitting in that bedroom, I felt a hundred miles farther away from Phel than ever before, farther even than when I thought I would never see him again.

Although I think it's still too soon to attempt going back to the house to find Hugh—since, knowing him, he won't be ready to look at me—I also think there's a reasonable chance he'll have escaped to the beach. Or at least I'd rather he be out blowing off some steam in the surf than the alternative; still don't wanna think about it. Hugh is a get-out-and-find-something-to-take-your-mind-off-it kind of guy, rather than the type to sit around and brood, and I suspect he does a lot of his best thinking out on the waves. I wouldn't mind it so much right now either, but to be honest, I don't feel drawn to the ocean the same way Hugh and Phel do. I like being in the water, but I prefer to feel my own two feet on solid land or see it racing past me beneath the wheels of my bike, especially when it feels like everything else is falling away. So home it is. I can't really think of where else to go.

Except that when I trudge home and walk into the living room, I can't bring myself to sit my ass down on the couch and count the minutes until Hugh comes home. A bit too much like counting down to the executioner's axe, if you ask me. Part of me wants to pick up the phone and demand that Phel be here—no fucking way is he off the hook on account of his beef with me—but I'd also kind of prefer to gouge my own eye out with a toothpick. Whether that's anger or embarrassment talking doesn't matter. I won't call him. But hanging around with a finger up my ass ain't much my style either, so I recruit Callie, who's been pretty much ignored all morning, poor girl, and decide to go spend some quality time with the other love of my life, the one who never talks back or kicks my ass to the curb.

Being in Cardiff, where everything is just about within walking distance, I haven't given Lucy the kind of TLC she deserves lately. She's not particularly dirty, just dusty from sitting in the driveway all these weeks, but a little soap and water never hurt anyone, especially not with all the care I've put into her detailing. Besides, pampering my baby always manages to take my mind off everything from indigestion to the colossal fucking smoke show my life has recently become. Phel used to make fun of me for how much I babied my bike, but I didn't give a shit then and don't give a shit now. Hugh's not the only one who uses escapism and diversion as a means of getting his shit sorted out, and this is better than the way I used to handle stuff, which was to throw myself into as much sex and alcohol and women as I could get my hands on. While sex and alcohol don't seem like such a bad deal right about now, part of the problem is I only want to fuck and drink if I can do it with Phel.

I go wash the fucking bike.

It's a warm enough day out, if a bit windy and overcast, and within minutes of filling a bucket with water and soap and going to work on the pipes, I'm starting to sweat. I strip off my shirt, as much to stay cool as to avoid soaking myself through with the hose. I can already feel it working, the tension draining out of me, bringing me to that quiet place where I can think about where I am and what I have to do without feeling suffocated. Fuck meditation: give me a sponge and some quality Ducati time and I'm calmer than a Hindu cow. Well, almost.

I'm maybe halfway through scrubbing the rims when Callie gets excited and starts running around with the goofiest of expressions on her face. I peer around the end of the bike and see my brother's mile-long silhouette loping up the street. His surfboard is tucked protectively under one arm. I stop what I'm doing and get to my feet, balling up the rag in my hands and tossing it into the bucket so he can see I'm open and—what? Unarmed? If Hugh wanted to end me, he could clunk me over the head with the surfboard and that'd probably be it. I know he won't, despite the fact that we've exchanged our share of punches over the years, but hopefully he'll get the picture I'm ready for whatever he wants to dish out.

Instead he just comes up and stares at me for about a minute before he scritches one hand behind Callie's ears and disappears inside the house with her in tow, not even a word spoken. What the hell?

When he doesn't come back out again in the next few minutes, I try to throw off my growing sense of unease and go back to washing the motorcycle. Then I hear his voice from the front door.

"Nate?"

I'm back on my feet again in less than a second, shoulders tight with anticipation. "Yeah?"

"Can you come in here for a sec?"

Swallowing, I nod; makes sense he'd want to do this inside, where none of the neighbors can hear. Back into the bucket goes the washrag. "Yeah. Okay, Hugh," I tell him. "Be right—"

He's gone again before I even finish my sentence. That's also a bit weird, but I suppose the guy is upset enough that I can cut him some slack, and mostly I'm just relieved to see him steady on his feet and showing no signs of intoxication. Of any kind.

Inside, I find him huddled on the living room sofa with his head almost between his knees, while Callie, picking up on his distress, prances around nervously and flashes us both worried looks. Normally one of us would be trying to soothe her, bartering for calm with comforting pats, reassuring words, and the odd doggie treat, but considering my brother's demeanor is why she's all worked up, he's the one I'm most concerned about. Not knowing what to expect, I sit down next to Hugh, close enough that he knows I'm here, but not so close he'll feel hemmed in.

Silence floats between us for an agonizing few moments until I find my balls again and manage to start, "So listen, Hugh—"

But that's as far as I get, again, before my brother's head comes up and he says, "Nate, stop."

My mouth clicks shut and I can't do much else besides stare at him helplessly.

Now that Hugh's looking straight at me, I notice for the first time since he found us at Phel's house that he looks like shit, tired and pale and like he went three rounds with a tsunami. Considering he just came back from surfing, maybe that last one ain't far off. He takes a deep breath. "I know you've got a lot to say to me, Nate, and trust me when I say I want to hear it. No way am I letting you off the fucking hook—you *or* Phel. But right now…."

"What?"

I see my brother take a long, deep swallow, like he's physically trying to hold back vomit. "Right now I need you to sit here with me for a little while. We don't have to talk, but we can if you want, as long as it's about anything other than you or Phel or the incident from earlier I'd really like to just bleach from my mind, okay? That's all I ask."

A shiver travels down my spine and makes all the hair on my arms and legs stand on end. I try to hide the shudder that follows. "Hugh, what—" Voice catching, I dare to ask, "Did you… did you go out and do something? You know… something—"

"No." At that, he looks away and purposely won't meet my gaze again. "But I really want to, okay? And for the first time in a while, it went a hell of a lot further than just wanting to come home and have a beer and try to unwind. I wanted to obliterate all of this morning and everything else along with it." He doesn't say any more than that, but he doesn't have to. His meaning is pretty clear, and suddenly I'm the one fighting back vomit as the realization that I fucking drove him to this drops in my stomach, even though Hugh will claim otherwise till he's blue in the face. "Just sit here with me awhile," he says again.

Not knowing how to respond, I reach over and put an arm around his shoulders, and he lets me. His hand drops to my knee for support. Though his fingers tighten around the cap of bone a bit more than is comfortable, the last thing I can think about doing is complain he's squeezing too hard. "Okay, I'm not goin' anywhere," I eventually force out. "We can talk about anything you want. Let's just sit right here, Hugh."

Despite the offer, we don't talk, except when I notice Hugh's eyelids starting to droop after about an hour and I suggest he go to sleep. Reluctantly, he does, curling his large body up on the couch with far less awkwardness than I should ever expect from him. Within minutes he's asleep, probably worn out from surfing and whatever fight is going on inside him at this very moment. Watching him sleep makes tiredness overcome me, too, but I'm still too restless and would feel bad nodding off when he asked me to keep watch. Obviously he can't do any damage while he's asleep, but symbolically, I need to stay awake, keep an eye on him. If Phel comes by, and it occurs to me he might, I want to be able to send him home, since I know Hugh probably won't, not even if he's still spitting mad when he wakes. Much like his brother, Hugh has a hard time telling Phel no.

I do, however, allow myself the luxury of slipping into the kitchen for a snack when lunchtime—even a late lunchtime—comes and goes. I debate waking Hugh up to make sure he gets something to eat, then decide against it since he probably spent most of last night sleepless and worrying about Phel like a damned fool. Hugh needs the shut-eye, and a guilty part of me supplies he might be more amenable to conversation about the past couple of days' drama if he's well rested.

After a quick snack of peanut butter sandwiches, which makes me feel twelve again but manages to calm my jumpy stomach, I find myself sitting there at the kitchen counter, staring into space. I have no idea how much time goes by with me spaced out like that; it could be ten minutes or a whole hour. I don't snap out of it until I realize I've been holding my cell phone in my hand almost the whole time, clutching it in my fist like I'm either about to throw it or crush it like a beer can. My aching knuckles alert me to the fact I'm doing it at all, but I don't have to think real hard about why I took it out, even if I never acknowledged my own hand reaching into my pocket.

At first I hesitate, but after that it's a lot easier to dial the 740 area code than I would have thought, seeing as how I've avoided it all this time. The remaining digits follow practically on their own, memorized so long ago I don't have to think about which buttons I'm pressing. I deleted the speed dial setting before coming to Cardiff, to reduce the temptation of calling at every moment of weakness and doubt. I notice I'm starting to get a bit light-headed and lean my arms against the countertop for support. The rings stretch out for what feels like a century each, one after another until I know the answering machine's going to come on if someone doesn't pick up in the next two seconds.

Someone picks up.

This is okay, I tell myself. It's not a betrayal if I'm doing something I maybe should have done a long time ago.

There's a long pause before anything is actually said, but then Emilia tentatively asks, "Nate?" and I breathe an incredible sigh of relief.

"Yeah, Em," I answer raggedly. "It's me."

10

Phel

THE previous owner of Hugh's house had a thing for ostentatious doorbells, I think; it's not so much a chime as a chorus of barely musical noise approximating Handel's *Messiah*. It goes on and on and on, far longer than any doorbell should. Hearing it for the first time nearly changed my opinion of Hugh as a person, so offensive is the sound, and for weeks after he swore up and down it came with the house. Unsurprisingly, Nate is all too eager to mock Hugh about it at every available opportunity, and has been known to hammer on the buzzer whenever Hugh is particularly buried in work or if Nate happens to be cross with him. Childish, yes, but I admit to having been amused by such antics from time to time, since I've often thought about sabotaging the damn thing myself.

As I lift my hand to press the button, it occurs to me I've rung Hugh's doorbell more in the past couple of weeks than I have in months. Once upon a time—and it really does feel that way now—I could walk in the front door and help myself to a beer from the fridge. As far as Hugh was concerned, it was less trouble for me to look after myself and treat his home like my own than potentially interrupt him in the middle of writing or, more likely, be ignored outright. While there has been no formal revocation of my no-doorbell privileges, I think it's fair to assume I no longer occupy such haughty status as to walk into Hugh's house unannounced. More than that, I'm scared to try, since I don't know what waits for me on the other side.

It's been almost a day since I spoke to the Fessendens, except for an ominous text I received from Nate this morning: *Meet me @ Hugh's 2nite. 8pm. Need 2 talk 2 U guys.* That's it. When I responded asking for clarification, all I got was *Plz just come.* I took it as a measure of his seriousness that the expected innuendo was never made. Not knowing whether or not Nate has already spoken to Hugh about the series of unfortunate and stupid events that have led us to this point, I can't be sure whether this meeting is to discuss the matter at hand, or something else. Whatever the case, anticipation sent my stomach plummeting to my knees as soon as I received the message, and there it's remained all day. I'm early, I know, but I couldn't bear another minute of sitting around my house doing nothing.

Hugh opens the door still glowering at the doorbell chime, and his expression darkens that little bit more when he sees me standing there. The only one unequivocal in her greeting is Callie, who shoves past him to come sniff around my hands, tail wagging joyously. For a moment Hugh looks at her in betrayal, then says to me, "Nate's not home yet."

I try not to scowl. Even if that's the case, does he expect me to go home and come back again, or maybe wait on the front stoop like a dog? Surely Hugh can't be that disgusted with me. Besides which, there's a reason I came a bit earlier than Nate specified in his text. "I wanted to speak to you before Nate lets us in on whatever surprise he's hiding," I tell him. "If that's acceptable."

Hesitating, Hugh continues to block the doorway with his body until I give up and start to turn away, sighing heavily. He grabs my arm unexpectedly. "Wait." I glance back at him, and he shuffles his feet like he's the one who should be embarrassed and uncertain. "I'm sorry. I think it's probably a good idea if we have a minute to speak alone too. Come in."

I follow him into the kitchen with Callie in tow and see he's in the middle of fixing himself a modest dinner of spaghetti and tomato sauce. It's inadequate and boring, since Nate is the unabashed cook in the family, and it tells me there's still some distance left between them. The thought floods me with shame. Despite everything, I'm worried what will become of Hugh's relationship with Nate. Cut off from my own family, I don't want that for either of them. Nate has made bad choices, yes, and hurt people, but knowing as I do how much he loves his family, especially Hugh and Liam, it's not a fate I'd wish on him, not even at my most bitter.

As if he senses my assessment of the scene, Hugh courteously asks, "Have you eaten?"

I shake my head. "I haven't, but I doubt I could keep anything down right now anyway." He shrugs in sympathy. "Thanks, though."

"Uh-huh."

Forever ago, I used to excel in taking control of situations in which I felt like a fish out of water, using my suits and matching ties and expensive haircuts as a shield between myself and my fear of not owning a room enough to meet my father's standards. Hugh shouldn't instill me with this same worry, but right now he does. Right now, I know I'm not owning anything.

As if he understands, Hugh goes to the fridge and grabs a beer, popping the top off against the counter before he hands it over. Whether it's meant to be for liquid courage or a sign all is not lost, I can't be sure. Hugh grabs one for himself too and downs it considerably faster than I could even attempt. Soon enough, the silence begins to stretch out as long and thick as syrup.

Just as quickly, it becomes too much. "How was I supposed to tell you it was your brother who ruined my life?" I blurt out, and I don't miss the way Hugh's fists clench in response. He doesn't answer, though I can tell he wants to, and I'm so desperate to have out with it all I can't help but goad him a little. "Well?"

"You should have just... *told me!*" he finally explodes. Such an overly simplistic declaration would normally be enough for an eye roll from me, but I know Hugh knows this isn't the most eloquent response he could have given either. Likewise, it's usually the simplest of statements that require the most complex answers.

I try to consider what it might sound like to come out and tell Hugh the whole thing. Of course, it would all be different now than if I'd explained it weeks ago, more different still if I'd done so before I knew he and Nate were related, but before I can think too hard, I find the words falling from my lips. I speak slowly, as though my brain is unsure of the story. Unable to watch Hugh, I focus on my hands instead, pulling and twisting the hem of my plaid shirt—one of Nate's? I no longer know what I own anymore—between my fingers.

"I met Nate in Columbus over a year ago. He was the most beautiful man I'd ever come across and just... the way he looked at me was so unlike how anyone had ever looked at me before. We fucked. That was supposed to be the end of it." I pause and look up at Hugh to find him watching me in a fixed way, though his expression is uneasy.

"I had no idea he was married, no idea about Liam or anything else, I swear."

Hugh says, "I know. Nate told me."

I resist the urge to grab Hugh's arm and shake him, fighting hard to remain where I am. "I'd never... *been* with someone before like I was with Nate. Never had a boyfriend, never was a part of something longer than one night or maybe a weekend. I didn't think I was cut out to love someone the way I wanted to love Nate; it scared the shit out of me. But every time he came to me, it was like he knew my mind was just waiting for him to change it, like it was impossible he was the only one who wanted what he thought we could have."

I swallow at the memory the same as I always do, feeling the weight of that love pressing down on me until I couldn't tell myself apart from it. The constant anticipation of suffocating to death with it, but finding each breath easier than the last. "You don't know what that's like, Hugh, because you're the type of man who's always known you could have a family—you probably knew the second you met Nell you would marry her. I grew up thinking I'd never have any of that until I met Nate, and then I started to want it more than I wanted everything else. I was *ready* to throw everything else away for him because of how badly I wanted that dream."

"And you had it taken away from you," Hugh finishes, voice tight. "I know how that feels, Phel. You don't have to tell me what it's like to have the rug swept out from under you and all your dreams with it."

"But do you know how it feels to have to look at the person who caused it?" I answer. "What it would have felt like if you came face to face with the person who fired that shot?"

Hugh jerks like I've slapped him in the face, but recovers quickly. "But you went back to Nate, Phel. You've been saying for months how your life was totally wrecked, and yet I bet almost as soon as he showed up, you went crawling back."

"*He* was the one who begged me to come back," I counter, but the minute the words are out, I know how stupid this distinction sounds. "But yes, I was foolish enough to fall for it a second time."

"Fall for what?" Hugh asks. "You already knew everything, didn't you? Did Nate surprise you with something new?"

I shift my weight from foot to foot and look back down at my hands. "No. There was nothing new."

"Then you went back in with your eyes open, man," Hugh answers. "Whatever decisions you made were all up to you. I'm not saying Nate gets a free pass for what he did, but you coulda walked away this time and didn't, same as you coulda chosen to tell me the truth, and didn't." I knew that was going to come back around in short order.

Trying hard to say exactly what I feel, however difficult, I grimace. "Admitting I'd gone back to him was no less difficult than breaking the news to you about our history," I say quietly. "Because I knew you'd say exactly this. And I knew you'd be right."

"Then why the hell *did* you go back?"

Still hesitant, I shrug, since the inadequacy of the gesture is no different than the inadequacy of the English language to describe everything I've been feeling these last few weeks, or months, or year. The word "madness" doesn't quite cut it. "I wanted to rewrite history, I think."

"That's not possible," says Hugh with rigid certainty. "What happened, happened, and trying to do it over with the kind of baggage you've been hauling around is hardly going to help. Even I know you aren't that stupid."

I flinch. "Well, I *was*. Or just very good at convincing myself while I was at it." We both let that hang there a while, neither of us willing to touch it, and when I break the silence, it's not to apologize or to offer more excuses as to why I've been such a fucking idiot, in all respects. "We're not so different, Hugh," I tell him. "What I said to you on the phone yesterday wasn't a complete lie—I do value this friendship, and I want to salvage whatever bit of trust might be left. Or better yet, rebuild it. I don't know how, but that's what I want." I can't bear to say out loud that I probably won't be around much longer to do it, since I know Nate isn't going to be the one forced out of Cardiff in this equation, but Hugh probably knows that already too. "I was afraid the truth might do more damage. I didn't want to lose you either. Not in addition to everything else."

"Lying to my face isn't the horse I'd have chosen to bet on," Hugh deadpans.

"I know," I answer raggedly. "And you have to know how much I regret it."

Whatever Hugh might have said is cut off by the front door slamming, a warning, however insufficient, that Nate is home. Any bombshells still in store are about to make themselves known. My stomach tries to launch itself from my knees up to my throat, and I have to turn away from Hugh to hide how nauseated I must look. From his pained expression, I know he catches it anyway, but instead of commenting, he goes to meet Nate.

"So what's with all the secrecy, dude?" he asks, not bothering with pleasantries as I hear Nate's footsteps approach the kitchen. I don't blame the man, who must be thoroughly sick of surprises by now. His tone suggests there's already been some kind of a discussion between him and Nate, but I'm startled to find he knows as little about the topic of today's surprise discussion as me.

"No secrecy here," says Nate, and by the lengthy pause that follows, I know he's waiting for me to turn around and look at him. Like he needs my permission to continue. I do, very hesitantly, because his gaze itches and burns between my shoulder blades. For several long moments our eyes meet and he doesn't smile. "I have to talk to both of you," he explains, more to me than Hugh, it seems. "Together."

"So talk," snaps Hugh, clearly antsy.

Nate nods. "Let's go into the other room," he suggests and, off the blank look shared between Hugh and me, adds, "It's just more freaking comfortable, okay?" He then turns and walks away with the clear expectation for us to follow. Exchanging another glance, Hugh and I do just that. I inhale sharply when I feel his hand brush reassuringly across my shoulder. The gesture of support comes out of nowhere and could crumple me where I stand.

In the living room, Nate gestures for us to take the sofa while he himself paces awhile before settling lightly on the edge of the coffee table. His fingers drum an anxious tattoo against the wood. It makes me uncomfortable that Nate sits closer to me than he does Hugh, slotting our legs together in a way that's loose and perhaps even unintentional, for his thigh barely brushes my knee unless I jostle it around. A little voice suggests he's trying to be close to me, and I know then that this conversation won't be good, not if he's steeling himself like this, reaching for whatever support he can get. Why does he think I'm the one to give it? But still, when I catch his knee bouncing nervously, I want to reach out and still it with my hand. After all this time, it agitates me to see Nate in a state of struggle.

He clears his throat a little. "I know it's weird to call a meeting like this, considering we all practically live here...." *Or did*, I think. "But I've been thinking through some stuff in the last twenty-four hours and made a few decisions I couldn't sit on any longer. I'm sorry if this seems out of the blue," he adds.

Oh Christ. Not only is this bombshell going to be bad, but it's going to be *big*, because Nate doesn't give these types of wind-up speeches for anything. It's clear he's working himself up to it as much as he's trying to ease us in.

Surely Hugh must know this, too, but he groans and says, "Jesus, Nate, just spit it out," like the anticipation is killing him too much for the warm-up. He wants it ripped off like a Band-Aid, no preliminaries and no courtesy. I'd understand, except I know that whatever comes out of Nate's mouth next won't affect Hugh half so much as it affects me. *This is it. He's going to ask me to leave*, I realize, and my hands tighten on the sofa cushions as my stomach flips violently.

Sure enough, Nate's eyes flicker over to mine, confirming that Hugh is here to receive the information, but otherwise this conversation is between Nate and me. "This isn't working," Nate says, voice catching, and he gives a little shake of his head. "Guess that ain't no surprise, but one of us has to get the fuck on out of here before someone gets hurt even worse. I can't do it anymore." The silent *Phel* tacked on to the end of that statement is terribly clear to me; clear to Hugh, too, since he glances over once. I swallow and open my mouth to speak, but Nate shakes his head again, with more firmness, and says, "Don't. Just... no more arguing."

"What are you trying to tell us?" asks Hugh, sounding unsettled. I don't know what he and Nate talked about last night, or any of the conversations they've had since Nate came to California, but from the way Hugh's jaw tenses, I get the feeling his thoughts are a lot closer to my own. Pieces start to click into place about why Nate has called us both here. "You can't just ask Phel to leave, if that's what this is about," he says. My breath catches, because that—that I didn't expect. "Obviously you guys have got problems between you I wouldn't touch with a ten-foot pole, but you can't expect him to pack up and go because you can't deal with it anymore."

To my surprise, Nate doesn't respond angrily to this decree—doesn't even seem taken aback. He just nods. "I know," he answers, then meets Hugh's eyes for a brief instant before turning back to me. "I'm not asking anyone to take off or give up their home. I came here to tell you *I'm* the one leaving."

"*What?*" I assume the cry comes from Hugh, because my stomach is so busy twisting itself into knots that it's a miracle I don't vomit all over myself. But Nate and Hugh's heads both swivel in my direction, suggesting that I, in fact, am the one responsible for the protest.

Nate smiles at me in the least happy way imaginable, and sighs so his eyes fall shut for a moment. "I called Emilia yesterday," he tells us gruffly. "At the time I didn't exactly know why I did it, but I managed to get her on the phone for the first time since this all started and... we talked. I realized we're at a dead end here, and I for one can't keep chasing after things that are never gonna happen, not when there's a whole stack of problems back home I need to stop running away from too." We lock eyes again, Nate and I, and I notice his are starting to go glossy and wet with tears. He reaches out and slides a hand against my cheek, calloused fingers catching against the stubble on my chin.

"I love you, Phel," he murmurs, and my heart wants to clench around the words so hard I think I actually flinch. I don't know how I can want to hear him say that so badly, and yet not want to hear it at the same time. Meanwhile, this moment is so painfully private that even Hugh shies away, letting Nate continue. "I love you, and you know deep down I'd give anything to make things right between us. Anything." Nate swallows, forehead deeply furrowed, and my throat contracts in sympathy as I lean forward into him. "There's nothing left to prevent us from being together, Phel—no secrets, no marriages, no reason to be afraid someone will find out and try to come between us. For the first time ever, we actually have a shot at being together the way we wanted from the beginning." Nate's fingers stroke against my jaw one last time before his hand withdraws.

"But you're still so angry, man. I can't say or do anything right, and I don't know what will make you let go of that. Hell, you don't ever have to; you deserve to feel how you want after what I did. But this is how *I* feel, and we're just gonna go on floggin' the dead horse until we're both even more miserable and Hugh can no longer stand the sight of us. So maybe it's time we call it quits for good. Before things get any worse. You got a life here in California you should go about building; I want that for you. And I got a son back in Ohio who needs a father. It's time we both do what's best for us. The last few weeks haven't been good for anyone."

Hesitantly—for a moment I'd forgotten entirely he's still here—Hugh speaks up. "So… you and Emilia are gonna forget all this ever happened?" His tone suggests what he thinks of that plan, and I silently thank him for buying my spinning mind some time to continue its useless whirring.

With a grunt, Nate rubs his palms against his thighs, and I see the faint dampness left behind as further proof of his anxiety. "No, we're still getting divorced," he answers. "Nothing else for it. But after two hours with Em on the phone yesterday, she eventually admitted she doesn't want Liam to grow up in a broken home any more than I do. We don't need to be married or in a relationship to raise our son together, and the rest… we'll figure it out when I get there. She told me I could take the guest room while we decide if we should stay in the house, or if I should get my own place. It's not perfect, but it's a start. I know Liam will be happy." To Hugh alone, he says, "You know I'll always be around when you need me, Hugh. Right? Whatever it is, I'll be there, and you got Phel to make sure you don't do anything too stupid out here when I'm gone."

It shouldn't escape Hugh's attention that we haven't decided—or he hasn't—whether this is a possibility. Whether it's what we both want. Do I wish to stay in California and build a new life that is finally my own and not the structured false security of a rehabilitation program? Persuade a couple of rough, hippie craftsmen to let me buy out their surfboard business on the beach? Make a name for myself? Yes, that's what I've wanted for months now, to be past this whole debacle. But it isn't so simple, and both Hugh and the hard knot of fear in my stomach know it.

"Well, aren't you going to say something?" Hugh asks me. Though the words are harsh, his voice isn't, and before I can speak up with an *I don't know*, Nate spares me the effort.

"No, Hugh, it's okay," he says, looking right at me. Like last time, there won't be a good-bye, and even though I'm no longer the one who's running, I know I'm still the one who could stop this all right now by taking Nate's hand in my own and saying, *No, stay*. It's all he's ever wanted to hear from me. Those two little words, proof there's someone who will fight for him. But I can't get them out, can't pull them into the light through all the mess of anger and heartbreak and pain still swirling inside me. Nate knows. With a penetrating look that strips me of whatever capacity for speech I might have still possessed, he says, "It's better if he doesn't say anything."

TODAY is my last day at Palermo. Nate left a couple of days ago, heading north along the I-5 on a route that will take him through Eastern California, Arizona, New Mexico, Texas, Oklahoma, Missouri, Illinois, and Indiana, then up into Ohio. As I've been largely unable to sleep at night, or any other time for that matter, I've followed his route in my head out of a sense of pique aimed at no one but myself. Not long before that, Nate was still a warm weight in my arms. Now he's so far out of my reach, so far beyond what I can see, there's not much else for me to do besides stand here and take stock of what's left.

 The bedroom closet yawns open before me in sharp throwback to a time, not so very long ago, where I stood in much the same position in Columbus and thought about all I'd be leaving behind, the majority of my worldly possessions no longer necessary to my life. I once had two apartments' worth of belongings and more suits than a Seville Row tailor, and now, having culled most of my old wardrobe, everything I own fits into a single suitcase. There's nary a pinstripe in sight, while the softness of Italian leather shoes and silk ties are completely unsuited to the sand and surf of California. I kept a few items for sentimental reasons and discarded or donated everything else.

 Certainly it's a rude awakening to realize how little I owned in my old life beyond what I needed for work or making myself presentable to my parents. I had no hobbies, no personal memorabilia outside my relationship with Nate, no family heirlooms I cared enough about to take with me except a single picture of Aurelia and me as children. Even my collection of movies and music felt secondary, and reminded me far too much of Nate to warrant keeping. My sister, in addition to helping me unload what I could and arranging for my properties to be put up for sale, promised to safeguard the rest until I had my life back in order. But I now know I'll never be that Phelan again. More importantly, I don't want to be. If the past few days have taught me anything, it's this: that man is dead. Pity I wasted so many months trying to revive him, with zero success. It's in packing up the bare minimum of what I need to survive that I realize how hard I was hanging on to a ghost.

Contrary to what Nate probably thinks, I didn't run out on him out of spite on the day Hugh discovered us; rather, I hightailed it because I knew another second alone with him in my house would shatter every last iota of willpower I had. How close I was to giving in terrified me—I wanted so badly to lose myself to the fantasy Nate conjured for me.

Of course, having failed to impart this to him, it's an empty excuse—as empty as any of the excuses I could possibly come up with for how I've treated him. I was hurting, yes, and angry, and at the time it was easy to pretend I didn't care what impression I left him with, or how angry or hurt I left him in return. "Let him think I'm lost to him forever" was my original idea, like this was the all-important big picture I wanted to make him see all along. But I barely made it down the road before I realized how absurd that was, that I was striking out at an enemy that no longer existed, if it ever had. Never mind integrity. Never mind trying to be the kind of man I'd so wanted to be, once upon a time, for Nate. For myself.

Immediately I wanted to march right back there and apologize, only to discover the chutzpah had deserted me. Instead I chose to wander the grounds until I thought it was safe to go home, alone except for my shame. Now I have even less than that, naught but a bitter taste in my mouth that isn't likely to go away anytime soon. No matter how much I try to reassure myself that pride isn't an easy demon to buck, that better men have destroyed themselves for less, it's a hollow comfort. I should have tried harder, realized sooner what—and who—I was turning my back on. This entire time, I've told myself that person is Nate. It never occurred to me the real answer might be myself.

You know what they say about hindsight.

By the time Nate made his big announcement, I was desperate to go to Willa for advice. She was my mirror, though I was afraid of what I would see looking back at me. Our next and final appointment was scheduled for the following morning, thank God, but I wondered how much flak I would get for canceling so many of our previous sessions. She and I hadn't spoken in a couple of days, not since our debate about the power dynamic in my relationship with Nate. So much had happened since then, it felt like it'd been several years rather than a few days. Because I was still sore about that last conversation, and too caught up in everything else after that, I wasn't much in the mood for a sit-down chat. But after Nate announced he was leaving, I found I just... didn't care. It was a conclusion, after all, to my time with Willa and my stay at Palermo, and in the midst of everything, I realized I was compelled to apologize.

Of course I was wrong about everything. I'm not such an asshole that I can't admit it. I felt guilty about what I said the last time I saw Willa, and not only because she was on the money. Going into that conversation with Nate and Hugh, I had a sinking feeling I would find out how much the power balance had shifted in Nate's favor, though the whys and wherefores were still largely unknown to me. He didn't know it either—still thought I was the one in control. But I've never been that person. By day's end, there were no illusions about who held the reins, not for either of us. I just wish it hadn't happened so late.

Once again, however, I'm getting far ahead of myself. I went to meet with Willa, and in about thirty seconds flat, we moved away from small talk about my upcoming emancipation and on to the subject of Nate, Hugh, and the unceremonious revelation of the whole affair. Much to my surprise, Willa didn't ask me how I felt about it. It was as if she knew starting with the most obvious subject would only result in further tension and confusion between us.

Instead she folded her legs beneath her on the soft, comfortable chair she liked to sit in during our formal sessions, which were held in her office, and tucked her hair back behind her ears in that habitual way of hers. "Earlier today I was going through all our session notes from the past few months," she began. "I realized there's one thing we've never talked about this whole time."

There was something we hadn't talked about? I was surprised. I probably said as much in the glance I shot her, but for her benefit, I asked, "And what's that?"

Willa smiled at the dryness of my tone. "Your interaction with Nate's wife, Emilia," she explained. "You once mentioned she was how your family found out about your affair with Nate, but never elaborated. I thought, since this is our last session, you might be willing to talk about it now. You have to admit it bears some thematic consistencies with your current predicament."

Snorting, I cocked my head. "Is that a polite way of saying I fucked up both times in the exact same way?"

With a soft chuckle, Willa shook her head. "You're giving yourself too much credit, Phel. You don't deserve all of the blame, though I do think history was bound to repeat itself in light of some of the choices you've made. Most people don't realize how much their lives will follow a certain pattern until they make one small change, a simple adjustment to their reactions or way of thinking that can put everything onto a different track entirely."

I fought the urge to get my back up at that. "Willa, you've made it abundantly clear you don't approve of the decisions I've made with Nate." Swallowing, I then add, "And you were right. He's gone—left me behind. Is that what you need to hear?"

She smiled. "That's where you're mistaken, Phel. You respond to these conversations as though I'm someone you have to impress or justify yourself to—I have my opinions, obviously, and objectively speaking I recognize where you have certain patterns that keep repeating themselves. But I'm not here to tell you right from wrong. What the heck do I know? I've made plenty of mistakes in my life. My only purpose here is to be your friend and help you understand the choices you make. *Maybe* to help you make better choices in the future too. That's all. No judgment, no preaching, just rigorous honesty like we agreed at our first session. Right? Whatever it takes to get you back on track and happy again."

Back on track to what, I wondered? Everything's gone. And if I was honest with myself, I wasn't all that happy before either, unless I counted the delirious year I spent with Nate. No, the most I could hope for was a blank slate and some assurances my best friend wasn't going to take out a hit on my life before the end of the day, and maybe after that I could hit the road and find a new dream. First, however, I had to get through this conversation. "Talking about Emilia Santos-Fessenden makes that possible?"

With another chuckle, Willa sighed and tapped her pen against her writing pad. "No," she said wistfully, "maybe not. But I must admit I'm curious, myself, as to how things unfolded. And also why Emilia is the one person in this whole affair, other than Hugh and Liam, you don't bear any ill will towards."

Shrugging, I hesitated to answer. "I've had time to feel many different things towards Emilia," I began, "but ill will isn't one of them. She's what my father would call a class act. Despite being in a position to make my life even more of a living hell, she never did. Not like I would have done. She never gave any sign she resented me either."

At this, Willa frowned. "I thought you said she's the reason you were outed to your family?"

"She is," I answered with a nod. "It wasn't intentional on her part. I guess Nate must have given her the details after she caught us, told her who I was... which I suppose is only fair, since I'd want to know too. Even though I did everything in my power to keep Nate from contacting me after we broke up, Emilia practically made it her life's mission to track me down. It wasn't hard—just about everyone in the Midwest or on the East Coast knows who my family is. And anyone with a passing familiarity with Columbus could tell you exactly which building I worked in, since my last name is written on the side."

"So she came to confront you," Willa concluded. I half expected her to write that down, but she didn't.

"Not at first. Emilia didn't storm into my office like a jealous housewife—she went about trying to contact me the traditional way, with phone calls and messages left with my secretary."

I thought back to those couple of weeks and the dozens of messages and missed calls I found waiting for me every time I sat down at my desk. I'd disconnected my home phone and changed my mobile number, even the locks on my apartment, but there was no way to prevent Emilia from calling me at work except to keep avoiding her. Word got around the office pretty fast, and everyone, including William Carpenter, a visiting executive from my father's offices in New York, assumed she was the jilted woman with whom I'd been having an affair. It was almost enough to make me smile, remembering the lecture I received from Mr. Carpenter about keeping business and pleasure separate, the potential scandal that could rock my family's Christian values if it came out I'd been carrying on with a married woman, not least one with a family. Despite all that, I was pretty damn nervous when Carpenter threatened to contact my father if I didn't clean up my mess and the news became public.

Willa considered this for a moment. "Did she seem agitated that you were avoiding her?"

I shook my head. "That's just it… she never did." I'd listened to some of those voice mails and Emilia never sounded anything but sad, desperate to talk to me and get some of the answers we'd both been denied, but still calm. Maybe she did yoga too. I had no idea how much Nate had told her, but it obviously wasn't enough. "I felt bad for her. Then one day I guess she decided to put an end to things for good and came to the office in person."

"Yikes." Willa inhaled sharply.

"No," I corrected, shaking my head again. "It wasn't like that at all."

Emilia walked into our offices with her head high and asked to see me in a voice so calm and composed that my secretary, Amy, didn't think twice about letting her in to see me. Smartly, Emilia had dressed in a conservative pantsuit and had her hair pulled back in a neat ponytail; she looked every bit the high-powered businesswoman, not at all out of place. When Amy rapped on my door and ushered Emilia inside, even I had to admit she was a beautiful woman, tall and with striking Mediterranean features I immediately recognized from Liam. She could have been the dark lady of Shakespeare's sonnets. I suppose she was exactly as I pictured, though in that moment I couldn't decide whether or not to be threatened. It was necessary to remind myself she wasn't the one Nate had the affair with, though all that thought accomplished was to send me back into another tailspin of guilt. I couldn't help but notice the shadows that crowded beneath her eyes, the faint puffiness that came from days of crying, which no makeup could hope to conceal. I recognized these things because of what I saw each time I looked in the mirror. No doubt Emilia took one look at me and knew I wasn't handling the situation much better. It gave me an odd sense of solidarity I didn't want to feel.

"Mr. Price," she said, voice even. "I hope I'm not interrupting anything… I know you know who I am."

Defeated, I slumped back in my chair and gestured for her to close the door of my office behind her, though not before asking Amy to hold my calls and suggesting she go get us both coffees from the bakery a few blocks away. It would keep her away from the office for a good twenty-five minutes. Amy, as much as I was grateful for her talents as an assistant, was an incorrigible gossip. I knew she'd otherwise be listening in to every word.

Turning back to Emilia, I attempted a smile. "Mrs. Fessenden." I swallowed heavily around the name, which felt like lead on my tongue. "I—I'm sorry I've not returned your calls. I just didn't...." No ready excuse came to mind, and I shrugged. "I had no idea what to say to you. Though it's obvious you're far more certain as to what you'd like to say to me."

To my surprise, Emilia chuckled. "I'm not Mrs. Fessenden," she said, irony heavy in her voice. "My last name is still Santos. And no, I have no idea what to say to you. But I'd like you to call me Emilia anyway." She paused, watching me, and as the seconds ticked by, I could feel her thinking, *What the hell is it about this guy that made my marriage worth destroying?* I had no answers for her. "Can I call you Phelan?"

I rather appreciated the use of my formal name, since Nate and Aurelia were the only ones who ever called me Phel. Everyone else, even my parents, called me Phelan or Mr. Price. I nodded and gestured for her to take a seat on one of the Barcelona chairs in front of my desk. "Can I get you anything to drink?" I asked, compelled to carry on with as many pleasantries as possible before all hell broke loose.

Not fooled, Emilia crossed her legs and folded her hands in her lap, a gesture I read as quiet determination not to appear defensive. It mostly worked, except I could see her fingers trembling. "Phelan," she began, "we can just cut to the chase. I know it was rude to barge in here, but it became clear after the fourth or fifth missed call that you knew exactly who I was, and had no intentions of speaking with me. I get that, but—I deserve more than the brush-off from your secretary. This is my family we're talking about. My family that's ruined."

"Because of me," I offered, voice tight.

She shook her head, surprising me yet again. "No, *not* because of you." I caught her blinking rapidly in a sure-fire sign she was fighting off tears, and the pain in her face was almost enough to make me choke up too. "Nate has been pretty sparing of the details," she said, "and yet the one thing he made pretty clear is you had no idea about any of this—that you were just as surprised to find me at the house that day as anyone. He's defended you from the start, so know that. Whatever the reason we're here now, it's not because of you—it's because of Nate.

At least he isn't trying to deny it." Her mouth twisted. "Funny time for him to start showing a sense of chivalry; I might have appreciated it more if I hadn't just found out he'd been screwing another man for over a year."

I flinched.

Once we got down to it, the information Emilia wanted to know was pretty basic—I got the impression Nate had already given her most of the answers, but she seemed disinclined to trust them until she heard it from me: where Nate and I met, how long we'd been seeing each other, whether I'd ever had any idea he might still be married. If I thought he was really gay. I told her everything without hesitation, only pausing when I found myself too overcome with emotion to continue talking without breaking down entirely. Truth be told, I was afraid not to, not trusting the lengths to which such an emotionally exhausted woman as Emilia might go to find some peace of mind. As I sat there trying to compose myself, a hand came out and covered mine on top of the desk.

"Do you love him?" Emilia asked frankly. She was crying too, albeit in more of a controlled way, and her voice didn't waver. In fact, it was such a mixture of hard and worn-out I almost wanted to ask what was going through her head at that moment. Her face betrayed little, or rather, so much that I didn't know where to begin.

At that point, at least, I wasn't yet able to lie, not to myself or anyone else. It had to have been pretty damn clear on my face how I felt about Nate. "More than anything," I answered, and she sighed, not with impatience, but resignation.

"That's what I thought," she said. I must have looked confused, because she gestured vaguely and settled back against the chair rest with a far-off expression on her face, which looked ready to crumple at any moment. "When I walked in and found you together, that was the first time I really realized, without a doubt, that something in my marriage was irreparably damaged." She paused to look down at her hands, then back up at me, biting her lip. "I know Nate didn't marry me because he thought it was true love," she stated. "We were both too young when Liam was born; Nate wanted to do what was best for everyone. He's been a good husband and an amazing father, but I know it's not what he'd have chosen for himself if things had worked out differently." Grimacing, she added, "Sometimes I wish he had. Sometimes I wish I'd never told him about Liam at all."

Such a bald statement made me shift uncomfortably. "I don't think that's what he thinks about," I told her. "He's never regretted being a father to Liam, and I doubt he's ever resented being there to support you either."

When I said it out loud, it seemed to fit. Even if Nate truly wasn't attracted to women, to Emilia, there was a sense of duty about the man that would have overridden everything else, every regret and secret desire he was too scared to acknowledge, let alone pursue. I knew this because I felt the same conflict within myself whenever I thought about disappointing my family. It wasn't a simple matter of choosing one over the other, nor was it a case of erasing my sense of grief and bitterness just because I didn't envy Nate his position. At the end of the day, he'd done this with his eyes open. Maybe if I hadn't been the one to get burned, I'd have been a lot more understanding—being with me in secret was incredibly cowardly, but in some ways also the single biggest act of bravery he'd committed.

"I know all that," Emilia assured me, smiling weakly. "But that doesn't change the fact that when I saw him with you, there was this look on his face I've never seen before except when he looks at Liam—real love. You can't fake that, and you can't hide it. At first I didn't quite know what it was, because he's never looked at me that way, ever. But that's how he looked at you, Phelan. You know I have absolutely no reason to lie about that."

"I'm sorry."

"'I'm sorry' doesn't change the fact that I'm not the one my husband's in love with, does it?" she shot back.

Her words made me squeeze my eyes shut until she got the message and stopped talking. We were both silent for a while until I opened my eyes again and found her watching me. "It doesn't matter how he looks at me," I forced out. "Just like it doesn't matter what he says or how many times he says he loves me, wants to be with me. What matters is honesty and trust, and knowing the person you're with. I don't know Nate at all." Inexplicably, this made me angry with Emilia. "How can you just sit there and be so calm when he ruined those things with you too?"

Emilia hesitated, but when she spoke, her voice was still steady. "Because deep down I knew there was something going on," she replied. "I didn't know what, but obviously you don't have your husband carry on an affair for a whole year without picking up on *something*. I just couldn't get any proof there was another woman. If I'd known Nate had found someone he cares about so much, I wouldn't have tried so hard to ignore all the signs—"

Despite knowing how cold I sounded, I cut her off. "I don't want him," I snapped. "Whatever Nate and I had is broken, do you understand? You might as well just keep him. Or throw him back, for all the difference it makes." Broken certainly didn't mean the same thing as forgotten, but I pushed onward, determined to sever myself from the whole business as cleanly as possible. "It's over. But you—you're still married to him, and what Liam needs most is a strong family who loves him. Whatever your ideas about how Nate feels, he obviously values your marriage far more than he valued his relationship with me. You should fight for it. I certainly won't be one to stand in your way."

Whatever Emilia had to say in response, I never got to hear it.

To Willa, I said, "All hell broke loose after that. Next thing I knew, Nate was storming into our firm—not like he was on the warpath, but like he was scared half to death of me talking to his wife. He must have figured out Emilia came to see me, and I guess he thought if he got there in time, he could stop us from meeting or my coworkers from hearing the truth. But that's obviously not what happened."

Consideringly, Willa said, "You fought with him?"

I chuckled. "Quite the opposite—we left my office to see what all the commotion was about, and I stood there dumbly and watched as Emilia came to my defense. She tried to get him to leave, accusing him of trying to keep more secrets, which only upset Nate more. He was aware no one else knew I was gay, but as soon as he started arguing with his wife, it was pretty clear which of them was my lover. No one had any doubts after that as to which team I played for. When I snapped out of it enough to try and get them to leave quietly, Mr. Carpenter had already called security. Not long after that, he was on the phone to New York to tell my father everything."

How quickly word could spread, and how quickly I found myself summoned to New York to explain myself. In the end, it was a short conversation: my father asked if it was true, if his only son was really a faggot like the society papers claimed, and an adulterer and home wrecker, no less. I was too tired and miserable to deny my sexuality any longer, and confessed to everything.

Funny, but I always expected that conversation to be a lot more explosive, whereas in reality it was such a controlled thing, such a simple dismissal. My family very quietly withdrew their acknowledgement of me at the same time they withdrew their financial support and their love. Perhaps the two had ever been indistinguishable. I was asked to pack up my offices in Chicago and Columbus, and others were hired in my stead. Mr. Carpenter's son was promoted to my old position. I didn't dare approach my father, but for three weeks I left messages and begged my mother to pick up the phone and talk to me, to no avail. Considering how I'd first refused to acknowledge Emilia, my mother's response seemed a cruel irony. Eventually even Aurelia called to say she had to sever contact, citing threats of disownment from my father if she continued to associate with me. She cried as she said it, but sever contact she did.

Pausing, I sighed and met Willa's gaze, surprised to find myself dry-eyed at a memory I hadn't been able to summon for months, not without feeling my stomach flip or the unpleasant churn of anxiety or my ears ringing with the force of an impending panic attack. In a way I almost missed it, since at least those things were concrete, definite, better than the weird void in which I now existed. "You know all the rest. Does that satisfy your curiosity?"

Seeming to understand my exhaustion, Willa reached out and took my hand. "I'm sorry, Phel. Thank you for telling me. You should be proud for facing this chapter of your history so bravely; I don't think you thought you could do it."

"I didn't," I admitted, "but it's behind me now." The answer sounded lame and unsatisfactory, but I had none better to give.

Though she nodded, Willa cocked her head. "If I can say so, Phel, you seem far less… hostile than you did a couple days ago. About Nate or any of this."

I grimaced, thinking of the way I stormed out of our last session with all the grace and entitlement of a four-year-old drama queen. Not one of my finer moments, to be sure, and I felt the blush that heated my cheeks. "I apologize for what I said to you. That was unnecessary and unfair. I didn't want to admit you were right, though in retrospect I wouldn't have been so angry if what you said wasn't true."

"I've heard worse," answered Willa, shrugging, but then she flashed a smile. "Thank you for the apology, though." I didn't always understand her, and it still made me uncomfortable to think she knew so much about me without the favor being returned in kind, but all things considered, I rather liked this woman. After hesitating, she added, "Am I to take it that your feelings toward your relationship with Nate have changed?"

It was the question I'd been dreading, as much from Willa as myself or anyone. "I don't know," I admitted. "I'm just so damn tired, Willa. Too tired to be angry with anyone, including Nate, but that doesn't mean I know how I feel about any of it. I just...." A juddering breath escaped me. "It doesn't matter now. He's gone."

Unwilling to let me leave it at that, Willa straightened and set her mouth into a determined line. "Keep going, Phel," she urged, reading my tendency to shy away from difficult admissions.

Frustrated, I sighed. "I feel like I laid down this giant minefield between Nate and myself," I began, still uncertain as to where I was going with this. "It seemed like the only way to keep myself safe was to keep him at a distance—by any means necessary. I don't know half of what was going through my head. But somehow Nate still managed to find his way through all that without acknowledging the personal danger to himself."

I wondered, then, if Nate really felt as uncertain as he acted around me, tiptoeing across eggshells like I was the very mine he might trip at any moment. I knew how full of uncertainty he was at times.

"He just kept getting closer and closer and, finally, when he decided to come out to Hugh, I thought, 'This is it. He's going to destroy everything for sure this time, starting with himself.' I couldn't let that happen, when it came down to it; I couldn't handle the idea of Nate coming out unsupported or, worse, me trying to force him to stay closeted. So I tried to push him out of harm's way and wound up hurting myself more. But that's...." I paused, starting to lose the tail end of the analogy even though it felt right in my head. "That's why

Nate was always so dangerous," I concluded. "He made me forget how to protect myself."

Although Willa acknowledged this with a nod, I knew she wasn't going to come out and agree with me. Not because I was automatically wrong, but because agreement was too easy and didn't do much by way of forcing me to grow. "Did it ever occur to you you're protecting yourself from the wrong things?" she asked.

In spite of myself, I laughed, the irony making it a hard, joyless sound. "I think it's pretty clear by now the only thing I need saving from is myself," I told her.

Myself, maybe, and a few other people that needed saving from me as well. Nate never came out and said I was the reason he left, not really, but he and I both knew I'm what pushed him to it, me with my anger and my spite and the need to wound, so strong that I was half-mad with it. In that much, Willa was right—I would never have felt so angry if I didn't still have feelings for him. If I didn't still love him. It's a shame that while I could have been trying to fix our relationship, I was set on punishing us both. And it hurt, more than I thought it could, since we'd been through this once already and I should have known what to expect. But just like the first time, the reality of not having Nate was a shock. Despite everything, I don't think I ever truly expected to be without him, even now. Like someone who has lost a limb, Nate's absence gave me the sensation of waking up from a dream of being whole, only to find a space where there was once an arm. Whatever my fervent longings, I knew I would never get it back again, and a replacement would never do.

A solid rap on the door of my cabin jerks me out of my daydreaming, and when I turn, I see Hugh standing there at the bedroom door, having let himself in. In his arms are several broken-down cardboard boxes and a roll of packing tape.

"Hey," he says, and the wide-eyed look on my face must speak volumes, since he adds, "I thought you could use some company, maybe some help packing up your stuff. Today's moving day, right?"

I nod. "Yes." I want to add that I'm not sure where I'm moving *to*, but that Hugh is here at all makes my knees weak with surprise and relief. The last thing I want to do is spoil it with my complaining. I'm a grown man, after all, and presumably if I've survived this long, I should be able to accomplish finding myself a place to live without help. "There isn't much to do," I tell him, "but thank you for coming."

Hugh smiles and sets the boxes down on the bed, then comes to stand beside me to survey my closet. "I would have thought there'd be more," he says. After a pause, he chuckles. "No offense, but I always kind of got the sense you were a bit of a...."

"What?"

"A label queen." Hugh shrugged. "I thought I'd find a closet full of designer jeans and custom suits. Instead your wardrobe looks about the same as Nate's." He sucks in a sharp breath at that, realizing his mistake, but I just smirk and shake my head to let him know it's alright, and hold back on mentioning half the clothes in here could very well have belonged to Nate at some point, considering the amount of wardrobe migration that seemed to occur while we were together. Not a lot, but some; in any event, I was spared having to go hunting around for many T-shirts and casual clothes when I arrived in Cardiff. Not for the first time, I wonder if Nate suddenly found himself digging up pocket squares and cuff links among his things after we broke up. The first time.

Putting that out of my mind, I resist the urge to put my hands on my hips in a way that would only give Hugh more ammunition to tease me. "I *am* a label queen," I assure him, sassing up my tone a little for his entertainment. "Or was. I had considerably more to pack up when I left the Midwest than I brought with me."

"What'd you do with it all?" he asks curiously. Hugh doesn't have what I'd call impeccable style. I don't always appreciate the volume of the patterns he chooses in his shirts, but I must respect his taste in designers, if nothing else. He has an eye for quality Nate could never quite bring himself to give a shit about. It isn't as though Hugh could ever make use of my old clothing, given the considerable difference in size between us, but I know he'd be appalled to learn I'd thrown anything out.

"I no longer had use for any of it," I explain. "Much as I appreciated a well-cut suit or a fine silk shirt, it would have been rather superfluous to drag all the trappings of my old life with me out here. I sold most of it or gave it away."

Hoping to get on with it, I resume emptying my closet into the suitcase I brought with me, and a moment later Hugh starts to pitch in, using the boxes for the odds and ends scattered about that don't really belong next to my jeans. We work in silence for a little while, and then he asks, still sounding perplexed, "What if you need it all back again?"

I stop to look at him, holding a pair of Nate's old sweatpants I never had the heart to get rid of, since they were softer and more comfortable than my most expensive cashmere sweater and never lost their scent of him even after dozens of washes. "I think that if I end up needing those things again," I say, "I'm doing something wrong. I don't want to go back to that life."

Saying no more, Hugh and I finish packing up the rest of my belongings in silence, and in less than an hour's time, the closets are empty and the dressers are bare. The last thing to disappear into my suitcase is the leather journal I've kept for a long time, since before meeting Nate, though the entries became rather few and far between when our affair took up again. I suppose I couldn't afford the level of self-reflection that required, knowing what I'd find, but I think I'd like to start writing in it again.

I want to comment on how utterly unnecessary it was for Hugh to offer me assistance in this task, since I completed it the first time around on my own. But all I say is "I appreciate your help, Hugh." There are two suitcases and three boxes, which Hugh hefts on his own without looking remotely inconvenienced by it.

"No problem," he answers, then jerks his chin at the door. "How about we get this stuff loaded up into my truck and hit the waves for a bit?" I hesitate, and he catches my reluctance. "Come on. It's a nice day out. I'll even let you buy me lunch."

I snort at that, but can't argue. Surfing sounds like the perfect way to put everything else out of my mind and give me the bit of Zen I've been craving for days. Then I remember my surfboard is still currently sitting in pieces in Hugh's garage. "I don't have a board," I remind him.

"There's an extra one at the house," he says. "Don't worry about it, let's just go."

As if he knows how much I'm dying to question the vagueness of his plans, Hugh doesn't give me much opportunity to argue as we go, first herding me into his Range Rover, then shoving a surfboard—Nate's, I recognize immediately—into my hands and telling me to change for the beach. This little reprieve from thinking has me grateful, in a way, not just because I begin to feel more secure that things might actually stand a chance of working out between me and Hugh, but because for once it feels wonderful not to know what's going to happen next and be denied the opportunity to fret. Ironically, I recognize this as yet another missing element in my recent affair with Nate. Rather than embracing the sacrifice of control or, alternately, the complete trust that was placed in me, I spent the whole time worrying about how it might be turned on its head. I don't know how Nate ever let himself go enough to trust that I wouldn't hurt him when I so badly wanted to. In the end, I couldn't give either of us what we wanted, because it wasn't a true give and take—it was simply losing, and losing, and losing.

But. The objective here is not to think, and already I'm spectacularly missing the point. We go to the beach, bare feet padding across the warm asphalt as we make our way through the streets of Cardiff, and true to Hugh's word, the waves look nothing but succulent from the shore, rolling out in a wash of white-tipped blue and green, the water dotted with wetsuit-clad bodies and brighter splashes of color off their surfboards. We struggle into our wetsuits, the wind bordering on chill, and clip the leads on our boards to our ankles before heading into the water.

Eagerness has me dashing straight into the waves, paddling out with furious strokes of my arms that Hugh seems to match without the slightest quickening of his breath, his long limbs sluicing easily through the water. Hugh might be the more natural athlete among us, but not the most daring surfer. His big body is unfailingly confident as he drops in and out of waves, but perhaps also because of his size, he is more likely to dither before rushing out into a swell that could pose an unexpected challenge.

I don't share his hesitation. I go for the first one I see, trusting the subtle lift of the hairs on the back of my neck as though it's possible to sense which wave will follow through on its faint promise of greatness. Unlike when I started, the swells no longer intimidate me, not even the big ones. I crave the moment of free-falling and the sudden lurch of my stomach that follows, same as whenever Nate's lips met mine, when he held my body still and showed me how it could sing.

The tide shifts and clashes faster with its constant ebb and flow. I catch another ride and am forced to bail before it can tumble me on my ass. Hugh finds a few more waves, but I can tell that he, along with the few other surfers out here in the lineup, is growing impatient with the inconsistency of the waves. Sure enough, they turn back one by one to head for home or a more reliable section of the reef, like the Suckouts. That leaves Hugh and me sitting out in the middle of the water alone, perched on our boards with not much choice other than to catch our breath and maybe talk. I don't mind. It doesn't feel like we've been avoiding it, exactly, but when Hugh looks at me I'm momentarily stricken and don't know what to say. He saves me the trouble, as usual.

"Nate called this morning to say he arrived safely in Ohio," he says, staring off in the direction of the horizon. He slicks his hair back away from his face. "Thought you might want to know."

Solemnly, I nod and fight off the sudden thickness in my throat. "Thanks. I'm... glad. I'm glad he's safe. I was wondering about that. That damn bike of his—it was a long way to travel alone at this time of year."

My response makes Hugh sigh angrily, and I recoil slightly. Before I can ask, though, he says, "You still don't have anything else to say about it? After *everything*?"

"I don't know what else there is *to* say," I admit. "Nate was right in that much; sometimes it's better to not say anything."

Hugh grunts, and I can't tell whether it's a noise of agreement or denial. "Well, I figure since I was going to ask you to come live with me, we should probably talk about it at some point."

I jerk in surprise. "You were going to—what?" Surely that offer got snatched off the table ages ago.

He meets my eyes steadily. "You heard me, Phel. I know you've probably been thinking about where the hell you're going to go after this, and, well... Nate was also right about what he said: you should stick around California. It's good for you to be out here, and... it's good for me for you to be out here too." He pauses, and I have a hard time deciphering the look that flickers across his face. "Assuming, of course, you want to be."

There is so much wrapped up in these few sentences that I scarcely know where to start. Of course, I've been hoping against hope for Hugh to accept my apology and plea for forgiveness; I'm not so stupid as to think I don't have work left to do in earning his trust back, but this is both such a significant step forward and a point of such confusion that for a moment I'm speechless. I don't understand how Hugh still wants to be my friend after I betrayed his confidence and, ultimately, broke his brother's heart. There's no question that's what I've done, on either count. I destroyed Hugh's trust and inflicted upon Nate as bad a turn as I felt had been done to me. What stalls me is the suggestion that I could want anything other than to stay here.

Enough time passes that Hugh seems to read my silence, for he gives a heavy sigh and splashes idly at the water near his knee. "Look," he begins, "I'm not gonna deny I'm hurt by how you and Nate carried on behind my back, but this whole situation has been a fucking kaleidoscope of messed up. I don't know if I'd have acted much differently if the roles were reversed."

I'm unable to resist the urge to fidget, even though the movement sends me listing a little to either side on my board. "That's nice of you to say," I answer. "But I don't think you're the kind of person who'd get yourself into that kind of mess to begin with."

There's a low laugh that's full of irony, and Hugh is back to pinning me with his stare. "That's where you're wrong, Phel. Maybe I don't have many gay love affairs in my past, but I'm not exactly what you'd call squeaky clean. I've had my share of fuckups no one else knows about besides Nate and the counselors at Palermo."

"The counselors at—" I stop dead, hesitating for a moment even to let go of my breath, while Hugh, on the other hand, seems to have trouble finding enough air for a breath of his own.

"Listen, Phel," he says, and starts pulling at the neoprene on his thigh, "there's obviously a lot of stuff you didn't tell me when we became friends, and—well. As it so happens, there's a lot of stuff I didn't tell you either." Catching the terrified expression on my face— *what now?*—he quickly holds a hand up. "It's nothing, like... *personal*," he explains in a rush. "Personal to me, okay, but not personal to you. I didn't tell you because it was a while ago, and you didn't have any real reason to know. But I think I should come clean now since we're in a sharing mode."

His face is so serious and pained that my mind immediately leaps to the worst possible scenario. "Did you kill someone?" I ask, half-joking but mostly not, and to my great relief Hugh blanches and barks out a laugh so relieved that it almost circles right back around to anxious.

"Jesus, no," he exclaims. "Is that what you think?"

Feeling awkward, I try to shrug. "No, but when you give me an introduction like that... and your books are *awfully* violent...."

"Okay, okay."

He still looks so nervous. I can't not try to help him out in some way, though I still have no idea what he's about to say. "You can tell me, Hugh," I encourage. "By now there's probably not a whole lot you can say that will shock or otherwise scandalize me."

"I know." He sighs again. "It's not that. I just... don't talk to people about this. Ever." Our eyes meet again before his gaze flickers away like a skittish bird's. "After Nell died, I sort of went crazy." Off my expression, he butts in, "Not crazy like *that*, but... I definitely got messed up in some stuff as I was trying to shut it all out."

"Stuff, as in...."

"Drugs." The word plunks between us like a dropped anvil; all that's missing is the splash. "It wasn't, like, super dramatic or anything, but it definitely would have gotten a whole lot worse if Nate hadn't intervened. I was pissing away a lot of money on coke, and I guess the effects were pretty obvious to my family. I was a huge dick to everyone and impossible to be around. Nate flew out here to try and get me sorted out. That's how I wound up in Cardiff, to get clean." In a purely restless gesture, he lifts his hand to scrub through his hair again. "Mostly I'm pretty good; I have to pay attention, obviously, which is why I don't drink all that much beyond a couple beers here and there, but sometimes... it's hard." Hugh bites his lip. "The last few days have been hard."

Unconsciously, I flinch. "Hugh—I'm so sorry," I splutter, unable to come up with anything better or more adequate. "I had no—"

"I know." He attempts a smile. "That's not your fault, and not really the point I'm trying to make. The thing is, Phel, it's not my place to judge what people will do in a time of grief or when they hit rock bottom, because I know all about it."

The next breath I try to take comes out sounding more like a sob. "But you never hurt anyone," I cry out, even though I don't know for sure if this is true. In my gut, I feel it is, because Hugh's more the type to hurt himself first before putting someone else in harm's way. "I let my grief drive me to hurt Nate as well as myself, and there's no excusing that." Struggling to explain something I still don't fully understand myself, I go on. "It's like I'd lost a part of myself when I came here, the Phel who was confident and proud and *alive*. And then that Phel was gone, and I felt fucking afraid all the time, like my own shadow could jump out at any second and take away everything I had left to lose."

Aware my outburst isn't close to being done, Hugh stays silent and continues to watch me, the atmosphere oddly calm with the gentle lapping of the waves around us and the calling of sea birds in the sky. "When Nate showed up, I felt this thing inside me that wanted to break away and be free again. And hurting Nate—subjecting him to every kind of cruelty and humiliation I could think of—was the only thing that made me feel like a shadow of my old self again. I wanted it so bad, Hugh, and I let myself be carried away with it. In trying to get back to the middle, I let myself get lost all over again. And hurt Nate in the process even worse than he hurt me, because I did it with my eyes open."

"Nate's an adult, Phel," Hugh reminds me gently. His hand comes out and covers my knee across the water. "If you'd really done anything so bad that he couldn't take it, he would have just walked away."

"He *did* walk away," I remind him. "He's gone."

Hugh nods his acknowledgement. "And that's why I'm trying to help you out, man," he says. "I don't want to judge you for that stuff you did or might have done—quite frankly, I don't wanna know—because it won't solve anything. Obviously it doesn't sit right with you, so what'd be the point of me telling you what you already know? You fucked up; so did Nate. It happens, 'cause no one's perfect. It's more important for us to help each other get back up again. I sure as hell would be nothing and nowhere if Nate hadn't done the same thing, helped me find another chance."

"I don't think I've got any chances left."

"Well, I'm sure that's not true." Hugh sounds so much more certain than I feel; I could almost ask him for his secret. "I'm sorry I couldn't be a bigger help to you throughout this whole thing, just like I'm sorry you and Nate couldn't work things out between you. But don't say there're no chances left, because if there's anything I don't doubt, it's the fact that Nate loves you, dude. I've known that much from the start, even before I knew you were the one he was so crazy about; he told me himself."

Far beyond the point of tears threatening to spill, I hug my arms around myself and just let them fall to blend with the salt spray on my face, their taste indistinguishable from the sea. "He left," I say again.

For a moment Hugh looks like he wants to slap me. I almost welcome it. "Don't be such a goddamned idiot, Phel," he snaps. "Nate wanted to find some kind of happiness out here as he tried to figure his life out, no different than you. Do you honestly think he would have just walked away and gone back to Ohio if he wasn't willing to give anything for you to be happy instead?" He lets that sink in for a while, though my brain seems to have a hard time absorbing the words, before giving my knee another gentle squeeze to draw me back.

"You really need to stop living in such deep denial about Nate's feelings, or your own. I know you love him too, and quite frankly it's sort of retarded for both of you to go on being miserable on principle alone. At some point you're going to have to give up on thinking there's nothing else out there, because that's a fucking choice, not a reality." Unspoken is the reminder that Hugh spends a fair time of his own being miserable about Nell, and that's certainly not by choice. "I mean... look. You're a surfer, even if it took you a while to know it, and anyone who looks at you can see how naturally you come to the water. Half the waves you spot look like nothing but unbroken water to me, but somehow you always know when it's gonna be good, and you go for it. Any true surfer knows when they've found the perfect wave. So why trust your intuition in the water, but not out of it? What makes you think you can be right about a wave, and not how you feel about Nate?"

"Because I've been wrong too many times before." Pathetic, I know, but Hugh's faith in me makes me so stupidly hopeful that I don't know how to trust it.

Sharing my disbelief, Hugh scoffs. "And I was wrong about how awesome the waves were going to be out here today," he deadpans. "Does that mean I'm not going to come back out surfing again tomorrow?"

No, of course not. Hugh says the words, and I can't imagine not getting back up on my board after a miscalculated drop leads to a spill, or better yet, not coming back day after day until the tide is just right and the waves, however broken, carry you right on up like you're a part of the water. That faith is what makes it okay to admit defeat one day and keep on trying the next, anticipating the moment when things are just right and you trust yourself enough to do things properly. The water doesn't care if you aren't ready; it'll wait until you are. Is it the same with Nate and me? Can I admit to still needing him in my life, to wanting to try again, without feeling like I've betrayed myself or anyone else? Could I be anything but unhappy if I continued to stay angry and alone?

These questions unanswered, Hugh and I remain a while longer in the ocean until it becomes obvious we should call it a day. The other surfers have all but deserted the beach, and it's a long paddle back to the shore in becalmed waters. In silence, we walk back to Hugh's house, where he moves my meager collection of things into the spare bedroom. Like it's a choice I can accept, or not. There's no one forcing me to stay or go but myself.

After dinner, I'm alone in my room doing what amounts to staring into space when Hugh knocks on my door and enters with an envelope in his hand, Callie a shadow that trails close behind. He comes over to where I'm sitting cross-legged on the freshly made bed—Callie, forever lacking in propriety, leaps on top of the mattress to settle herself at my feet—and passes it over with a small, crooked smile that's indecipherable in the dim lighting.

"I got this the other day, after Nate left," he tells me and with a nod indicates I should open the envelope and see what's inside. "Dunno whether it was out of hopefulness or frustration, but there's no date on it. So you can just... do whatever you think is best. Whatever your gut tells you."

Hugh is gone again when I look up. The only company left in the room, aside from my misery—if I'm allowed to be really maudlin—is Callie and the plane ticket she's curiously trying to sniff in my hands. I stare disbelievingly. There's no departure date specified, as Hugh said, and no doubt it cost him a small fortune to arrange it that way, but what's clear as day is the destination: Columbus International Airport. My breath catches audibly in the quiet room, and the tumble in my gut is precisely the same feeling I get when crashing over the edge of a monster wave, the perfect ride sweeping up out of nothing but hope and a prayer.

It's there for me to take it, if I'm strong enough. *If I have faith*, I think. If I could walk up to the man I love with forgiveness in my heart and certainty in our future, and say, *Hello, Nate. Remember me?* The yearning is so strong that I can feel it vibrating through the core of me like a tuning fork struck to the perfect pitch, can feel it the way I felt something click into place as I looked across a crowded bar and saw him standing there, looking back at me like he already knew my name and where'd I'd been. It feels like holding the whole ocean in my hands, all its terrifying danger and fathomlessness and possibility; it feels like looking over the edge of a cliff of water. I can go forward, or I can remain as I am. I know this.

So I close my eyes and let it carry me over.

11

Nate

THERE is only a slim—really slim—possibility that I will ever write a book of relationship advice for women, but if I had to come up with something, I would probably include this nugget of wisdom: When your ex-husband finds his way back to you on the tail of a yearlong queer love affair and immediately starts restoring every piece of furniture in sight, you are absolutely within your rights as a woman to start drawing conclusions about the relative insanity of gay men. Or carpenters.

Emilia, to her credit, doesn't make any loud noises about what my little adventure might have done to my mental faculties, but there are times I can tell from the look in her eyes that she isn't sure it's anything good. My son is a bit more forthcoming in his opinions, the way ten-year-olds tend to be, but the first time he comes out and says, "Dad, you were a lot less crazy before you were gay," I can't really refute his observation. Trying to explain that I've always been gay—and crazy—probably wouldn't help much either.

While driving across the country, I had some time to think about what I wanted to do first after California. Too many miles and too many empty roads made it impossible for my mind not to wander, but on some mornings, when I woke up to face another day of seemingly endless highways, it felt like I could keep driving until the singularity and still not find any answers. The great unknown is a scary place to be with too much on your mind; you begin to wonder if it's possible for the human psyche to swell and swell until it has no choice but to collapse in on itself, a psychic supernova. Afraid of creating any black holes out there in the desert, I stuck to trying to figure out the stuff I could, like where I would live or what I would do for a job once I reached Ohio. Definitely not anything along the lines of *Will Phel ever talk to me again?* or *Will I ever meet another man like him? Do I want to?*

Admittedly my big plan turned out to be a little anticlimactic. The most I could decide was that I probably needed to find a hobby and should get back into carpentry. I didn't care what—furniture, cabinets, the old countertop Emilia and I had been meaning to replace for ages.... If it had a surface that could be sanded down and refinished, I wanted to restore it. Of course, this decision seemed sensible as I drove through the southern states, but I realized a fatal flaw somewhere around Missouri: it ain't exactly balmy in the Midwest this time of year, and the garage, while insulated, is still cold enough to make my nuts shrivel to the size of kidney beans. Not what you'd call ideal field conditions. Even Lucy became a target for my resentment when the weather got real nasty.

But where there's a will, there's a way, and on most days, I had enough willpower to distract myself from what I'd left behind in Cali and the recurring full-color fantasies of wearing nothing but a smile and Phelan's mouth. Once home, I cherished the opportunity to hug my son whenever I felt like it, despite his protests, and being back on familiar turf filled me with a not insignificant sense of relief. Nevertheless, it wasn't long before a feeling of crushing depression reasserted itself, a familiar specter from my days alone on the road. Every tall dark-haired man to cross my path made me do a double take, and that was all the reminder I needed that yep, I was back in Ohio and the love of my life was still a week and thousands of miles away. While traveling, I couldn't begin to count the number of times I almost turned Lucy around and drove back the way I'd come, needing Phel like a fish needs water. But the water didn't need the fish, I guess, because he was never there swimming after me in all the backward glances I spared.

"Cut your dad some slack," Emilia told Liam one night when she didn't think I was listening. She had crept into his room before bed under the pretense of wishing him good night, not realizing I was only a few steps outside the door and perfectly within earshot of their conversation. "If you'd been through all the same things as him recently, you'd be feeling a little crazy too."

When I started my first restoration project, all she said was "Do what you need to do, but you better not track any wood shavings into the house."

So I got to work refinishing the dining room table first, thinking Emilia might like it prettied up before Christmas. In actual fact, I was distressing the wood and going for a more rustic antique effect, having gotten it into my head that the old farmhouse look was exactly what our house was missing. The table, a hand-me-down from my dad, was the right size and shape to pull off what the folks at Restoration Hardware charged thousands of dollars for. Emilia didn't say much to dissuade me, although she did often shake her head in disapproval on the nights she caught me buried in sawdust out in the garage, dressed in a parka, wool hat, and gloves to fight off the chill.

In a familiar scene, I caught her watching me from the garage doorway, a robe pulled tight around her middle and a mug of hot coffee ready for me in her hand like a peace offering. "I think you should call him," she once suggested, her voice encouraging. I considered it an achievement that I'd let coffee and manual labor replace my hankering for a shot of whiskey or five, but in lieu of a *fuck no*, I thanked her for the drink, turned the sander back on, and readjusted my safety goggles to let her know I wasn't ready to talk about it yet.

She stopped mentioning it after that, for which I was grateful. I mean, not only is it hella weird for your wife—even soon-to-be-ex—to start offering you relationship advice about your gay lover, but she had to know I couldn't think about it anymore. I'd explained the situation over the phone while I was still in Cardiff, so it's not like she didn't know how things ended between me and Phel the second time around. It cheered me up to know she wanted me to be happy, but even Emilia's cautious optimism and strange unflagging faith in gay love stories weren't enough to keep me going. I was emotionally and mentally wrung out. Phelan had chosen his anger over me, and that was that. I couldn't argue with him over the ghost of our first relationship, no matter how much it haunted my daily (and nightly) existence months later. I just couldn't.

A few weeks went by. Nothing major in the grand scheme of things, but enough for me to start to feel settled in my routine again and take over a side of the responsibility for Liam I'd never experienced when working all the time and, oh yeah, forever driving to Columbus to be with Phel. It's not like my kid is particularly high maintenance, but it felt good to make his breakfast in the mornings and be the one to drop him off and pick him up at school each day. I turned into the kind of father and partner who had dinner on the table ten minutes after his co-parent got home.

My days were spent tinkering with things around the house and looking for work to last me until the spring, at which point I felt reasonably confident Craig would give me a job again. I knew I didn't want my old position back. There were various reasons for it, but mostly I didn't want to go back to Columbus and see all the places Phel and I had been together. Instead I found myself wanting something simple that would give me more time with Liam. I hoped there were still spots left among the laborers so I could continue on with the carpentry. Working with my hands and creating things felt cathartic and required enough focus to keep my mind from straying into more dangerous territory.

From what I learned on the phone with Hugh, things seemed par for the course in California. Writing was going well, Callie was great, the surfing was as awesome as ever. He missed having me around. All he ever said regarding Phelan was that he was quiet but otherwise okay, but I could tell from Hugh's voice that he was as worried about Phel as he was me. Sometimes he made frustrated noises about how stupid we both were, at which point I usually shut the conversation down or changed the subject to something else. I never asked whether Phelan said anything about me, because I didn't want to know either way. Eventually Hugh shut up about it altogether.

I should have known better than to trust my brother or a period of such calm—it ought to have been damn near conspicuous—but after so much drama, I think I was happy to latch on to the illusion of normalcy, let myself become complacent and resigned and numb. This is a life, I told myself. Eventually I would be happy again, because the human capacity to heal itself and move on is nothing to sneeze at. Then one day the doorbell rings, and the routine I only just started to enjoy again goes down the shitter.

It happens on a perfectly average Thursday night, the way these things do. Since most of my friends are either shared with Emilia or not the type to make house calls, I don't get much by way of visitors in Mount Vernon. Fewer since I got back. Emilia knows how much I hate being interrupted when I'm at work in the garage, so she can usually be counted upon to get the door or phone when she's home and I'm busy burying myself beneath a pile of sawdust. Still, I pause in the middle of varnishing a table leg to listen for the sounds of the door being answered, then return to what I'm doing once I hear her voice, muffled through the door, brighten in greeting. The male voice that answers is indistinct and all too easy to ignore, but by then I'm already back to dipping my paintbrush into the thick amber goo and smearing another coat onto the wood in thin, even coats, taking distinct pride in my work as I see the color grow dark and rich like good whiskey.

Ultimately it's the quiet moan of pain coming from the doorway between the house and the garage that pulls me away from my work yet again. At first I'm not sure I've heard anything at all, except maybe the howl of the wind clawing its way beneath the garage door, but a prickling instinct has my hair standing on end before I can truly convince myself that's all it is. The sound is a soft, low note of misery like a wounded dog might make. Or like someone swallowing reflexively to prevent anyone from hearing. Maybe I've been a dad too long not to respond viscerally to a thing like that, not to want to find whatever's hurt and make it better. Or maybe it's a pang of recognition that'd strike me anywhere, the way twins sometimes know when the other is injured or sad. I can't ignore it, at any rate, so I turn. My breath catches and I push my protective goggles up my face so I can see better. Of course it's *him* standing there in the doorway, bundled in a wool overcoat and jeans and gloves, flecks of melting snow dotting his dark hair and chimney chute eyelashes. And just like that, I'm back to thinking my dreams have come to life to haunt me during my waking hours.

I almost *do* rub my eyes to clear my vision, but I notice Emilia standing behind Phelan, her figure half-silhouetted in the light that spills into the garage from the house. She gives Phel a little shove in my direction and steps back with a quirk of her lips, the latter aimed at me. "I'm going to take Liam to the mall for a while," she says. "Leave you two to talk."

I don't know whether I want to thank her or beg her to stay, wrap my arms around her knees like a kid terrified of being left alone in the dark. I'm still half-convinced I'm hallucinating, maybe from having inhaled too many fumes from the varnish.

Phelan watches her go with a similar expression on his face, then turns back to me. There's a fucking interminable pause as we stare at each other. Finally he shifts and says, "Hello, Nate," awkwardness seeping through the crack in his voice and the way he shoves his hands deep into his pockets. With a small self-deprecating huff and a ghost of a smile, he adds, "Remember me?"

Ever the picture of intelligence, I blink. "Are you for real?" I manage to force out after another drawn-out silence. I take a step forward with my hand outstretched like I expect it to pass through him. For all I know, it will, because even though I know he isn't actually an apparition, it's a hell of a lot easier to convince myself I'm stuck in a deleted scene from *Ghost* than figure out what the fuck Phelan is doing in my garage.

Clearly misinterpreting my question, Phel falters and takes a step back just as my fingers brush the lapel of his coat. "I'm sorry, I didn't—" he begins, swallowing when I grab a fistful of the thick wool to pull him back. "Nate?"

"How are you here?" I ask him. Still searching for a tangible explanation, I slide my hand up his chest to cup his face. His skin is warm almost to the point of feverish, and the whiff of sunscreen and sand and *Phel* that comes off him tingles straight from my nose down to my dick. It's a sensory association I didn't realize I'd developed while in California. Part of me wonders if I'm going to spring a boner every time I smell salt water or Hawaiian Tropic from now on. "*Why* are you here?" A terrible thought strikes me and manages to break through my stupor. "Is Hugh okay? Is he hurt?"

"What? No!" Phel's eyes widen—obviously he felt the way my fingers jerked in worry. "Hugh's fine, everyone's fine. I'm just...." A sudden flush of red darkens his cheeks, and he bites his lip, eyes lowered, embarrassment screaming through his body language. Problem is, his current expression looks a hell of a lot like something else, something that typically gets me from zero to turned-on in about five seconds flat. The sight is more than I can take, and for a second I want to pretend he *is* a mirage, the ghost of sexy-as-fuck lovers past come to torment me with shy looks and doe eyes.

"I'm just here," says Phelan at last. He lifts his eyes to meet mine, and no, that definitely isn't coquettishness I see. It's insecurity. Fear. Whatever reasons compelled Phel to darken my doorstep, he came with an as-yet-undetermined heap of personal reservations.

Don't you go getting your hopes up, asshole, I order myself. *Hope is the kiss of death.*

The thought is enough to sober me, snap me out of my mind's sex- and Phel-deprived musings and back to the situation at hand. I take a step back, away from him. My mistake has always been that when I get too close to Phel, I'm incapable of seeing anything else clearly. Naïve though it might be, I tell myself keeping a safe distance will calm my racing heart and racing thoughts, will settle the desperate urge to fling myself at Phel's feet and beg and beg and beg. For what, I don't know. That's sort of part of the problem and always has been. "You sure are," I answer with my best shot at keeping the quiver out of my voice. "Again I ask: why?"

Phel laughs self-consciously and finally manages to hold my gaze, miserable but resolute. As he opens his mouth to speak, he also wrings his hands, and the small action draws my attention down to his fingers, makes me see how badly they're trembling. His teeth, too, are chattering. A voice in my head, which mysteriously sounds like a combination of my mother, father, brother, ex-wife, and every Southern-blooded, etiquette-obsessed woman I've ever met, chastises me for being such a shitty host that I'd let a guest stand outside in the cold garage and freeze his nuts off. Even Liam would probably know better than that. I know Phel isn't shaking just from cold, but it's enough.

"Come on, we shouldn't be talking out here," I say before he can begin to elaborate. Sighing, I strip off the protective gear I'm wearing and slap my gloves down on the workbench, then take Phel's elbow to lead him back to the house. "Let's go inside where it's warm," I tell him.

Lips pressed into a bloodless line, Phel nods and allows himself to be led. But he knows the way and ultimately doesn't need my guidance, and pulls away to reach the living room before I do. For a moment he stands there staring off in the opposite direction, which happens to be out the front window. Snow has started to fall gently. It blankets white over everything, except there's already so much snow on the ground that it does little more than disappear and fade into the landscape like nothing has changed.

Pausing to watch Phel, I swallow hard around a sudden blockage in my throat that would probably give me away were I to speak. Phelan looks so small there, silhouetted by the window, thin and hunched and silent, and yet somehow he still manages to block out everything else in my life by his presence alone. But I guess even the moon eclipses the sun sometimes. "You should sit down," I suggest, my voice rough. "I'll make some coffee." Caffeine is the currency of stalling and bad news.

Since I'm the only one in my family who drinks coffee, Emilia purchased one of those single-cup coffee makers that come with the little discs. Normally I get kind of excited over the process, because I'm easily impressed that way, but at this very moment I curse the machine's existence. I wish it took longer to brew a couple of cups so I'd have more time to think.

I tap my fingers anxiously as I hear the hum and bubble of the machine, the tinkle of steaming liquid into the cup. Once the drinks are ready, I can't help but feel I've squandered the opportunity to figure out what the fuck Phel is doing in my living room. Despite my every instinct, hope still clamors in my chest like a canary down the mine, desperate to burst free. I tell myself this visit isn't like the last one, isn't Phelan come to patch things over and get us back on the right track. A lot has changed since then. For one thing, I'm not the one who fucked up. I left, yeah, but leaving was the best and smartest thing I've done in a long time. Refusing to believe otherwise is the only thing that's kept me remotely sane since I left California behind in Lucy's rearview mirrors.

After dumping several teaspoons of sugar and half a cup of cream in Phelan's coffee—it's hard not to remember just the way he likes it, even now—I reenter the living room and see him fumbling with an orange bottle of pills, struggling to remove the childproof cap. Startled by my reappearance, he curses and drops the whole thing just as he pops the lid off, sending the plastic bottle and a couple dozen tiny salmon-colored pills scattering across the surface of the coffee table.

"Fuck." Lurching forward onto his knees, he attempts to gather them all up before I can make it across the room.

I set the steaming mugs of coffee down on the table. Although he manages to chase most of the pills into the cupped palm of his hand, I kneel beside him to snatch the bottle up off the floor.

"Xanax?" I read off the label. Busted. Phelan's eyes drift guiltily closed. "Phel, what the fuck? I thought you stopped taking this shit?" I don't mean for it to come out that way—I know Xanax helps people and has helped Phel in the past—but drugs, prescription or otherwise, have done so much to fuck up the lives of the people I love that I can't help but be a little distrustful of them in any form.

"Easy for you to say," he snaps, and finally, there it is, some of that old fire coming back into his eyes. I want to snort at how predictable and unpredictable Phel is all at once. His mouth hardens. "You're not the one who just flew across the country to make an ass of yourself."

At that, I grunt. "No, but I guess that brings us right back to the question of *why* you are here."

As I pass over the prescription bottle and watch Phelan deposit the pills back into it, I can't stop myself from reaching out to cover his hand with my own, if nothing else to stop its shaking and fumbling as he attempts to replace the cap. At least he's not trying to dope himself up anymore. The whole scene is a little pathetic and a lot absurd, considering the terms we parted on, but he's such a mess that it makes my heart hurt.

Keeping my voice gentle, I urge, "Phel, talk to me." The canary's all but in my throat now.

He looks up at me.

"I assume that's what you came for, right?" I ask. "To talk?" About what, I can't fathom. There's a distinct possibility Phel spent the last month and change cataloguing everything I did wrong and is here to read me the riot act. Get in the last word, as it were.

"No."

Wait... no?

A bone-weary sigh hisses out of Phel as he carefully withdraws from my grasp. As if not knowing what else to do with himself, he stuffs his hands between his knees and sits there. The two of us kneel together on the floor until he feels comfortable enough to talk again. No more than a couple of minutes tick by. "I didn't come to talk, because there's nothing to talk about," he says at last. He sounds awkward but resigned. "You said everything there was to say in Cardiff. Not much else for me to add, really. I just... I came to apologize. Set things right."

Intrigued, surprised, hopeful, disbelieving—my emotions run the gamut from one extreme to the other in the space of seconds. All of them must show on my face as Phel watches me guardedly. His expression most of all lets me know I didn't mishear him.

"Try not to look so shocked," he deadpans. Giving a weak chuckle, he pries his hands out from between his knees and wipes his palms on the legs of his jeans. Nervous. "I don't know where to start. I know I'm doing a shitty job of this, on top of showing up out of the blue. But I'm trying to make it right. In whatever way I can, I want—I *have* to try."

The earnestness of Phelan's words and the sudden ferocity in his eyes releases some of the knot in my chest, lets me draw a proper breath for the first time this evening since I turned around and saw him there. Maybe even since the first time I turned around and saw him, period. *What the fuck are we beating around the bush for?* I finally ask myself. *You know what he wants to say, so why are you letting him choke on it?*

I guess the simple answer is that I'm scared. And I'm not so great a person that I can swallow down the months of sadness, anger, confusion, and loss I've suffered over this man, as much for him as because of him. I'm not so forgiving that part of me doesn't want to hear those two little words come out of his mouth, not after the months I've spent screaming myself hoarse to make him hear my own apology. It has to end somewhere, but not yet. Leaving California didn't end shit, and Phel knows it too.

Squaring my shoulders ever so slightly, I find his gaze and hold it for as long as I'm able, ignoring the quiver in my gut. "Why?" I ask him with an edge of belligerence. "You made it pretty clear, Phel, where you stood on the whole issue of you and I. So why do you gotta try now, after everything?"

I expect the question to cow him or embarrass him or *something*, make him blush and stutter at the very least, but to my surprise he seems galvanized, a deliberate straightness creeping into his posture. Not unlike the day we first met, Phelan's eyes are the softest thing about him, so deep and blue that I want to tumble into them from a great height.

"Because I love you," says Phel, his voice clear as day and without a waver or trace of uncertainty. With a tiny tilt of his head, he searches my face momentarily before fixing back on my face. "And because I was so very, very wrong."

Thousands of tiny razorblades slice down my throat when I attempt to swallow. I want to speak, even though I don't know what the hell one says to that, and something in Phel must recognize that only I could try to make a joke or a derisive comment when I ought to be verklempt. He places a hand between us on the edge of the sofa cushion as though he wanted to reach out and then thought better of it.

"I—I've been so sharp," he continues. "This whole time you've been cutting yourself on me like I'm covered in shells. It's no wonder you left, Nate, and in the end, I—I don't blame you for that. It's what I deserved. But I should have stopped you from going. I should have known it was time to give up the fight and put my fucking knives away, and for that, for everything, I'm asking you to forgive me." Biting down on his bottom lip to stop it from trembling, he leans forward slightly. "Even if you can't take me back, I need to know that at the very least, you don't hate me. Selfish, I know, but I have to hear it from you either way."

I twitch back in surprise. "Phel—how can you.... Is that why you think I left? Because I *hate* you?"

A shoulder lifts, his gaze drops, and I sigh. Unthinking, I reach out and take his hand again, the one on the sofa cushion. This time he lets me keep it, lets me curl my fingers around his palm and hold it tight. The brief squeeze I give startles a little gasp out of him, and he looks up—not at me, but up somewhere into the middle distance—with moisture glistening against his bottom lashes. As he tightens his jaw to stave off further tears, the cleft of his chin seems even sharper than normal.

I suppose I should take a stronger stance here, gather together all the angry thoughts that have crept up on me in the last few months and finally let Phel have it, but all it takes is a quivering lip for me to realize how fucking stupid that would be, how totally beside the point. Because Phel is *here*, and God damn it if I'll allow either one of us to walk away again, not without letting him hear the one freaking thing that matters.

Emboldened, I reach out and cup his face in my hands, then draw him closer so our noses are only a few inches apart. "No matter the stupid shit you say or do, I could never hate you," I hiss at him, resisting the urge to shake him. "Sure, I left, but it was for the exact reasons I told you, Phel. Because I didn't see a way forward the way things were going. Feeling like you hated *me* almost as much as you hated yourself. You just.... Nothing I said or did seemed enough to get your to put your goddamned fists down. I couldn't stick around and watch you keep beating yourself up, and me in the process. Not with a son waiting on me back here. Not thinking we could still be in the same place fifty years from now and none of it would matter. It wasn't fair to anyone."

"I don't want to fight anymore," Phel whispers. "I'm so tired. I'm so *sick* of missing you all the time."

Our foreheads press together when I incline my head just the slightest bit forward. He leans into me like every ounce of energy has flown out of him. "Then stop." I feel the tickle of lashes as he squeezes his eyes closed, and he exhales a shaky breath against my face. It is surprisingly cool, and I realize it's because tears have started to leak from my eyes. "You're the love of my fucking life, jackass, and I surrendered to you a long time ago. So just… stop attacking me, yeah?"

Phel's nod registers as a rushed bob of the head, followed by a loud sniffle and something that resembles a choked laugh, a little hysterical, by the sound of it. I try to squash down my nervousness that Phel will suddenly freak out at me again, and put my arms around him, holding him tight. He allows it, melts into the hug like muscle memory hasn't let him forget how good it feels for us to be together like this. His hair, when I bury my nose in it, smells like minty shampoo and snow.

"I'm sorry, Nate," he says again, his voice muffled in my shirt. A shudder runs through him before he lifts his head, showing me his wet eyes and lashes spiked together with tears.

Christ, he looks so goddamned beautiful like this, and I don't feel guilty for thinking it, for relishing the delicious ache that springs up deep in my chest over the knowledge that his tears are *for* me, not because of me. I know what it feels like to see someone cry on account of something horrible I've done, but I never gave much thought to how good it would feel to have them cry for joy. Saying that doesn't feel arrogant, since I'm crying too. Maybe Phel is a little sad right now, yeah, but he's here, and I'm here; he's asking me to keep him, and there's no way in hell I'm turning him away.

"Can I kiss you?" Phel brushes at the tears on my cheeks with his fingertips and meets my eyes, not even bothering to hide the hopefulness of his gaze. A look like that, so much love and expectation all wrapped up in one devastating expression, would knock my feet out from under me was I not kneeling already.

I force a chuckle to hide how painfully my breath caught in my throat at Phelan's question, and let my hand come to rest at the back of his neck, a gentle hint that he isn't going anywhere. "Never ask me anything like that ever again," I tell him a moment before I bring our lips together.

Maybe for the first time in his life, Phel doesn't have a smart response, but I feel the spark of his smile come to life against my own. For once, and for a long while after that, there's not a damn thing else to be said.

THE rustle of the hotel shower curtain makes me turn my face away from the spray just as Phel steps into the tub and sidles up next to me, a quick flash of teeth as he grins and proceeds to steal my hot water. I can't help but smile back even as I roll my eyes at him, then hook an elbow around his neck in a playful headlock so I can angle us both in a better position to share the shower.

Barely more than ten minutes have passed since I felt his lithe body against mine, and perhaps an hour before that I had him underneath me, begging me to make him come for the third time tonight. Still, the warmth of his body and the slick slide of his wet skin sends a shiver through me, elicits an exhausted but optimistic jerk from my cock like I haven't felt since, well… the first time I took Phel to bed, really.

"I thought I made sure you were unconscious," I say teasingly, then let out a happy sigh as Phel grabs some soap and begins lathering it up on my chest. I've washed myself already, but no way am I gonna tell him to stop. "Your last words were, I'm pretty sure, 'You're going to kill me if you keep this up.'"

Phel snorts and gives one of my nipples a vicious enough twist that I yelp in surprise and flinch to protect myself. "I might be older than you, but I bounce back quickly," he drawls. "Last I checked, you're the one who gets winded after twenty minutes of surfing."

"Fuck you, that was *one time*." I hope Phel will enjoy being reminded of this exchange the next time he's in the mood for athletic marathon sex. That there *will* be a next time makes me want to sigh in relief again, a quiet joy that's finally starting to seem real and solid and *here*.

Following the initial rush of excitement, the hastily scrawled note to Emilia that Phel and I were going someplace more private, and the ensuing drive to the hotel, during which Phel probably broke a few land speed records, I started to feel a bit wary. I began to wonder if I might jolt awake and realize none of this had really happened. If hope is an elevator, I wanted to stop the ride before I figured out I had that much farther to fall in the inevitable crash. The paranoia alone was enough to make me feel stupid on top of feeling like a jackass—there are better ways to react to your lover chasing you clear across the country to make a statement—but my reservations must have revealed themselves in a single unguarded expression when I thought Phel wasn't looking.

He crossed the hotel room to take my hand in his; apparently I spoke too soon when I said we had nothing left to talk about. It was starting to become clear that wasn't true, and that we would probably both be doing some talking for a while longer if we wanted things to get better. I reminded myself it didn't have to happen—couldn't—all in one night, but the shadow was hard to shake.

"We both feel like we have something to prove right now, or need to have something proven to us," he said quietly. "Let's not make any promises except to say that we both want this to work, okay? I'm here, and I'm not going anywhere." His brave smile let me know he was on the same page: trying not to become mired in the doubt that killed us the first time around. "I'm trusting that you aren't going anywhere either. Is that enough?"

Unsure of my voice, I nodded and let him put his hands on me. Surprisingly, the heat of his touch was all the reassurance I needed. It *was* enough.

Still is, and I interrupt Phel's lazy attempts at soaping me up to get my arms around him again and bear him back against the shower wall. Definitely trying this later, I think. He hisses as his butt hits the chilly tiles, but smiles at me ruefully.

I love seeing his hair all wet and plastered to his forehead like this, those great blue eyes blinking up at me from under his lashes. Fuck, he's sexy, and I want to go on being reminded of that fact every day until I die. I always want to feel this greedy and uninhibited as I slide my hands down his slippery sides to his ass, then bend my head to kiss his neck. Knowing I can do these things whenever I want is exhilarating, and an opportunity I don't plan to pass up again. It's crazy, but my dick is already getting hard again as it brushes Phel's thigh, and he only has to take one look at the state I'm in around him to know I will always be his, for anything and everything. Tonight is only the beginning. Hell, the past year and a half will have barely scratched the surface if I have anything to say about it.

"When do you suppose Emilia and Liam will expect you back?" he asks, teasing, the smile evident in his voice. I bite down a little on his collarbone just to hear him chase the question with a gasp. "I might not be done with you for a while yet."

Even before I open my mouth to respond, when I lift my head to smirk down at him, I can tell from his unimpressed expression that he knows whatever I say next will make him roll his eyes epically. "Well, while you were busy recovering from that spectacular ass fucking I just gave you, Emilia sent me a text to say I shouldn't bother showing my face until I'm sure we've sorted things out." Enough years of marriage will make you pretty good at approximating tone of voice even through text messages, and I heard Emilia's amusement in every word. Knowing her, she called Hugh already to high-five him over the phone.

"And do you think we have?" Phel asks, a note of seriousness in his tone.

I try to let the force of my kiss speak for me, and based on how he slumps a little in pleasure, I think it does, but I pull back to touch his cheek in a fond gesture anyway. "I think there's a lot of crap still to discuss," I tell him honestly. "But we'll get there eventually. This thing of ours.... We knew what we were betting on from the beginning, even if it took us a hell of a long time to get it right."

Phel cocks a little smile at me that suggests he's thinking about some other conversation he's had. "Hugh told me something not long after you left, about how good surfers always know how to spot the best waves even if they don't always know how to ride them at first."

I smooth my hand over Phel's shoulder as he shrugs, partly just to touch him but also to encourage him to finish the thought.

"He said I was one of the best surfers he'd seen, in that way. Out of everything he's ever said to me, that might be the one thing that stuck."

"That kid knows what he's talking about sometimes," I admit and think that there might never be a way to qualify how much I owe my brother. For this, for being my Rock of Gibraltar. For helping me come back to myself when I always assumed I'd be the one taking care of him. I know Phelan feels pretty much the same way, that whatever lies in our future can only include Hugh as well, and I'm over the mood at the thought. It feels like that's how it should be. Everything in its right place, to quote a song.

I press another kiss to Phel's forehead and then reach out to shut off the water. We're both clean enough, I think, and there's a whole pile of blankets and pillows calling to us. Right now all I can think about is loving him again and then falling asleep while I stare at his face. I'm eager to wake up and see him there in the morning. It's a deep, bone-tingling excitement better than the rush of crashing out on a really spectacular wave—a full-body high.

"Come on, sunshine," I say. "I'm not done catching up yet. Let me take you back to bed. We can talk about the rest of our lives tomorrow."

Epilogue

Hugh

LET me just start by saying that Liam is not, and has never been, a shy kid. He has every ounce of his father's cockiness and charm and a heaping dose of Emilia's poise and good sense, so it would surprise me little—as in not at all—if he someday went on to become the kind of lawyer students read about in their textbooks and dream of one day becoming. A real killer in the courtroom, the kind of prosecutor who goes on to take down every Don Corleone type there is. Arguing with that kid puts me on edge; I always lose. Then, to make matters worse, Phel went and buoyed up every last remaining insecurity he could find, so my nephew now has roughly enough self-esteem to go out and become the next Brad Pitt. Loosely put.

More specifically, Liam is really goddamn good at surfing for a kid his age, and knows it. I'm all for confidence out on the waves, but it makes teaching him safety and technique all but impossible.

Liam looks at the foam training board like it's personally offended him, happily uncaring that he hasn't surfed in months and oblivious to my God-given right to play the overprotective uncle. It's a gorgeous June morning, the breeze crisp and the sun bright, and it was more or less unanimously decided that today should be spent down at the beach, same way we unanimously reach this decision every morning. As such, no one needed much convincing, least of all Liam, who I know has been dying to get back on a surfboard for ages. It's his second summer out here with us in California, and he won't be heading back to Ohio until the end of August.

I'm all for letting him at the waves, but I need to know he can handle himself out there before I let him anywhere near the water. Nate, Emilia, *and* Phel will all string me up by the nuts if something happens to him out there. But the only response I can get out of him is an exasperated "I'm a better surfer than my dad, Uncle Hugh—for one thing, I'm not afraid of big fish *or* mermaids," followed by the kind of eye roll perfected by eleven-year-olds the world over.

"Stop mouthing off and show me another pop-up," I snap good-naturedly. "You can show off later when I'm sure you're not going to be feeding any fishes on my watch." There's another exhausted roll of Liam's eyes before he gives up and does as I say. I have to admit he's doing really well, young body springing up to the proper surf position with complete ease. The only unusual thing is that Liam surfs goofy, like Phel, and I have to mentally flip him around to adjust his legs here and there.

As I leave Liam to practice a few more times, I glance over to the water and see Nate and Phel coming in from the surf with their respective boards under their arms, bickering and shoving one another like they're ten. Like I've seen happen a million times before, Nate, who rarely wins his arguments with Phelan the honest way, stops Phel midsentence by grabbing him around the waist and hauling him in for a kiss. A childish part of me still wants to blush and look away whenever they do that, and I hear an echoing "*Gross*" from Liam's quarter. I make a face at him to show my agreement, though I've definitely caught Nate and Phel in more compromising positions before. And I'm not even just talking about the first time.

Holding hands (which, by the way, will never not look weird coming from my macho-as-shit brother), Nate and Phel wander over to where we've laid our towels and gear on the beach. Almost immediately, Liam starts whining to Phel about how overprotective I'm being.

Phel snorts and turns, a signal for Nate to unzip the top part of his wetsuit, then flicks an amused look my way. "Much as I enjoy seeing your father and uncle made out to be the bad guys," he says, "I got the same treatment from Hugh before I was allowed into the ocean with a surfboard too. You better get back to practicing if you ever hope to prove them wrong."

Liam grumbles some more about how this isn't his first rodeo, but complies.

"How'd you do that?" I ask incredulously, amazed that Phel can get Liam in line without batting an eye. Not that I've ever seen Nate or

Emilia struggle with him to any great extent, but with me it's like pulling teeth to get my nephew to do anything he doesn't want to. I think the kid knows I'm a pushover, though Phel spoils him more than anyone else.

It's Nate who answers, stooping to ruffle his son's hair. He playfully plants a foot in the middle of Liam's back as he's lying across the board, laughing as Liam whines and struggles to get back up like a turtle who's been marooned in the sand. "Liam doesn't like it when Phel gets pissed," says Nate, grinning. "He knows it'll just lead to a lecture with lots of big words he doesn't know."

It occurs to me this is precisely how I used to lecture Nate as a kid, how much it used to annoy him then too. Like father, like son, I guess. But this, I think, is why Nate is the perfect dad: his parenting style would probably get Child Services called on him if witnessed by the wrong person, but the fact of it is, he ignores the adult/child dynamic most of the time, treating Liam with the same amount of roughhousing and silliness as two kids would each other. I'm reminded how little physical attention—or affection—our own father paid to us as we were growing up, and I know why Nate does it. I know why Phel spoils Liam rotten, too, though he's not so much the roughhousing type. Instead he appeals to Liam's desire to be taken seriously, which earns him major brownie points in Liam's book.

I see this look pass between Nate and Phel, a quick flash of smiles and locked gazes that suggest a lot of making out is probably imminent, so I sigh in resignation and look down to where Liam is currently trying to wrap himself around Nate's leg like an octopus and bring my brother to the ground. "C'mon, Liam," I beckon, and go fetch both our surfboards where they're lying a few feet away. "I think we better get in the water unless you're in the mood for a free show from these two."

"Ew," yelps Liam, and he pretends to fling himself away from Nate as Phel leans in for a kiss to prove my point.

Considering Liam spent the first ten years of his life exposed to nothing but displays of heterosexuality from his dad, I have to give him credit for how cool he is about Nate and Phel, even when they're at their most obnoxiously affectionate. Obviously it wasn't always like that—it's clear Liam struggled to adjust to the new relationship at first, trying to balance his like of Phel as a person with the dissolution of his parents' marriage and Nate's identity as a gay man. That would be tough on any kid; hell, it was even tough for me at first, and I had plenty of time to adjust to the idea. Now, though, you'd never know it was once otherwise, with Liam adapting to Phel's new role as co-parent and, most of all, friend.

This explicit acceptance is how Nate and Phel can get away with playing up public displays of affection just to watch Liam squirm. He never fails to be as dramatic as possible about it, but I see no difference from the exaggerated show of disgust he used to put on whenever he caught Nate and Emilia kissing. Liam treats all demonstrations of adult affection as equally horrifying, and that, I know, is a sign of his approval of Phel and Nate's relationship.

Helping Liam into his wetsuit before we jog out into the surf together, that Nate settles down next to Phel and Callie on their towels, his arm slung around Phel's neck, doesn't escape my notice—they're always touching in some way or another, which, after over a year of being back together, is both the most astounding and ridiculously sappy thing I've ever seen. It's a difference in Nate I can't help but double take over each time. The fact that I've never known him to be so openly affectionate clearly doesn't mean he's never wanted to be; and if the way he looks at Phel is anything to go by, he wants it all the time. (Whatever else Nate happens to want all the time is strictly not for me to comment upon.) Taking into account everything they went through, it's a damn miracle he and Phel can be together this way. I'm definitely not the one to accuse them of being too gooey around each other and, given the alternative, would never ask them to stop.

I guess it's what one might call an unconventional arrangement, but after Phel went to go find Nate in Mount Vernon, they were able to work out a system that allowed the unlikely family unit to split its time between California and the Midwest. Things are finally really good between Emilia and Nate, who have taken to the role of joint parenting with an enthusiasm I both respect and admire. They make it look easy, really, and personally I think Emilia seems a lot happier too, having started dating this chiropractor called Chris who Nate says is really nice. Rather than spending all their time flying back and forth, he and Phel tend to spend longer stretches of time in each place, including summers exclusively in Cali with Liam, who seems to have taken to the SoCal lifestyle like a duck to water.

Meanwhile, the surfboard business Phel and I took on as partners is going great; it took about five seconds for me to realize the untapped goldmine we had in Max and Logan, who produce some of the most beautiful and technologically advanced surfboards I've had the pleasure of trying. Even Nate got in on the game, starting off as an apprentice before taking on his own share of projects in the shop. He's a natural to the craft with his artistic eye and background in carpentry. In one way or another, we're making a real name for ourselves in the industry, and between the four of us, work can get done pretty much anywhere. Phel still has contacts to help with the marketing aspect back in Chicago, and Nate even has a workshop set up in the basement of their house in Ohio in addition to the one here. Max and I keep things running smoothly while they're away—after all, he's the founding partner of the business—and so far I think we've got a promising future ahead of us.

I know Phel would say things could only be more perfect if he was back in contact with his family, but we all know that's probably not going to happen. Even Aurelia, who always seemed pretty cool from Phel's stories about her, limits her contact to a few texts and phone calls every couple of months. It's obvious how much it pains him to still be cut off, but he claims not to blame her for being unable to sever the ties to their family for Phelan's benefit alone. I would certainly do that much for Nate, and vice versa, but if Phel's family refuses to come around, the most we can do is try to compensate with love of our own. Where Nate is concerned, I know how happy he makes Phel; they effect such a recognizable difference in each other, I'm almost at a loss as to how they managed before.

Obviously Nate is a different person now that he no longer has to pretend to be what he's not, but it's Phel who seems the most changed out of everyone. He's so confident and self-possessed, finally in control of his life, and with such calmness and ease I actually feel envious sometimes. It's obvious he's found the balance he struggled with so much when he and Nate were apart. Seeing that guy, I think I know what attracted my brother in the first place, and it's amazing how Nate, just by being in proximity to Phel like this, is so much more open and unguarded and vibrant, where he always seemed to be on the defensive before. They saved each other, I guess.

And me? Well, some days I feel like everything has changed, others like it's exactly the same. My last book was a hit, the fans seeming to enjoy the addition of Agent Jacob as a new character to the series, with critics calling him a welcome counterbalance to the

Manderfeld twins. I've even started dating again, though I'm aware that my love life is the laughingstock of this family. It's still a work in progress, but I'm here in Cardiff with the people I love most in the world, drawn together, however weirdly, by surfing and some sleepy town in the middle of nowhere.

I've since changed my opinion about Cardiff: it isn't just a place for people to go with all their baggage and when their lives feel the most broken, though I do think it rescued us, in its way, from a lifetime of real misery. It might have started off as a home for my grief, but now it's the only place on earth where I've ever felt perfectly happy, and like things have worked out exactly as they're meant to. In one way or another, I can't think of anyplace else I'd rather be.

MAL PETERS's first complete story was a retelling of *The Tortoise and the Hare*, co-written at age six with her father and set in the Welsh countryside of her birth; it involved the conspicuous use of vintage muscle cars. Although she's since gone solo due to creative differences, in the past twenty years she hasn't forsaken her love of sweet rides or writing fiction, having completed degrees in creative writing, English, and information studies, and has published her work in a small (very small) selection of Canadian university journals. Simultaneously a librarian, freelance editor, and fencing coach in Toronto, where she has lived more than half her life, she also enjoys cooking, music snobbery, soldering things, loudly pontificating the superiority of Piedmont region wines, and talking bollocks. If she can't be overheard making sarcastic remarks or working on her trilogy in four parts, she's probably asleep.

Visit her on the web at http://www.malpeters.com.

Also from DREAMSPINNER PRESS

NOTHING Ever HAPPENS

SUE BROWN

http://www.dreamspinnerpress.com

Also from DREAMSPINNER PRESS

ANDREW GREY

LEGAL ARTISTRY

http://www.dreamspinnerpress.com

For more of the best M/M romance, visit

Dreamspinner Press

www.dreamspinnerpress.com